He was being pulled across the room, toward the window. An irresistable pull, growing stronger, faster, and suddenly he was jerked across the room as though on wires, leaving his feet like an adagio dancer. He witnessed himself flying, *flying* toward the window, and he screamed. A woman screamed, too. And then Laycock was driven through the glass, feeling excruciating pain as shards of thick, broken glass tore at his flesh. For a second he hung suspended eight stories above the ground, then fell still screaming toward the parking lot, feeling and hearing the rushing wind, feeling himself being suffocated by the wind pouring in his face, and then came a great pain that filled his mind and body as he felt nothing more.

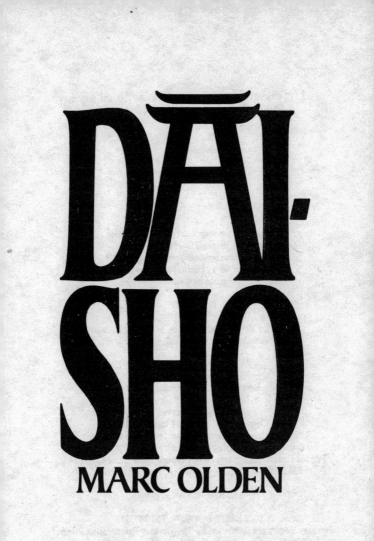

DAI-SHO

MARC OLDEN

BERKLEY BOOKS, NEW YORK

For my mother Courtenaye, with all my love

This Berkley book contains the complete
text of the original hardcover edition.
It has been completely reset in a typeface
designed for easy reading, and was printed
from new film.

DAI-SHO

A Berkley Book / published by arrangement with
Arbor House Publishing Co., Inc.

PRINTING HISTORY
Arbor House edition / October 1983
Berkley edition / January 1985

ISBN: 0-425-07657-1

A BERKLEY BOOK ® TM 757,375
Berkley Books are published by The Berkley Publishing Group,
200 Madison Avenue, New York, New York 10016.
The name "BERKLEY" and the stylized "B" with design
are trademarks belonging to Berkley Publishing Corporation.
PRINTED IN THE UNITED STATES OF AMERICA

Acknowledgments

Diane Crafford, for her creative contributions; and Valentina Trepatscheko, for fulfilling demanding typing requirements.

DAI-SHO. TWO SWORDS, ONE
LONG, THE OTHER SHORT,
CARRIED BY SAMURAI OF OLD
JAPAN. SOMETIMES TRANSLATED
AS A GREAT AND A SMALL.

BUT MY HEART'S LEANING WAS
FOR DEATH AND NIGHT AND
BLOOD.

Yukio Mishima
Confessions of a Mask

PROLOGUE

Karma: THE CONCEPT THAT
WHATEVER ONE DOES IN LIFE
BECOMES THE SEED WHICH
DETERMINES ONE'S DESTINY IN
THE NEXT LIFE. REBIRTH IS THE
ENDLESS RECREATION OF LIFE IN
OBEDIENCE TO MORAL
NECESSITY. WHENEVER A PERSON
DIES, THE KARMA IS LEFT. A NEW
LIFE MUST FOLLOW TO WORK
OUT THE RETRIBUTION
INVOLVED. IT IS A MATTER OF
ACTION AND REACTION. THE
PROCESS NEVER ENDS.

St. Elmo Nauman, Jr.
Dictionary of Asian Philosophies

Few men dared carry such a sword.

It had been forged by the legendary Muramasa, a brilliant but unstable swordsmith.

His blades, said to hunger after men's lives, were so bloodthirsty that they maddened their owners, compelling them to kill or commit suicide.

The way of the sword, kendo, was to protect the righteous and punish evil. But those who owned a sword of Muramasa were said to be unable to live without killing. A Muramasa blade, whispered the superstitious, could never rest peacefully in its scabbard.

IKUBA CASTLE
EDO, JAPAN
AUGUST, 1585, 2:00 A.M.

THE SAMURAI Gongoro Benkai walked to the castle window, stepped to his left and merged with the darkness before looking down on the walls rimming the moat. He did not hear the chirping of crickets that lived in chinks between the rough-hewn boulders forming the castle walls. His right hand dropped to the hilt of his Muramasa *katana*, his long sword. The silence could mean intruders.

He waited for geese and ducks that nested on the far side of the moat to cry out in alarm, but they remained silent. And the frogs continued to croak. Two signs that no intruder was attempting to cross the moat.

Benkai's long sword remained sheathed—a bared blade had the right to blood. Returning a sword unused to its scabbard insulted the weapon and branded the wearer as impulsive, unworthy to be a warrior. The sword was a divine symbol; long ago a god had dipped his sword in the ocean, held it up to the sun and the drops that fell from the blade became the islands of Japan.

Thus the sword was the warrior's link to a sacred tradition and a symbol of his royal ancestry. The sword was a samurai's soul.

As samurai, the ruling class, Benkai carried the *dai-sho*, the long and short swords, worn thrust through his sash, the cutting edges up and on the left side of his body. Both were in lacquered scabbards and tied to his sash by blue silk cords.

His skill as a fencer and the reach of the long sword made it a murderous weapon. Its hilt was covered in white enamel and gold, dotted with six emeralds and trimmed in red silk cord. The thirty-six-inch blade was slightly curved, with a razor-sharp cutting edge achieved by folding together and hammering twenty paper-thin layers of steel of varying hardness. The result was a sword both beautiful and well crafted, a sword that could slice through iron as though it were a melon. With it Benkai had killed more than sixty men.

At midnight a strong southern wind had sent a heavy rain horizontally against the castle and its stables, archery courts, shrines, barracks and pavilions. Two hours later the rain stopped and a humid darkness hid everything beyond the towering castle walls: the canals that drained low-lying marshes and rice fields; the thatched huts of the poor sprawled between the rice fields and the Sumida River; the luxury villas that rested on low hills ringed by pear, peach and cherry orchards.

Then the blind musician had come to the *dojo*, the fencing hall, with an urgent message for Benkai, who each night practiced one thousand cuts and two hundred fifty draws with the long sword. At the *dojo* entrance the musician dropped to his knees in fear, his head touching the mat. All samurai had the privilege of *kirisute gomen*, the right to kill any disrespectful commoner on the spot without fear of penalty.

"Honorable Lord Benkai, my mistress Saga asks please that you come to her quarters. Please at once. She knows of a plot by traitors here in the castle to murder our Lord Saburo. Mistress says that you alone can be trusted. You are the most faithful of any who served our beloved *daimyo*. Only you can prevent our merciful and gracious Lord Saburo from being murdered three days hence."

The blind musician did not see Benkai's eyes narrow into dark slits. If the musician spoke true, then Benkai's honor was at stake; honor demanded that a samurai serve his master with unswerving loyalty, whether in adversity or defeat. And loyalty had been known to continue past the grave. Because

Benkai's loyalty matched his swordsmanship, Saburo had made him his bodyguard. Benkai was his lord's teeth and claws and the *daimyo* could not have chosen more wisely.

Gongoro Benkai was fifty, a bearded, squat, muscular man with dark hair worn samurai fashion, the back braided, then oiled and pulled forward in a queue across his shaven skull. Dark skinned and ugly, he was called Land Spider behind his back. His eyes had a wolflike brightness that believers in black magic swore came from eating human flesh. He fenced with such fanatical skill that he was said to be the son of Shini-gama, Lord of Death-desire and a fox, the animal capable of inducing demonic possession.

The most frightening rumor about Benkai, more frightening than his willingness to kill, credited the speed of his Muramasa blade to an *Iki-ryō*, an evil spirit created by Benkai's dark thoughts.

Shi-ryō, ghosts of the dead, those lost souls who haunted at night, were not as feared as an *Iki-ryō*, a ghost that sprang from the living and who could kill. Sinister and vile thoughts —anger, hatred, vengeance, bloodlust—were strong enough to send the *Iki-ryō* from a man's mind and into the world to destroy.

Benkai was icy nerved, with an assurance that came from self-knowledge. In combat he neither panicked nor showed mercy; he was what Lord Saburo called a tiger who had tasted blood and was therefore always dangerous. He also possessed the warrior's contempt for death.

At a time when all believed in demons, ghosts, goblins and spirits, only an invisible and deadly *Iki-ryō* could account for swordsmanship so beyond that of ordinary men. How else could the dreaded Land Spider fight and defeat as many as twelve attackers at once.

The crickets were silent.

An alert Benkai eyed the castle ramparts topped with pine trees and spears that allowed armed sentries to come and go without being visible. The massive walls were made of "hundred-man stones," named for the number of men needed to move each one, and were too thick for the crude cannon to penetrate. Benkai himself had chosen the expert archers stationed in the *yagura*, the corner towers, men rewarded with triple rice rations for any infiltrator killed between dusk and dawn.

The grounds within the walls were patrolled by armed guards and fighting dogs, mastiffs crossbred with bulldogs. Both drawbridges were made of iron and the moat was deep and wide.

Benkai's fingers toyed with the silken cord dangling from the hilt of his long sword. *Hai*, yes, a strong defense. Efficient. Impregnable. But most castles were not conquered from outside; they were betrayed from within, which explained the secret tunnel that led outside, if the *daimyo* was forced to abandon his fortress. A wise rat did not trust his life to only one hole.

Lord Takemori Saburo had need of such defenses, and of Benkai. By his treacherous conduct and vain posturing the *daimyo* had made an enemy of Toyotomi Hideyoshi, and a more dangerous enemy did not exist. Despite the presence of an emperor and royal court in Kyoto, the country was actually ruled by Hideyoshi. Until three years ago he had been a brilliant general under the shogun, the military dictator Oda Nobunaga. Aided by Hideyoshi's wisdom, Nobunaga had ended three hundred years of civil war by crushing the arrogant warlords and bringing most of Japan under his control.

After Nobunaga's assassination Hideyoshi, an ugly, dwarfish man of great cunning and charm, had vowed to surpass his dead master. "I shall make a single country out of China, Korea and Japan," he boasted. "It will be as easy as rolling up a straw mat and putting it under one's arm."

He began with Japan. Those he did not destroy, he won over with diplomacy. The Crowned Monkey, as he was called, was a born leader, gifted with the ability to win the confidence of others. Even those who had been prepared to fight Nobunaga to the death found themselves won over by the charismatic Hideyoshi. And as more of Japan came under his domination it became apparent that he had forever changed the way the country fought its wars.

He retained a huge army of spies and sent them to every Japanese province, village, valley, port and island. One group of agents sometimes observed another, and a detailed comparison was made of each report. Hideyoshi was the first to gather military intelligence far in advance of a planned campaign. He collected maps and information on rice harvests and fishing fleets, on troop movements and morale, on weather and military supplies, and he used the information unerringly. He also prepared psychological studies of warlords and their generals. A brave soldier and an excellent judge of men, Hideyoshi was gifted with two other valuable traits—patience and a superb sense of timing.

The Crowned Monkey was all that Lord Saburo was not, reason enough for the ruler of Ikuba Castle to hate him. The weak and sensual Saburo, who was forty, obese and completely hairless, outwardly pretended to be Hideyoshi's ally while plotting behind his back. Hideyoshi, meanwhile, pressured Saburo to join the growing number of lords who acknowledged him as Japan's sole ruler.

"The Monkey has asked me to tear down the walls of my castle, walls that have stood for over a hundred years," an angry Saburo protested to Benkai. "He claims it would be my gift to peace, that in the new Japan there is no need for such fortresses. Curse him! And in the same letter he dares raise the taxes and amount of tribute I must pay him. *Hai*, he plots my ruin. Yes, yes, my ruin."

Benkai nodded in silent agreement.

Saburo flicked his thick wrist, snapping open a large gold fan. Nervously fanning himself the bald *daimyo* rolled his eyes. "If I am cruel it is because I am forced to be. Hideyoshi, who does not even know his own father, presumes to elevate himself above me, *me*, whose ancestors are royalty descended from gods. Let this maggot-eating dwarf bow to me, not I to him."

He tapped Benkai on the chest with the fan. "He is a snake and if I . . . if we have our way, one day he will cease to hiss."

The two men were alone in the council room, yet Saburo looked around to make sure he wasn't being overheard. "I have talked to others, you know, and they too are desirous of removing the Monkey. The Monkey's appetite must be curbed. And soon. Yes, yes."

"With respect, honorable Lord," said Benkai, "Hideyoshi is too strong to face in open battle. He has many men and he has many lords on their knees to him. All have sworn to follow him unto death, as I have sworn to follow you."

"Yes, yes. Hideyoshi is the head and those who follow him
are the body. But you see, Benkai, when the head is removed
the body is useless."

Saburo brought the gold fan to his mouth and giggled coquettishly behind it. "*Ninja*. Yes, yes. *Ninja*."

Ninja. Clans of spies and assassins employed by rival warlords during the ceaseless power struggles that had torn Japan
apart for hundreds of years. Men and women dressed in black,
physically fit, and skilled in the martial arts. Masters of espionage, killing, blackmail. Masters of disguise, capable of
assuming a thousand different faces.

The name meant "stealers in"; their trade, *ninjitsu*, was the
art of stealth or invisibility. Both terms were a tribute to their
training, which allowed *ninja* to perform feats perceived as
supernatural by the frightened and ignorant.

The different *ninja* networks offered their services to the
daimyos and military chieftains; it was the Koga clan, a network powerful enough to rule its own province, that Saburo,
on behalf of himself and two other warlords, had petitioned to
murder Hideyoshi.

"Our Monkey has been quite busy," said Saburo. "Let
death bring him rest and eternal sleep."

"*Hai*." Again Benkai bowed his head in agreement. It was
not for him to question his liege lord. Nor did he give any
thought to the fact that three hundred years of brutal power
struggles were coming to an end because of men like Nobunaga and Hideyoshi. Benkai had received rice, land, horses and
servants from the *daimyo*, and he served him because he had
vowed to do so, whether right or wrong.

Hideyoshi was a great lord, with qualities that Benkai admired. But he was Saburo's enemy, thus making him Benkai's
enemy as well. Karma had ordained that Benkai serve Saburo,
not Hideyoshi, and karma offered no escape. A man had to
drink the wine in his glass.

* * *

THE CRICKETS WERE SILENT.

Benkai turned from the window to look at the woman

who sat on the floor, stirring the tea brewing in a pot over a hibachi with a bamboo whisk. She lived in lavish quarters decorated with exquisite wooden sculptures, wind chimes, painted folding screens and lacquered redwood chests. Here, as in the *daimyo*'s quarters on the floor above, the straw mats were changed daily. Such luxury was not to Benkai's taste; he was a simple man who preferred plain things.

The woman was Saga, a seventeen-year-old concubine given to Saburo two years ago by one of the lords with whom he now plotted to kill Hideyoshi. She was elegant and exotic, a small woman with fashionably blackened teeth, shaved eyebrows and fragile combs of engraved oyster shells fastened in cocoons of black hair. Benkai found her insolent and too sure of herself. She neither wavered nor hesitated in her actions and either loved or hated, with no middle course.

Benkai looked down as Saga, kneeling on a straw mat, poured the green tea into drinking bowls. With extraordinary grace she bowed her head, picked up his tea bowl in her hands and extended both arms toward him. Her face, with its white lead makeup and small rouged mouth, was expressionless.

Benkai knelt opposite her, resting on his heels, palms down on his thighs. After long seconds he took the tea from her but did not drink.

He said, "I have decided. It is better that you write down the names of the men you accuse as traitors and sign it. I will see that it reaches my Lord Saburo."

"*Hai.*" She bowed, then rose to her feet in a rustle of silk and walked to a folding screen painted with golden herons and silver hawks. She disappeared behind it, then emerged seconds later holding her writing box. Kneeling opposite the samurai she opened the box, prepared the inkstone and ground the ink.

She selected a new brush and a sheet of yellow paper. "The men I shall list are important. They stand between me and my Lord Saburo. Each is a man of authority and position. They are pleased that he has found a new favorite."

Benkai almost permitted himself a smile. Tonight Saburo was taking his pleasure with Hayama, a beautiful twelve-year-old boy, a gifted actor, singer and dancer. Benkai, among other warriors, fancied the boy and would have enjoyed him had not the *daimyo* claimed him first.

"How came you by the names of these men?"

"When you stepped to the window, I was about to—"

"I am here now. Proceed."

"Less than an hour ago my slave Ichiro overheard men talk-ing in the stable where he sleeps. Certain men hiding there from the rain were careless with their words. Ichiro listened. He listened well."

"He cannot see. He makes music and he grovels."

Saga held his gaze. "He hears with the ears of a hawk, my lord. And he can only come to me. A slave cannot approach the *daimyo*."

"You can approach him."

She lowered her head. "I no longer please him. To him I am a jealous woman, nothing more. And would not such a woman do anything to be received back into her lord's favor? Is it not wiser for you to approach him?"

"Such a woman," said Benkai, "might even lie."

Saga's smile had an edge to it. "*Hai*, such a woman might prove deceitful. But I shall prepare the list and hand it to you. Let our Lord Saburo be the judge of my loyalty. Even to speak to you of this places my life at risk. If these men learn you and I have met, I am undone."

Sighing, she laid down her brush, picked up her tea bowl and brought it to her mouth. She sipped, then eyed him across the bowl, waiting for him to drink.

Benkai brought his bowl to his lips. Saga held her breath, her eyes suddenly widening. The samurai tasted the tea and frowned.

Suddenly his head snapped toward the painted screen Saga had walked behind to get her writing box. Mosquitoes swarmed in front of the screen. Mosquitoes drawn by the pres-ence of someone hidden behind the screen.

And the surface of the tea was cloudy. *Poison*.

Instantly Benkai hurled the tea bowl aside.

A *trap*.

Saga scrambled to her feet. The smile on her face was now cruel and triumphant. Reaching into a sleeve of her kimono, she took out a *tessen*, a war fan. A flick of her wrist and the fan opened, the light from a paper lantern reflected from its iron ribs and cutting edges.

There was pride in her voice. "It is too late. You will never reach him in time. Never."

Benkai now knew who she was. *Kunoichi*, a female *ninja*. And he knew why the crickets were silent.

To know and to act were one and the same. In one move Benkai was on his feet, the long sword quickly out of its scabbard and held overhead in a two-handed grip.

Two strides brought him to the screen where the sword, its blade a bluish-white sheen of steel, sped downward to splinter the bamboo and rice paper and cleave the skull of a crouching *ninja*. As the dead man tumbled forward Benkai pivoted left, his bloodied sword biting into a masked charging *ninja* wielding a *bo*, a hardwood staff. The stricken *ninja* stared down at the wet crimson line now dividing his body. Then as the *bo* slipped from his fingers, he dropped screaming to his knees and tried to push the streaming gray mass of his intestines back inside his body.

Three more *ninja* leaped through the open window and dropped noiselessly to the mat-covered floor. Benkai, the rage to kill roaring in his blood, hurried to meet them, short sword now in his left hand, long sword in his right. The first *ninja*, lean and swift, squatted on his heels and swept his *shinobi-zue*, his bamboo staff, in front of him, keeping it close to the ground. From inside the staff uncoiled a six-foot-long chain with a steel weight at the end. Before the weight could wrap itself around his ankles, Benkai leaped high and to the left, letting the chain pass beneath him. A single thrust and the point of his short sword was deep into the chain wielder's throat.

One backstroke of the long sword and a *ninja* poised to hurl a *shuriken*, a flat, star-shaped knife, had both arms severed at the elbows.

The third *ninja*, sword in hand, charged with his arms extended, blade aimed at Benkai's heart. Using his long sword Benkai parried the attack, knocking it aside so strongly that the *ninja* was off balance, his left side defenseless. A vicious thrust and the samurai's short sword was buried to the hilt in the *ninja*'s unprotected armpit.

Benkai whirled around and in that instant his skull almost shattered with pain. He willed himself to stand, to continue fighting, drawing on an inner fury, a maniacal strength that allowed his mind and body to accept the pain caused by the arrow embedded in his left eye.

The way of the warrior was death. Only by concentrating on this idea day and night could a samurai discharge his duties and maintain the dignity that was part of his honor. A samurai's life belonged to his master. To lay it down without regret or hesitation was the warrior's glory.

Half-blind, Benkai inhaled through his nose, then let the air out through his mouth. It was the rasp of a wounded, cornered but still dangerous animal. Across the room the *ninja* who had fired the arrow quickly notched another to the *hankyu*, the half-bow that could be concealed on the body. Bringing the bow up, he pulled back the string and released a second arrow. Benkai, his beard bright with his own blood, brought up the long sword and scornfully flicked his wrist, knocking the arrow aside. For the moment, death must keep its distance.

Four *ninja* remained. Benkai saw the open space in the floor where they had hid. He saw Saga, standing among them, whisper to the leader and point her war fan at Benkai.

Shouts rose from the courtyard, the ramparts, from a tea pavilion near the north drawbridge. The castle had been betrayed by Saga, who had gained Lord Saburo's confidence in bed, and by false friends, who cared nothing for loyalty and honor. Before he died Benkai would drink of the black wine; he would have his revenge on the traitors. Retribution was sacred. Until Benkai returned evil for evil there would be no freedom for him in this world or the next.

Saga aimed her chin at the bodyguard. "Kill him! He must not reach Saburo!"

The *ninja* edged closer, emboldened, yet nervously intimidated by the arrow in Benkai's eye. No ordinary man could suffer such a wound and still stand. An ordinary man would be lying on the floor in agony, or already dead. But Benkai remained on his feet, sword at the ready.

Saga's voice was a low hiss. "He bleeds. He is no demon; he is an ordinary man. Kill him and you will be rewarded. I swear this."

Her words gave them courage; they fanned out, attempting

to surround Benkai. He looked at their weapons with contempt. A hand sickle, hardwood staffs, weighted chains, climbing spikes, swords, a blowgun with poison darts. Weapons that could maim, blind, kill. But none that could equal Benkai's Muramasa blade.

There was no time to remove the arrow or stop the bleeding. Saburo was in grave danger, perhaps even dead. Honor demanded that Benkai hasten to the *daimyo*, or see the gods and his ancestors turn their faces from him. Better to be reborn five hundred times without his hands than to suffer eternal shame.

He had to fight his way to Saburo or die trying.

With the blood-coated arrow jutting from his eye like a wooden horn, a screaming Benkai leaped at a *ninja*.

* * *

A week before the attack on Ikuba Castle the Koga ninja had infiltrated Edo disguised as horse traders, Buddhist monks, beggars and rich farmers. They concealed themselves in homes and businesses owned by Hideyoshi's agents, who gave them reports on Saburo, the castle, its troop strength and the weather. To prepare for the night raid the ninja spent the final twenty-four hours in total darkness. On a Friday midnight, with the southern rain as cover, the attack began.

First, the moat. After poisoning the geese and ducks, black-costumed ninja entered the water, submerged and breathed through bamboo tubes as they swam to the base of the castle's sixty-foot wall. Hidden by darkness and the heavy downpour they began the dangerous climb to the top. Each man bore, besides his weapons, the weight of metal spikes on his hands and feet, the better to grip the rain-wet stone. Strength, stamina and agility made the ninja a superb athlete and flawless killing machine, as well as a resourceful secret agent.

The Koga ninja knew about the corridors in Ikuba Castle called "nightingale floors," intricately sprung floors that "sang" or "squeaked" when anyone walked on them, reducing an assassin's chance of approaching the daimyo's quarters unawares. They also knew that one could cross these floors soundlessly if shown how. They knew, too, of castle corridors deliberately leading to dead ends, of rooms with trapdoors that opened onto bamboo spikes, of rooms rigged to drop nets down on an infiltrator.

And they knew about Saburo's secret tunnel.

East of Ikuba Castle, in a small wooden building that was a Buddhist shrine, four ninja stripped nude and rubbed oil over their bodies. Then they walked to an opening in the floor, where the leader stepped onto a ladder and descended into a tunnel. They carried no weapons, lanterns or torches. The last man closed a trapdoor over his head, leaving behind a dozen ninja standing in the light of a single oil lamp.

In a corner of the bare shrine lay two robed monks, the leather thongs that had strangled them still around their throats. A signal from one ninja and the monks were stripped. Minutes later two ninja wearing the Buddhists' robes, their faces hidden deep in the saffron hoods, sat near an open window and fingered lacquered beads. From a distance the shrine appeared peaceful, its caretakers silently meditating to the sound of the heavy downpour on the tiled roof.

Within the tunnel that was Saburo's secret escape route the four naked ninja ran over volcanic ash and mud, each step taking them west toward Ikuba Castle. Although the ninja had excellent night vision they trailed one hand along the dampened earth wall for direction and balance. Each had stuffed a cotton rag in his mouth to muffle his breathing.

Somewhere between the shrine and the castle, according to espionage reports, half a dozen guards were on tunnel duty. In the darkness, where it was impossible to distinguish friend from foe, the ninja using bare-hands would kill anyone wearing clothes.

They would change into the uniforms of dead

guards and wait to be linked up with the ninja *back at the shrine. Then the attacking force would make its way into the castle to kill Saburo and Benkai. Saburo, believing he was protected by his bodyguard's Iki-ryō, had boasted that not even the gods could make their way past Benkai's sword.*

In the tunnel, the four naked ninja *lay stomach down on the ground and listened. Ahead of them a spear brushed against a shield. There was the creak of leather armor and someone complained about the soldiers' poor rice ration. A sixteen-year-old guard, on tunnel duty for the first time, was teased by his sergeant about his lack of beard. Six voices were heard from ten feet away in a low-ceilinged, earthen room lit only by a pine torch stuck in a mud wall. This was the beginning of the secret tunnel, the entrance into Ikuba Castle.*

The beardless guard dropped his sword and was severely tongue-lashed by his sergeant. Another guard used his knife to sharpen the tip of his spear. Weapons made noise, especially in the confined space of a tunnel, and the guards' weapons had become a disadvantage. It was the responsibility of the ninja *leader to give his men the final advantage.*

He removed the wet rag from his mouth, raised himself into a runner's crouch and looked over his shoulder to make sure his men were still lying down. Then without a word he raced forward with extraordinary speed, his muscled body glistening with oil and sweat. In seconds he was past the relaxed guards and reaching for the torch. He tore it from the wall, hurled it far back into the tunnel and over his prone men, throwing the earthen room into darkness.

The young guard screamed in agony and then the scream abruptly died.

* * *

IT WAS A GRAY and muggy dawn over Ikuba Castle. On the horizon a rising sun outlined the top of blue hills and the muddy Sumida River, now rain swollen and overflowing its banks. On all sides of the castle rice fields, roads, marshes and plains were black with Hideyoshi's cavalry and foot soldiers, an army made confident by an unbroken string of victories. Like the Koga *ninja*, the Crowned Monkey had used rain and darkness as cover to "steal in." Ikuba Castle was surrounded, its garrison outnumbered and cut off from any escape.

In Lord Saburo's quarters Benkai, the arrow still in his eye, watched his *daimyo* prepare for *seppuku*, the cutting of the stomach, the ritual suicide that was at the heart of the samurai's discipline. A frightened Saburo stepped onto a thick red rug enclosed on three sides by a white screen and dropped clumsily to his knees, his trembling hands fumbling with his kimono. Benkai waited until Saburo had bared his chest before nodding to one of the four guards in the richly ornamented rooms. Stepping forward, the guard squatted behind Saburo and removed the *daimyo*'s sandals. A man about to commit *seppuku* sometimes let his sandals fall off, due to nerves. This gave him an undignified appearance, something to be avoided.

Benkai's own appearance was harrowing. There was the arrow, and the blood on his face and chest, and there was Saga's head, tied to his sash by her black hair. And there was the Muramasa. He had cleaned it with white tissue paper and now it was held in his right hand, dangling at his side, menacing in its sinister beauty. The guards had just witnessed the Muramasa chop down half a dozen *ninja* sneaking out of the secret tunnel, slashing and cutting until the infiltrators were driven back.

On the other side of the barred tunnel door the *ninja* taunted and threatened Saburo. Benkai knew they would eventually find another way to break through. This time, however, there would be no Saga to open the door for them.

The guards found Benkai more terrifying than the idea of death at the hands of the *ninja* or Hideyoshi, and they obeyed his commands without question. Fear had robbed them of all judgment; nothing mattered except to obey Benkai.

He told them that *seppuku* was the only way for Saburo to retain his honor and avoid the shame of capture and disgrace. Defeat was certain. The chain of destiny, with all its sorrows, was now wound tightly around the *daimyo*'s throat. Taken alive he faced crucifixion or a slow, torturous death from his captors cutting into the nerve centers of his spinal cord.

"A samurai must choose between disgrace and glory," said Benkai. "*Seppuku* is the way to glory."

"*Hai*," shouted the guards.

Saburo's rooms gleamed with the lavish use of lacquer and gold. Gilded ceilings, luxuriant with sunken panels of painted waterfalls and seashores, looked down on intricate ivory carvings, bamboo and redwood furniture, porcelain pillows, teakwood chests of jewelry and cedarwood folding screens inlaid with mother-of-pearl. The air was sweet with the smell of burning incense and the perfume of fifty-foot-high wild camellias growing south of the castle wall.

Near the barred oak door to the *daimyo*'s quarters the air smelled of smoke from fires burning on all three castle floors. Smoke poured from the courtyard and from buildings throughout the compound. There was the stench of the dead *ninja* and the corpse of the boy Hayama, who had taken a blow from a hand scythe intended for Saburo. The *daimyo* wept for the dead boy, a sign of weakness in Benkai's eyes.

Benkai had decided that his master must die before his spirit weakened further, before the *ninja* could take him alive. He signaled to the four guards he had ordered to act as *kenshi*, official witnesses to Saburo's suicide.

Asano, oldest of the guards, lit two candles that had been placed in front of the white folding screen. Each candle was four feet high, was wrapped in white silk and rested on a bamboo stand. White was the color of purity and of death.

A second guard brought Saburo a *hachimaki*, a white headband that symbolized readiness for a great spiritual or physical effort. As Benkai wrapped a white silk cloth around the hilt of his sword, a guard brought Saburo a bowl of rice wine; the *daimyo* took four swallows. The word for four and death was the same, *shi*. A guard placed Saburo's trembling hands behind him, where they could not be seen.

The warning drums, conch shells and gongs that had attempted to rally the *daimyo*'s men were now silent. Suddenly there was a new sound that made Benkai turn from Saburo and stare at the window. Humming arrows. Shrieking like crazed birds, they soared high from somewhere within Ikuba Castle, then floated against a gray sky before dropping among Hideyoshi's forces. The arrows carried messages, and Benkai knew what they were.

The *ninja* had Saburo trapped in his quarters. They had slain his three generals, leaving his troops demoralized and leaderless. Wearing the uniform of the *daimyo*'s men, the *ninja* had moved around the compound and killed at will. Some of the garrison, terrified and not knowing which of their own to trust, had locked themselves inside a barracks, refusing to fight.

"Beware the day when cowards act on what they believe," said a bitter Saburo.

Outside Saburo's quarters, on the other side of a tall oak door, the nightingale floors squeaked under the sandals of the cursing, shouting *ninja* attempting to break in. Benkai, whose indifference to the torment in his skull chilled the four guards, turned an ear toward the door. There was a sudden silence in the hall, then the sound of running men. The door shook from the thrust of a battering ram.

Saburo, kneeling, hugged himself and bit his lip hard enough to draw blood. Since it was no longer possible to live proudly, he must die proudly. Would his courage hold out long enough to do what must be done?

At a black-and-gold lacquered cabinet Asano removed a white wooden tray on which lay a long knife wrapped in white tissue paper. Forcing himself to stay calm he crossed the room to Saburo, bowed, then placed the tray on the floor at the *daimyo*'s knees. Asano's part was finished. He looked at Benkai and willed himself not to flinch.

Benkai was to be the *kaishaku*, the executioner and second. His skill with a sword would lessen Saburo's agony; *seppuku* was excruciatingly painful, the strongest test of a samurai's courage. The Japanese believed that the soul rested within the abdomen and to open it would reveal if the soul was clean or polluted. The stomach was the center of a samurai's will, the focus of his spirit, boldness, anger, kindness, all that he was and held sacred. Stomach cutting was an ordeal requiring such composure and dispassion that only the true *bushi*, the warrior, the most controlled and bravest of men, could accomplish it.

The battering ram again pounded the door as Benkai walked behind the white screen and knelt facing his master's left side, his left knee on the ground, his right knee raised. He held his sword high in both hands in accordance with Saburo's rank.

"My lord, do not turn around," whispered Benkai. "Please bring the tray to your forehead, then place it back on the floor. After that you may reach for the knife at a moment of your choosing."

This was a merciful lie. There was no time left. The door would give way any second and the *ninja* would do anything to capture Saburo alive, to stop him from dying at his own hand.

Benkai knew too that his master's self-control could break at any time and that he would disgrace himself. Let the way of the sword show compassion. Some might call it a violation of the rites of *seppuku*, but Benkai was determined that his master should receive this last kindness.

Saburo, his eyes bright with tears, leaned forward to pick up the tray. When his fingers touched it Benkai, who had been watching his every move, leaped to his feet, paused only a second, then brought the blade down upon the *daimyo*'s neck.

There was a thud as the head, completely severed from the body, fell to the rug. In the silence blood poured from the neck while the body remained kneeling. Benkai bowed low in respect, then wiped the blade clean with a piece of tissue paper from inside his kimono. After sheathing his sword he reached down and pulled out Saburo's feet, causing the body to fall forward. He took more clean paper and a small dagger from inside his kimono, walked over to Saburo's head and shoved the dagger deep into the left ear. Picking up the bald head—there was no topknot to grip—Benkai placed it on the clean paper laid over the palm of his left hand and held it up to the witnesses.

One guard averted his gaze, and another fouled himself and had to clutch the man beside him for support.

"Look at it!" commanded Benkai. After each man had stared at the severed head Benkai placed it by the *daimyo*'s shoulders. On the rug Saburo's blood was a widening dark stain.

The oak door shattered, but the bar and hinges held.

Taking the knife from the tray Benkai walked from behind the screen and knelt facing the damaged door. Behind him the guards watched as he removed his *dai-sho*, placing both swords to his right. Then, opening his kimono, he waited.

It was time for him to open the seat of his soul, to prove his honor before the dogs. It was time for him to join his master. When the gods saw Benkai's sincerity they would grant him what he wanted most—revenge on those who had betrayed Lord Saburo. Even if it meant being reborn a thousand times Benkai would return evil for evil, blood for blood.

The door gave way, tearing itself loose from the hinges and sending shards of wood flying into the room. Masked *ninja* ran forward, then stopped at the sight of the composed Benkai. Instantly they knew what he planned to do. The sight of the arrow in his eye kept them rooted in place.

Laying the knife aside Benkai gripped the arrow in both hands, breathed deeply and broke it off close to his forehead, leaving a piece still in his eye. Contemptuously he threw the blood-coated shaft aside. His face was knotted with pain, but he refused to cry out.

After breathing deeply he said, "I will show you how a true warrior dies. None of you will ever tell of how you carried my head back to Hideyoshi, the monkey whose dirt you eat. I could kill many of you easily, but my master is dead and so the taking of your lives is a meaningless task. It is as useless as building a house on quicksand. I die to join my master. I die so that the gods can see the courage and purity of my release from this body and grant me the right to punish those who have betrayed my master. I die willingly, at a time and place of my choosing."

Without hesitation he took Saburo's knife in both hands and plunged it deep into his left side. His body shook slightly, but he uttered no sound. He drew the knife slowly across his stomach to the right side. Then he turned it in the wound, and brought it slightly upward in the crosswise cut called *jumonji*. This was an indication of even greater courage.

Benkai paused, his forehead beaded with perspiration, his

neck rigid with corded veins. With trembling hands he yanked the knife out, placed the blood red blade in his mouth and fell face down on the floor.

As the silent *ninja* stood in awe the skies blackened, darkening the room. Lightning flashed across the black sky and thunder rumbled, then boomed, echoing and reechoing. A sudden downpour pelted the castle and the land around it with sheets of chilled rain and hailstones. In the courtyard horses reared out of control, pawing the air with their hooves, terrifying their handlers.

When the earth shook, the *ninja* in Saburo's quarters screamed and turned to flee. *Earthquake*. It could kill in seconds. The land vibrated and swayed, then roared and dipped and murdered the things upon it. Within the compound Ikuba Castle, resting on a stone base, stood firm against the quake. But most of the other buildings collapsed into open fissures or were flattened. Here and throughout Edo, the quake killed men and animals and destroyed shops, roads, rice fields. Fires followed and so did plague and in two days Hideyoshi lost a third of his men and half of his supplies.

It was then that he rescinded his order for Benkai to be given a warrior's burial. Following his instincts and the advice of his chief astrologer and sages, he ordered the bodyguard cremated and the ashes scattered to the four winds. With that the rains stopped and Hideyoshi's troops ceased to die.

But before the year ended the *ninja* leaders who had taken part in the Ikuba Castle raid died violently and only with luck did Hideyoshi, the supreme spymaster, survive an attempted assassination.

A few years later he tried to conquer Korea and failed. He lost thousands of men in a long and dismal campaign that was the biggest disaster of his life. Aiding the Koreans were the Chinese and leading the Chinese, it is said, was Benkai.

With his Muramasa and the *Iki-ryō*.

one

ZANSHIN

*A STRONG MENTAL
CONCENTRATION; A
DETERMINATION TO FIGHT
UNTIL THE END AND
WITHOUT CARELESSNESS.*

Hong Kong, June 1982

AT NOON IN ABERDEEN HARBOR a gunshot signaled the start of the race. Eleven-year-old Todd Hansard, watching with his mother from the deck of a moored yacht, immediately felt a fear in his bowels.

The women around him paid little attention. They were wives of the businessmen meeting below in a conference room, whose entrance was guarded by two gigantic Japanese with oiled topknots that identified them as *sumotori*, former sumo wrestlers. Smaller Japanese with Ingram M-11s guarded the gangplank of the yacht, which was registered to a Tokyo conglomerate and called *Kitaro*. The guards eyed the boats docked on either side and the crowds milling on the pier. For them the excitement of a twenty-five-hundred-year-old race in memory of a Chinese ghost did not exist.

The race was Tuen Ng, the Dragon Boat Festival held each June in honor of Chu Yuan, an honest Chinese statesman who had drowned centuries ago to protest the corrupt government of his time. Competing in the all-day event were dragon boats, long, narrow war canoes with a dragon's head carved at the bow and its tail carved on the stern. Each craft carried a rowing team of twenty men sponsored by police, firemen, unions, journalists, racetracks and banks, both Chinese and European. The event, one of Hong Kong's most popular, was a tribute to the vain attempts by sympathizers who had rushed to the river to save the doomed Chu.

On the *Kitaro* Todd Hansard breathed in the odor of sawdust and wood chips. The yacht was anchored on Apleichau, the tiny island that housed Hong Kong's great boat builders, and the wood smells came from their greatest and most traditional work—eighty-foot junks made from teak logs without blueprints, built entirely on instinct. Out of respect for Chu's ghost, construction in the shipyard had temporarily stopped. So fervently did the Chinese believe in ancestor worship, as well as in the occult and the supernatural, that once a year the bones of ancestors were removed from their graves and lovingly washed. Construction had also stopped for another reason. The Chinese were gamblers and the workmen wanted to watch the race, on which they had bet heavily.

In Aberdeen, a village on Hong Kong island's south coast facing Apleichau Island, crowds of Chinese and a sprinkling of Europeans watched the race from white beaches, rocky coves and from the tops of parked cars and buses. They cheered their favorites in Cantonese, Mandarin, Shanghainese and English, and threw silk-wrapped packets of rice into the water to feed Chu's ghost. Some carried caged birds, a colony status symbol. Others sported caps, T-shirts and paper pennants in the colors of their favorite team and carried joss sticks for luck.

Noodle and meatball vendors had set up stalls on both sides of the harbor. Aberdeen's famed floating restaurants refused to allow more people aboard their already densely packed decks. On thousands of sampans and junks bobbing in the bay, the Tanka, the boat people who lived and died on this floating slum, banged cymbals and gongs to drive away evil spirits.

Todd Hansard watched his mother and the Japanese, Chinese and European women around her fan themselves and chatter rapidly in Oriental dialects and English. He was the only child and the only male among these *tai-tais*, women who belonged to wealthy men. A couple of them had flirted with Todd, a gesture he found uncomfortable and embarrassing. The helicopter saved him from further attention. It rose from behind Aberdeen's glass-and-steel high-rises, then swooped over the *Kitaro*; it carried police identification. Seconds later it banked left, hovering over some sampans that had strayed into the racing lane. The Chinese pilot, in mirrored sunglasses and a cowboy hat, used a loud hailer to order the small one-oared boats back to their flotilla.

Todd cringed and placed both hands over his ears. *The drums*. The dragon boats carried them to time cadence for the oar strokes and now their pounding filled his head with a throbbing pain that seemed to have been with him forever. A sudden raw iciness, brought on by the din from cymbals and gongs, left him quivering.

The nightmares had started two months ago, terror fraught and harrowing, followed by apparitions and specters during the day and always the omens, chilling forecasts of something ill-starred and malignant.

He swayed and felt himself about to pass out. Gripping the railing he focused his gaze on the sun, giving himself up to its heat and blinding whiteness. *He must not close his eyes*. Sleep had become a dark suffering, a look into hell that hid the un-finished tasks of past lifetimes. He believed in karma and knew that life was the sum of all of one's lives prior to birth. But he did not know what his unfinished tasks were. He knew only that a bygone horror was reaching out for him, and he did not know why.

He spoke of it to no one, not even to his mother. How could he tell her that he was terrified by the evil in his dreams, yet drawn to it by a promise of power.

* * *

TODD HANSARD was the son of a Chinese mother and a white father. He was a tall, thin boy, with straight black hair and a sad-faced, sloe-eyed beauty that was almost feminine. His eyes were unusual—one was a startling blue, the other a deep violet. There were similar contrasts in his disposition and energy. His moods alternated between friendly and with-drawn, while his energy had recently gone from low level to hyperkinetic and overactive.

To determine his future Todd's mother had consulted as-trologers, seers, numerologists and spiritual advisers, a deci-sion that angered her husband. "Good God, woman," he said. "When are you going to learn what not to believe?"

He scoffed even more when one seer noted that Todd possessed psychic powers, a mystic otherworldliness that so frightened the sage that he cut short his interview with the boy and fled the Hansard home.

Until a year ago Todd had been bullied and beaten by Chinese youngsters his own age. The Chinese sense of superiority and contempt for *gweilos*, foreigners, had made the half-caste Todd a target until he discovered the martial arts. His first teachers were the Chinese servants at his parents' home on Victoria Peak, Hong Kong's most exclusive enclave. They taught him kung fu and how to use weapons. In the early morning they took him to the Botanical Gardens where, surrounded by stunted Chinese pines and forests of bamboo, he joined hundreds of Chinese who were practicing the slow, balletlike movements of *tai chi chuan*. This was the boxing exercise derived from the calisthenics of ancient Buddhist monks.

But for reasons Todd himself never understood he preferred Japanese fighting forms, especially kendo, which he practiced obsessively. He progressed quickly, showing such skill that his instructor refused all payment and began to teach Todd privately, an honor bestowed rarely and only then to a student with extraordinary potential.

His fights away from the *dojo*, the fencing hall, now took a different turn. One which occurred a month before the dragon-boat race brought a police inspector to the Hansard home, a nineteenth-century mansion with bay windows, Chinese blackwood furniture and a veranda shaded by hanging bamboo blinds. He spoke with Todd's mother, a tall and lovely Shanghai woman whose black hair reached down to the small of her back. Such beauty actually depressed the inspector; he knew he could never possess it.

"Broke the leader's hip and fractured his cheekbone, you see," he said. The inspector was Welsh and had trouble reading from his notepad. He refused to wear his glasses in front of Katharine Hansard. "Knocked a second youth unconscious and tore the ligaments in the right knee of a third."

He flipped the note pad closed and smiled. "Day's work for any man, I should say. And your son is how old?"

Katharine Hansard did not return his smile. "Eleven. Inspector, I don't understand why you've come here. You've said these boys were members of a street gang, thugs who attacked my son without provocation.''

"Thugs with knives, if you will. Boy of yours gave 'em a good thumpin'. Used a broom handle, he did. Snatched the broom from some old lady as she was sweeping the sidewalk in front of her shop. Witnesses said your son fought like a wild man, like one possessed, you might say. Appears you have a miniature Jekyll-and-Hyde on your hands, Mrs. Hansard. From what I've been able to learn from school and from friends he's usually quite well behaved. Quite respectful. No trouble at all.''

The inspector combed his thick, red mustache with manicured fingertips and thought of her writhing beneath him in bed. "We must ask ourselves why he's become the belligerent lad of late." He tapped the note pad in the breast pocket of his jacket. "Not the first time, you see. Past three months he's had more than his share of punch-ups. Recent pattern of sorts. He's—''

"He's half-white.''

"I've noticed that, madam." Another smile. Ignored.

"That is the reason he's been beaten," she said.

"Not lately, he hasn't. Your boy's come out on top every time of late. Hurt the other lads quite severely in every instance.''

She touched her black hair with a slim, golden hand. The gesture made the inspector's heart jump. "My son has never attacked anyone, inspector. You probably have that written somewhere in your notes. Todd fights only in self-defense.''

"Agreed. What brings me here, however, is the severity of that defense. Your son inevitably comes down hard on his attackers and always with a weapon.''

He saw it in her eyes, a quick hardening, a slight lifting of the head. Just like your bloody father, thought the inspector. And a right nasty piece of work he is.

The inspector corrected himself. "Let me amend my last statement, if I may. Your son's used his fists but seems to prefer a weapon. *Prefer* is the operative word here. A stick, the branch of a tree. A *shinai*, the bamboo sword used in kendo. Appears to be a right little demon on occasions. Especially when there's something in his hands to fight with. Peaceful enough when left alone, but the moment the black flag goes up, he bloody well loses control."

The words were barely out before he knew he had gone too far. Katharine Hansard rose from her chair. "The houseboy will see you to the door."

"Mrs. Hansard, I didn't mean—"

"If there's anything further you wish to discuss, please contact my husband. You know who he is, I'm sure. And you know where to reach him."

Angered at being reminded of how powerless he was compared to the Hansards, the inspector coughed into his fist and looked through a bay window at a white-jacketed Chinese servant using a long-handled net to scoop leaves from a swimming pool. With just one year to retirement a policeman did not need the Hansards for enemies. What was it his coal-miner father used to say? *If you can't impose your terms on life, you must accept the terms life imposes on you.* In any case, it could have been worse. Mrs. High-and-Mighty Hansard could have threatened him with her wog father. That slant-eyed bastard was one of the most dangerous men in Hong Kong and had been responsible for a few deaths in his time, policemen among them.

As for Mr. Hansard, he was definitely a man to be reckoned with. He was a banker, and bankers, not the governor or the Queen's representatives bloody well ruled Hong Kong. A word from Ian Hansard in certain quarters could be the inspector's ruin.

He took his bifocals from an inside pocket, perched them on the end of his nose and tilted his head back to look at Katharine Hansard. She was even more beautiful than he had imagined. And then he saw the look on her face. Hatred. Hatred aimed at him for having tried to harm her son.

The inspector cleared his throat. "It won't be necessary to contact your husband, Mrs. Hansard. The last thing I wish to do is to disturb a man in his position. As a matter of fact, I suppose you might bring charges against Todd's attackers, should you choose to do so." He hesitated long enough to assert his independence, then added, "After all, he was the injured party."

At the window Katharine Hansard watched the inspector's car pull out of the graveled driveway, then turned and walked upstairs to look in on Todd. A hand went to her mouth in shock as she watched the sleeping boy toss and turn and moan. Suddenly he shot up in bed, drenched in perspiration, his chest rising and falling with his frenzied breathing. Rushing across the room she dropped onto his bed and took him in her arms.

She asked him about his dreams, but all he could remember was fear.

* * *

KATHARINE HANSARD at thirty no longer worked as a nurse but devoted herself to sculpting and to her son, whom she had practically raised alone. She had been born to wealth and power; her father was a Triad leader, a power in Hong Kong's underworld. She had married a wealthy Englishman, Ian Hansard, president of a Hong Kong bank with branches around the world. She lacked for nothing and yet the quiet, reserved Katharine Hansard had lived a life of great pain, which lately she had come to see was self-chosen.

In defiance of her father she had an affair with an American, Todd's father, whom she had not seen since the boy's birth. To give the child a name Katharine had married Ian Hansard, whom she did not love. He was a small, blond Englishman with the good looks of an aging choirboy and a burning determination to lead a remarkable life. Depressed by his father's failed dreams in Socialist England, the ambitious Hansard had emigrated to Hong Kong, where business was all that counted.

In an environment where principle and morality could be harmful, he avoided both and prospered. At thirty-five he was the youngest of the colony's major bankers and only occasionally showed a private displeasure at what he had become.

He was never close to Todd. The boy, after all, was not his son, and in any case Hansard had the English reluctance to showing affection. What did annoy him was the closeness between Katharine and the boy, especially when they spoke in Cantonese, a dialect he neither understood nor ever intended to learn. He had married his wife for her exotic beauty and the envy it inspired in other men; he had no tolerance toward rivals for that beauty. What belonged to Hansard was his and not to be shared, particularly in his own household. Besides, Todd, while respectful and well behaved at home, was too intelligent for Ian Hansard's liking.

"Chap's a real genius," Hansard had said to his wife. "I don't pretend to understand the workings of his mind but he's got a brain cell or two between his ears. Function of a genius, I'm told, is to furnish us cretins with ideas twenty years later. I'll say this about his sudden interest in things Japanese: one can't be inquisitive without being malicious, don't you think? Not that I'm saying the boy's bonkers, you understand."

Hansard had to be careful when he talked to Katharine about the boy. One wrong word and she could be as unforgiving as fire. Hansard decided to go after the Japanese, a much safer target.

"Mind you," he said, "the Japs are malicious enough in their oh so polite way. I could tell Todd a thing or two about the bloody Nips, doing business with them as I do. Ian Fabian Charles Hansard knows facts about the Japanese that would make very interesting reading, should ever I decide to put them down on paper. But some things are best left unsaid. One never regrets one's silence, only one's words." He looked at his wife and thought of her father, one more wily Oriental gentleman with secrets to keep.

* * *

ON THE SUN-WASHED deck of the *Kitaro* a white-uniformed crewman wheeled a trolley of steaming bamboo baskets to an empty table shaded by an oversized deck umbrella. The baskets contained hors d'oeuvres, steamed dumplings, minced pork, rice flour balls, custard tarts and red bean paste soup. A second trolley followed with bottles of cognac, champagne, club soda, ice buckets, cans of soft drinks and bowls of fresh fruit. Murmuring approval the perspiring women seated themselves around the table. Todd remained alone at the rail and ignored his mother's call to join her.

The drums. The cymbals and gongs.

He dropped to his knees, hands over his left eye. A sudden pain in his head gnawed at his brain with sharp animal teeth. He fell back to the deck and rolled from side to side in a futile

attempt to shake it off. His shirt was damp with cold sweat; he
was fast losing consciousness. Katharine Hansard called his
name, but he was falling swiftly now, dropping into a red
darkness and frozen mist. The last thing he remembered
before passing out was the warmth of his own blood on his
hands and face.

* * *

*He was in Japan, inside a castle lit by paper lanterns
and pine torches. The castle was under seige and
ninja had found a way inside. Now they edged closer
to him, black-clad phantoms bringing silent death.
He drew his katana and held it overhead with both
hands, waiting. He too wore black, a kimono of
black-and-gray silk, with a mons, his family crest, on
the back and sleeves. But something was wrong. The
pain. A hideous pain in his left eye. But he must not
falter, he must not give in to it. Stand and fight. Hai.*

*From other rooms came the sound of sword upon
sword and the screams of wounded men. He smelled
smoke and heard footsteps racing across the singing
floors. Something was tied to his belt. The woman's
head, its eyes closed as though in sleep, the lips
parted as if to speak. When had he killed her and
why? A new urgency seized him and he knew he must
get to a room on the upper floor. He must cut his
way through the ninja. Someone on the next floor
needed him, but who? He didn't know. He knew
only that he must go forward, that he must kill.*

* * *

TODD OPENED HIS EYES. He lay on deck, bone tired, his
shirt soaked in perspiration. There was a life preserver under
his head and his mother knelt beside him, her hand on his
forehead. His stepfather, the *tai-tais*, and a few Japanese
crewmen looked down as a small Japanese in a business suit
squatted to take Todd's pulse. He spoke to Todd in Japanese.
An annoyed Ian Hansard said, "Well for God's sake, Todd,

answer the man. How many times does he have to repeat himself?"

The boy frowned.

"Minute ago you were chattering away like a bloody magpie," said Hansard. "First I knew of your being able to speak Japanese."

Dazed and weak, Todd tried to push himself off the deck and failed.

"Don't, don't know Japanese," he said. "Can't speak—"

Hansard rolled his eyes upward. "Lord help us. Todd, we distinctly heard you speak Japanese. There's no need to lie. We don't give a damn what language you babble in, just don't waste our time lying about it, that's all."

Hansard felt his wife's eyes burn into him, but he refused to look at her. Damn them both for pulling him from a meeting that meant millions to his bank. This time he was going to speak his mind and tell the world that dear little Todd was as mad as a hatter. Definitely in cloud-cuckooland, that boy. It wasn't Hansard's style to dust Todd's jacket, to beat him, but this playacting nonsense could not go unanswered. And if Katharine didn't like it, she could bugger off.

Hansard suddenly saw an advantage in Todd's dockside charade. It was just the excuse he needed to pack the little blighter off to school in England or Switzerland where if the teachers were cruel, it was only to be kind. And Hansard could get his own back for the letters his wife continued to write to Todd's natural father in America.

True, she hadn't seen the American since Todd's birth and she made no attempt to hide the letters, which she kept in her studio. Hansard had secretly read a few, and knew the two still shared a closeness he could only envy. His own infidelity did nothing to ease his jealousy. Hansard might own Katharine, but he could never possess her. And as Todd grew older the banker looked into his face for signs of the American: all he saw was a reminder that he himself was not loved by the wife with whom he was obsessed.

"Todd," Hansard said, "below deck I was told that you were half-blind or something. Instead I see you with two eyes in working order. Wouldn't you say an explanation is called for?"

Katharine Hansard brought her son's hand to her cheek. "He was bleeding. The doctor—"

Hansard shook his head. "Katharine, dear heart. Doctor Orito said there's nothing physically wrong with Todd and that includes his eyes. Both eyes. Need I say that the doctor is not on board to indulge anyone in their fantasies. Is Todd going to come down with the same sort of mysterious attack at the party we're having next week for the film people? Could prove embarrassing to both of us. Very, very embarrassing."

He brushed imaginary lint from his shirt, one of dozens made for him at a cost of one hundred pounds each at Turnbull and Asser in London. "Katharine, darling, when we return home you and I must have a little heart-to-heart about Todd's future. There are places that will discipline a boy in a manner to make him much the better for it. Now if you'll excuse me, there are people waiting downstairs."

He crossed the deck and stepped into a passageway leading below. He was not happy with the discomfort he sensed in his wife at the thought of Todd being sent away. But Hansard did feel better for it.

Doctor Orito snapped his black bag shut and spoke to Katharine Hansard in English. "Please, your son, he has illness recently?"

She did not take her eyes off the boy. "He has trouble sleeping, yes. And bad dreams. Very bad dreams."

"Has he taken medication of any kind, anything that perhaps might cause him to hallucinate?"

"No."

"I see. He has a most strong imagination. He speaks of *ninja* and castles and a battle in which he fought." Orito smiled. "Perhaps he heard a little Japanese somewhere and remembered it, but did not know he remembered it."

"He studies kendo with a Japanese teacher. But he has not studied the language."

"Mmmm, yes." Orito looked at Todd, who held his gaze. "Strange eyes, your son. Most strange. Please take him inside, away from the sun and the excitement of the race."

Todd had been holding Katharine's hand and when his grip relaxed she looked down to find his head in her lap. Their eyes

met; she smiled and then his eyes closed and he slept. Not
the sleep of rest, but of exhaustion. In sleep he looked more
vulnerable than ever, and she wondered if she had enough
strength to continue to bear his suffering.

When Orito saw her tears he knew there was nothing more
he could say to her; tears softened stones and tamed tigers. He
had looked into the boy's eyes and heard his words and in
both had read pages of danger. But he could not talk to the
mother now. Tomorrow was in the hands of the gods and
while the worst was not always certain, it was often very likely.
He left without warning Katharine, without telling her that
soon, according to her son, the *ninja* would kill her and her
husband.

2

IN MODERN TOKYO one still finds shrines to Inari, the rice god, and the mysterious white foxes that served as his messengers. Most of them are kept up by businessmen and industrialists who pray for a harvest of corporate profits and unlimited wealth instead of an abundant rice harvest. On the edge of the city, in overcrowded neighborhoods of cheap houses and wooden shacks now resting on ancient rice fields, a modern version of the *Ta-asobi* ritual, an ancient fertility rite, is played out.

Here on a dark, cold February night, in front of a timeworn Shinto shrine, old men in white kimonos shove four bamboo stakes into the ground and encircle them with a straw rope. This is now the sacred rice field and in its center stands a large drum. Spring will come soon and the gods will leave their mountain homes to live in the rice fields. Demonic spirits and goblins will attack them. The *Ta-asobi* rites are a help to the gods in this conflict.

Inside the holy enclosure the old men till the ground with imaginary hoes. Then, as one of them thumps the drum, the others dance and scrape bamboo sticks one against the other to pantomime driving away birds. A prayer is sung to accompany symbolic plowing and fertilizing. Finally, four small boys playing the role of *saotome*, girls who plant the rice seedlings, are led to the enclosure. As onlookers clap and shriek, the boys are tossed over the large drum. The rice has been planted.

This pantomime allows the Japanese to deal with man's two selves: flesh and spirit, body and soul, material and metaphysical. Life and death, god and man, good and evil, the old and the new. All form an uninterrupted cycle, an eternal play, with neither beginning nor end.

There is also the rice ritual observed once a year, in secret and alone by one man. It occurs in the heart of Tokyo, within sight of luxury hotels, blocks of high-rises and garish nightclubs. The man is the emperor, who tends a tiny rice field deep within the walled gardens of the historic Imperial Palace. No one is allowed to watch him, but what he does dramatizes the inseparable connection between Japan's frenzied present and her mystic and savage past.

* * *

SHORTLY AFTER SUNRISE two men carrying the black leather cases of kendoists stepped from Ikuba Castle into the castle courtyard. One was Kon Kenpachi, Japan's most famous and controversial film director. Behind him was Zenzo Nosaka, a wealthy industrialist and a power among the *zaikai*, the country's big business interests. Both men wore summer kimonos and *geta*, Japanese clogs that clacked against the cobblestones as the two crossed the courtyard and stopped at a garden.

The garden's stark beauty came from polished black rocks arranged in a semicircle on sand that had been skillfully raked to express a calm lake. At its edge stood a small Shinto shrine made of green bamboo. Resting on the shrine's single shelf was a round polished mirror and a sword, symbols of the wisdom and courage of Amaterasu, the Sun Goddess from whom Japan's early rulers claimed descent. To keep out evil spirits a braided straw cord was strung across the shrine's entrance.

Kenpachi and Nosaka bowed their heads in silence, then walked on. The film director, anxious to begin their fencing match, led the way.

Ikuba Castle, which belonged to Kenpachi, rested on a hill between an expressway and a public park in Shinjuku, Tokyo's Greenwich Village. The district's elegant shops, first-run movie theaters, bath houses and jazz clubs drew artists, homosexuals, the young and the *yakuza*, gangsters, who helped shape Kenpachi's image of himself.

The castle moat had been filled in with grass hundreds of years ago. Reflecting Kenpachi's love of luxury the compound included a swimming pool, twin guest cottages and a movie theater seating seventy-five with an elaborate film-cutting room. Three gardens ringed the three-story, white wooden castle building; one was designed around an ornamental pond spanned by a slender redwood bridge taken from Hideyoshi's four-hundred-year-old Osaka Castle. The stables, long gone, had been replaced by garages housing a British Morgan, a Mercedes, a 1929 Daimler, a Silver Cloud Rolls Royce, a Lincoln Continental and several motorcycles.

Only two buildings remained from Lord Saburo's day—the castle, with its black-tiled, horned roofs and the *dojo*, the original fencing hall used by Benkai, Saburo's bodyguard.

At the *dojo* entrance Kenpachi stopped to look east at the sun-reddened Tokyo Tower in the heart of the city. Later in the day the tower, fifty-nine feet higher than the Eiffel Tower on which it was modeled, would be hidden by pollution so thick that at major street intersections, billboards would flash electronically computed pollution levels.

As a boy Kenpachi had been able to stand anywhere in Tokyo and see Mount Fuji many miles away. Then the air had been clean and clear. The land had been respected and loved. But that had all changed. Today the beauty of the sacred snowcapped mountain and the blue sky above it were hidden by smoke from thousands of factories and by exhaust fumes from millions of cars and trucks. Wild flowers and smaller, weaker animals were dying.

In recent years Kenpachi's anger had grown at a Japan made morally bankrupt by a westernization, by greedy Japanese and Western businessmen, by the spread of American culture. He had come to hate modern Japan and those responsible for it. Months ago he had decided to deal with these people. His response had been that of a samurai, one of blood and death.

Kon Kenpachi stood five feet seven inches with straight

black hair, brown eyes and a scar between his left ear and
cheekbone that gave his full-lipped, sullen handsomeness a
dangerous edge. He was thirty-eight, slim yet muscular, and
flat waisted from years of body building, from practicing
karate and kendo. In exercise he acted out the role of a samurai, a warrior standing alone against the erosion of Japan's
traditional values based on Bushido, the code of honor, loyalty and courage. It was a pose born of a desire for glory.

The flamboyant Kenpachi added theatrical flourishes to the
martial arts and Bushido; when he hosted a party or press conference he would wear a kimono, *dai-sho*, jeweled bracelets on
both wrists and dark glasses.

Though married he did not hide his obsession for *onnagata*,
the male actors who played women's roles in the kabuki
theater. In reporting on a party where a drunken Kenpachi
and his *onnagata* lover hacked poolside lounge chairs to bits
with samurai swords, a critic wrote, "Aeschylus was correct.
A prosperous fool is a grievous burden. If anyone can be said
to be an ass in a lion's skin, it is our Mr. Dai-sho."

Dai-sho, in this case, was slang for bisexual.

Kenpachi the film director had won two Oscars, plus numerous festival awards in Asia, Europe, and South America.
His movies were intense and mesmerizing, violent and erotic,
personal statements of a dark vision that had made him a cult
figure from Tokyo to Beverly Hills. As man or director he was
charismatic and arrogant, an intellectual with a touch of the
hoodlum who shamelessly courted celebrity while living in
eight-hundred-year-old Ikuba Castle in the manner of a feudal
daimyo.

The versatile Kenpachi was also an actor, poet, playwright,
artist and composer, and lived life as though it were a prize to
be taken by winners. He lost himself in his work and in his
pleasures. The perfect life, he knew, was not doing all you
were able to do; it was doing all you would like to do. Now, at
the peak of his powers, he was directing his first film with
Hollywood backing and a Japanese and American cast, a film
which he boasted would be his masterpiece. Only Kenpachi
and a handful of trusted associates knew that this movie was
also to be his last.

When it was completed Kenpachi planned to commit *seppuku*.

* * *

THREE MONTHS AGO the American film proposal had been one of three Kenpachi was considering as his final work. That was when he had gone to the sumptuous mansion of Zenzo Nosaka, located near the Imperial Palace. Nosaka was eighty-two, in excellent physical and mental health, an elfin, gray little man with the cold looks of a pitiless cat. He had become the most ruthless and feared of the *zaikai* by identifying the enemies of his interests with the enemies of humanity.

Nosaka, a descendant of one of Hideyoshi's most important captains, was Kenpachi's longtime mentor. In the director's early years Nosaka had rescued him from degrading poverty and backed his films. When scandal had threatened Kenpachi it was Nosaka's money and power that had saved him from blackmail, prison and disgrace. The *zaikai* leader, an excellent kendoist and noted collector of samurai swords, had introduced Kenpachi to fencing and even now remained his toughest fencing opponent. In the tradition of older to younger samurai, Nosaka and Kenpachi had once been lovers.

Throughout his life Kenpachi's choice had always been danger. This recklessness had brought him wealth and fame and saved him from failure and shame. To experience the maximum danger, *seppuku*, was all that remained to him. For this he needed Nosaka's help, but it would do no good to flatter the old man. Flattery was for the weak and Nosaka was not weak. For Kenpachi's plan to work he would have to show Nosaka that there was something in it for him.

"I speak of my death first, Nosaka-san. It will be a grand one, with a grand purpose. I propose a suicide of *kanshi*, one of protest and censure. *Hai*, of condemnation. I condemn Japan for what she has become and I die to arouse her. I give my heart's blood to free her from America. Someone must shame our country into changing course. I will open my *hara* and shock Japan into returning to the glorious Imperial Nippon of the past."

He closed his eyes. "The sanctity of our royal family is worth dying for. Let my death return the emperor to what he once was, a divine symbol of authority, a god here on earth. Japan cannot be great so long as the emperor is seen as mortal. Glory, Nosaka-san. I say glory is to be achieved through blood and death."

Nosaka fingered a long string of tiny black pearls that dangled from his neck. Attached to the pearls was a gold-rimmed monocle, which he now inserted into the socket of his left eye. He studied Kenpachi for long, silent seconds. Nosaka, descendant of samurai, was never surprised by death. Death was the embrace, the eternal night, that could not be avoided.

There was no happier man than he who knew when to die. Was Kenpachi-san such a man?

The film director poured tea into a pair of bowls, then handed one to the old man who sat across from him on the floor in a room with walls covered with samurai swords and other medieval weapons. Nosaka had given him much and guided his professional and personal life. But he could not take away Kenpachi's regrets. Regret at not having been born a samurai. Regret at not having fought for Japan in the last great war.

Kenpachi worshipped the royal family while hating them for what they had become since the occupation. It was disgraceful that the crown prince, heir to the throne, had married a commoner. Loving and hating at the same time was a contradiction, but not in one with Kenpachi's passions.

Kenpachi's main passion was his belief which tied death to youth and beauty. He was obsessed with finding a way to preserve beauty in the face of *mujo*, impermanence and inevitable change. And against all odds he had found a solution; beauty could be sustained forever, but only by dying young when beauty was at its most alluring and seductive. From this point on he romanticized death, bloody death, in his life and work. For him the death of the young was the ultimate in beauty.

Kenpachi's vanity about his own beauty was an open secret. There was the intense daily exercise, the constant examination of face and form for the slightest flaw, the fierce rededication to discipline following each instance of debauchery. It was this beauty that had brought him into Nosaka's life and to the *zaikai* leader Kenpachi had been son, disciple, lover. Nosaka had never loved any man or woman as he had the sensuous Kenpachi. Only the two of them knew how much pain this desire had brought the businessman; it had almost become Nosaka's slavery.

Kenpachi knew that Nosaka, with the wisdom of a samurai, would one day prefer to see this beauty which had given him such acute pleasure preserved through *seppuku*. Better to remember what you once loved as timelessly beautiful than to see it wither and die.

And Nosaka knew that Kenpachi's failings, his destructive excesses and indulgences, would one day exact their toll; pain followed pleasure and every action had its reaction. Nosaka was that rare man, one who knew how to be old. Kenpachi wasn't.

It was time to give Nosaka a reason to join Kenpachi in his grand plan.

"Nosaka-san, I have learned that the American, Jude Golden, is dying. For this and other reasons which I will explain, I ask your help in bringing back to life the Blood Oath League."

A stunned Nosaka pulled sharply on the string of black pearls, sending them bouncing on the straw mat. To calm himself he looked at a wall where he had hung a collection of *tsubas*, sword guards, the thin metal disks that protected a sword user's hand. Excited, Kenpachi watched the old man's eyes glaze over, and knew what was happening. The years were falling away; Nosaka was young again, a junior officer in the Kempai Tai, the dreaded military police. It was the 1930s, Japan's most eventful and violent time. The country was a fascist state, controlled by a military elite openly seeking war with China and secretly preparing for war with Britain and America. The military also controlled the emperor, clung to a rigid foreign policy and dreamed of an empire stretching through Asia and across the Pacific.

Supporting this dream were men like Zenzo Nosaka, who formed secret organizations with the backing of wealthy industrialists and retired military officers. The White Tigers, the Black Dragon Society and the Blood Oath League were a few such groups, all of which worked outside of the official security agencies and were often more feared. They posed as patriotic clubs, cultural societies and martial arts clubs and dealt in espionage, blackmail and murder. Their targets were union leaders, journalists, foreign diplomats, liberal politicians, businessmen.

Nosaka, an expert kendoist and judoka, helped found the Blood Oath League. Unlimited funds from right-wing businessmen and his own talent for leadership enabled him to recruit the best fighters from Tokyo's *dojos* and weld the Blood Oath League into one of Japan's most efficient terrorist and espionage units.

When the war ended, Nosaka's ties to the league and his brutality against allied prisoners of war while a Kempai Tai officer brought him a death sentence from an American warcrimes tribunal. Jude Golden led the American prosecution team that won the conviction. The sentence, however, was never carried out.

By means of the martial arts Nosaka managed to cheat the hangman who still took the lives of his close comrades. Judo and kendo had toughened his body and mind, leaving him with an iron will, so that while others cringed before the conquerors or emerged from the war as broken men, he survived beatings, solitary confinement and attempts to starve him into submission.

Trial and imprisonment, however, had been a loss of face. The man Nosaka held most responsible for this and never forgave was Jude Golden.

The Blood Oath League. Neither time nor distance could erode such a memory.

When Nosaka looked at Kenpachi once more the old man's face was a stern mask. The film director grew uneasy; he feared, needed and loved the *zaikai* leader at once. Nosaka's gaze made Kenpachi feel as feeble and as deceitful as a woman. Kenpachi leaned forward and began to pick up Nosaka's pearls.

"What do you fear?" asked the old man.

"I wish to wipe away the shame the Americans have brought upon you, Nosaka-san. I—"

"I find it quite easy to deceive people who believe they are deceiving me. You have had my help and my affection over the years and though I sometimes find your self-love flagrant and notable, I will not turn my face from you. However, do not seek to manipulate me."

"Forgive me, Nosaka-san," whispered Kenpachi, his eyes cast down. "I do speak the truth about Jude Golden, but you are right about me, as always. I greatly fear old age, disease, decay. With each day I fear them more and more. I cannot face the idea that each day brings the putrefaction of my flesh hours closer. I have definitely decided to die by my own hand, at a moment of my own choosing and soon. There is in me less fear of death than of old age. Having accepted this, I now speak to you of the Blood Oath League."

He looked up. "I want the league to kill ten men, the killings to be done before I die."

He waited for a reaction. There was none. He continued, "You are familiar with them. They are Japan's enemies, certain bankers, a particular journalist, certain businessmen and politicians of whom neither you nor I approve. Some are here in Japan, others are presently in the West, in America and Europe. I blame them for what Japan has become, a polluted and mercenary extension of the West."

After a while Nosaka said, "Please place the pearls in an empty tea bowl." He held out his hand for the monocle, took it from Kenpachi and examined it for cracks.

He looked at the film director. "If I refuse to help, will you still proceed . . . with all of it?"

"*Hai*."

"I see. Well, we both know men who kill, do we not?"

Kenpachi bowed, aware that Nosaka's remark held a sinister implication: the old man was one of the few who knew that Kenpachi himself had killed twice, once in a secret ritual, once for the thrill of it.

Nosaka picked up the tea bowl of black pearls and began to stir them with a forefinger. "Men who hide behind high walls and bodyguards with the smug assurance that theirs is the final truth and must be accepted by all. A past and present danger to Japan. Your words were my words at another time and I

believed them as sincerely as you seem to now. Yes, I know the
men you wish to kill and I despise them, perhaps more than
you do."

He selected a pearl and rolled it between a thumb and forefinger. "We, the league, were fearless. We were made brave
by knowing that there was nothing more glorious than to die
for Japan. We believed in *geba*, the cult of divine violence,
which promised a dying warrior immortality as a star in the
constellation of Orion."

He stared into the small bowl of pearls as though seeing the
past and the future. "We were heroes with but a single burning impulse, to lift Japan to a glory *higher* than the stars. Yes,
higher. It was, I can tell you, a great experience and a great
time in our history. Never have I felt as fulfilled, as alive as I
did in those days with the Blood Oath League. I have thought
of it often, especially now that I am old and have almost done
with life. I, too, must prepare for death, for the day when the
gods cut the cord binding me to this wheel of birth and
death."

He looked at Kenpachi. "There are things I do not wish to
leave undone."

There was a slight taunt in the film director's voice as he
said, "There were three Americans who prosecuted you at
your trial. Jude Golden was their leader. I have not forgotten
their names."

Nosaka placed the tea bowl of black pearls to one side. "We
forgive when it suits us and it has never suited me to forgive
them. One can close one's eyes to everything except memories.
On the day I was sentenced to hang I vowed to kill the three
Americans. That vow kept me alive. *Hai*. No sooner had I
thought those words than I knew that death would not come
for me until I had disposed of Jude Golden, Salvatore Verna
and Duncan Ivy."

He looked past Kenpachi to the wall beyond, at a *hora-gai*,
a conch shell used hundreds of years ago as a horn to give
notice of an attack. *Yesterday's enemy, tomorrow's friend*.
By a twist of fate, Nosaka and the three Americans had been
forced to become allies. That twist of fate was the cold war, as
Japan joined forces with America against Japan's old enemies, Russia and China. Suddenly Nosaka's espionage skills

were needed by an America bogged down in the Korean War and by a Japan anxious to keep communism at bay.

He had been allowed to live, given a pardon and gone on to prosper in business. The three Americans had even become his secret business associates. One was now an important labor leader in New York; the other two had become bankers. All three were corrupt and greedy and unaware that in his mind the unforgiving Nosaka had killed each one a thousand times. The impending death of Jude Golden was a sharp reminder that Nosaka still had an unfinished task. Or he himself could die and face the gods with nothing to offer but broken vows.

Nosaka's eyes returned to Kenpachi. The old man's catlike features grew more predatory. "You say Jude Golden is dying. How do you come to know this?"

"From his daughter who is called Jan. She is the producer of the American film which I have been offered, which would be done here, in the Philippines and in Hong Kong. She was to have come to Tokyo tomorrow to discuss the project with me, but she had to cancel our meeting. Her father was suddenly taken to the hospital with serious heart trouble."

Nosaka closed his eyes and sat rigid, hands down on his thighs. Kenpachi watched and remained silent. Finally the old man murmured, "Accept the American offer."

He has agreed to help me, thought an elated Kenpachi. He bowed. "*Hai, sensei.*" Master.

Nosaka opened his eyes. "I want the names of those you feel are fit to do the task you now propose. Give me only warriors. When I have investigated them thoroughly, we shall then move on to the next step. Also, give me the names of the ten you wish to have killed. We must also begin to investigate them. When we strike there can be no room for error. As to your *seppuku*, when do you propose to do it?"

"I shall complete one last film, my masterpiece, and then I shall offer my life to Japan."

Nosaka bowed his head. "Let your *seppuku* follow the proper form. Traditional wine, witnesses, the sword handle wrapped in white and such. Above all, give much care to the choice of a *kaishaku*, he who will end your pain before it becomes unbearable. It is a special position, one to be filled only by a skilled swordsman and true *bushi*."

Dizzy with elation Kenpachi returned the old man's bow. For Kenpachi the weapons room became a meteor carrying him to an infinite and unimagined joy.

Bushido. The word coming from Nosaka had the force of a blow across the face and Kenpachi flinched as though he had just been struck. Suddenly he was afraid without knowing why.

"By joining you," said Nosaka, "I have not given you the right to amuse yourself at my expense. You will follow my instructions without deviation. Is that understood?"

"*Hai, sensei.*"

"True knowledge is being and becoming. No truth is yours until you have experienced it for yourself. In prison I was forced to unlock the powers trapped in my mind, or I would have died at the hands of the Americans. I released forces hidden in my soul, hidden in every man's soul if he would but seek them out. You must do the same. You must go beyond your limits and in doing so you will obtain absolute strength of body, mind and will."

"How?"

"Bushido. By the practice of kendo and karate, combined with *zazen*, meditation. Reach deeper within yourself than you ever thought possible. Look into your soul and explore death and become truly fearless. Above all, find a way to touch the universal mind, the one mind that we all belong to. For there you will be able to find him who would be your *kaishaku.*"

Nosaka sighed. "Hundreds of years ago, one had to practice *zazen* for a minimum of ten years before being allowed to begin the practice of the fighting form. Ah, the warriors of those days. They had such wills as to make mountains crumble before them and oceans dry up at a word. What is the first truth about Zen?"

"That there is no unity or One, that One is All and All is One. Yet the All remains All, the One remains the One."

"To know and to act are one. All of your past lives are in the One. Body and mind are to function as one . . ."

Kenpachi, now high strung with excitement, barely heard Nosaka's words. He vaguely saw the old man rise and walk to a pinewood chest, lift up the top and from inside remove several objects. Then Nosaka was kneeling in front of Kenpachi and handing the objects to him one by one.

"Benkai's Muramasa," said Nosaka, passing over the long sword.

Kenpachi's eyes were all whites.

"Saburo's knife," said Nosaka. "The one Benkai used to commit *seppuku* four hundred years ago. These are the jewels of my collection. All great weapons have souls of their own, powers of their own. These weapons have given me power which I have used to become successful. Now I give them to you. Use them with pride and never forget the glory and honor which they represent. When you do *zazen* keep both the sword and the knife at your side. Always."

Kenpachi, eyes bright with tears, could only nod.

"And now this." He handed Kenpachi a small black lacquered box edged in gold and silver. The top of the box had a grainy finish rough to the touch.

"Place your hand on it," Nosaka commanded. "Benkai's ashes are lacquered into the top."

Kenpachi, eyes closed, shivered.

"Do not open it," said Nosaka. "First purify yourself. Become fit for your *kaishaku*. Be worthy of him. You will know who he is when he tells you what is in this box. The man who is to be your second will be drawn to you by what is inside this. After you meet him you will then open the box, for you will immediately know the truth of what he is saying. Do not disobey me in this, for merely by looking at you I will, as always, know of your weakness. And this time I shall turn my face from yours forever."

"*Hai, sensei.*"

"If you must kill to keep this box do so without hesitation."

"*Hai.*"

"You have only a short time to acquire a new way of looking at reality. Practice Bushido and as I did in prison, send forth your spirit to meet that of the past samurai and beg their help. If your faith is strong you will receive what you wish for. Let the spirits of past warriors choose your *kaishaku*. Believe and they will come to you."

Nosaka smiled, remembering what he had accomplished in prison while living in the shadow of death. "I will show you how to use the way of the sword to make your spirit strong. I will show you how to find the hidden powers within yourself. That which you least know you will come to believe.''

Kenpachi, holding the lacquered box in a tight grip, opened his eyes. He felt a new and vigorous force inside him and he now understood the need to consecrate himself. He would have to know his heart and mind as never before. He would have to deal in truths other than those he had always made for himself. Without knowing where the words came from he said, "Benkai will come to me. *He* will be my *kaishaku*. Honor and glory will be mine. Benkai will bring them to me.''

* * *

THE IKUBA CASTLE *dojo*. Kenpachi had kept the old fencing hall as plain and as simple as it had been in Benkai's time. The one-room building had neither modern locks or electricity; the only source of light came from two windows and half a dozen paper lanterns hanging on bare walls. There were few decorations: there was a list of ancient swordsmiths on one wall and on another, two framed ink drawings of priests and birds done with exceptional skill by Benkai. Leather and wooden scabbards hung above the entrance, their lacquer dried and cracked with age.

It was a place that smelled of sweat and straw, a place where one felt the dead cold of the past.

Behind the *dojo*'s barred door and windows Kenpachi and Nosaka faced each other in the center of the floor. Both were in *seiza*, the formal kneeling position, buttocks on heels, back straight, hands palms down on thighs. Over kendo training clothes, a quilted cotton jacket and skirtlike trousers made of lightweight black cotton, each now wore the kendo armor—waist and hip protector of dark blue heavy cotton; a chest protector of heavy bamboo and leather which gleamed under a dozen coats of black lacquer; a hooded face mask with a leather flap to guard the throat and a steel grill to protect the face. Hands and forearms were protected by long leather gloves. The overall look was both medieval and futuristic.

With the left hand both men reached down to the mat and picked up the *shinai*, the lightweight, three-foot-long bamboo foil that was respected as a real sword.

They rose, still facing each other, and bowed from the waist, the *shinai* pressed against the left hip as though in a scabbard. For a few seconds they watched each other before sinking into a deep knee bend, to finish in a crouch, knees spread wide. Here Kenpachi and Nosaka slowly drew the *shinai* from its nonexistent scabbard and in a two-handed grip, right hand over left, pointed the weapon forward.

The bamboo foils touched and crossed at the tip.

Kenpachi's face was beaded with perspiration; a vein throbbed in the center of his forehead. *Zazen*, meditation, had not relaxed him. He was edgy, the result of a twenty-four-hour fast and a hard week's shooting on the American film called *Ukiyo*, the floating world, where pleasure was taken without a thought for the morrow. This was the first time in two weeks he had fenced with Nosaka, who had been out of Japan on business. Kenpachi would have to show a strong spirit.

The film director had also grown increasingly irritated over the matter of the black box. He wanted to open it now, today, but did not do so because he feared Nosaka's anger. Recent weeks of intense Bushido training, including long hours sitting in *zazen*, had left Kenpachi agitated and strained. Without telling Nosaka, Kenpachi continued the use of drugs, believing they heightened his awareness during meditation.

In sleep the director, exhausted by long hours on the set and by his increased martial-arts practice, saw into the dark caves of his own mind, saw evil at its most beautiful and ugliest and knew that all things were possible. Asleep, he enjoyed a profane and terrifying freedom.

Awake, he wondered if it was not madness to expect a stranger to describe the contents of a box he had never seen.

In the *dojo*, flickering light from the paper lanterns darkened the straw mats with long shadows which closed in on the two men. Saburo's knife and Benkai's long sword, still in scabbard, rested on a small wooden table near the door. Under dancing yellow flames from a lantern the scabbard's twin red dragons seemed to uncoil and slither about on the lacquered black wood.

The *shinai* of each crouching fighter was pointed at his opponent's throat. Each man's back was straight, his eyes unblinking, the head erect and both elbows held close to the chest. A slight grunt from Nosaka was the signal to begin.

They rose, each pushing the right foot forward, the *shinai* now aimed at the opponent's eyes, blocking his view as much as possible. Eyes first, said the ancient swordsman. Then footwork, followed by courage and strength. The eyes allowed you to detect your opponent's weakness, his fear, his technique, his spirit. Footwork enabled you to attack him with the speed and savagery of a hawk.

There were seven target areas in kendo: the left and right side of the head; the top of the face mask; both wrists and the left or right side of the chest protector.

Kenpachi attacked at once.

He leaped forward, *shinai* held high, then brought it down swiftly, aiming for the left side of Nosaka's head. The old man easily blocked the blow, knocking it away. Without stopping Kenpachi slashed first at Nosaka's right wrist, then at the left side of his chest. Each attack was blocked by Nosaka, who continually circled to his right, increasing the distance between him and his opponent.

With a shout Kenpachi pressed the attack, driving the old man back with a dozen quick, vicious strokes to the head, chest, wrists. Nosaka blocked, evaded and when he had knocked the last attack aside, stepped obliquely to his left and scored a clean slash against Kenpachi's right side.

His anger barely held in check, the film director aimed a thrust at Nosaka's throat; the old man sidestepped and at the same time tapped Kenpachi's right wrist. Kenpachi turned to face Nosaka only to have the old man make a small circular movement of his *shinai* that parried Kenpachi's weapon upward and to the right. A second later Nosaka again struck the director in the right side of the chest.

Kenpachi charged; this time his *shinai* was parried downward to the left. He never saw the next movement but felt the point of Nosaka's sword push hard against his throat flap.

"Patience," said Nosaka, stepping back out of range.

Patience. Kenpachi remembered the words which Nosaka had him memorize years ago, the words of the great Hideyoshi to his successors. *The strong, manly ones in life are those who understand the meaning of the word patience. Patience means restraining one's inclinations.* Reluctantly the director slowed the pace of the fight, attacking but not forcing an opening where there was none. Now he began to apply what he had learned in recent practice sessions with the Blood Oath League.

He began to score on Nosaka, each strike, clean, strong.

The two were in close quarters, weapons crossed waist level at the hilt when Nosaka shoved his hands forward to push Kenpachi back. At the same time Nosaka took one step back himself, weapon now raised high and Kenpachi, seeing the opening, quickly stuck him at the top of the face mask.

Ecstatic, the director pressed the attack, striking three more times at the head. A retreating Nosaka blocked each attack, his weapon held high. Increasing his speed Kenpachi leaped forward, faked a head strike, then struck at Nosaka's open right side. Score.

The old man countered immediately, going for Kenpachi's right wrist, forcing him to drop his hand low to avoid the strike. Nosaka, however, never followed up the wrist feint. Instead he scored twice—a thrust to the throat, followed by a head strike.

Neither man spoke. Talk was unnecessary. There was only the focus on combat, on the full use of body, mind and soul in a fighting form that traced its history back almost two thousand years. Kenpachi and Nosaka were aware only of the moment, that the difference between life and death lay in one quick movement of the wrist, that through kendo they were more alive than at any other time.

Sounds. The rhythmic clack-clack-clack of the bamboo weapons striking one another. The soft shuffle of bare feet across the straw mats. The *kiai*, the ferocious warrior cry designed to terrify the enemy and give courage to the attacker.

Nosaka, with his tigerish, implacable spirit, scored more frequently, mixing feints and evasions with a skillful combination of offense and defense. Kenpachi, more emotional and reckless, scored less. But it was obvious that in the past three months he had improved his technique and above all his *shin*, his spirit.

The match ended. An exhausted Kenpachi removed his face mask, breathed deeply and waited for Nosaka's criticism.

"Good," said the old man. Nothing more.

It was enough.

A jubilant Kenpachi bowed from the waist. "*Domo arigato gozai mashite, sensei,*" thank you very much, master.

"Your spirit has become stronger. Even now I feel it. The *seppuku* of such a man is a worthy gift to Japan."

"Your words mean much to me, Nosaka-san. But I am no closer to finding my *kaishaku*. It has been three months since you gave me the box, which as you know still remains closed. The film goes well. I shall finish it on schedule, perhaps a day or two sooner. It is my wish to die within twenty-four hours of its completion. The league will have done its work by then and my death would have much meaning. Some men in the league have said they would be honored to be my *kaishaku*. But when I mention the box, they have no answer."

Nosaka placed his *shinai* in a narrow leather carrying case and zipped it closed. "The league has killed five times for us. Two deaths here in Japan. One in Rome, one in São Paulo. And Duncan Ivy, first of the three Americans who put me on trial thirty-seven years ago, is now dead. Five deaths for the new Japan. What of the next killings?"

Kenpachi, who had knelt down and was folding his armor into a round leather carrying case, stopped and looked up at the *zaikai* leader. "Our men are already in Paris. Within twenty-four hours the Frenchman Henri Labouchere will no longer be alive to finance and construct atomic reactors on Japanese soil. And the American Salvatore Verna will die before this week ends."

"Ah yes, Mr. Verna." Nosaka had a special hatred for Verna. The New York union official had not only tried to hang him but Verna's greed had recently forced Nosaka to abandon the building of a $600 million auto plant on Long Island.

The old man fixed his gaze on Kenpachi. "You will listen carefully to what I now tell you. Today is Sunday. Tomorrow you are scheduled to meet with the American producer Jan Golden, Jude Golden's daughter. There is to be some discussion as to whether or not you will do location filming in Hong Kong."

"*Hai.* She is against it. Each day's filming costs fifty thousand American dollars and we would be in Hong Kong for a week, perhaps ten days. She wants to save money. And time."

"You will insist on going to Hong Kong as scheduled. Do whatever you have to, but see that you go as originally planned."

"Miss Golden arrives in Tokyo from Los Angeles tomorrow afternoon. We are to discuss our differences over dinner."

"She is a woman and will be whatever you wish her to be."

Kenpachi smiled. "It disturbs her that she is attracted to me."

Nosaka carefully folded his *hachimaki* into a neat square. "Let your power over Miss Golden be equal to your longing for a glorious death."

His eyes went to Kenpachi. "Now I shall tell you why it is urgent that you go to Hong Kong as soon as possible. My business took me there, as it did to Manila, Singapore, Seoul and Jakarta. But it was in Hong Kong, during a meeting aboard my yacht, the *Kitaro*, that I first saw the boy."

"Boy?"

"Orito, my physician, was called to treat him. It seems the boy had some sort of trance or vision. One could even call it a rather lurid daydream. After Orito told me what the boy had said while supposedly in this trance, I came on deck to look at him. I didn't approach him. That I will leave to you."

The old man patted his neck with the folded *hachimaki*. "His name is Todd Hansard. Come, let us bathe while I tell you about him."

3

ON A HOT JULY afternoon Frank DiPalma stepped into an air-conditioned 1927 Rolls Royce, the most magnificent car he had ever seen.

The elegant interior took his breath away. It was an eighteenth-century drawing room on wheels, with a painted ceiling of rococo cupids and upholstery of Aubusson tapestry, with scenes of chateaux, trees and gardens woven in silk and wool. Once the property of Victor Emmanuel III, the Italian king who had made Mussolini his prime minister, the Rolls belonged to Salvatore Verna, a New York union leader who entered the back seat after DiPalma and slammed the door behind them.

The front seat was empty. A chauffeur wasn't needed; the Rolls wasn't going anywhere. This afternoon the car was a meeting place.

It was parked in the garage of Verna's home, a Long Island oceanfront mansion lying between a hilly ridge and the sand dunes and shallow lagoons fringing the Atlantic shore. Not too long ago DiPalma and Verna would have punched each other out on sight. Then DiPalma had been a much decorated New York City narcotics detective, responsible for Verna's only prison term, a one-year sentence for refusing to cooperate with a grand jury. In retaliation the mob-connected Verna had put out a contract on him.

Now Frank DiPalma was a popular television crime reporter and Sally Verna was still a corrupt labor leader. He was looking to DiPalma to keep him alive.

The garage door was raised, allowing DiPalma to take in the grounds of Verna's luxury home. Straight ahead was a collection of topiary scupture—a large bear, lion and rhino expertly clipped out of dark green hedges. To the right three of Verna's grandchildren played in a swimming pool of Carrara marble edged in imitation Greek columns and black sphinxes. DiPalma had seen the mansion from the outside after being passed through the gates by a pair of armed guards. It was constructed of white marble, with a grand staircase visible through open french doors, and a patio ringed by stone cherubs riding stone dolphins.

A goddamn ice palace, DiPalma thought.

A private dock, a cabin cruiser and a pair of motorboats came with the estate, which had been built by a twenties bootlegger for his sixteen-year-old bride. Sally Verna had it all.

DiPalma stroked a silver-topped black oak cane, his trademark and favorite weapon; he was an expert kendoist and skilled in *escrima* and *arnis*, the Filipino stick-fighting arts. His mind wasn't on this meeting with Sally Verna; it was in Hong Kong with Katharine Hansard, the Chinese woman who had given him the cane, the woman he had once loved and had not seen in eleven years.

His mind was also on Todd, his son by Katharine. DiPalma had never seen the boy, only photographs of him. Yesterday DiPalma had received an urgent telephone call from her, begging him to come to Hong Kong immediately. Katharine feared for her life. And Todd's. The boy had had a vision indicating they were both in danger.

DiPalma was bone tired. There had been a piece of film which had to be edited and an assignment which had to be postponed and a station manager and producer who had to be convinced that if they didn't let him go he would go anyway, even if it meant getting fired. The script for an already filmed piece had to be rewritten and recorded in a hurry.

DiPalma had little time for Sally Verna. A half hour, no more. After that the limousine which had brought the former detective to Long Island was going to take him to Kennedy International Airport for the fourteen-hour flight to Hong Kong and Katharine. A sleeping memory awakened within him, thoughts of another woman who had once needed his help. Lynn, his dead wife. She had died in a hostage situation gone wrong, the result of a plot against DiPalma by a crazed and vengeful drug dealer.

Something else nagged at him. Katharine's father, a Triad leader, had vowed to kill DiPalma if he set foot in Hong Kong again. Her pregnancy by a white man had been shameful, a disgrace to a man in her father's position. But he could not abandon Katharine. DiPalma had already failed one woman, burden enough on his conscience.

Frank DiPalma was in his mid-forties, six feet tall and bulky, a graying bear of a man with hooded eyes and a flat-faced look that women found handsome. He walked with a barely perceptible limp and had a sleepy-eyed, threatening sexuality. He had been a New York City cop for twenty years, most of it on the vice squad where he worked narcotics. Rising to the rank of detective lieutenant, he had served on DEA and FBI task forces and been an adviser on drug crimes to police departments throughout the United States and overseas.

Even after leaving the department DiPalma's reports on drug trafficking were required reading among drug enforcement officials worldwide.

Two years ago he had gone into television broadcasting. Capitalizing on twenty years of police experience, street smarts and an uncompromising honesty, he had become a media star at an unexpected age. With his polite menacing calm, the husky-voiced former detective reported on crime as TV audiences never knew it, speaking without exaggeration or sentimentality and always with a terrifying clarity. His sources of information, drawn from his past, were unmatched by rivals: from a mob hit man to a senator's mistress, from the chief of a Rome film studio to the head of the Justice Department in Washington.

The results were prize-winning investigative reports, high ratings, fan mail and enemies. The enemies were the Suits, the television and advertising executives whose advice he ignored while continuing to report what he considered was the truth.

"You let yourself be influenced by people you want to please," he had said to his attorney. Because of DiPalma's popularity and critical acclaim the attorney had twice been called in by the network to renegotiate a new contract. The most recent one was for six figures a year, with a three-year guarantee.

DiPalma said, "You *allow* yourself to be influenced. And it's usually because you're anxious to have somebody's goodwill. Well, I'll let you in on a little secret. I don't fucking care about the Suits' goodwill."

"Right now you don't," said his attorney. "When you're hot, you're hot. And when you're not, you're not. What happens when it stops, when the ratings go into the toilet and you stop winning prizes?"

DiPalma lifted his cane to his mouth, breathed on its silver top, then polished the metal with a black silk handkerchief. When he had achieved the desired luster he said, "Am I correct in assuming that I have lived over forty years without the Suits? And in that time did I not eat three meals a day, wear clean socks and cross the street without getting hit by an iceberg? I could walk away from broadcasting tomorrow if I had to and never look back."

For sure, thought the attorney. When the Suits had tried to get DiPalma to dye his hair, wear horn-rimmed glasses and a vest, he had walked. When they had told him he was overweight, needed to smile more and should take speech lessons, he had walked. Now they left him alone. Now they believed he did not need them. And so they wanted him all the more.

The attorney stroked his nose with a pinky finger. Independence wasn't for everybody. Frank DiPalma, on the other hand, wasn't everybody. Frankie boy knew the secret. Have the strength to stand alone in the midst of others and if you had to, against others. The attorney envied him for that. He disliked the big man for it, too. DiPalma reminded the attorney of what he himself might have been and wasn't.

* * *

IN THE ROLLS, DiPalma watched Sally Verna light a cigarette with a trembling hand. Verna was a balding, sawed-off bull of a man in his mid-sixties, with a small nervous mouth and a physique kept hard-muscled through weight lift-

ing. For almost thirty years he had headed a New York automotive workers' union, one of the largest in the country. The
union had become completely mob dominated; it had also
formed alliances with other Eastern unions to give Verna and
the mob extraordinary power.

In addition to controlling thousands of Eastern automotive
workers, Verna and his underworld associates controlled
freight handlers, security guards and clerks at half a dozen
major Eastern airports. They also owned banks, real estate
and mortgages in several cities, had investments in Atlantic
City, Las Vegas and Caribbean casinos and administered a
pension fund worth billions of dollars.

Verna himself held paying positions in at least six mob-
dominated unions—local, regional and international—all of
which allowed him to sell sweetheart contracts, with sub-
standard wages and benefits.

Men in Sally Verna's position usually had others do their
killings for them. But Verna was different. DiPalma knew
that the cunning and unforgiving union leader had killed at
least twice. Not because he had to, but because he wanted
to. An associate had once betrayed him, then fled New York.
Eighteen years later he returned, his appearance changed; he
believed he couldn't be recognized and the trouble between
him and Sally was forgotten. As he sipped beer in a Queens
bar, a man came up behind him and put three bullets in his
head. Twenty patrons in the bar, however, never saw Sally
Verna pull the trigger.

The informant who had helped DiPalma bring Verna before
a grand jury fared worse. Verna learned his identity and had
him taken to an Astoria warehouse and hung on meat hooks.
The labor leader then personally tortured him with an electric
cattle prod; to make the informant's death as painful as possible he was doused with water to give the prod a stronger
charge. It took the man three days to die and Sally Verna was
there each day, watching the informant scream and flop
around on the meat hooks, which dug into his flesh whenever
he twitched.

DiPalma wondered if Verna feared punishment for either
crime.

Verna screwed his half-smoked cigarette into the ashtray of

the Rolls and immediately lit another. "Wasn't sure you'd come." He picked up a hand radio lying on the seat between his legs. "I'll have somebody bring you a drink."

DiPalma shook his head. He hadn't had a drink in eleven years, not since that night in Hong Kong when a shotgun blast had shattered his left hip, almost torn his left arm from its socket and left him with a stomach that could not tolerate booze or spicy foods.

He said to Verna, "I'm here because I get paid for reporting. On the phone you said something about a very big story, something you could only talk to me about. And we both know you've got nothing to gain by lying to me."

"What's with lying? Hear me out, then decide for yourself. Think I'll skip that drink, too. Stomach's acting up. Before I go into this thing, we're meeting out here in the garage 'cause I don't want my wife seeing us together. She knows you and me bumped heads in the past. She's getting over a heart bypass and I don't want her worrying. She's out sailing with my daughter and son-in-law. Gives me a chance to enjoy my grandchildren. *Enjoy*. Shit."

Verna blew smoke at the polished redwood steering wheel. "Understand you're going to Hong Kong."

DiPalma's eyes narrowed. "Since when did my travel plans interest you?"

"Hey, don't get me wrong. What you're doing over there is your business. I didn't ask and I don't want to know. I just heard you're going, is all."

"Nobody knows why I'm going and you're right, it is my business."

"DiPalma, it's not easy for me to come to you. I did it because the trouble I'm in might come down on my family and I'd like to stop that if I can. I got no right to ask you for a favor, but I'm asking. You're going to Hong Kong and you're the one guy I know can't be bought or scared off. Truth is, you go with this thing and you could run into problems."

"Such as?"

Verna studied him carefully. "Such as some very heavy people in Japan and their American friends coming down on you. People with money and power like you wouldn't fucking believe."

DiPalma looked at his wristwatch. "Sally, you have twenty-seven minutes. After that, I'm on my way to the airport."

Verna rubbed his balding head with a calloused hand. "Okay, okay. I want something from you, but I'm paying off with the biggest story you'll ever come up with. I want you to pick up a package for me in Hong Kong. It ain't what you're thinking, so don't jump salty. No dope, no jewelry, no cash. Nothing illegal. I'm not running a game on you. Sally Verna's brains ain't in his ass."

DiPalma turned in his seat until he faced the labor leader. The former detective's smile was chilly. "Sally, if I even *thought* you were setting me up or trying to get even for that fall you took, I would tear you on the dotted line right here and now."

"Hey, if it makes you feel any better, you can check out the package."

"As sure as the bear shits in the woods, I'd check it out. What's in it?"

"It's a file. Some records. Bank records, reports, correspondence. A lot of papers."

"So what's wrong with the mail? Or having one of your bent-nosed friends go and get it for you?"

Verna took his time answering. He didn't look at DiPalma. "There's an inside guy at a big bank over there who's been collecting stuff on the way the bank operates. It won't do him any good to be seen with me or any of my people. He wants like a third party, somebody neutral between him and me. He also ain't giving it away. We'll be paying plenty for that file."

"We?"

"I got a friend whose name I ain't gonna mention. Not yet, anyway. In any case, this stuff's too valuable to put in the mail or trust to just anybody to carry around. The guy who brings it back should be able to take care of himself. He's gonna need king-sized balls."

So you're warning me, thought DiPalma. He watched Verna drag deeply on his cigarette and saw the fear in his eyes. DiPalma had never really stopped thinking of himself as a cop, and much of a cop's knowledge was primarily guesswork. You combined that with speculation, supposition and you threw in a few "what ifs." This meant trusting your instinct.

Instinct said that Sally Verna, a man who did not scare easily, was, at the moment, too terrified to lie.

DiPalma said, "About this story, how big is big?"

"Fair enough. I swear on the heads of my grandchildren it's the biggest story of your life."

"And to get it I have to bring you back a package from Hong Kong. What's wrong with just sending you back a postcard?"

"DiPalma, there ain't no free lunch in this world. You play, you pay."

DiPalma tapped Verna's knee gently with the cane. "You're forgetting something. You came to me, I didn't come to you. That means *you* pay. And I'm not a player. Not yet."

Verna snorted, sending twin spears of smoke from a heavily veined nose. "Have it your way. Ever hear of the Blood Oath League?"

DiPalma had to stop himself from laughing out loud. "Sounds like friends of yours. White on white shirts, bent noses and diamond pinky rings."

"Very fucking funny. A few weeks ago in San Francisco a banker named Duncan Ivy was killed."

DiPalma yawned and nodded. "Cops feel that one could be another Manson-type killing. Yeah, I remember. Ivy, his wife, and Ivy's lawyer and his teenage daughter, who apparently just happened to be visiting. Wrong place at the wrong time. Everybody sliced to pieces with knives, swords. Maybe machetes. No suspects, no motive."

Verna stuffed out an unfinished cigarette. "You don't know the half of it, buddy boy. The president of a Japanese aerospace company was down in Brazil for a business conference—"

"Saō Paulo. Same thing happened to him and two bodyguards. We've got a newsroom down at the station, Sally. Stuff coming in over every kind of machine you can think of. I've been known to read some of it now and then."

"So you know. You know about the Japanese reporter in Tokyo? Or the Japanese construction guy in Osaka? Or the Italian count in Rome who was trying to sell the Japanese government on building an airport that would have been the largest in the world?"

DiPalma rolled the cane between the palms of his hands and waited.

"The Blood Oath League," said Verna. "It killed them all."

"You make it sound like gospel. Maybe you'd better tell me where your information comes from."

"My information's righteous. Believe me, it's good. But like you said, you ain't a player yet, so let's just go easy on names. You don't go around giving away your informants, so don't expect me to be no different. Not 'til you come on board. Let's just say I got a friend who's an expert on Japan. He's also tight with what you call 'the intelligence community,' He's fucking good at getting the facts, my friend. For now we call him Mr. O. 'cause he's always organizing."

"And Mr. O. has contacts with the French police?"

"Mr. O. is pretty fucking wired, let me tell you. You asked me about the Blood Oath League. For openers, it's Japanese."

Verna told DiPalma about the league, the old and new versions.

"Who's calling the shots on the new version?"

"Zenzo Nosaka. Same man who called the shots on the old one."

"Jesus." DiPalma's head flopped back against the seat. He focused on a pair of entwined cupids directly above him.

"You know Nosaka?" asked Verna.

Not just Nosaka, thought DiPalma, but Kon Kenpachi, his great and good friend. The two Japanese were inseparable and shared a deep interest in right-wing politics. DiPalma had never met Nosaka, but he had come face to face with Kenpachi more than once. The American and the Japanese hated each other. Both were linked by *ken*, the sword; it was the sword which had made them enemies.

Following the almost fatal attempt on his life in Hong Kong, DiPalma had regained his strength and the use of his left arm through kendo. His health had improved and kendo had become a fixation with him. He had a natural talent for sword and stick fighting. This, along with a cop's persistence, had led him to become an expert on samurai swords, their history, the men who forged them, the emperors and warriors who owned them.

With a growing reputation as a kendoist and sword historian, DiPalma was asked to speak before Japanese history groups in American colleges and universities, before groups of American businessmen and others interested in Japanese culture. He began collecting swords and writing his own history of their pedigrees, traveling to Japan to research the weapons and their makers. Then he wrote a book on Japanese swords and swordsmanship, which made his reputation. Western collectors, antique dealers, even Japanese, sought his opinion on a sword's authenticity.

Skilled at detecting forgeries DiPalma, while in Japan, pronounced a famed sword as merely an excellent copy. The sword belonged to Kenpachi, who denounced DiPalma as an ignorant and publicity-seeking *gaijin*. DiPalma was proven right and Kenpachi never forgave him. No white man could be superior to a Japanese kendoist in knowledge or fighting skill.

Kenpachi's hatred of DiPalma took a peculiar form. In the former detective's kendo club in New York, a mysterious fighter challenged him to a match. DiPalma accepted. The match was hard fought and dangerous but DiPalma defeated the man, who left without unmasking himself.

Later he learned that his opponent had been Kenpachi, who had flown to New York to challenge DiPalma. It was the flamboyant Kenpachi's style to make such a trip, to protect his pride by fighting masked. The defeat, however, was never forgotten. DiPalma became his sworn enemy.

DiPalma asked, "Did Kon Kenpachi's name come up in connection with the Blood Oath League?"

"No. Who's he?"

"Friend of Nosaka's. You asked me if I knew Nosaka. I don't, but I know of him. Son of a bitch is over eighty, wears cloaks and derbies and is one hell of a kendo man. Kendo's—"

"I know what it is. I spent time in Japan after the second World War. That's where I met Nosaka."

DiPalma, alert, sat up straight. It wasn't knowing a lot that made you smart; it was knowing what was necessary. The killings in Rome and San Francisco were facts and the other murders could be checked out easily enough. And Zenzo Nosaka was alive and well and fencing his ass off. On the surface, Sally Verna's story seemed to be coming together. His fear had to be caused by something or someone very special. Such as Zenzo Nosaka.

Why did Nosaka want Sally Verna dead? And how could bank records and correspondence in Hong Kong keep Sally alive?

DiPalma wondered about the two players Sally was protecting. There was Mr. O., who collected information, and there was the mystery man in Hong Kong, who was sitting on a special package Sally wanted brought to him.

Verna said, "I give you Nosaka and the Blood Oath League. You bring me back those records from Hong Kong. Like I said, check 'em out. Make sure you're not smuggling dope into the country or something."

"I have a question about your little package. Say I check out the papers and find you and your Mr. O. implicated in something naughty."

"For Christ's sake, DiPalma, ain't it enough you already put me in the slammer one time? Okay, okay, maybe, just maybe, my name and my friend's might turn up in those records. A few bucks may have changed hands, but that's it with us. For what I'm giving you on Nosaka, you can afford to forget about me and Mr. O. Fact is, I want your word that we ain't mentioned in any story."

I bet you do, thought DiPalma. Which was worse—breaking his word to Sally or keeping it? "Tell you what," he said, "let's put any promise like that on hold."

"What fucking choice do I have? Look, Nosaka's the big guy. Bring him down and you'll be doing the whole fucking country a favor, considering the way he does business over here."

"What about the way he does business?"

"Buddy boy, it's an offense against Jesus, I'm telling you. Payoffs here and in a dozen countries. Bribes to different governments, to guys down in Washington, to customs in any country you can name. Industrial espionage, blackmail. How the fuck you think Japan got to be so rich?"

DiPalma grinned. "I hate to tell you this, Sally, but he sounds a little like you and the boys."

"Listen, I didn't bring you out here to get zapped. I'm telling you about Nosaka, about him killing people, about him paying off half the fucking world. Japs call it *shieh lei*, bribes. Except nobody does it like Nosaka. And to do that he's got to move a lot of money around, I mean a lot."

"Through his bank?"

"You got it, buddy boy. And through a few other cute maneuvers, too. That's what I meant when I said you got to be careful on this thing. He's got heavy friends, people he's been payin' big bucks to for years. Bring him down and you can write your own ticket for the rest of your life, I'm telling you."

Easier said than done, thought DiPalma. Nosaka was one of the richest men in Japan, hell, in the world. He controlled companies that manufactured cars, trucks and electronic products. He owned international real estate and controlled a bank with branches in over fifty countries. He did indeed have friends in high places, including Washington. The price you paid for taking on somebody like that was to see a close-up of his ugly side.

DiPalma, an expert at reading faces and masks, knew that up until now Sally Verna had been doling out the truth in small doses. The labor leader seemed undecided as to which bridges to burn and which to cross. DiPalma gave him a push.

"Sally, we're running out of time. You're in bed with Nosaka, I don't know how, I don't know why, but you are and that's why he wants to ice you. From the top, Sally, and straight. What's joining you and the old man at the hip and why does he want to put out your lights?"

Verna turned from DiPalma to stare at a coiled hose hanging on the garage wall. The cigarette between his fingers was forgotten. "It was 1946. I was still in the army and in Tokyo working with the International Military Tribunal for the Far East. We went after Japanese war criminals. I bounced back and forth between the Central War Crimes Agency and the War Crimes Prosecuting Office. Shit, we were all hot to trot, a bunch of young wiseasses who were going to make the world safe for democracy.

"Me, Mr. O. and the others. We went after the worst of the Japs. Tojo, Dohihara, Hirota, Itagaki, Kimura, Muto. And Nosaka. We found the evidence, witnesses, we did the prosecuting. Nosaka we went after especially because he was with the Kempei Tai, a bunch of pricks. They were the army police, the Japanese gestapo and nothing but animals when it came to torturing people, especially American flyers. During the war Nosaka got around. Tokyo, Hong Kong, Malaya, Singapore. He was everywhere, dealing out pain and torturing for information. Men, women, children. Didn't matter."

Grinning, Verna turned to DiPalma. "On the day he was sentenced to hang Nosaka says to us, 'Your favor shall be remembered and the recipient is grateful.' Cute, huh? The Japanese don't come right out and say what's on their mind. They have to be polite even when they're mashing your balls between two bricks. What he was saying was he was going to kill us for what we had just done to him."

"How come he survived?"

"Hey, goombah, you're a big boy. Yesterday's enemy, tomorrow's friend. Comes the cold war and Russia and Japan change places. Russia's now the bad guy and Japan's the good guy, 'cause the fucking Japs hate communism. Nosaka was worth his weight in gold. A real smart cookie. All the time he was waiting to be hung he was giving us information, I mean real good shit. First he gives up some of his own people, guys we never knew about and couldn't locate until he tells us."

Verna stuck a hand under his T-shirt and scratched his chest. "America was scared of communism and Nosaka knew the names of all kinds of Communist agents, people in China, throughout the Pacific, all over. And his information was righteous."

DiPalma said, "One thing led to another, I bet. First his execution gets postponed, then his sentence is commuted and next thing you know Nosaka's on the street with pockets full of American money."

"What the fuck can I tell you? Russia grabbed all of Eastern Europe. North Korea and China went Communist. Then Russia gets the A-bomb, and now Washington is peeing in its pants. Nosaka became the greatest thing since sliced bread."

According to Verna there were many reasons why the little man in the cloak and derby was suddenly indispensable. He knew the names of the Japanese spies in Afghanistan, who for years had crossed the border into Russia and brought back information. The Japanese who operated in Switzerland and spied on Russia during the entire war. The Russian military men who, fearing Stalin, had defected to Japan starting in the late 1930s. The Japanese who, before Pearl Harbor, had been go-betweens for German spies in England and who knew about Russian agents buried deep in the British Secret Service.

"Another thing," said Verna. "The Germans captured a lot of Russian files, photocopied the stuff and passed it on to the Japs. And don't forget, it's always been official Japanese government policy to plan thirty years ahead. They did it back then and they're doing it today. Whether they won the war or lost it, they were ready to deal with whatever they had to deal with. And for them that meant knowing every fucking thing they had to know about everybody. That's a tradition which goes way back in their history."

"A man called Hideyoshi started it," said DiPalma. He looked at his watch. "How did Nosaka come to own you?"

"What makes you say that?"

"Because that's why he let you live. Men like Nosaka don't make threats lightly. He means every word he says. If you're telling the truth about his threat, you're only alive because he needed you."

Verna chewed on a thumbnail. "When he went into business, he needed connections in America. Private bills passed in Congress allowing him to do what he wanted to do in Japan, which was still under our occupation. We introduced him to people. Congressmen, bankers, lobbyists, businessmen willing to invest in Japan. In Nosaka. Paid off for him."

"And for you, Sally. For you and your friends."

"Like I said, no such thing as something for nothing in this world. Look, some people in this country wanted to see Japan on her feet again, with guys like Nosaka in charge. Japan was one country that would never go Communist, not with guys like Nosaka around. We had no trouble getting him together with the right people."

DiPalma rubbed his chin with the knob of his cane. "This

bank of his, how much of it do you own?"

Verna blinked. "Son of a bitch. How did you figure that out?"

"You want me to take your name out of those papers I'm supposed to bring back. So-called bank papers. You're not that hard to read, Sally."

"With you around, I feel like I'm fucking made of plate glass. We're on the board of directors, me and Mr. O. We bring in other Americans, mostly military people. Everybody gets paid, stock, bonuses, whatever. The military guys are tight with the Pentagon and the CIA, so the bank's used to pay out money for American spy operations nobody's supposed to know about."

"Such as arm deals," said DiPalma. "What about drugs? Guns and drugs go together."

"Hey DiPalma, what do I look like? You expect me to answer a question like that? Anybody who wants to put money in Nosaka's bank can put it in. The bank does a lot of other things, too. Like it's a collection agency for Nosaka. Industrial espionage. The bank has branches around the world and the people who work in it are fucking spies. They steal business secrets and pass 'em on to Nosaka."

DiPalma nodded. Now that would make a good story. Industrial espionage. The dark side of Japanese business success and Nosaka right in the middle of it. One more question for Sally Verna.

"I get the feeling you did something recently to remind Nosaka of that little promise he made to you almost forty years ago. What was it?"

Verna stared straight ahead. His grandchildren were tossing a Frisbee near the topiary menagerie. "You might say I pushed a little too hard."

"I'd say you got greedy. That's your main character failing. And this time you did it to the wrong guy."

A look at Verna's face confirmed DiPalma's educated guess. Sally's explanation made it official.

A Japanese car manufacturer, Soami, had wanted to build a plant on Long Island. Soami was Nosaka's biggest rival, so he ordered Sally Verna to stop the plant, and he stopped it cold. He threatened Soami with strikes, with political trouble in

Albany and in Washington, with trouble from the local zoning commission and unions allied to Verna. He threatened Soami's management with immigration problems. Soami pulled out in record time.

"That cleared the way for Takeshi, Nosaka's company, to come in. But I had my own ideas about that. I wanted to be taken care of."

DiPalma grinned. "You tried blackmailing Nosaka. You told him pay off or you'd blow the whistle about Soami."

Verna lifted a corner of his small mouth in a smile, in which his eyes did not participate. "Whatever I tried to tell him, he didn't buy. He ain't happy. Leave it go at that."

"I get the feeling he's a lot more than unhappy."

"He's not the only one. The emperor of Japan's not happy either. Last week this wacko Blood League sends him a letter saying that these killings are being done in his honor. Ready for that? The names of all the guys who've been killed so far are in this letter."

"Including Duncan Ivy?"

"Including him. Why did you bring up his name?"

"Because when you spoke about his death it seemed to bother you more than the deaths of the others. A lot more."

Verna pounded his thigh with a clenched fist. "Ivy worked the war crimes tribunal with me. He was also my daughter's godfather. When they got him and when his name turned up on the Blood League's list, I knew for sure the cocksuckers were after me. Letter to the emperor says it's all being done to bring back the old Japan. What the hell does killing half a dozen people have to do with the old Japan, I'd like to know."

DiPalma stretched. Time to go and leave Sally Verna alone with the dried flowers of his bad memories and even worse judgments. "Maybe you should ask Mr. O. about the old Japan. He seems to have pretty good connections with the Tokyo police. Here's the deal, Sally. Take it or leave it. No decision now. I want to think about our little talk. When I get to Hong Kong I'll call you and let you know if I'm in or out. If I'm in, you have your boy bring the file to me at my hotel. I'll be staying at the Mandarin but I don't want to get involved in paying this sucker, whoever it is. That's your problem. I don't want to be within ten feet of your money for whatever the reason."

Verna shrugged. "You're calling the play. If you agree to bring it back, I'll wire him the money."

"I'm in only if there's enough to stick it to Nosaka. Otherwise I'm not about to get involved. The network doesn't like libel suits, which is the least we can expect from Nosaka."

"What about keeping me out of it?"

"What about it?"

"You said—"

"No I didn't. And you know it. But if I can, I will."

Verna came as close to pleading as he ever had in his life. "DiPalma, if you don't keep me out of it, I'm a dead man."

The former detective thought of Katharine. And Lynn. And Sally Verna's wife, who had just had a heart bypass. He said, "You're out of it. Just one more thing: you've got good security here. Gates, walls, probably a first-class alarm system and enough headbreakers walking around on the grounds to start a small war. I've noticed a few guard dogs as well. That should be enough to stop anybody."

Sally Verna's voice was a pained whisper. "Those people are *ninja* and they don't give a shit about getting killed. What do you think the name Blood Oath League means? These guys are stone crazy and they deal in blood. My grandchildren are in and out of here all the time. I don't want anything to happen to them, but what can you do against *ninja*? Tell me, what the fuck can I do?"

* * *

IN THE BACK SEAT of his limousine, heading for Kennedy, a tired Frank DiPalma stared through tinted glass at narrow sailboats slicing through a choppy Atlantic Ocean and wondered which boat contained Sally Verna's wife and daughter. Sally, of course, would not be grateful for DiPalma's promise to keep his name out of it. It was the union leader's style to hate those he owed. He couldn't stand to owe. But he owed his wife and grandchildren. This was the debt which DiPalma had agreed to help repay.

Frank DiPalma closed his eyes and settled back against the

limousine's plush interior. Sally was a drowning man and his reaching out for DiPalma could pull them both down. The former detective turned his mind to Katharine and Todd. In Hong Kong he would go to them first, then deal with Verna's banker friend. If Verna was righteous, the man in the bank faced as much danger from Nosaka as DiPalma faced from Katharine's father.

Minutes later DiPalma slipped into an uneasy sleep and dreamed of a beautiful Katharine, who remained just out of his reach, a silent Todd in her arms.

And in the background Kenpachi and Verna's banker friend, his face masked, linked arms and laughed insanely and together beckoned DiPalma closer.

4

In Paris, a contented Henri Labouchere sipped Kir Royale, a mixture of champagne and crème de cassis, then closed his eyes and slid down into his scented bathwater, his broad back against the side of the huge, half-sunken rose marble tub. Tonight he shared the tub with his three-year-old son Nicholas, who with intense concentration was floating a black-and-white soccer ball between himself and his father. The ball was a birthday gift from Paul Gaspare, Labouchere's Corsican bodyguard.

Sliding doors on two sides separated the bathroom from the terrace where Gaspare now stood looking down on Avenue Foch. The bodyguard, who had been with Labouchere for years, enjoyed watching the whores on the elegant street work pedestrians and motorists for quick trips to the nearby Bois de Boulogne.

Of the twenty rooms in his Avenue Foch duplex, Labouchere's favorite was this bathroom. Ten years ago he had given this room to his first wife Delphine as an anniversary present, a bedroom converted at a cost of almost a million francs. There were gold faucets shaped like mermaids, authentic Louis XIII baroque mirrors, tables and chairs covered with a thin layer of gold. Delphine had chosen everything.

Over her objections Labouchere had selected the bronze and ebony empire style for the rest of the duplex, which comprised the top two floors of a ten-story building facing the Bois de Boulogne and the Metro station designed by art nouveau

architect Hector Guimard. Riding the subway, however, was
not for Labouchere or his Avenue Foch neighbors, who included Prince Ranier, several Rothschilds, deposed Iranian
royalty, Christina Onassis and at least a dozen billionaire in-
dustrials from as many countries.

Avenue Foch, a four-fifths-of-a-mile stretch running between the Étoile and Bois de Boulogne, contained the greatest
concentration of wealth and power in the world. It was Paris's
Golden Ghetto.

In the tub Labouchere opened his eyes. His empty glass
was being pried from his fingers by his adored Nicholas. The
Frenchman smiled and allowed his thick hand to be separated
from the thin stem of the glass by tiny fingers. No one else was
allowed to take anything from Labouchere with such ease. He
smiled as Nicholas filled the glass with bathwater and poured
it on the golden mermaid faucets, performing the task with a
seriousness that amused his father.

Labouchere tilted his head back and inhaled deeply, trying
to catch a whiff of Paul Gaspare's cigarette smoke from the
terrace. The doctor had forbidden Labouchere to smoke and
had cautioned him against rich foods, to help lower his blood
pressure. He was allowed two glasses of wine at dinner and
had to walk three miles every other day.

Labouchere had stopped smoking, but he kept an unlit
Cuban cigar in his mouth for hours at a time. He avoided rich
foods five days a week. Then, on weekends, he ate and drank
as he pleased. Had he not done as he pleased throughout his
life he never would have become a wealthy man. Nor would he
have won the most lucrative contract of his life, a deal to build
two atomic reactors in Kyoto at a cost of twenty-one billion
francs.

Tomorrow morning a helicopter would fly him and
Nicholas four hundred miles west to the port of Le Havre.
Here father and son would join French and Japanese government officials and salute the three ships heading for Japan
with construction supervisors, equipment and material and a
dozen atomic technicians. On board would also be several
hundred bottles of red wine from Labouchere's private
vineyard near Bordeaux, his gift to the French workers who
would be away from home for almost a year.

Tonight Labouchere had celebrated at Le Moi, his favorite Vietnamese restaurant, dining on pork with caramel, chicken with Chinese cabbage and crisp noodles. He felt entitled to enjoy himself; in securing the Kyoto contract he had attempted a difficult objective and achieved it. The doctor's orders cautioning restraint could wait until another day. In any case, a man who did nothing and caused no offense died as surely as the man who did as he wished and broke every rule.

Henri Marie Labouchere was in his late fifties, a beefy, horse-faced Frenchman with thinning brown hair parted in the middle and the hard, dark eyes of a man who preferred to distrust everyone rather than be deceived by them. His company, Canet-Banyuls, was France's number-one producer of nuclear power plants and its third leading manufacturer of turbine generators for conventional power plants. Canet-Banyuls's one hundred thousand employees also built transformers, electric motors as well as radar for combat aircraft and lauching systems for French nuclear missiles.

Besides electricity and defense, Labouchere had guided his company into land-development projects in ten countries, the development of a French cable-television system and had recently concluded a licensing agreement with a major American soft drink company to bottle and sell its product throughout half of Africa.

Henri Labouchere's strength lay in his boldness, in his knowing what weapons to use and against whom to use them. Having decided to prey rather than be preyed upon, he found himself at home in an unjust world. He felt no guilt at his cut-throat business tactics, seeing a mirror of them in nature, where only the strong survived and the weak went to the wall. He had learned from the mistakes of his father, a man who had been betrayed by relying on the courage of others rather than trusting his own courage.

In love Labouchere had shown the same courage, choosing as a first wife a plain, unattractive woman who had been an assistant to his plant manager in Marseilles. The marriage, a shock to those who had expected him to marry for beauty or social position, had been a success until Delphine's tragic death from an aneurysm. She had been affectionate and loyal, with the courage to stand up to him and the sense to do it in private. She supported his every plan, became his most trusted confidante and disappointed him only in her inability to bear children. When she died it shocked Labouchere to realize how much he had depended on her.

At fifty-two, Labouchere married a second time. Sylvie, twenty, was a glacial, green-eyed beauty, who wanted to be important and admired as much as her husband. She was offered film and modeling contracts, all of which she turned down. Labouchere later learned that she had turned them down out of laziness, not out of a desire to be constantly at his side.

When Labouchere was fifty-three, Sylvie presented him with his first child, Nicholas. The industrialist found great joy in the boy, but also regrets over the childless years with Delphine. And guilt over the regrets.

Tonight in the tub Labouchere smiled and thought about his bold reaction when he had learned of Sylvie's infidelity two days ago. He had spoken of her betrayal to his bodyguard Paul, his only confidant since Delphine's death.

"Tomorrow I am sending her to New York to play among the wealthy Europeans and South Americans who infest Manhattan. I used a ruse. She is to select furniture for our Fifth Avenue apartment and, of course, do a little shopping. She suspects nothing. While she is gone, I shall make arrangements for the divorce and to secure permanent custody of Nicholas."

"How long will madame be in America?"

"At least two weeks. Should she find something or someone to amuse her, she will undoubtedly stay longer. In her absence I want you to gather all of the information I need regarding her lovers. There are two."

Labouchere's eyes held Paul's. "Get written confessions from each man. I do not care how, but I want from each one a written admission of his adultery with my wife."

"It is done, monsieur."

"*Bon*. When she returns, she returns to nothing. She will never set foot in this house again, nor will she anymore set eyes on Nicholas. Her settlement from me will be minimal.

I will leave my mark on this whore. Can I rely on you, old friend?"

"Have I ever failed you, monsieur?"

* * *

WHETHER IT WAS HIS failed second marriage or the Kyoto contract, Labouchere acted according to his belief that a successful man was always proud, aggressive and cunning. Above all, he was never to lack boldness at any decisive moment of his life.

To be the one French power company allowed to deal with the Japanese meant securing the permission and cooperation of the French president, prime minister and foreign affairs minister. It meant bribing French officials to withhold the necessary export licenses from Labouchere's competitors, leaving the way clear for him to obtain such licenses. And it meant being smart and tough enough to deal with the Japanese.

"You cannot bring the Americans into this Kyoto project," a Japanese businessman had told Labouchere. "You must understand this about Japan: there is a high sensitivity in my country to nuclear weapons, especially to nuclear weapons belonging to the Americans. Three atomic bombings of my country by America—"

"Three? *Mais non*, there have only been two. Hiroshima and Nagasaki."

"You are forgetting Bikini, my friend. In 1954 the American fallout from an atomic test at that Pacific island came down on a Japanese fishing boat, the *Fukuryu-maru*. One crewman died. With the memories of the war still fresh, it was as if a hundred thousand had died. As far as we were concerned, the Bikini test was the third atomic bomb to fall on us. Every August sixth the Hiroshima bombing is commemorated by demonstrations, protests, antinuclear speeches. You would do well to forget borrowing an American nuclear-powered ship to demonstrate the peaceful use of nuclear energy on the high seas."

Labouchere shrugged. "It is forgotten. Let me say that I had no intention of bringing nuclear weapons into the picture. The Americans, however, have made great progress in peaceful uses of atomic energy. I merely wished to show—"

"Henri, listen to me. The contract was awarded to *you*, not to the Americans. We do not wish to involve ourselves at this time with the United States regarding atomic matters. Japan suffers from what you might call a 'nuclear allergy.' "

"Caused by the Americans."

"Dear friend, even French reactors for peaceful purposes will cause trouble in my country. There will be protests, angry newspaper editorials, even threats to your life."

"I am willing to accept this."

The Japanese said, "Certain people in my country feel that nuclear power in Kyoto will be of benefit to both business and to the consumer. That is why we are going ahead with this project."

Labouchere knew who those certain people were. In Japan, business dictated to the government, guiding it through the Sanken or council composed of two dozen of Japan's most powerful industrialists and bankers. The legislature, prime minister and all government agencies took orders from the Sanken, who represented the *zaikai*, the big business circles. This made Japan the ultimate corporate state, with big business deciding government policy at home and abroad. Any politician or government worker who disagreed with big business was booted out of office immediately.

The backing of the Sanken did not eliminate Labouchere's having to pay *shieh lei*, a way of life in Japanese business. Thirty million American dollars had been delivered in cash or placed in secret bank accounts by the Frenchman, who looked upon bribery as a legitimate corporate expense. In any case, the cost of the Kyoto project would probably double before its completion, yielding Labouchere windfall profits. Thirty million in *shieh lei* was peanuts compared to what the Frenchman would eventually take out of Japan.

As for Japanese opposition to the Kyoto project, Labouchere's friend had been correct. Antagonistic editorials, demonstrations at Labouchere's Kyoto and Tokyo offices and even threats to his life all materialized. None had the slightest effect on him; he had survived similar opposition in France and saw no reason why he shouldn't survive this.

These days the world was filled with crackpots, most of

whom ended up with a policeman's club across the face. Labouchere was too rich and too powerful to concern himself with bearded crazies in jeans who preferred slogans to thought and rhetoric to an honest day's work. There was no way a handful of Japanese would stop the Kyoto reactors from being built.

But a few days ago a worried Paul had said, "Something's happening, monsieur, and I do not like it. It is a pattern and it concerns the Japanese."

The bodyguard told Labouchere of the killings. "Five, monsieur. Three Japanese, one American, one European. All businessmen, all killed recently and not by guns or explosives. They were killed with swords, knives or bare hands. *Ninja* style."

Paul Gaspare neither worried needlessly nor scared easily. He was almost sixty, a small, dark man with a bulbous forehead and eyes which, in an enemy's words, were as hard as an erection. He wore in his jacket lapel the red ribbon signifying his military decorations for bravery at Dien Bien Phu and in Algeria. On his watch chain was the heavy gold medallion embossed with the Napoleonic eagle and Corsican crest. This indicated membership in the *milieu*, or Union Corse, the powerful Corsican underworld organization that made the Sicilian Mafia seem childish by comparison.

Gaspare, who had been with Labouchere for over twelve years, had also served with the Service d'Action Civique (SAC), which did the dirty jobs for DeGaulle that neither the national police nor SDECE, the French CIA, would touch. Labouchere had chosen his bodyguard not only for his bravery, but for his connections in intelligence, law enforcement and the underworld.

Labouchere paid attention when Paul said, "Your security is my concern. I have to look into every threat, no matter how trivial it may appear to be. A day or so ago I had a friend in the SDECE contact Tokyo about the threats you have received. He says we shouldn't worry about them, but there is something else he feels we should be careful of. It appears that Tokyo police feel a group called the Blood Oath League is operating again. It was pretty big around the second World War. Strong-arm stuff for businessmen, killings, spying, even a little blackmail. The Tokyo police don't have much, but they hear that the league might have been resurrected."

"Why? And by whom?"

"They don't know who's behind it. But they feel the reasons are the same as they were in the thirties and forties. Back then the targets were businessmen, reporters, politicians. The new league is just supposed to be after businessmen, Japanese and westerners. But at the moment Tokyo authorities can't get close to the group. They can't line up informants nor even infiltrate the league."

"The usual thing, I suppose," said Labouchere. "Kidnappings and ransom in addition to bloodletting."

"They kill. That's all they do."

Labouchere reached for a cigar and a lighter.

Paul said, "With your permission, monsieur, I'd like to put on a few more men, especially when you're traveling outside of France."

"But of course."

"I would also like a twenty-four hour guard on the flat. Say a couple of men with automatic weapons. They would be in a parked car downstairs. No one would notice. I can fix that up with the police so there would be no trouble. Building security is light, unfortunately. Some friends will make available hand radios and I think you should, perhaps, vary your routine. Leave for work at a different time each day and take different routes."

"I leave that to you, Paul. I shall do whatever you say."

The bodyguard looked up at the ceiling. "I'm wondering about the roof."

"Seems safe enough to me."

"It should be. It's more than twenty feet down to the top window. A sheer drop, too. Nothing to hang on to. No fire escapes, no ledges. But if we're talking about *ninjas*, these Blood Oath guys, I mean, we're talking about first-class athletes. Each of the men they're supposed to have killed all had tight security."

"But they didn't have you, my friend."

In the tub Labouchere struggled to his feet, waded over to the faucets and lifted up a giggling Nicholas. Holding the boy under one arm, the Frenchman leaned over and pressed the

lever releasing the bathwater, then straightened up and kissed
his son on both cheeks. Nicholas had noticed the extra bodyguards around the flat, but had said nothing. He was observant, like his father, and showed every sign of taking the
changes in stride. Labouchere liked that.

Labouchere was also pleased that for now Nicholas was too
young to go to school. This reduced the chances of the boy's
being kidnapped. At the moment let him stay home under
guard. When a nurse took Nicholas for a walk, at least one
armed man accompanied them.

Labouchere looked around the bathroom. *Merde*. No
towels. The lack of efficiency in small things annoyed him. He
expected perfect service in his home and no excuses. He was
going to give the maid hell about it tonight. He turned toward
the terrace to summon Paul to search the flat for bath towels.

Labouchere's mouth was open to call Paul when the industrialist saw three black-clad figures drop silently onto the terrace behind the bodyguard's back. Two rushed Paul; the other
spun around and sped into the bathroom toward Labouchere,
who was too surprised to move.

On the terrace one attacker kicked Paul in the back of the
knee, then threw a wire over the Corsican's head and yanked it
tight against his throat. At the same time the attacker jammed
a knee hard against Paul's spine, pulling back on the wire with
all his strength. The bodyguard, his air gone, the wire slicing
into his throat, threw himself backward, sending himself and
the attacker struggling toward the sliding glass door.

Both men collided with the glass at the same time, shattering
it and sending shards flying into the bathroom and onto the
terrace. They crashed to the bathroom floor simultaneously,
both bleeding heavily. Paul, the wire embedded in his neck, attempted to push himself off the floor; his back was to his
attacker, who lay writhing from side to side. When the bodyguard reached a sitting position he pulled at the wire with one
hand and with the other clawed for the .38 Smith & Wesson in
his belt holster.

The second attacker on the terrace moved faster. He wore a
samurai sword slung across his back and in one motion unsheathed it, lifted the weapon high, then brought it down. The
blade hit deep into the bodyguard's skull, sending pieces of

bone and brain into the glass sprinkled on the yellow tiled floor. Paul, his head and face a mass of blood, slumped across the legs of the first attacker. The bodyguard's right arm twitched as he fought for life.

In the bathroom, the attacker who had rushed Labouchere came to a sudden halt, surprised by the sight of the naked Frenchman holding his son. The hesitation was brief. He also carried a sword across his back; in a second the naked blade was in his hands and he swung.

Labouchere turned his back, using his body to shield his son. The blade dug into the beefy Frenchman's bare shoulder and he shrieked, then stumbled and fell forward into what was left of the bathwater. The attacker stepped into the tub, kicked his way through the now bloody water and lifted the sword high. He brought it down once, twice. Nicholas screamed. A bleeding Labouchere, still attempting to save his son, crawled toward him. The sword was raised again. And still once more. And then silence.

The attacker sheathed his sword, stepped from the water and looked down at his masked comrade lying under a dying Paul Gaspare. He was dragged aside and the two *ninja* examined the bleeding man in black; his throat, side, neck and wrists had been badly cut by glass.

There was a brief conversation in Japanese before they carried the third man out to the terrace. Here he was tied to one of two ropes they had used to lower themselves down from the roof, with a makeshift harness around the bleeding man's chest and under both arms. Then they climbed the ropes and together pulled him up.

One slung the wounded man over his shoulder and, followed by his comrade, silently crossed the roofs of Avenue Foch, two shadows that soon blended into the June night.

* * *

IN THE BOIS DE BOULOGNE the two Japanese, still masked, stood behind the dying third man. He was unmasked and bare chested and sat in a formal kneeling position, buttocks on heels, hands palms down on his thighs. He trembled with pain and his body was dark with his own blood, but he did not cry out. His eyes were closed and after a while he began to chant a prayer. His voice was strained, harsh, barely audible.

When his head slumped forward with pain, one of the two behind him stepped forward, sword high. A single, quick stroke and the wounded man's head flew off, disappearing into the darkness.

The butchering of the corpse continued. The executioner chopped off the dead man's hands, then wrapped them and the head in the corpse's black sweater. Next, the two attackers dropped to their knees and used their hands to scoop out a shallow grave in the soft earth beneath a nearby bush. The mutilated corpse was then placed in the grave and covered with earth, twigs, leaves.

Minutes later the two Japanese, one carrying a grisly bundle of the dead man's head and hands over his shoulder, jogged across a moonlit clearing and vanished into a grove of pine and birch trees.

5

WHEN TODD woke it was almost dark. Instantly his eyes went to the *bokken*, a wooden sword with the curved, tapered blade and carved hilt of an actual samurai sword, that lay bathed in moonlight on a chair beside his bed. Todd used the *bokken* in Koryu, an ancient fighting form practiced without armor in order to develop an exact and beautiful fencing technique.

While the lack of armor made the movements freer, Koryu placed greater pressure on the fencer to avoid being scored on. A higher form of fencing than *shinai* kendo, Koryu was performed with intense concentration. Each movement was executed with fierce pride.

A perspiring Todd sensed the threat of rain in the humid night. Nude, he pushed aside his sheet and mosquito netting, swung his feet to the floor and stood up. Both hands went to his throat. The throbbing pain that had sharply awakened him from a troubled sleep was still there. His skin tingled with an unnatural heat. His face smarted as though it had just been singed by fire.

When he had first opened his eyes there had been a horrifying second when he felt himself immersed in flames. Night and solitude now held only demons.

Something drew him to the *bokken*. He lifted it from the chair, hands on hilt and blade, and walked to the window. From behind bamboo blinds he watched guests step from expensive cars and enter the Hansards' Edwardian mansion or stroll its well-tended grounds, which were lit by paper lanterns strung between tall hedges, bamboo poles and red pines. Near the pergola, a covered walk formed by climbing plants, Todd's mother, lovely in a white Grecian tunic belted at the waist by an ultrathin Ciani gold lariat, was chatting with Hong Kong's governor, his wife and two of the American actors.

Todd's stepfather, several feet away, was talking to the film's attractive producer, Jan Golden, and a pretty Japanese actress in an Elizabethan knot garden of clipped shrubs and herbs. The boy noticed that his stepfather deliberately kept his back to the circular driveway as guests applauded a Chinese couple who arrived in a one-hundred-year-old horse-drawn hansom cab, complete with top-hatted driver. Todd watched them step down from the carriage and pose for photographers before disappearing inside the mansion.

The boy had seen the couple at his stepfather's bank. The man was a popular movie actor who produced and starred in one kung fu film a month and gambled away his profits. His wife was the beautiful star of a top-rated television soap opera shown in Chinese communities throughout the world. Todd knew she slept with his stepfather in exchange for the low-interest loans which financed her husband's movies. Ian Hansard had a craving for Oriental women.

Todd gripped the *bokken* with all his strength. There was a frightening bond between the boy and someone here at the party. *Who was it? And why?*

And there was the *ninja*. He had not told his mother what he had seen in his dream on the boat; it was a dream after all, a fleeting shadow on which no one could lay a hand. He feared for his mother, but he knew that he and all others were powerless in the face of karma. Destiny was destiny. Even the gods were forced to submit to fate.

Suddenly the pain in his throat grew keener. At the same time a deep impulse consumed him and he turned his back on the window. *Hai, someone connected to his nightmares, someone responsible for the uneasiness that he now lived with, was here in the house. Not on the grounds but here in the house.*

Todd faced the door and began to move instinctively. He crouched on his heels, knees spread wide, *bokken* gripped tightly at the hilt and aimed at the eyes of an imaginary oppo-

nent. Then he rose slowly, his gaze fixed straight ahead, his
bare back streaked with silver moonlight.

With a cold ferocity he began the practice of Koryu.

* * *

KON KENPACHI stood beneath a cut-glass Georgian
chandelier in the crowded Hansard living room and forced a
smile for the photographers who had motioned him closer to
Tom Gennaro and Kelly Keighley, the two American male
leads in *Ukiyo*. Unlike Kenpachi, who disliked being ordered
about by anyone, the actors seemed reconciled to the ordeal
of popping flashbulbs and shouted questions from reporters
representing Hong Kong's myriad daily newspapers. The Japanese director also found his surroundings disturbing. His
aesthetic sense was offended by the clutter of the Hansard
mansion, with its quilted white silk ceiling, red damask chairs,
Meissen porcelain and bay windows of Tiffany glass.

Any visit to China, and he had made several, always unnerved Kenpachi and left him uneasy. In his heart he knew the
truth, that Japan had built her civilization through the theft of
China's secrets. Japan's food and art, its music and science,
its religion and even its martial arts, all originated in China.
For a time the Japanese people, having no written language of
their own, had spoken Chinese exclusively, as Western medieval scholars had used Latin. Today's Japanese language used
several thousand Chinese characters. Even the word *seppuku*
represented the Chinese characters for suicide.

The result of these centuries of pilfering was psychological
dependence and a cultural inferiority complex, which all of
Japan's military aggressiveness and claims to superiority had
failed to eliminate. Only one of Japan's three invasions of
China, in World War II, had come close to succeeding. But
when America had come to China's aid that invasion too had
failed, leaving the Chinese as conquerors of the people they
called "the monkey thieves," a slur on the Japanese who, a
myth said, were born of a Chinese princess kidnapped by a
monkey.

Kenpachi knew that a case could be made for the Japanese
as thieves of other nations' technology and cultural ideas. The

Japanese were imitators, not innovators; their strength lay in duplication or improving on the achievement of others. China's existence reminded Kenpachi that truth was too often a whore, someone you knew but did not want to encounter in public.

An impatient Kenpachi had now been in Hong Kong for twelve hours without seeing the boy Todd. Had the director purified himself these past weeks only to be forced to bring the box to a half-white, half-Chinese child? Yes, Nosaka was to be obeyed. The superior man was easy to serve, said Confucius, and difficult to please.

Kenpachi's curiosity about the small black box, carried to the party in a shoulder bag, was at fever pitch. Would he learn its contents tonight? Was his search for a *kaishaku* at an end?

To Kenpachi's right a second group of photographers had posed Jan Golden arm in arm with Ian Hansard and Hong Kong's governor in front of a cast-iron fireplace. Hansard was a member of the legislative council, which made Hong Kong's laws, set its economic policy and granted film-making permits. Kenpachi, who had been willing to do anything to avoid poverty, recognized that same wretched compulsion in Ian Hansard and therefore knew the banker was never to be trusted. As for the governor, Kenpachi had already posed with the pink-faced Englishman, whose bad teeth and malice were barely concealed by good manners.

Across the room Kenpachi and Jan Golden's eyes met briefly before she looked away to smile at the governor. She was in her mid-thirties, a tall, long-nosed woman with green-gray eyes and the habit of throwing her head back, causing her mane of auburn hair to swirl glamorously about, a gesture Kenpachi knew compensated for her short sight. She was ambitious, a hard worker and more knowledgeable about the Far East than any western woman he had ever met.

Kenpachi admired her willingness to allow a sort of nasty intent to surface, as he admired her talent for restraint or exaggeration when either suited her purpose. What interested him most about Jan Golden was her sexuality, which appeared offhand but which the observant Kenpachi knew masked a fear that her true and hidden sensuality was too strong for compromise. She was, he sensed, both repelled and attracted by him.

Kenpachi shaded his eyes against the popping flashbulbs and searched among the crush of reporters, photographers, dinner-jacketed men and elegantly gowned women for Wakaba, his Japanese bodyguard and chauffeur. The young, burly Wakaba, with kendo and karate skills matched only by a high-strung belligerence, was one of the first to meet Nosaka's strict requirements for membership in the new Blood Oath League. He worshipped Kenpachi and was insanely jealous when anyone came close to the director.

Wakaba had already offered to serve as Kenpachi's *kaishaku*, then join him in *seppuku*. But the bodyguard had failed the test of the box.

Kenpachi, increasingly edgy, glanced at the ceiling. One way or another, with or without Wakaba's help, he was going to find the boy and find him tonight. The box was a hot coal on Kenpachi's hip.

He felt a hand on his right shoulder and turned to see Tom Gennaro aim a finger at the reporters and photographers crouched in front of them. "Tell your people what I think of this man. I made the deal for this movie without seeing the script. And that's something I never do. I mean never."

A smiling Kenpachi bowed his handsome head, his mind still on Wakaba and the boy. Such praise was his due; all the Americans should be honored to work with him, especially on his final film. Still, there was respect for the talent of the Oscar-winning Gennaro, a dark, sad-eyed little man skilled at playing lethal outsiders. There was also admiration for Keighley, white haired and knife thin, who had a sinister sexuality popular with Japanese audiences.

Gennaro had undergone an immediate infatuation with Japanese culture and spent his off-camera hours touring temples, walking with geishas and practicing kendo with Kenpachi and Wakaba. Keighley's time was spent with his "secretary," a statuesque Venezuelan who was only seventeen and had been the actor's mistress for four years.

And there was Jan Golden, a woman of force who saw only a world of possibilities. Kenpachi and Nosaka were using her, but the situation was not without its small ironies. The American woman had shamelessly used Kenpachi's artistic reputation to get the high-priced Gennaro and Keighley to work for what she called "short money." With these three names on contracts it had been childishly simple to get whom she wanted for *Ukiyo*.

The original script, written by a former Vietnam war correspondent, had impressed Kenpachi, but it needed rewriting. The director was not satisfied with the story of two GIs, on leave in Tokyo from Vietnam, who become involved with a Japanese prostitute and steal money from the *yakuza*. Kenpachi's version, a brilliant rewrite instantly accepted by Jan Golden and the American stars, saw a young GI (Gennaro), team with the prostitute to steal money hidden by her lover, a Japanese gangster serving a prison term.

Both the American and the woman were now pursued across Japan by the *yakuza*, a mysterious and corrupt American (Keighley) and a female American journalist anxious to report the story. In the end it was Keighley and the journalist who betrayed Gennaro and the prostitute he had come to love.

"I'm wiped out," a tearful Jan Golden said after reading Kenpachi's version. "It's romantic, violent, sad, funny, it's everything. And I really care about the lovers. You've made it high tragedy and it works. At least I think it works. I mean it's, well, a bit downbeat. Couldn't we have one bit of hope at the end? A lighted match at the end of the tunnel, so to speak?"

Kenpachi shook his head. "As you have said, it is a tragedy and the essence of tragedy is sadness. We are dealing with the inevitability of events, destiny set in motion by the actions of those in the script. If you look closely, you will see a small triumph, the triumph of a man over those forces that seek to destroy him. Death cannot take away that tiny victory. The lovers, the American and the Japanese girl, now have convictions, beliefs. Convictions must bring suffering."

Jan Golden was silent. She had complete belief in his talent and besides, she couldn't deny a gnawing desire for him.

* * *

KORYU.

Todd Hansard, chest rising and falling, held the hilt of the *bokken* close to his abdomen, the tip pointed at the throat of an imaginary enemy. In the moonlit room the naked boy paused before attacking again. The burning in his throat was ignored; he was in a dream state, free from mind and body, all other existences forgotten except that of *do*, the way.

He filled his lungs with air, then exhaled slowly. Then he attacked with a strong spirit; his life depended on a fraction of an inch of movement, on a single stroke of his blade. All that he was flowed from a secret place within him into the *bokken*.

He took three steps toward the door and stopped. He waited. Then, in Todd's mind, his opponent lifted his own *bokken* overhead and slashed downward. Quickly the boy stepped back on his left foot and struck the opponent in the head before the enemy's sword could complete its move. As the opponent took one step back, Todd, maintaining concentration, brought his *bokken* overhead. He held it there and waited. Then he and the opponent lowered their swords to point at each other's faces, held that position for seconds before pointing the weapons at the floor.

Each now took five small steps to the rear, brought up his *bokken* to point at the other's face and waited.

Todd attacked again. Three long steps forward. Stop. Watch the other man's eyes. Suddenly the opponent's *bokken* sped downward toward Todd's right wrist. Without thinking the boy stepped back diagonally on his left foot, evading the enemy's weapon. Then a step forward and Todd's *bokken* had cut the enemy's right wrist.

Five small steps to the rear and again the boy had his back against the window, *bokken* aimed at his opponent's throat.

Forward once more. Three long steps and stop. Eyes to eyes. This time the opponent delivered a two-handed thrust at Todd's solar plexus. The boy parried the attack to the left and countered with his own thrust to the throat.

Spellbound, Todd had gone beyond time and space, beyond is and is not. He had transcended all existences to reach the plane of consciousness where thought neither mattered nor was necessary. He believed the enemy in front of him existed and sought to take his life. And because his own life could now end within the space of a heartbeat, the boy fought with a tension unknown to modern swordsmen.

Suddenly the room in front of him was filled with light. A second later it was dark except for a path of moonlight between the window and the door. But Todd retained his concentration. For him there was nothing between earth and sky but the sword. And the man he must kill.

* * *

Kenpachi quickly entered Todd's bedroom, then closed the door behind him. Wakaba remained on guard in the hall while the director pursued a paradox. Kenpachi was excited because he was about to see the boy recommended by Nosaka, the most clever of men. Yet common sense told Kenpachi that an eleven-year-old boy had no place in his plans. It was time to put an end to this business. Simply show the box to Todd Hansard and . . .

A shocked Kenpachi almost cried out, terrified by the power emanating from the naked boy across the room. Because he was half-hidden by darkness, the boy's spirit seemed all the more intimidating. Never had Kenpachi experienced such unity of body, mind and technique; not in Nosaka, not in the best of the fighters in the Blood Oath League. A boy. Was Kenpachi dreaming?

So completely had Todd given himself to his sword play that Kenpachi sensed danger; if he approached the boy now, the director would be killed. Frightened, yet willing to embrace danger, the Japanese did not run. Instead he stepped back deeper into the darkness, his hands fumbling with the shoulder bag.

* * *

TODD TOOK THREE STEPS forward and stopped.

This time the enemy struck with all his strength, making contact with the tip of Todd's *bokken*, then sliding his blade along it in a thrust to the chest. Stepping back on his left foot, Todd parried his opponent's weapon. Immediately both fighters brought their weapons back to point at each other's throats.

Todd struck first. He sidestepped to the right and without hesitating leaped forward on his left foot and sliced the opponent's right side. Kenpachi inhaled sharply, marveling at a move of such outstanding skill and beauty.

The director could wait no longer. He stepped forward into the moonlight, the black box extended in both hands. He pushed the box toward Todd.

The effect on the boy was immediate; his cold savagery vanished and he dropped the *bokken*. Eyes bulging, he clutched his throat and backed away from a stunned Kenpachi. That was when the Japanese knew what the box contained.

Todd's face twisted in pain and he shook his head violently from side to side.

Kenpachi, overjoyed, bowed and said in Japanese, "It is yours."

Todd answered in Japanese in a drugged voice. "I do not want the bone."

According to ancient Buddhist rites, after the cremation of a body its ashes were searched for the *Hotoke-San* or Lord Buddha, a tiny bone found in the throat. The shape of such a bone foretold the soul's future. If the next birth was to be a happy one, the bone would resemble a tiny image of Buddha. But if the next birth was to be unhappy, the bone would be either shapeless or ugly.

Kenpachi's hands shook as he lifted the lid of the box.

The bone was half the size of a pinky finger and rested on red silk the color of fire.

It was yellowed. Hideous. Shapeless.

Kenpachi could only breathe the name. "*Benkai*."

Todd shivered. His eyes were closed and his arms extended, as though keeping Kenpachi at bay. "Keep the *Iki-ryō* away. Don't let it return to me. Please don't let it return."

With these words Kenpachi knew the pleasure of power. His practice of *bushido* and his meditation on death had brought forth the *Iki-ryō*, which now disturbed the boy. In life one dominated or one served. Therefore it was right and necessary that Todd obey the one who had assumed control of his existence. He had to obey Kenpachi.

He said, "You will answer. The point on Benkai's, on your Muramasa. Is its edge straight or curved?"

Todd's voice was a croak. "*Fukura-tsuku*." Curved.

"What is written on the tang?" The tang was the part of a blade which fitted into the hilt.

"D-date. The name of Muramasa. Province of Muramasa. My name. My-my . . ."

Todd, head back on his shoulders, dropped to his knees. His eyes remained closed.

"The five relationships," said Kenpachi. "Name them."

"Fi-five. Father and son. Husband and wife. Brothers, older to younger. Friend to friend. And . . ."

"Say it. I order you."

"Master and servant."

Kenpachi's eyes brightened. "Karma has said that the relationship between master and servant is to be found in the three worlds. What are they?"

"Three. Past life, this life, future life."

"You have lived many lives. On the normal plane of consciousness you remember nothing. But tonight is different and so I ask you: give me the name of two of Hideyoshi's chief spies."

Todd's breathing grew louder and he pressed clenched fists to his temple. Blood trickled from his left eye. "Spiiies." He drew out the word. "Spiiiies."

"Two."

"Hirano Nagayusu. Kasuya Takemori. They worked with the Buddhist priest Kennyo."

Nagayusu was the name Kenpachi wanted to hear and had doubted the boy could know. Nagayusu was Nosaka's ancestor. Kenpachi had found his *kaishaku*, his second. But while destiny had given him the half-Chinese boy, Kenpachi had yet to know what he had received.

What he did receive next was a warning. "The woman is a danger," said Todd. "Guard yourself well, mas—" He hesitated. The word came hard, but he said it. "Master."

Master. In life one could rarely ask for more than the happiness of a passing moment, and for this one moment Kenpachi was the happiest of men. Master.

"What of the woman. Who is she?"

"She was yours when I served you. Since then she has taken many births and is once more beside you. The woman is from the West."

There was only one Western woman in Kenpachi's life at the moment—Jan Golden. But how could she be a danger to him unless, yes, unless she was Saga, Saburo's treacherous concubine. And had been reborn to again betray the lord of Ikuba Castle. I am lord of Ikuba now, thought Kenpachi, and she shall not betray me.

If Nosaka didn't kill Jan Golden, then Kenpachi would. It was the only way to avoid becoming Saga's victim as Saburo had been four hundred years ago.

Wakaba opened the door. "She comes, Kenpachi-san. The mother."

Kenpachi snapped the black box shut and turned in time to see Todd, still on his knees, lose consciousness and fall forward to the floor. Frustrated, the director took a step toward the boy, then stopped. He didn't want to leave, but there was no choice. No matter. The boy was his.

Thousands of lives had prepared Todd for this moment. You are mine, the director thought. And I will have you. Nothing or no one shall prevent this. But first you must be purified, made ready for your role in my destiny, my *seppuku*.

Kenpachi stepped into the hall where Wakaba was staring at Katharine Hansard, now almost on them. Her eyes were narrowed with unspoken questions. Kenpachi had an answer. He slapped Wakaba's face.

"Fool," hissed Kenpachi. He spoke coldly in English. "You have wasted my time. You lead me from room to room and it is obvious that you have no idea where this telephone is. Meanwhile an important caller waits and I stand to lose a great deal of money because of your stupidity. Did you look in this room before summoning me?"

Wakaba, a hand to his cheek, shook his head.

"Of course not," said Kenpachi. "Had you done so you would have found nothing more than a sleeping boy. And please, do not blame the servant for your stupidity. You should have brought him with you instead of subjecting us both to your inability to remember correctly. For now I advise you to keep as far away from me as you can, at least until I find this caller.''

Continuing his pretense of rage, Kenpachi walked away from Wakaba, leaving him in front of Todd's room. He strode past Katharine Hansard as though she did not exist.

Wakaba finally moved, following Kenpachi. He, too, ignored the woman, who watched the two men until they disappeared down the staircase leading to the ground floor and the party.

CHIKAI

*IN KENDO, FACE TO FACE
WITH AN OPPONENT.*

6

IN HONG KONG Ian Hansard arrived at the snake restaurant shortly after 5:00 P.M. The restaurant, which served only snake meat, snake wine and snake bile, was in the western district, the area his wife was fond of calling "the real Hong Kong." Katharine loved the old three-story buildings with their carved balustrades and ornate balconies. And she enjoyed exploring the narrow side streets and alleys jammed with hawkers' stalls and shops of jade carvers, herbalists, calligraphers and coffin makers. Hansard found the district an eyesore filled with crumbling housing, toothless old whores, squatter shacks and foul-smelling slaughter houses.

More to his pleasure was the beautiful Oriental woman he was to meet in the snake restaurant. Dear God, what an absolutely smashing creature she was. Japanese, lovely and blessed with an eye-catching figure. Her name was Yoshiko Mara. Two days after the Kenpachi party, she had presented herself at Hansard's bank and requested his help.

"I am a designer," she said, "and I plan to relocate here from Tokyo. Labor costs in Hong Kong are cheaper and there is not the competition I face in my country from more established designers."

"Well, Miss Mara, what can I do to make your stay here in Hong Kong profitable as well as pleasurable?"

She crossed her legs before answering and Hansard's mouth went dry. Her hair was blue black and her almond-shaped eyes were made more alluring by silver eye shadow. She wore a

tailored gray suit with a slit skirt which showed a fair amount
of thigh when she sat down. There was white lace at her throat
and, God in heaven, she had on those ankle strap shoes that
Joan Crawford always wore, the sort that put Ian Hansard instantly in heat. Yoshiko Mara was an extremely nice bit of
crumpet.

"I have some money," she said, "but I shall need a small
loan and perhaps advice on setting up one or two corporations. At least four businessmen in Tokyo spoke highly of you
and recommended that I seek you out."

She gave Hansard their names. Ian Hansard smiled;
damned if he didn't have her now. She knew he could help her
and if she wanted that help she would have to be very nice to
him. "I may well have a solution to your problems," he said.
"Where will your showroom be?"

"Oh, I intend to have more than just a showroom, Mr.
Hansard. I want to do both couture and ready-to-wear line. At
the moment I can't discuss it, but there is some property in the
western district which I may be able to get at a reasonable
price. The property includes an abandoned factory which I intend to renovate and use for my ready-to-wear line."

"I say, that sounds exciting. By the way, do call me Ian.
And since you're new to Hong Kong, perhaps I can show you
around. It so happens I'm free for dinner tonight and we
could discuss your plans over some rather excellent Cantonese
chicken at a restaurant owned by a friend of mine."

Yoshiko Mara touched her small pink mouth with green-
tipped nails and smiled shyly. She seemed most anxious to
please. Ian Hansard had every intention of giving her that opportunity.

* * *

EXCEPT FOR HANSARD and a trio of Chinese waiters
engaged in a vigorous game of Mah-Jongg near the kitchen,
the snake restaurant was empty. He had been to such restaurants before, but never one quite as unappetizing as this little
room, with its dim lighting, low ceiling and stained, creaking
floorboards. There were only a half dozen wooden tables,
which Hansard suspected had been looted from a trash barge.

One wall was lined with built-in cupboards, whose drawers contained live snakes. Hansard could hear them hissing and thrashing about, which did little to soothe his nerves.

On either side of the cramped kitchen, walls of shelves were lined with large glass jars of snake wine, which was nothing more than clear alcohol containing decomposing snakes. While uneasy around reptiles of any sort, Hansard had come to share the Chinese belief in snakes as medicinal and rejuvenating aids. In the cold months he too ate snake to ward off influenza and had yet to become seriously ill during a Hong Kong winter. The meat tasted somewhat like chicken, only more succulent.

As for the aphrodisiac qualities of snake bile, Hansard had to admit there was something to what he had always treated as an old wives' tale. A drink of snake bile in Cognac did make him feel more amorous and ready for the old in-and-out. Perhaps one day he would be like those Chinese in their eighties and nineties, who claimed that snake bile enabled them to make love regularly and even father children.

Since Yoshiko had selected the snake restaurant for a drink Hansard guessed that the property she had in mind for her factory and showroom was nearby. Hong Kong's real estate speculators and their wrecking balls had already begun to reshape parts of the western district. As Hansard saw it, he and Yoshiko would have their drink; then she would undoubtedly take him over to the site she proposed to purchase and ask his opinion. Over the telephone she had hinted as much.

Professional matters out of the way, the two would then take the ferry across the harbor to Kowloon for dinner. Hansard had seen Yoshiko two days running and while he had not yet taken her to bed, he was certain that little pleasure would be his tonight. He screwed a Senior Service cigarette into a black ivory holder, then lit it with a thin gold lighter. A waiter looked at him, but Hansard shook his head. When Yoshiko arrived he would order. As the waiter turned back to his Mah-Jongg game, Yoshiko stood in the doorway. The Englishman's face brightened and he rose from his chair.

"You look absolutely lovely," he said.

Yoshiko wore a high-necked, long-sleeved dress of lavender

silk, with a matching lavender headband to hold her lustrous hair in place. Her legs were bare and she wore gold sandals with wraparound gold laces that reached the knee. Fingernails and toenails were painted silver and she smelled of jasmine. Hansard stared at her with open longing and when she touched his arm, he coughed to clear his throat. He felt like a randy schoolboy, tongue-tied and nervous.

"I could use a drink," she said in a throaty voice that made Hansard tremble. "I have been rushing madly about all day, seeing people and trying to make decisions that could affect the rest of my life. Tonight, I just want to relax."

"Well, I must say the rushing about certainly seems to agree with you. Not a hair out of place and your beauty appears to be completely intact."

"You are very kind. You have made my stay here in Hong Kong most enjoyable."

"The pleasure has been mine, I assure you. Well, let's summon a waiter and get ourselves squared away, shall we?"

Her hand reached across the table for his. "I've heard so much about snake bile. I wonder if it's all they say it is."

Hansard removed the cigarette holder from his mouth. "And what do they say it is?"

"Oh, they say it relaxes you, removes your inhibitions." She laughed. "They even say it makes you live longer."

That wasn't what she meant and they both knew it. Hansard squeezed her hand. He could afford to be bold from here on. He lifted a hand, and a waiter with hair like polished wood left the Mah-Jongg game to come over to their table. Hansard, his stomach knotted with excitement, ordered snake bile. Yoshiko's hand rested in his; the odor of her perfume, and thoughts of the night ahead, pushed aside his apprehension of snakes.

The waiter returned from the kitchen with a tray containing four small teacups and a bottle of Remy Martin. Then, as Hansard and Yoshiko watched, he went to the wall cupboards, where he slowly opened one of the sealed drawers and carefully removed a live, six-foot cobra. The waiter held the hissing, twisting snake at arm's length, his left hand tightly squeezing it just beneath the expanded hood.

Returning to Hansard's table, the waiter jammed his foot

down on the snake's tail, stretching it taut. As the snake hissed louder and bared curved fangs, the waiter reached into a shirt pocket and removed a thin metal piece with a small hook at one end. Placing the metal piece between his teeth, the waiter ran his free hand down the length of the cobra's stomach, his fingers feeling for the bile sac.

When he found it he used the metal piece to make a one-inch slit over the sac, causing the cobra to tremble with pain and rage. Now the snake was at its most dangerous. Dropping the bloodied metal piece on Hansard's table, the waiter used two fingers to probe the opening in the snake. In seconds he plucked out the wet, thumb-shaped yellow sac that was the cobra's gall bladder, and dropped it into one of the teacups. Still squeezing the cobra below its flattened hood, the waiter now stepped back as a second waiter moved to Hansard's table. This one broke the sac, poured the clear bile into another teacup, then filled the cup with Cognac. Finished, he bowed, then stepped back to join the waiter holding the twisting cobra.

Yoshiko dipped a forefinger into the Cognac and bile, then slowly licked it, her eyes on Hansard. Again she dipped a finger into the teacup and this time touched Hansard's lips. He took her hand in both of his, licked the finger as she had done and devoured her with his eyes. She withdrew her hand and brought the cup to her mouth. She sipped, then held the cup out to him. She kept her hands on the cup as he took her hands in his and drank. There was a gentle pressure on Hansard's lips; Yoshiko held the cup against his mouth, urging him to drink more. Hansard, wanting her as he had wanted no other woman for a long time, drank all of the warm and bitter liquid, feeling its fire race through him, feeling his penis harden.

His eyes were closed and he never saw Yoshiko nod to the third waiter, who quietly locked the front door and stood with his back to it. A second nod to the two waiters near the table, one of whom still gripped the cobra, was returned.

Hansard swallowed the last of the Cognac and bile, opened his eyes and smiled at Yoshiko.

"Dear Ian," she whispered, placing the cup to one side and taking both of his hands in hers.

He leaned forward to kiss her. Suddenly with surprising strength, she yanked him forward toward her, leaving Hansard stomach down on the table, too startled to cry out. Leaping from her chair, Yoshiko then drove her elbow into his right temple, almost knocking him unconscious. As she stepped back, he rolled off the table and fell to the floor on his back, squeezing his throbbing head.

The waiter holding the cobra stepped forward and dropped it on Hansard.

The reptile struck without hesitation. Its head, the hood spread wide in frenzy, sped forward, fangs biting deep into Hansard's cheek. He screamed and pulled at the snake, but it clung to the Englishman's flesh, shooting its deadly venom into his face. Hansard twisted and writhed on the floor and desperately tried to push the snake away. His legs lashed out, overturning the table, sending teacups and the bottle of Cognac crashing to the floor. The venom worked quickly; Hansard's thrashing was followed by a seizure and then there was a muffled cry deep in his throat. He stiffened and spittle dribbled from his mouth. Then his eyes went up into his head and he relaxed and lay still.

The snake coiled and uncoiled over Hansard's chest and face, leaving traces of blood on the dead banker's clothing.

The waiter who had held the cobra went into the kitchen and returned with a garden rake and a meat cleaver. He handed the rake to another waiter and the two cautiously circled the cobra and the dead man. The hissing snake crawled away from Hansard's body, its gray hood red with the banker's blood, then stopped and rose in the air, swaying left and right, preparing to strike again. The waiter holding the rake struck first; he brought the iron end down quickly, pinning the cobra's head to the floor. Instantly the second waiter leaped forward and beheaded the cobra with a single stroke of the cleaver, driving the cutting edge deep into the floor.

Both waiters then rushed to Hansard's corpse and began to rifle his pockets.

Yoshiko picked up her purse from the floor and walked toward the door. The looters were forgotten; her mind was on the second person she had to kill tonight. At the door she stopped and turned. Her nostrils flared in disgust as she watched a waiter pick up the dead cobra's head and drop it into a jar of clear alcohol. The other waiter chopped up the cobra's body into sections for edible snake meat.

In Hong Kong nothing was allowed to go to waste.

Outside, Yoshiko walked to the edge of the western district before finding a cab. The driver understood English and she smiled and gave him Katharine Hansard's address on Victoria Peak, then opened the rear door and stepped inside.

* * *

IN A KENDO *dojo* above a tea merchant's shop on Queen's Road, Todd Hansard kneeled and concentrated on the practice matches. He wore kendo armor, but his mask and *shinai* lay on the mat. Suddenly his eyes widened and he flinched with pain; something was happening to his mother miles away on Victoria Peak. His head jerked under the impact of a blow to the temple, then snapped backward from a strike to the throat by a bare hand.

Todd clutched his throat and fought to breathe. And then the pain was gone. Now he felt the heat from the fire.

He leaped to his feet, raced across the *dojo* floor and disappeared down the stairs. The *sensei* and a few kendoists walked to the window and looked down the street, but Todd Hansard had already disappeared into the rush hour crowd.

* * *

STILL IN HIS KENDO ARMOR, Todd stood alone under the pergola on the grounds of the Hansard home. The climbing plants of the covered walk and the deep twilight hid the boy and his tears. Across the grounds flames had engulfed the bungalow behind the Hansard mansion, the bungalow his mother used as a sculpture studio. Hoses from the fire trucks were trained on the small burning building, their streams of water white arcs against the darkening sky.

Todd's mother was in that building, and he knew she had been murdered. The police, the servants and neighbors who whispered about a tragic accident were wrong.

Todd looked at the great white house, untouched by the fire, its windows now glowing a bright red. Her house. "Mother," he whispered.

Grief made the boy shrink from human company and cling to night and shadows. With an understanding that was becoming a curse, he knew that he could never share the sorrow of Katharine Hansard's death with anyone. It was a weight he must carry by himself, a sad endurance that would stay with him.

Yet within him was an awareness that pain and death could never be separated from life. To reject them was to reject life itself.

* * *

A deeper wisdom pushed its way into Todd's consciousness. It spoke to him of mujo, *the impermanence to be found in all things. Whatever lived and was to be found between heaven and earth was subject to disease, decay and death, to inevitable and inexorable change. A samurai must remember* mujo *and be strong. All of life was a preparation for death. A warrior must contemplate* mujo *every day of his life.*

* * *

BUT TODD HANSARD was still a boy, living partly within a normal adolescence, partly within an ancient destiny that sought to control him. His mother's love had offered the hope that he might one day escape his fate. But now she was dead and Todd was alone. And so it was the boy, not the warrior, who dropped sobbing to his knees, overwhelmed by a pain which clung cruelly to him.

7

A WEARY AND UNSHAVEN DiPalma carefully picked his way out of the blackened ruins that had once been Katharine Hansard's studio. On the grass he looked back over his shoulder at the scorched chimney, at the iron sculptures twisted and melted by intense heat, at a charred, water-soaked couch. After a few seconds he turned forward and looked down, his attention caught by something on the ground. A pair of eyeglasses in a puddle, lenses smashed, a stem torn off. Katharine's.

He picked up the broken frame, placed his cane under one arm and wrapped the frame in his handkerchief. After pocketing the handkerchief he walked the several yards to where Todd stood beneath a cypress tree. DiPalma, eyes hidden behind mirrored sunglasses, had never taken a longer walk in his life. What the hell do you do when you don't know what to do?

At the tree, father and son stood side by side. Todd ignored DiPalma and continued to stare at the burned-out bungalow. He was taller than Frank had imagined, with something of Katharine's beauty in his face and with the strangest eyes. One blue, one violet, each vivid and deep colored and his gaze as pointed as an ice pick. Katharine had written of his intelligence, his interest in kendo and Japanese culture, even his having a touch of psychic powers. In recent letters she had called Todd *different*.

When they met for the first time earlier that day DiPalma

had seen just how different his son was. Failure to save
Katharine, which triggered new guilt over the death of his
wife, Lynn, had left DiPalma depressed and suffering from
his own ghosts. And so he had expected to meet an equally
despondent Todd, a boy also saddened by two deaths. Instead
Frank had met a composed, self-possessed and dry-eyed
youngster, who had coolly shaken his hand and called him sir.
Was the boy in shock or somehow managing to imitate the
samurai he admired? Whatever the reason, Todd's composure
was disturbing. And *different*.

DiPalma had been met at Kai Tak Airport by Roger Tan, a
Chinese-American DEA agent he had known and worked with
in New York and who was now stationed in Hong Kong.
Roger had whisked him through customs and immigration
without a baggage check, then taken him off to the side and
told him about Katharine and Ian Hansard. Without saying a
word DiPalma walked away. Roger Tan knew enough to leave
the big man alone.

Tan walked to the newsstand, purchased a copy of the
International Herald Tribune and turned to the sports pages.
Fifteen minutes later the drug-enforcement agent, his head
still buried in the paper, heard DiPalma say, "Let's go." Tan,
who knew about Katharine Hansard and Frank, saw that
DiPalma had been weeping. He also saw guilt and anger on
that flat face and knew that the big man was at war with
himself. Katharine's death would plunge him into war with
others. Tan was glad he wasn't among them.

In the car Roger Tan had done most of the talking. He was
in his early thirties, a short, broad-shouldered man with a
round, boyish face and perfect teeth which he cleaned with
mint-flavored dental floss several times daily. A federal drug
agent for ten years, Tan was convinced that the agency was
holding him back because he was Chinese and married to a
white woman. He enjoyed passing on damaging or unflatter-
ing gossip about his superiors. He was also the only born-
again Chinese-American DiPalma had ever met and held the
highly original theory that Jesus had married, raised a family
and spent time in China.

Roger Tan was correct about being the victim of bigotry.
The bigotry, however, came not from DEA, but from the

British on the Hong Kong police force, who had a racist dislike of working with the Chinese. For that reason Washington was reluctant to send Chinese-American drug agents to the colony. Unfortunately for Roger, DEA now needed intelligence on Asian drug dealers badly enough to assign him to the Far East.

Roger Tan was a good agent; he was also a vain man, one in constant need of praise from superiors and co-workers and a nuisance to them when he didn't get it. Frank DiPalma had failed to convince him that, race aside, insolence and abrasiveness did not help anyone's law-enforcement career. In the end DiPalma decided that Roger Tan would rather complain than not talk about himself at all.

As the car pulled away from the airport DiPalma said, "Forget the hotel. Take me to the Hansard place." After a long silence he added, "She telephoned me two days ago. Said she was afraid. Asked me to come as soon as I could."

"Figured it was something like that. Yes, sir, that's exactly how I figured it. You know Ling Shen hasn't forgotten his promise. The minute your plane touched down he knew about it. Bet a month's pay that somebody at customs or immigration's on the horn to him now, telling them you're back in Hong Kong."

DiPalma ignored the reminder that a death sentence hung over him in a land where such promises were always carried out. "Why does everyone think her death was an accident?"

"The evidence says so. She did metal sculpture and she used an acetylene torch. So you're talking about mixing gas and fire. Figure it out for yourself. The odds are strong that something can go wrong, especially, say, if she was a smoker."

"She wasn't."

"How can you be so sure? You haven't seen her in eleven years."

"Katharine was a nurse. She'd watched people die from lung cancer and she never forgot it. She hated the smell of tobacco and she wasn't the kind of woman to change her mind easily. What about Hansard?"

Roger Tan leered. Talking about Hansard was a chance to gossip, a chance to show off. "Found that sucker over in Kowloon, face down in Yuamatei Harbour. That's boat-people territory and most of them are illegal immigrants. They live like pigs, let me tell you. It's worse than any slum we've got in the States and twice as dangerous. They have these floating whorehouses if you're looking for cheap nookie, but I don't recommend it. Most of them are one-woman sampans and man, that boat does not stop rocking while you're pumping away. Ain't a day goes by some turkey doesn't get taken off over there or killed. Hey, they didn't just take Hansard's wallet and jewelry. They took his pants and shoes. I mean, shit.''

"Cobra venom," said DiPalma. "Isn't that way out even for Hong Kong?"

Roger Tan chuckled. "Man, nothing is way out for Hong Kong. This town is in-fucking-credible. I'm not surprised at anything that happens here. Look, the boat people never leave the water. So they keep pets. So maybe somebody kept a cobra. Cops tell me the venom puffed up Hansard like he was a float in some parade. Face was bloated, purple, skin torn off. The man goes over there to play hide the wienie and ends up playing feed the cobra. Fucking funny when you think about it.''

DiPalma looked out the car window at the ferris wheels of the Kai Tak amusement park. "You would think a guy as smart as Hansard would know better than to go strolling through Yuamatei any time, let alone late at night."

"I know a lot about this country," bragged Tan, "and I'm telling you the old guys knew how to run things. I'm talking about Genghis Khan. A mean fucker, but he made the country so safe they say a virgin with a sack of gold could walk from one end of China to the other.''

He grinned. " 'Course, there's no record of any virgin having started and finished the walk, but what the hell. Frank, Ian Hansard was a chaser. I know what I'm talking about. Strictly Orientals. No whites, no blacks, no plaids. Orientals only. So maybe he had something special going for him in Yuamatei.''

DiPalma slowly turned his head and gave Roger Tan a hooded look. Tan, his eyes on the road, felt the weight of the former detective's gaze. After a minute Tan stopped chewing his lip and sighed. "All right, all right. So he was killed somewhere else, then taken across the harbor and dumped. So a dude in his position doesn't put his ass on the line chasing bimbos in a neighborhood that's worse than Newark and Detroit combined."

Tan made a left turn onto Lion Rock Road, slowing down for the flood of Chinese who came there daily for the Kowloon city market, a huge concentration of indoor and outdoor stalls. He was still right about most of what he had said about Hansard's death, and set out to prove it.

"I know what I'm talking about when it comes to the boat people in this town. If they saw anything happen to Hansard, we won't hear about it. Like I said, they're illegal aliens from the mainland, with no papers, no ID, no visas, no nothing. The last thing they want to do is talk to the police. You said something about Katharine Hansard being afraid, that she had asked you to come to Hong Kong."

DiPalma used the fingertips of both hands to rub the sleep from his eyes. "Why were you investigating Ian Hansard?"

"You don't miss anything, do you?"

"You know a lot about his death. Cobra venom, the way his face looked, what was taken from his corpse. You said yourself Hansard had no wallet, no ID and not that much of a face. I think you were interested in him for some reason and ended up helping to identify him. Hong Kong is a hustler's town, the name of the game is get rich anyway you can. This place is money mad and Ian Hansard was in the money business. Since he and Katharine died at the same time—one hell of a coincidence by the way—I'd like you to tell me about Ian Hansard and the money business."

"That's your trouble, Frank. You don't come out and say what's on your mind. Okay. Hansard was chairman of the board and chief executive officer of Eastern Pacific Amalgamated Limited Bank. There are almost five hundred banks in Hong Kong, and Eastern's one of the biggest. It's got branches in over sixty countries. Hansard made a damn good living from Eastern and he was not very particular how he did it."

"So he was washing money. Who for?"

"The world. For openers, the Chinese underworld here and on the mainland. The Chiu Chau used him, which made Hansard a heavy hitter when it came to drug deals."

Hong Kong's Chiu Chau syndicates, named for a dialect spoken in southern China, had controlled most of Asia's narcotics traffic for over a hundred years. It was the Chiu Chau, protected by South Vietnamese politicians and military officers, who refined and distributed the powerful number-four heroin which created over twenty thousand addicts among American troops in Southeast Asia. The purity of heroin sold on American streets rarely exceeded 2 percent; number four's purity ranged from 80 to 99 percent.

Protected by Hong Kong's top government officials, the Chiu Chau also controlled much of the colony's organized crime. There were other secret societies in Hong Kong, along with criminal clans and gangs, but none matched the Chiu Chau for wealth, power and brutal efficiency. So tightly structured were the Chiu Chau that even the names of its half dozen leaders were unknown.

DiPalma said, "What about the Big Circle and the Red Guards?"

The Big Circle was a Chinese crime syndicate based in Shanghai; it had pulled off major bank robberies and hijackings in the colony, then invested the money in Hong Kong real estate, trading companies, dance halls, brothels and narcotics. The Big Circle was even rumored to own a few of the colony's banks.

As for the Red Guards, who had fallen out of favor on the mainland after Mao's death, some had drifted to Hong Kong and used their military training to pull off spectacular bank robberies and lucrative kidnappings. Hong Kong police had captured many of them, but not all.

Roger Tan said, "There was only one thing Hansard was concerned about and that was whether or not you could meet his price. He charged one percent of anything he handled. Usual shit. Shift the money from one account to another, from one phony company to another, then maybe from one bank to another, from one country to another. And back again. Jesus, I'm telling you after that nobody could find the money. And that was only part of what the dude was into. The man was very heavy, and I mean heavy, into industrial espionage."

DiPalma took his hands away from his eyes. "Who's behind Eastern?"

Tan laughed. "Used to break me up. I mean Hansard pretending that Eastern was an English bank. Queen's picture on his office wall, British flag in the lobby, bagpipes playing in front of the bank. And every afternoon tea and cakes served to the bank officers in the conference room. Fucking joke. Eastern is owned by a man called Zenzo Nosaka."

DiPalma's eyes narrowed until they were almost closed.

"You've heard of Nosaka, I'm sure," said Tan. "Man's got more money than God and is older than water. We've got photographs of him and Hansard together. Couple of weeks ago Hansard drove down to Aberdeen for a business meeting on Nosaka's yacht, the *Kitaro*. That was around the time of the dragon-boat races. We had a couple of people in the crowd with telephoto lenses, but just to make sure we had a police helicopter fly one of our guys over the yacht and he gets a few shots of them together. Hansard's tied into traffickers, so we thought we might get lucky."

"Did you?"

"Bet your ass, got pictures of Hansard with known Chinese and European traffickers."

"And with Nosaka."

"And with Mr. Zenzo Nosaka."

"You mentioned something about industrial espionage."

"Yeah. See, Hansard could run his little laundry on the side just as long as he took care of business for Nosaka. That meant Hansard had to steal business secrets. And he had to wash and distribute money Nosaka used for bribes and payoffs. And he had to wash money for Nosaka's right-wing Japanese friends. I mean, I didn't go looking for any of this industrial espionage shit. I just tripped over it and included it in my report."

DiPalma said, "So you got lucky. You traced dope money to Hansard and that led to Nosaka. Don't knock it. You just might get lucky and get promoted."

"Sure. And hell could freeze over tomorrow morning."

"What I'd like to know is how a bank can be used to cop business secrets."

Tan pulled the car in a line behind other cars waiting to board the ferry that would take them across the harbor to Hong Kong island. "Shit, that's easy. A bank's always getting requests for loans. First thing they do is run a credit check. In no time at all they know all they need to know about you. Now if you just happen to work at a certain company and can get your hands on certain information, then maybe a deal is worked out. You come up with the information, you get the loan."

"And maybe you don't have to pay it back."

Tan shrugged. "A secretary needs money for her mother's operation. So she turns over her notes from a very important meeting. A guy in the research department wants a new sports car. So he turns over a file on a new product that's supposed to be top secret. A junior vice president wants to take his girlfriend to Bangkok, so he makes a tape recording of a certain sales conference and passes it on. Look, it can go down in a lot of ways, especially if a bank knows you're hurting for money and who isn't? You know how hard it is to get credit these days? You take a look at interest rates lately? Shit, Nosaka came up with a good idea."

"And Hansard was responsible for collecting that information for him?"

The car inched forward, then stopped. "From all over the world. Sixty-odd branches. Super-industrial-spy network. Real dynamite shit and I wasn't even looking for it."

"Who's on the board of directors?"

"Heavy hitters. Heavy, heavy hitters. Strong on American ex-military. Former generals, admirals, Pentagon, Defense Department and Intelligence people. A few European military brass in there, too. They bring in millions to Eastern."

"Where's the money coming from?"

"Money to be used in arms deals, private wars, expensive dirty tricks, drug sales. Money that must not be traced to anybody. And let us not forget tax dodging and a few other scams and schemes these heavy hitters are into and don't want U.S. banks to know about."

Roger Tan drove the car onto the ferry and turned off the ignition. "For the sake of argument let's say Hansard and

Nosaka find themselves sitting on fifty million dollars of somebody else's dirty money. What do they do? They invest it in some stock or bond issue, but only overnight. In the morning they pull out with the interest on fifty mil, which is a nice profit. Meanwhile the money goes back into the regular account and everybody's happy."

"Which is what they did."

"You got it, crime fighter. They did it a few times a year, no more. Wait until there was a shitload of money in Eastern, then make that one overnight investment and get rich. Gave them plenty of money to pass out to the board and keep those fuckers happy."

"And Eastern's board gives Nosaka some very special Washington contacts. Neat. Real neat."

"Congress, Pentagon, CIA. What more do you need? Throw in London, Paris, Bonn. Those Europeans, remember? And you have got a man with a lot of connections." Roger Tan snapped his fingers. "Didn't tell you. A guy you popped a few years back, Sally Verna, he's on the board."

DiPalma acknowledged that revelation with a grunt. No surprises. Roger Tan's rundown on Eastern and DiPalma had put it all together. Sally Verna was on the board and Ian Hansard had been his inside man. Hansard knew of his wife's relationship with DiPalma. Through her he had learned that DiPalma was on his way to Hong Kong. So he had called Sally Verna, who then decided he had his messenger boy.

"What do you know about the Blood Oath League?" DiPalma asked.

"Fucking crazies. Strictly off the wall. The new kids in town and making trouble. Tokyo police telexed us. Wanted to know if we had anything on the league dealing dope to make money for guns. PLO, Red Brigades, they all do it. Couldn't help them. Don't know where the league's getting their bread, but it sure ain't through narcotics. I guess it's coming out of Japan, probably from guys like Nosaka and other right-wing creeps. Besides, from what I hear the league doesn't use guns."

It all came down to Nosaka, thought DiPalma. Katharine's death. The death of her husband. The Blood Oath League, the

Eastern Pacific Amalgamated Limited Bank, Sally Verna and a file of incriminating information on one of the world's richest and most powerful men.

Roger Tan said, "What are you going to do about Ling Shen?"

"Fuck him. I want you to get me the names of Eastern's board and its chief stockholders. Also a list of the countries where it has branches."

"You think Nosaka had something to do with Hansard's murder?"

"Yeah." DiPalma squeezed his cane. "He's involved in Katharine's death, too. Somehow, some way, he is. Both were taken out in a hurry and probably for the same reason. Nosaka. He's the man. He's the one I'm going for."

The ferry eased into the dock at the Star Ferry Terminal. Roger Tan started the motor. "All of this is hard on the kid, him losing two parents at once. Well, at least Todd's got you and that should be some help to him. Poor kid. He's in a few of the pictures we took on the *Kitaro* that day. He fainted or something. Probably due to the heat. They had to get Nosaka's doctor to bring him around. Heat's a bitch in this town. A stone bitch."

* * *

ON THE GROUNDS of the Hansard home, Frank Di-Palma, growing increasingly clammy in the noon heat, unbuttoned his jacket and loosened his tie. He wanted to step into the shade of the cypress tree behind him, but that would have meant walking away from Todd. Blue magpies and kites chirped and flitted among the leaves. The heat didn't seem to bother them.

He heard but could not see the Peak tramway, the funicular railway which lay beyond a nearby forest of bamboo and pine trees. DiPalma touched the jacket pocket containing the eyeglass frames that had once belonged to Katharine. He desperately wanted a drink.

A glance over his shoulder at the house showed that Roger Tan was still inside telephoning his office. Move your ass, Roger. Don't leave me out here alone. Todd had neither been hostile nor friendly. But DiPalma was certain that Todd would neither forgive him nor permit DiPalma to forgive himself. Was it time to accept responsibility for the boy? How do you go about that?

DiPalma had stopped being a father when his three-year-old daughter had been killed by a drug dealer. But the past had reached out for him and he was a father again, forced to do his best. With Katharine dead and Todd alone, he had no choice.

The heat reminded DiPalma of how Katharine had died. He closed his eyes. There was no more painful way of dying than to be burned alive.

Todd said, "My mother was dead before the fire started."

DiPalma opened his eyes. "What did you say?"

"She did not suffer, sir." The boy's voice had a trace of an English accent. He was formal, with good manners. For a few seconds DiPalma had the weird feeling that Todd had read his mind.

"She never stopped loving you," said the boy. "She knew you would come. It gave her hope."

DiPalma forced a smile. "Like they say, I needed that. By the way, do me a favor and call me Frank. Nothing else makes sense. I haven't been a father to you and Mr. DiPalma is too formal."

Todd bowed his head. "As you wish."

"Your mother said you were different. She mentioned something about psychic powers."

Todd frowned. "Sometimes I see things. Different things. And then at other times I suppose I'm quite normal. Like the other lads."

"It's not easy for you to relate to other boys or even to most adults, is it?"

Todd smiled. "No sir, it isn't. You can't always tell people what you think. Especially if you yourself are unsure about what you're seeing. Am I being clear?"

"Perfectly. I want you to say exactly what you want to around me. Don't feel hemmed in or uptight. Be honest. And I'll try to be the same with you."

"I know you will, sir. I mean Frank."

DiPalma took a step toward his son. "Todd, you said that your mother was dead before the fire. How can you be sure?"

The boy hesitated and looked at the cypress tree. Then he looked at DiPalma. "You said be honest, did you not?"

"Always."

"I saw it, sir. I saw it in my mind. I felt it as well. The blow to the head and in the throat."

DiPalma studied his son. Todd had taken a chance and told the truth. He had risked being laughed at or dismissed. What DiPalma said next could keep communication open between them or cut them off from each other forever. "Todd, did you see who did it?"

"I did not see, but I know. I felt a presence."

DiPalma waited as Todd frowned. Then he said, "*Kunoichi.*"

"Women *ninja.*"

"Yes, sir. I felt it was a woman, one woman."

"Todd, your mother didn't smoke, did she?"

"No, sir. She hated cigarettes. She often tried to get my stepfather to stop, but he wouldn't."

"Thanks, Todd. And the name's Frank, remember?"

The boy smiled for the first time. "I'm awfully sorry. I shall try to remember."

DiPalma placed a hand on Todd's shoulder. He felt awkward, yet it seemed the natural thing to do. "Don't worry about the name. I've been called a lot worse things than sir. If you forget, it's not the end of the world. How do you feel about sleeping in that house alone?"

Todd's chin dropped to his chest.

"I thought so," said Frank. "I'd feel the same way. Why don't we go to my hotel? I can clean up and we can do some more talking, if you like. If you don't want to talk, fine. You don't have to. Truth is, I might not feel like talking myself."

The boy smiled at him again. Score one in the battle for hearts and minds, thought DiPalma. But from new truths new doubts grow. There was still tomorrow, next week, an hour from now. Each day meant dealing with an eleven-year-old son he had never seen until an hour ago. That was going to take some getting used to.

They walked toward the house and reached the mansion just as a limousine turned off the road and drove up the circular driveway. Roger Tan stepped from the veranda and joined

DiPalma and Todd on the lawn. The car rolled to a stop and a burly Japanese chauffeur with a close-cropped head and dark glasses opened the back door. Two men and a woman got out and walked toward them. Frank DiPalma's jaw tightened and his hooded eyes grew hard. It was a look Roger Tan didn't like.

The first man out of the limousine was Kon Kenpachi. The second was Geoffrey Laycock, a British journalist. Behind them the woman hung back, reluctant to move away from the car. She fingered the oversized sunglasses hiding much of her face and stared at DiPalma. Finally Jan Golden came forward, eyes down on the ground and stopped behind Kenpachi.

Smiling, Kenpachi said, "Todd." The boy stood rigid, as though awaiting a command. DiPalma didn't like that. When the film director looked at the former detective the smile vanished. Then he turned to Todd and the smile was once more in place. They shook hands and DiPalma, suddenly jealous, knew they had met before. He also knew he didn't want Kenpachi anywhere near his son.

Kenpachi spoke to DiPalma but kept his eyes on Todd. "I understand you are the boy's natural father."

"That's right," said DiPalma.

"He and I get along quite well, don't we, Todd?"

As though hypnotized the boy replied, "Yes."

"We met the other night at his father's party and we've seen each other every day since then. I was the first to comfort him after the unfortunate death of his parents. You're still coming to stay with me at Ikuba Castle as we agreed, aren't you, Todd?"

DiPalma took one step forward. "I'll decide whether or not Todd goes anywhere."

Kenpachi studied the big man. "Ah, yes, the natural father at last makes his appearance. And as always when others are asleep."

Before DiPalma could reply Geoffrey Laycock stepped forward, his hand extended. "Dear boy, it's terribly nice to see you again. How long has it been? Ten years? Donkey's years, actually, since we've last seen one another and you haven't changed. You wouldn't happen to have a portrait of Dorian Gray hanging over your mantelpiece, by any chance?"

Geoffrey Laycock, a stringer for several London newspapers, was in his late fifties and had been a resident of Hong
Kong since the end of the war. He was a potbellied little man,
effeminate and quick-witted, with a pink angular face and
thinning white hair combed sideways across the top of his
head. A self-proclaimed devout coward, it pleased him to
make outrageous statements and get away with them. Di-
Palma found Laycock's nervous vitality exhausting.

Laycock wore a polka-dot bow tie, a doughnut-sized gold
medallion suspended from a gold chain around his neck,
pleated pants and wing tip shoes. He carried a hand-painted
bamboo fan against the heat. He tapped DiPalma on the chest
with it, and with one eyebrow raised appraised the big man.

"I must say, Francis, you have become increasingly masculine with the years. Quite becoming. Quite. I can see the
women pouncing on you with the intensity of a lapsed vege-
tarian attacking a T-bone steak. And speaking of beautiful
people, I was interviewing these two on either side of me,
when suddenly they decided to terminate the interview and
dash up here to gaze upon your child Toddie. He does have
smashing eyes, our Toddie. Absolutely smashing."

Laycock, folded fan against his lips, leaned forward to stare
at the boy. "Jewels for eyes," he said. "Two exquisite and
flawless gems." The journalist straightened up, flicked open
his fan and began fanning himself once more. "Rude of me
not to have introduced you two. Frank DiPalma, may I present Miss Jan Golden, film producer extraordinaire. Miss
Golden—"

"We know each other," said Jan. "How are you, Frank?"

"Jan. What are you doing in Hong Kong?"

She smiled nervously. "I can see you don't read the trade
papers. I'm producing a film here. Kon's directing. Actually,
most of it's being made in Japan. We're only doing a week or
so in Hong Kong."

"How's Hollywood?"

"Like somebody once said, you can take all the sincerity out
there and stick it in a flea's navel. There are days when I'd like
to chop it into little bits and shove it all through a six-inch
hole."

"Sounds rough."

"Tide's always high and rising out there. For fear and loathing, you can't beat it. If nothing else, I've learned it's one place where sincerity definitely has its limits. But—" She smiled and shrugged. "It was my choice, wasn't it?"

There was something unspoken between her and DiPalma which caused Kenpachi and Laycock to watch them both. DiPalma broke the tension. "I'd like you to meet my son, Todd. Todd, this is Jan Golden."

As they shook hands she said, "Pleased to meet you, Todd. Geoffrey mentioned something about Frank being your father."

Todd gave DiPalma the warmest smile since their meeting. "Yes, he is my father."

With his back to Kenpachi, the boy looked up at Frank. "My mother wanted to be buried according to Fung Shui. Would you help me to do as she wished?"

It was a trust that DiPalma knew he must honor. "I will. We'll do exactly what she would have wanted."

Fung Shui, wind and water, were the unwritten Chinese spiritual laws which guided yin and yang, the female-passive and male-active elements in nature. It was an ancient Chinese custom applied to the construction of home, office buildings, highways or tombs. The most auspicious location had to be chosen and bad spirits appeased.

Kenpachi said, "Todd, is there anything I can do?"

"No," said DiPalma.

Before the film director could reply a police car entered the driveway and pulled up behind the limousine. Two British police officers got out, leaving a Chinese driver in the car. When the policemen reached the group on the lawn, the officer in charge looked boldly at Jan before stating his business.

"Inspector Jenkins. And this is Officer Cole. We've come for the boy."

Jenkins was the Welshman who had come to the Hansard mansion to speak to Katharine Hansard about her son fighting in the streets. Then Jenkins had been forced to bend the knee and bow his head and eventually crawl out of the Hansard mansion with his tail between his legs. Now he wanted his own back. Both Hansards were a lump of lead, leaving him only the boy on whom to take his revenge.

"I'm Todd's father," said DiPalma. "I'd like to know where you're taking him and why."

Jenkins combed his red mustache with manicured fingers and looked at his partner, a hawk-nosed Scot with tufts of hair sprouting from his ears and nostrils. Then he looked back at DiPalma with open contempt. Without a word Jenkins grabbed Todd by the elbow and almost jerked him off his feet.

DiPalma's speed and grace did not go with his size; the big man moved with a terrible swiftness. A blurred lifting of his right arm and the tip of his black oak cane dug into Jenkins's larynx. Eyes bulging, Jenkins gagged, took his hands off Todd and shoved the cane aside. A second later the inspector's right hand was inside his jacket and reaching for his shoulder holster.

DiPalma attacked again. A flick of his wrist and the cane cracked Jenkins on the right elbow. The Welshman yelped, jerking the hand back as though his gun were hot metal.

His partner drew his revolver, but Roger Tan stepped in front of him. "Stay cool, man," said the DEA agent. "This thing doesn't call for guns. Just stay cool."

The Scot spoke through clenched teeth. "Out of my way, bastard, or I'll put a hole in you."

Geoffrey Laycock, manicured white hands fluttering in front of his face, intervened. "Gentlemen, please. Must we have so much belligerence in this oppressive heat? Please, let us all take three very deep breaths and hold the last one for a count of ten before saying another word. Please."

For a few seconds there was only the sound of Jenkins's loud breathing. Red-faced with anger, he held his pained elbow and stared at Frank DiPalma with hatred. Finally he spoke with forced calm, the corners of his wide mouth flecked with spit.

"You, sir, are under arrest. The charge is interfering with a territorial officer in the performance of his duty. I understand that in the States you are Jack the Lad on telly. However, in Hong Kong you rank as high as whatever happens to be stuck to the sole of my shoe. Nor does your Chinese compatriot, who interfered with my partner, rank much higher. You fucking Americans think your money buys you the right to put your foot on our throats. Well, Jocko, I intend to put the lie to that. The ball's in my court now and when I get you down to headquarters I will personally make you pay for being so confident and stupid."

"Inspector?"

Jan Golden's smile was sinister, her eyes bright. "I witnessed what just happened. I saw you abuse Mr. DiPalma's son and I'll not only bring it to the attention of the American consulate, but I'll see that the governor is informed as well."

Jenkins shook his head in mock sorrow. "Oh dear, oh dear. Whatever in the world do we have here? Why it's the liberated American woman bringing her righteous anger to the Far East. Bloody decent of you to give us yabbos an intoxicating breath of freedom. Now let me inform you of something. As far as I'm concerned you can get stuffed. Stay the hell out of my way or I will make you wish you had."

Geoffrey Laycock opened his mouth, but Jan Golden, the smile still in place, silenced him with a lifted hand. Stepping closer to Jenkins until they were almost nose to nose, she folded her arms across her chest, then spoke softly.

"Mister, if you arrest Mr. DiPalma, I will telephone the governor and tell him I am pulling my production out of Hong Kong as of today. Then I shall call the American consulate and tell them what I am doing and why. Finally, I shall call a press conference. I think the press will want to know that one million dollars and five hundred badly needed jobs are going to go flying out of your little town. All that hard work by your local film commission down the tubes. And when I finish spreading the word no one will want to come here and make a picture."

Jenkins concentrated on Jan's nose. He had been intimidated as soon as she had walked up to him. There was no getting around it; women with power, like her and Katharine Hansard, easily intimidated him. And Jan, with an instinct for brutal infighting, knew she had beaten him. Still smiling, she gently patted him on the cheek, then walked away.

Geoffrey Laycock stepped forward. "Dear God, it's all so heartstopping. Inspector, allow me to point out that if Miss Golden leaves Hong Kong under these circumstances, it will be terribly bad public relations for the territory."

"So it's taking her side, is it?" An angry Jenkins aimed a

clenched fist at Laycock. "And I suppose your version of this little affair is destined to appear in those slimy rags you write for."

Laycock raised both eyebrows. "This is one of the governor's favorite projects, not to mention being a favorite of the legislative council. You'll not be first in their hearts for having botched it up. Furthermore, your opinion to the contrary, Mr. DiPalma is an important journalist and any difficulty encountered by him would undoubtedly be looked into by his American television network. Dear boy, we both know that the Hong Kong police department cannot stand close scrutiny at this time. Or at any other time. But, of course, you are free to do as you please."

Jenkins said to no one in particular, "There is a Chinese couple waiting at the police station who claim to be an aunt and uncle of the late Katharine Hansard. They have identification supporting this claim, which under Hong Kong law makes them the boy's sole kin."

DiPalma said, "I'm the boy's father. Besides, when Todd was born Katharine's entire family disowned her."

"We've only your word that you're the boy's father."

"Check hospital records. Check—"

Jenkins shook his head. "Mister, I don't have to check a bloody thing. My orders are to bring the boy down to police headquarters and that's what I intend to do. Any opposition from you is in clear violation of the law."

"I'm afraid he's right," Laycock said. "You'll simply have to let the boy go."

DiPalma shook his head. "Katharine's relatives cut off any contact with her years ago. There's no secret about that."

"Ah, but the law, dear boy, is, if not blind, then afflicted with a severe case of cataracts."

Roger Tan said, "To get custody of Todd, you'll have to let him go. You stand in their way and they'll have the right to come back here with a small army and do whatever's necessary. If that happens, Todd could get hurt. And you can't sneak him out of Hong Kong because that makes both of you fugitives. Your best chance is to find proof that you're the natural father."

DiPalma said, "Eleven years ago they ran me out of this

town. Ran me out. The game was played by their rules and I
lost. Wasn't allowed to see Katharine before being put on the
plane. Never saw Todd. And now I get here too late to help
Katharine. Too goddamn late. Even if I come up with papers
saying I'm the natural father, I'm going to end up playing by
somebody else's rules. Well, I think I'll change the rules.
Todd, go with them. I'll see you soon.''

DiPalma, followed by Roger Tan, left the group and walked
toward the house. At the veranda a knot of servants scattered
and made a path for them. When the two men had disappeared inside the house Jenkins said to Todd, "If it isn't asking too much, your worship, would you mind getting into the
fucking car?''

Todd slowly walked ahead of Jenkins and his partner to the
car. Kenpachi had drifted over to the limousine, where he and
Wakaba, the chauffeur, now talked quietly in Japanese. Jan
Golden and Geoffrey Laycock were left alone with each other.
And while Jan stared at the house, Laycock stared at her.

"My dear,'' he said sympathetically, "the only way to be
happy by means of the heart is to have none. You loved him
once, didn't you? I saw it in your eyes. They say there are two
great moments in a woman's life. The first is when she falls
hopelessly in love with a man. And the second, of course, is
when she leaves him. You, my precious, have obviously had
your great moments with Mr. DiPalma.''

"He asked me to marry him. I said yes. And then I walked
away.''

She looked at Laycock. "I'm sure you'd like to know why.''

Laycock, eyes bright with anticipation, leaned forward.

Jan Golden smiled through her tears. "I just bet you
would.'' And she walked away from him.

8

THE LIMOUSINE CARRYING JAN GOLDEN, Kon Kenpachi and Geoffrey Laycock entered Statue Square, the location of Hong Kong's most powerful banks. A tap on the window from Laycock's fan directed Jan's attention to the chunky gray silhouette of the Bank of China, whose doorways were guarded by forbidding stone lions. She drew deeply on her cigarette and allowed the British journalist to tell her what she already knew, what she had learned from her father: that China owned a dozen banks and controlled over 20 percent of Hong Kong's deposits; that China had billions of dollars invested in Hong Kong businesses; that China and not the British Parliament controlled Hong Kong's very existence.

"China can take back Hong Kong without firing a single shot," Laycock said. "A telephone to the Queen and it's done. Whole damn colony is nervous about the treaty coming to an end, you know. Fifteen years from now, in 1997, Britain's ninety-nine year lease expires and China gets the bloody territory back. All four hundred square miles and some two hundred thirty-five useless islands. The mere thought of a Communist takeover strikes the fear of death in us all, especially among the posh set. Having grave effects already, I must say. Stock prices dropping, Hong Kong dollar sinking, fewer investments being made and that rather telltale sign—money moving abroad in suspiciously large amounts."

Suddenly the limousine braked, almost throwing Jan out of

her seat. A cream-colored minibus had cut in front of them without warning. Fucking Hong Kong traffic. Worse than anything Jan had seen in Paris, Rome or New York. The minibuses were small, privately owned vehicles which were allowed to compete with regular buses and trams. They could stop anywhere. A prospective passenger had only to hold out his hand or stand in the road and flag them down. To get off, one simply yelled at the driver.

To calm her nerves Jan lit another cigarette, then opened the window to allow the smoke to escape. Twenty minutes ago the limousine had left the Hansard mansion to return to location filming in Wanchai, once a popular red light district for American servicemen on leave from Vietnam. Laycock had begun babbling about Hong Kong, past and present, while Kenpachi buried himself in a leather-bound copy of his script. He used a felt-tip pen to make notes in the margins. The notes were in Japanese, beautifully formed characters running down the left side of each page.

If the notes were to himself, fine. But if they were dialogue changes or called for new camera setups, Jan wanted to be consulted. Meanwhile, Kenpachi had shut her and Laycock out. A director had the right to concentrate on his work without being interrupted; Kenpachi would be in deep shit if he didn't take his craft seriously. Jan suspected, however, that at the moment Kenpachi simply wanted to avoid talking to her about Frank DiPalma. Christ, what a shock that had been. She hadn't known the two men knew each other, let alone hated each other's guts.

As for Geoffrey Laycock, the man would not shut up. Jan bore the brunt of his running commentary on Hong Kong; her mind, however, was on Frank DiPalma. Kenpachi and Frank. The story of Jan's life. The man she wanted versus the man she needed. And as always Jan would make her choice according to her passion.

She knew that the immediate pleasure was always her undoing, that it drew her into what was often nothing more than the encounter of two weaknesses. But like everyone else, she did what she wanted to do. For her, pleasure lay in the knowledge that love was only temporary, that it would not last. With Frank DiPalma, love had threatened to last and so a frightened Jan had left him. She had not wanted to change. And yet she could not forget him.

In the stalled traffic she stared through tinted glass at the domed and colonnaded Supreme Court Building on the east side of Statue Square. It was a lovely example of Edwardian architecture by Aston Webb, the man who had designed London's Victoria and Albert Museum and the facade of Buckingham Palace. The building reminded her of Frank DiPalma. Surrounded by banks, glass and steel high-rises and even a Hilton hotel, it went its own way with dignity and grace. And with strength.

Geoffrey Laycock covered a yawn with his fan, reminding Jan of something Kon Kenpachi had said about Frank. Something to do with sleep. She looked at Kenpachi, still wrapped up in his script. She wanted answers now, not when Kon was ready to give them to her.

She said to Geoffrey Laycock, sitting across from her, "Kon's in another world at the moment, so perhaps you can help me. Something was said back there about Frank only showing up when people were asleep. I understand that Japanese and even Chinese often disguise the truth in their remarks, especially if the truth happens to be unpleasant. Do you have any idea what that sleep business was all about?"

Laycock's eyes widened. The fan waved briskly. "Death, my dear. In this case, sleep is a euphemism for death. Surely you know Mr. DiPalma's reputation. People dying around him and all that."

Jan could have kicked Kon for making that crack about Frank. But right now she didn't want to risk an argument. Making a picture was tough enough without antagonizing your director.

Laycock frowned. "I believe, yes, it was three. Frank suffered the loss of three partners while serving as a policeman. And he himself also sent a few men to their eternal rest. Strictly in the line of duty, of course. Some people looked upon him as a walking albatross, rather a black cloud of sorts."

"He killed to save his life or somebody else's," she said. "There wasn't a cop in the department who wouldn't have been glad to have Frank DiPalma as a partner."

"I cast no aspersions, I fling no brickbats. I merely report what has transpired. You are aware, of course, of the deaths of his wife and daughter?"

"They were taken hostage by a drug dealer, then murdered. Are you blaming Frank for that?"

"Absolutely not. I'm merely answering your question. People around Mr. DiPalma do tend to fall into 'the big sleep', as they say in detective thrillers. New York Hispanics nicknamed him 'Muerte,' death. Another colorful street name for him, I'm told, was 'Mr. Departure.' May I ask how you and Frank became acquainted?"

"We met at the network. I was in charge of all series and made-for-television movies produced in New York. Frank was hired as an investigative crime reporter."

"Quite accomplished at it, I hear."

"The best. Surprised the hell out of everybody. No one has better contacts, not even reporters with ten times his experience. The camera doesn't scare him and his crew love him. They know he's good and that they'll get to work on some exciting stuff, so they walk through walls for him. You can't compare him to most of the people in television. What they lack in brains they make up in stupidity."

The limousine started up again, leaving behind white-clad Englishmen playing cricket in Statue Square Park. Kenpachi was still buried in his script.

"A few of Frank's stories have gone on to make the newspapers," said Laycock. "Our English-language papers here have carried one or two. There was that rather odd one where he solved the murder of a young black child. She had been struck in the head by a bullet while lying in her pram. Somehow Frank learned the killing had been done by a local drug dealer. Apparently the dealer had money stacked floor to ceiling in a closet, and the rats had gotten at it. Eaten almost a hundred thousand dollars, if I recall. Bloody dealer became enraged, drew his pistol and began firing at the rats. A stray bullet killed the child. Amazing how Frank was able to go into the ghetto and in hours discover who had done it."

"Frank knows everybody. I've never seen a reporter with a better information network."

"I concur. And he does take advantage of every opportunity to enlarge that network, doesn't he?"

"What's that supposed to mean?"

"Please don't take offense. I was merely referring to the way in which he handled the story on the killing of the three judges in Palmero, Sicily."

Jan said, "Frank risked his life to get the story. He could have been killed."

"Indeed. I mean, after all, it did involve the American and Sicilian Mafia. Three judges murdered while trying Sicilian heroin traffickers and our Frank finding out that the hit man was an American living in Manhattan."

"Frank used to be a narc, remember? Somebody he knew owed him a favor and gave him a tip. He followed it up at the risk of his life."

"And he was clever enough to bring in an important American senator to share the acclaim. If I remember, the publicity from this case aided the senator in getting reelected. Very, very clever of Francis. And you say he's had no journalistic training?"

"None. His parents were Sicilian immigrants who ran a small produce market in Queens. He drove a truck for his father, fought the head breakers who tried to muscle in on the family business and managed to get in a couple of years of college before losing interest. He left school, got drafted by the army and was sent to Europe to work in the army's criminal-investigation division. Got out, bummed around Europe for a few months, then came home and became a cop."

Laycock sniffed behind his fan. "Not much formal education, apparently."

"Mister, the army can be one hell of an education. I should know. My father was an army officer and I learned plenty being around him."

"Forgive me. I meant no offense. I merely—"

"Mr. Laycock, I was born in Japan. My father did three tours of duty there and I was with him on two of them. By the time I was fourteen I had lived in six countries and in seven American states. When I grew older, I attended three different colleges and never learned as much as I did when I was an army brat."

"How did you become a film producer, if you don't mind my asking?"

"No, I don't mind. I had a failed marriage on my hands because my husband preferred gambling to me. I also was rather sick to my stomach at the constant rejection that went with trying to become an actress. I wanted glamor, money, power, fame, freedom. They all seemed to go with being a producer, so I became one."

"And the husband?"

"A trip to the Dominican Republic and ten minutes in front of a sleazeball of a judge, who tried to get me alone in his chambers, took care of that little matter. I think I married Roy because he had a year-round tan and good teeth and made me laugh. The trouble was, that outside of knowing every head-waiter in Manhattan and being able to shuffle a deck of cards with one hand, the bastard couldn't pour piss out of a boot with the instructions printed on the heel."

Laycock giggled. "Oh, I say, that's marvelous. Absolutely marvelous. Frank must have been quite a change from your husband."

"Roy was a lightweight. Frank's heavy duty."

Kenpachi closed his script and placed it on the seat between him and Jan. "Why don't you tell her why Mr. DiPalma will never leave Hong Kong alive."

Jan's head snapped toward Kenpachi, then at Laycock. The cigarette slipped from her fingers and she quickly brushed it off her skirt. Laycock picked it up and stubbed it out in the ashtray.

"I'm afraid there's more than a bit of truth in that. I'm surprised Francis never told you any of this himself."

"He used to say never put your business in the street," said Jan. "It just wasn't his style to open up that much. There were some clips at the network, something about him being in a shoot-out here in Hong Kong. Does it have anything to do with that?"

"Sad to say, yes. I suppose you could call it an example of Laycock's law, which is to say that just when it's darkest, things go black. It all started some eleven years ago when Frank was investigating a Chinese drug dealer in Manhattan, a lad who was a right nasty piece of work himself. Definitely mental, he was. Had the tendency to burn people alive if they displeased him. Francis was in hot pursuit and Nickie Mang knew it. Our Nickie moved back and forth between Hong Kong and America and so far had managed to avoid arrest.

"Then one day Francis learned that Nickie was returning to America by way of Canada and was bringing with him a rather large consignment of heroin. In addition, Nickie was also bringing with him a lovely new Chinese bride. Well, the worst occurred. There was a shoot-out in the Canadian woods and several of Nickie's associates lost their lives, as did his new bride."

Laycock sighed. "Not to put too fine a point on it, our Nick was now in a foul mood. He escaped the ambush and made his way to New York, where he did the last thing anyone expected him to do. He showed up at Frank's home in Queens and took his wife and daughter hostage. Frank, unfortunately, was seen as the man responsible for all of Nickie's woes, not the least of which was the demise of the late Mrs. Mang. Laycock's law turned out to be very much in evidence from here on in. Frank was still in Canada tying up loose ends in this case. By the time he managed to get to New York, it was all over. Nickie had killed Mrs. DiPalma and the little girl. He then surrendered.

"Poor Francis. He suffered the tortures of the damned and didn't know there was more to come. Now you would think that our Nickie, having proven himself sufficiently antisocial, would have been retained in custody without bail of any sort."

Jan said, "Are you telling me they let him out on bail?"

"Laycock's law, remember? I believe the proverb goes 'Laws, like the spider's web, catch the fly and let the hawk go free.' Mr. Mang's bail was set at one million dollars, an astronomical sum at the time. No one thought he could meet it. They were wrong. Once unchained, our Nick fled what had now become America's inhospitable shores and went to ground in Hong Kong. Seething with righteous anger, Frank took off with the idea of returning him to American justice."

Laycock snapped his fan shut. "Somehow Francis catches up with our Nick and starts back to the airport with him. Between Hong Kong island and Kai Tak Airport some of Nickie's associates attacked them and fired off a shotgun at Frank. Wounded him grievously. Damned near killed the man. Believing Frank to be dead, Nickie and friends started to drive off. Ah, but Francis was not dead. He clung rather perilously to life. By a miracle he found the strength and will to draw his revolver. Emptied the gun at the villains. Didn't hit a soul. However, he did manage to hit the gas tank of the car containing Nickie and his friends. There was an explosion and Nickie and cohorts were scattered about the countryside.''

"What about the Hong Kong police? Where were they while all this was going on?"

" 'The gods are moved by gifts and gold does more with men than words.' Euripedes. There is a great deal of money to be made in Hong Kong and sometimes the making of it is helped by having the police on your side. This is an advantage which does not come cheap. Our local constabulary, sad to say, too often becomes corrupted. Alas, Francis was left on his own. Rumor had it that the police kept Nickie Mang's friends aware of Francis's whereabouts at all times. Another rumor says the police were paid handsomely to sit on their hands. Now we come to the romantic portion of our tale, equally as sad and as unfulfilling. While recovering in a Kowloon hospital, Francis met a lovely young Chinese nurse.''

"Katharine Hansard."

"At the time, Katharine Shen. Her father Ling Shen headed the important Triad here. A Triad is—"

"I know. My father had contact with them during the war. They began as patriotic societies meeting in temples. That was a long time ago. Today Triads are little more than thugs and head breakers. They live off extortion and payoffs and whatever else brings in money without working too hard."

Laycock studied Jan before answering. Then, "A taste for truth and she spares nothing. Be that as it may, Katharine Shen and Frank DiPalma were drawn toward one another, with the result that she soon found herself *enceinte*. Preggers. You know, of course, that the Chinese regard themselves as the world's superior race."

Jan looked at Kenpachi out of the corner of her eyes. "As do the Japanese."

"Quite. Well, then, you have some idea of just how embarrassing Katharine's pregnancy was to her father and family.

He, in particular, regarded it as an acute slur on the house of Shen. Fact is, Ling Shen was ready to kill our Francis. For that matter, the American government was not too fond of Francis either.''

"Why? Since when is falling in love a crime against the United States?''

"You see, dear girl, we were at that point in time, 1970–71, when your President Nixon and his secretary of state Mr. Henry Kissinger were opening China up to what they rather pompously called 'the free world.' Secret meetings, coded cables, scrambled telephone calls. Very high-powered goings on. Diplomatic relations between America and China, which had ceased when the Communists came to power, were now about to resume.''

"Christ,'' said Jan. "I can smell it coming. Go on.''

"Think of it. China in the American camp and keeping an eye on the Russian bear. Do you know how many divisions this is worth to your country? In the light of that fact, Francis and Katharine, of course, became expendable. Shen set the ball in motion. He had enough influence in mainland China and Hong Kong to have them pressure your country. Simply put, the powers that be combined to have Francis booted out of Hong Kong. Furthermore, back in the States he was denied the necessary visas to reenter Hong Kong. The White House, Peking and Hong Kong. A most unholy trinity and a most powerful one. Our Francis never had a chance. He was not allowed to make waves. Time passed and both he and Katharine settled into new lives. They kept in contact with one another over the years, but the damage had been done. The world had used them ill.''

"And Frank never saw his son until today.''

"Yes.''

"I don't care what you say, there was more than just 'contact' between them over the years. Frank came back to Hong Kong knowing what might happen to him. There has to be a reason for that.''

"I'm afraid I can't shed much light on the reason for his return. Katharine did save his life, more or less. The death of his wife and child had to be a shattering experience. And there was the severity of his wounds. The doctors despaired of his life. He was broken in body and spirit. Then along came Katharine and he had a reason to live."

Jan closed her eyes. "And he never told me any of this."

"It was Katharine, by the way, who encouraged our Francis to take up Japanese fencing. Quite good at it, he is. You saw the business back there with the cane. He knows a bit about Japanese swords as well."

"*Gaijin*," said Kenpachi. "Nothing more, nothing less."

"*Gaijin* means—" began Laycock.

"I know what it means," said Jan. "Outsider. Alien. It's the name Japanese give to foreigners. That's your mistake, Kon. If you knew Frank DiPalma, you'd know it doesn't bother him to be an outsider, that he doesn't care what people think of him."

"Shen thinks of him. At this very moment, I would imagine that Shen is thinking of your Mr. DiPalma."

"You sound like you want him dead. I don't like that, Kon. I don't like it one goddamn little bit."

Laycock said, "Mr. Kenpachi does not exaggerate. To save face, Shen must kill Francis. Things have not gone well with Shen of late. Triad chiefs hold power on the basis of performance, nothing else. A mistake here and there and a chief can still retain his position. Too many mistakes, however, and he would find himself removed. Often this means a permanent removal from the world as we know it. The word is that if Shen makes just one more mistake, he will be sent to join his celestial ancestors."

"And failing to kill Frank DiPalma constitutes a mistake?"

"Dear girl, in Hong Kong, life is real and indeed quite earnest. Recently someone sent Shen a message by way of reminding him how much his authority has eroded of late. They kidnapped one of his lieutenants, then returned the fellow to Shen the next day. He was still alive. However, both hands and feet had been cut off."

"Christ."

"I read it as a power struggle of some sort. Definitely a difference of opinion between incompatibles. Fascinating business, these local crime wars. A provincial form of amusement."

"Am I alone on this one?" Jan said angrily. "Frank's walk-

ing around Hong Kong in danger of being done in by some
damn weirdo and all you two can do is sit there."

"What do you expect us to do?" said Laycock. "I, for one,
am no threat and Mr. Kenpachi, for another, was hired by you
to direct a film, not flex his muscles on anyone's behalf. If
Frank wants help, I'm sure he'll ask for it. He didn't have to
come to Hong Kong and he most certainly doesn't have to
stay."

Jan sighed. "I know him. He's here for a reason and he's
not leaving until he's ready. He's filled with guilt over Katharine and the only way to get rid of that is by taking care of
Todd. You can put money on it. You won't get him out of
Hong Kong so easily this time. Shen or no Shen, Frank will do
what he came here to do. And he'll leave when he's finished.
With Todd."

She took her sunglasses from her purse, put them on and
looked through the window. She didn't see Kenpachi's face as
he stared at her with cold disdain. Nor did she see the eye contact between the director and Geoffrey Laycock and the tiny
smile on the journalist's face before his fan came up to hide it.

She now hated Hong Kong because of the danger it represented to Frank. A part of her knew that she had made a mistake in leaving him. But it was her style to persist in certain
mistakes, especially mistakes concerning men.

Laycock was right; there was nothing she could do for
Frank DiPalma. Except remember how much she owed him
and hope with all her heart that he would leave Hong Kong as
soon as possible.

The limousine slowed down. They were in Wanchai, on
Lockhart Road, the main thoroughfare, with its tattooists, its
pungent cooking odors, topless bars, massage parlors, gaudy
hostess clubs and Chinese ballrooms. "The Wanch," as it was
known to the locals, was shopworn and tacky, Times Square
with egg rolls, downtown Los Angeles with sweet and sour
sauce.

Jan could not wait to say good-bye to the neon lights, the
schlocky souvenir shops and particularly to the pushy bar girls
with their bared nipples. Kenpachi had insisted on shooting
here because The Wanch had played a part in the lives of

lonely GIs during the Vietnam war. He was right, but she still detested the place.

Ahead Jan saw the cameras and lights, the crew and actors in front of a cheap hotel which was to be the scene of a sad farewell between Tom Gennaro, a GI on leave, and the Hong Kong bar girl with whom he's spent the night. Jan was glad to be back on the set, in her own world and away from other people's problems. Especially Frank DiPalma's.

The limousine stopped. Jan took her compact from her purse, checked her hair in the mirror and touched up her lipstick. When Kenpachi's chauffeur opened the door, she left without saying a word to the director or to Geoffrey Laycock. She headed straight for Stephen, her production manager.

Smart man, Stephen. Always had a lid or two of grass stashed somewhere. Jan wanted something to make her worry less about Frank DiPalma, to give her some hint as to why she still wanted to go to bed with Kon Kenpachi. Bring on the Acapulco gold, she thought. There were times when reality needed fine tuning.

9

FRANK DIPALMA stood at a bay window in the living room of the Hansard mansion and watched the limousine carrying Jan Golden disappear down the tree-lined road from Victoria Peak. A telephone receiver was squeezed between his jaw and shoulder, and his little black book of addresses and telephone numbers was opened face down on a nearby jade cabinet. A seven-foot Martineau clock, its long trunk encasing a brass pendulum, struck one in the afternoon. Time. It had softened his anger toward Jan for walking out on him. It had even lessened the pain. What it hadn't done was free him from her.

From the start there had been this difference between them; DiPalma measured love by its fidelity and seriousness, Jan measured it in terms of sensuality and an almost theatrical compulsion. She was elaborate and inexplicable, and he loved her. She was ambitious, conniving, impatient and unreliable. She was also honest, caring, generous and loyal. The mystery which was Jan Golden was one that Frank despaired of solving.

And because in their courtship she had fled from him, he had instinctively pursued her.

In bed, on their last night together, Jan had warned him, "Frank, there's not enough time to do all the things I want to in this world. What I'm saying is, I can't give too much time to anything. Or anybody."

"So you expect a lot out of life. What you end up with is something else again. Meanwhile we've got something here and now. And you know it."

"Frank, with me you'll always be chasing two rabbits. And the guy who does that never catches either one."

"What do you want me to tell you, that I won't play the game unless there's an easy way out? Look, we come into the world crying, we bitch like hell while we're here and most of us go out terribly disappointed. There are no easy answers for anybody. My father told me that life's a choice between boredom and exhaustion. He ended up working himself to death, which is a hell of a way to prove a point."

"I'll exhaust you, Frank. God knows I don't mean to, but I will. The only thing I know for sure is that I'm always at war with myself. Always have been and can't tell why. But I've never met a man like you, a man stronger than I am. I don't know if that's good or bad."

"Do you love me?"

"Today I do."

"Today's the day I'm asking you to marry me."

"Jesus, what am I doing?"

"Yes or no."

"Yes." And then she was in his arms, her mouth on his, her tongue spearing his. By saying yes to DiPalma, to the moment, she now had a moment without fear, without uncertainty, without doubt.

In the morning when he awoke she was gone. Later that day he learned that she was en route to Los Angeles, to begin work on a three-picture deal she had quietly signed with a Hollywood studio. It would have done no good to call, so he hadn't. He recognized that Jan had done what she wanted to do, as always. All DiPalma could do was forget.

In the Hansard home Roger Tan was talking in singsong Cantonese to a pair of Chinese servants. Roger had learned something interesting about Ian Hansard's love life; days before his death the banker had been seen with a beautiful Japanese fashion designer, who had come to him for money and financial advice. Her name was Yoshiko Mara. *A woman ninja killed my mother, said Todd.* No matter how trivial or personal, nothing happened in Hong Kong without the Chinese knowing it. And the Chinese loved to gossip, especially about *gweilos*.

A telephone call to the DEA office had produced a list of Eastern Amalgamated's board of directors. There had been no time to read it. At the moment, DiPalma had something more important to do. To get what you wanted you made the other guy see the light or feel the heat. DiPalma wanted his son and he knew how to go about getting him.

He shifted the receiver to his other ear. Instantly he heard, "Hello, Frank? You there?"

"Yes, senator. Sorry to wake you, but I need your help."

"You must need it real bad. It's one in the morning. Unfortunately, I'm still up. Getting some things ready for a breakfast meeting with the vice-president. I owe you one, that's for sure. Wasn't for you I'd be drinking myself to death in some second-rate Washington law firm."

"You and my father were friends, senator. He would have wanted me to help you."

"Your old man and me were more than just friends, Frank. Couple of ginzos who started our dirt poor and ended up doing okay." He laughed, a deep, warm sound. "Hey, paisan, we did it, didn't we. Fucking bastards in the party thought I was too old to run. Told me I couldn't win. But you put me back on the Hill with that Palermo thing. Feel younger than I have in years. Hell, if it wasn't for you, I'd probably be a dead man by now. Being out of work can kill a man my age. Was my wife serious? Are you really in Hong Kong?"

"Yes, senator, I am."

"What's cooking over there?"

DiPalma chose his words carefully. "Biggest thing I've gone after since I became a reporter. Might be something I can bring you in on."

Silence. And static. Then, "Something in it for me, you say. Anything you care to talk about?"

"Not right now. But if it's what I think it is, it's going to be incredible. Right now I need you to do one thing for me. One phone call."

"It's done. Just tell me who."

DiPalma rubbed the corners of his eyes with his fingertips.

"First, let me tell you it concerns my son. Somebody's trying to take him from me."

"Jesus, I didn't know you were married."

"I'm not. The boy's mother is dead. Happened here yesterday. Senator, you've been to China."

"Three trips. Last one with the vice-president early this year."

"The papers say China wants U.S. arms."

Again the deep, warm laugh. "Like people in hell want ice water. What's that got to do with you?"

"Senator, I want my son. I'd like you to make that call for me now. Tonight."

"Where to?"

Frank touched the lump in his jacket pocket that was Katharine's glasses. "I'd like you to call Peking," he said.

10

IN HER HOTEL ROOM Yoshiko Mara showered, sprinkled perfume on her wet body, then toweled herself dry. After shaving her legs and armpits, she styled her wig with a blow dryer and painted her fingernails a pale blue. Forty minutes were spent on makeup, most of it on the eyes, Yoshiko's best feature. She used three different colors of eye shadow, starting with white in the corners, then mauve on the center of the eyelid and finishing with a dark purple as she moved deeper into the socket. Coloring completed, she added false eyelashes and carefully painted them a dark brown. The result was provocative and beguiling.

The makeup done, Yoshiko stood nude in front of the bathroom mirror. Her body was slender and hard, with broad shoulders and lean but muscled arms. Her legs were those of an athlete, with solid thigh muscles and developed calves. Smiling, she stroked her flat stomach, allowing her fingers to brush the top of her pubic hair. It was a body that had given pleasure to both men and women. It was a body that promised fulfillment, no matter how forbidden the desire.

She raised her arms shoulder high, the backs of her hands toward the mirror. Her smile faded. Both forearms were scarred. This was why she wore long-sleeved dresses and blouses, to hide her body's only imperfection. She was twenty-eight and the ugly scars, which ran from wrist to elbow, had been with her for half of her life. She had gotten them when she had not been called Yoshiko, when she had lived in Hakone, the mountain resort southwest of Tokyo.

Hakone, with the districts of Fuji and Izu, formed one of Japan's most popular recreation areas. Together the three districts were a huge national park, offering swimming, hiking, skiing, boating and saltwater springs. Hundreds of thousands of Japanese and foreigners came here, most of them drawn by Mount Fuji, the majestic, long-extinct volcano whose snow-capped beauty could be seen from every resort, hotel and lodge in the surrounding countryside. Hakone, famed for its therapeutic hot springs, lay at the base of Mount Fuji; the peninsula of Izu, with its beaches and rocky seaside cliffs, lay to the south.

Yoshiko was the only child of parents who owned and operated a small Hakone resort and souvenir shop near a centuries-old hot spring. Like others in the region, both parents were passionately Japanese, with a strong, almost mystical attachment to nature. Both were religious zealots and politically conservative. Years of living such a narrow life had made them prisoners of their own experience, no longer able to recognize their intolerance.

Despite her strict parents, Yoshiko grew up undisciplined and resentful of the restrictions placed upon her. From the age of eight she was forced to work in the resort, where she cleaned toilets, made beds, scrubbed floors and waited tables. When her work displeased her parents she was beaten or forced to go without food. Occasionally she was made to stand silently in her father's office, facing the wall, while he went about his business. During one beating Yoshiko fought back, breaking her father's thumb. In retaliation he blindfolded the child, tied her hands and feet and left her in a locked closet for three days without food or water.

At school Yoshiko was an indifferent student, with a reputation for defying authority. She arrived late, missed classes and hid movie magazines and photographs of professional athletes in her desk. She fought other students, sometimes played brutal pranks on them and wrote bold love notes to older boys. The more punishment was inflicted on her, the more defiant she became. Her only interests were drama and sports, especially karate and kendo.

At thirteen she became the resort guide for guests who wanted to explore the region. Yoshiko took them to Matsugaoka Koen, the pinewood park, to the Dogashima Walk,

the trail leading down the side of a ravine to beautiful
cascades; to the azaleas and cherry blossoms of Kowakidani,
and to Owakidani, the Valley of the Great Boiling, where the
air reeked of sulfur and clouds of hissing steam spurted from
crevices in the rocks and a stick pushed into the earth caused
steam to shoot up into the air.

Yoshiko enjoyed being a guide. It took her away from her
parents, whom she hated, and from the resort, where she was
treated like a slave. She took pride in her knowledge of the
trails, parks and temples and in her ability to walk tens of
miles without tiring. Above all there was the excitement of
meeting people from Tokyo and foreign countries and learning that there was a world beyond Hakone.

At fourteen Yoshiko was seduced by a guest at the resort.
He was Zenzo Nosaka, the wealthy businessman who came to
Hakone for the hot salt springs that would calm his nerves,
smooth his skin and prevent stomach trouble. Drawn by
Yoshiko's girlish beauty and unbridled energy, Nosaka found
her to be as invigorating as his twice-daily saltwater baths.

For Yoshiko the seduction was an electrifying experience,
an arousal beyond fleshly joys. It was the first indication that
she might have power over others, a power stronger than her
parents had over her. Nosaka was influential and rich, yet she
quickly sensed that his desire for her was so strong that he
would leave nothing undone to satisfy it. Despite his age he
was an expert and vigorous lover whose sensuality exploded
upon Yoshiko. From this point on, sex would not only become
a source of power for her. It was to be her greatest slavery.

Nosaka made several trips to the resort, delighting
Yoshiko's parents. Each time she secretly went to his bed,
leaving it at sunrise to return to her own room. By now sex had
become indispensable to her, a necessary function performed
without guilt. There was no question of having betrayed her
parents. No bond existed between them and Yoshiko, who had
long wished to see them dead.

Between Nosaka's visits she took lovers from among other
resort guests, giving herself to men and women for the only
reason which mattered, her own pleasure. Yielding to her
strong sensuality gave Yoshiko confidence as well as the endurance to survive a miserable life. To make love was to live.
To make love was to enjoy being cruel to those who loved her

too much. Now there was no longer any boredom. Yoshiko had found her own wisdom and her vision of the world would never be the same.

She was upset when Nosaka's visits stopped. But in his place came Kon Kenpachi, to whom Nosaka had spoken of Yoshiko. The handsome Kenpachi, a glamorous and famous film director, easily overwhelmed her with his sensuality. For the first time she felt herself a victim in bed, vulnerable to one who would always be her master. She became obsessed by him; his lovemaking increased her sexual hunger until her longing for him pushed aside any feelings she had had for anyone else.

During his visits to Hakone and Yoshiko's secret trips to meet him in Tokyo, Kenpachi not only taught her about sex but introduced her to drugs, art, music and the world of film-making. He gifted Yoshiko with new kendo armor and improved her fencing technique in private workouts at his castle. While it was one of many such affairs for him, it was the first true love affair for Yoshiko and became her whole life.

Toward the end of the resort season, when her parents left on a two-day business trip to Tokyo, Yoshiko and Kenpachi together climbed Mount Fuji. It was a demanding climb, 12,350 feet to the peak of what had once been one of the world's mightiest volcanos. During the climb they passed the ten rest stations and followed the custom of having their walking sticks burned with the sign of each station as proof of having reached all ten. At the eighth station they spent the night alone in a stone hut, where they ate a cold supper packed by Yoshiko, made love and fell asleep in each other's arms.

They arose before dawn and climbed to the top of the snow-covered peak. Here, with a handful of other climbers, they watched the incredible *goraiko*, the world's most beautiful and moving sunrise. They could see the blue Pacific Ocean, other mountains and strings of villages which lined the coast. But it was the *goraiko* which left them speechless. Yoshiko had never been happier.

That night, back at the almost empty resort, they lay naked and exhausted in Kenpachi's bed. Yoshiko did not want the morrow to come. Tomorrow her parents would return and Kenpachi would be off to Tokyo. She wanted to go with him, to leave the despised resort behind. She had tasted freedom with Kenpachi, and now she did not want to be separated from him.

At the sound of a key in the bedroom door Yoshiko and the film director froze. When the door opened, her father stood in the entrance, a carving knife in his hand. Paper lanterns on the walls gave his horrified face the look of a demon.

He walked toward them, speaking with terrifying calm. "You have shamed my house. I cannot allow either of you to go unpunished."

Reaching the bed he slashed Yoshiko, the nearest target. She covered her face with her arms, shrieking as the blade sliced into both forearms. From the other side of the bed Kenpachi rolled onto the floor, snatched a walking stick from a chair and raced around the bed to confront Yoshiko's father.

Holding the stick overhead the director yelled, "*Kiaiii!*" The father swerved toward Kenpachi, away from the hysterical, bleeding Yoshiko. When he swung the blood-stained knife and pointed it at Kenpachi's stomach, the director brought the stick down on the father's wrist, breaking it. No longer rational, Kenpachi used the stick as a samurai would have used a sword.

Kenpachi smashed the father in the temple, across the nose, in both sides of the rib cage. Bleeding from the nose and ears, the father dropped to his knees. Now completely out of control, Kenpachi stepped forward and dealt the father a final blow, in the back of the head.

Backing away from the dead man, Kenpachi reached the bedroom door and pushed it closed. When he tore his eyes away from the corpse to stare at the blood-covered Yoshiko, he blinked. She was composed, with a hint of a smile on her beautiful face as she stared down at her dead father.

Kenpachi saw only the ruination of his career and prison. He began to shiver and the walking stick slipped from his hand.

And then he remembered Nosaka, who had always been his savior.

On a deserted road several hundred yards from her parents' resort, Yoshiko, her forearms wrapped in strips of torn sheets, stood with Kenpachi in the chilled darkness and watched the two cars speed toward them. It had taken the cars only forty-five minutes to reach Hakone from Tokyo, normally an hour's drive or more. When the glare of the headlights blinded Kenpachi, he waved his arms wildly. Quickly the lights were switched off and both cars slowed down. One rolled to a complete stop and cut its engine. The other made a U-turn and stopped, its engine still running.

Kenpachi led the sprint to the car with the running engine. When they were in the back seat, the driver jammed his foot down on the gas pedal. The car leaped forward, racing back to Tokyo. Through the rear window Kenpachi watched four men leave the first car and start toward the resort.

He relaxed. He was going to get away with it. His fears slithered away from him like a whipped dog. Nosaka would erase the business at the resort as though it had never happened. The entire matter was made of sand; the tide of Nosaka's influence would wash it away. For Kenpachi, it was all in the past and the past was gone.

He looked at Yoshiko, dazed by a painkilling injection from Doctor Orito. Orito worked swiftly, silently. He had already cut the bloodied bandages from one arm and had almost finished cleaning it. As for Yoshiko, never had she appeared so alluring. Her beauty and youth were breathtaking. The thought of making love to her now, this instant, so aroused Kenpachi that his penis grew rigid. He looked out at the pine trees racing past the car window to calm his lust.

But the glass held Yoshiko's reflection and because she was denied to him, he had never wanted her more. Orito was working between them, his back to Kenpachi, who dropped both hands to his lap and squeezed his hard penis, feeling a joyful pain, squeezing, squeezing, squeezing until there was a blissful release.

Kenpachi closed his eyes. His head flopped back against the seat. He was still weary from the climb of Mount Fuji and so he drifted easily to sleep. *Yoshiko*.

* * *

IN TOKYO she lived with Kenpachi at Ikuba Castle for almost two years. She grew taller and more beautiful, a beauty improved by Kenpachi's advice on makeup and fashion. He decided that long sleeves would best hide her scarred forearms and that she should wear only the best wigs made of human hair. Yoshiko, however, remained undisciplined, with little patience for serious work and study.

Formal schooling bored her, with its Japanese approach to learning through endless repetition and imitation. Kenpachi tried and failed to teach her calligraphy, the ancient form of penmanship, and *ikebana*, the traditional art of flower arranging. She made several attempts to learn *sadō*, the tea ceremony, before giving up entirely.

Both Yoshiko and Kenpachi were reckless, sensual and short-tempered. But she lacked his intelligence and sophistication, his artistic gifts and capacity for hard work. Kendo and karate slightly interested her and she decided that when older she would work in films. She did not need schooling for that. In any case, she no longer had to account to anyone for her actions; she was free to do as she pleased. Both parents were dead, the victims of a fire which had all but destroyed the resort.

As her stay at the castle lengthened, she spent less and less time with Kenpachi. He had his filmmaking, composing, acting and circle of friends with whom Yoshiko had little in common. And there were his other lovers, none of whom lasted long for Kenpachi's promises were written on the wind. Left alone, Yoshiko explored the gigantic and supercharged city that was Tokyo. The crowded pavements and heavy traffic shocked her; the constant movement left her dizzy.

But at night the city was at its best. Then it became a gigantic pleasure palace wrapped in miles of neon lights. A dazzling richness of theaters, pachinko parlors, nightclubs, turkish baths, movie houses, restaurants, homosexual bars and bowling alleys. Tokyo after dark was a fleshpot, an unending orgy of sensual gratification.

On her own Yoshiko wandered the Ginza, the broad, long avenue of department stores, hostess clubs, bars and dance halls. In the Akasaka district she was befriended by geishas and dancers who frequented the coffee shops when they were not working in nearby nightclubs. In Akasaka she met strippers and homosexual prostitutes, who took her to the Sensoji temple to hear the one hundred and eight tolls of the great bronze bell. Here Yoshiko stood with hundreds of others crowded around a monstrously large incense burner and hoped that its heat would cure their pains and illnesses. She held her forearms in front of the burner, but her scars did not go away.

In Shinjuku, site of Ikuba Castle, she met students, homosexuals and young people drawn by trendy shops, foreign films, coffee bars and promises of sexual freedom. Here also she met Juro, the student who became her lover. Slim and handsome in his black school uniform, the twenty-year-old Juro brought her dolls and American-style hot dogs and made her laugh. He worked hard at his studies and played the guitar for her in his room and told her of his plans to enter government service. In bed Yoshiko educated him.

With Juro, her self-confidence was restored, her sensuality reawakened. Kenpachi had become bored with her; she could not see beyond a small circle, a weakness he could no longer tolerate. He made fun of her lack of education, calling her *yabo*, uncouth and peasantlike. The lovers he really preferred were *iki*, sophisticated and refined, men and women with elegance and experience.

Yoshiko retaliated by seeing Juro and others behind Kenpachi's back. But Kenpachi learned of her infidelity and took a horrifying revenge.

One evening, after a candlelit supper with Yoshiko in the main hall, something they had not done in weeks, he invited her to the master bedroom. Here he showed her the entrance to what had once been Lord Saburo's secret tunnel, which had been sealed off for years. Recently Kenpachi had commissioned the reopening of the entrance; it was once more possible to use the tunnel, to follow it from the castle to a nearby Shinjuku park.

Hand in hand the two stepped through a wall closet and entered the tunnel. Kenpachi held a flashlight as they went down a small ladder leading to what was once an earthen room. The room was at the mouth of the tunnel and, except for one unfinished portion behind the ladder, was now lined with cement and bricks. Yoshiko giggled. This was the sort of fun she and Kenpachi had enjoyed at the beginning of their relationship.

There was a little light in the room, but the section behind the ladder was dark. Kenpachi and Yoshiko faced it together, his arm around her shoulder. When he shone the flashlight on it, Yoshiko screamed. *Juro*. Wild-eyed with fear, the bound and gagged student whimpered at the sight of her. He was almost entirely walled up behind fresh bricks and mortar; only his shoulders and head were still visible. Two men stood beside the wall. Yoshiko recognized them from the car which had taken her and Kenpachi from her parents' resort.

She wanted to run, but was held by Kenpachi's iron grip. "I think this is one history lesson which will leave an impression on you," he said. "In the days when Tokyo was Edo, human sacrifice was common. It was also considered necessary. *Hai*, very necessary. Human pillars. People buried alive in the foundations of important new buildings. Castles, villas, temples, even courthouses. It kept evil spirits away. It ensured that the gods granted the building eternal life."

He brought the flashlight up to Juro's terrified face. "Officially, of course, such sacrifices were forbidden. Nevertheless, they were carried out, usually in secret. Flesh and blood added to a new building to give it life. Sometimes a servant would beg his master for the honor of pleasing him by being buried alive. Think of it. Tons of earth and stone slowly pressing every ounce of life out of you and you unable to move."

He shone the flashlight on Yoshiko. "I gave you life. I took you away from the pigsty into which you had been born. And you repay me by reverting to the slut you were when we first met. I own you. You are mine, to do with as I wish for as long as I wish. You need to be taught a lesson. I assure you it will not be boring. Please stand in front of your lover."

Too paralyzed to speak, Yoshiko shook her head.

Kenpachi shoved her away. She stumbled, tripped and fell to the ground.

"You will not die," he said. "But you will place the finishing touches on this human pillar. It won't be the first time, will it, my darling?"

Yoshiko blinked tears from her eyes. *The first time*. After Kenpachi had killed her father, Yoshiko, inflamed by bloodlust, had picked up her father's carving knife and run bleeding down the hall to her mother's room. And cut her mother's throat.

"Finish entombing your lovely little student," said Kenpachi, "or join him."

Juro whimpered, moaned and pleaded with his eyes, while a

weeping Yoshiko lay on the floor.

"If you're still on the floor twenty seconds from now," said Kenpachi, "the two of you will die together."

Slowly she pushed herself to a sitting position, then stood.

And began to complete the entombment.

As Kenpachi and the two men watched, she carried bricks to the unfinished wall, covered them with mortar and was almost finished when Kenpachi said, "Stop."

Kenpachi walked over to Juro, grinned, then placed gold coins on the student's head and shoulders. Money to spend in the next world. *But in this world there would be no reprieve.*

Kenpachi backed away from the wall and said without looking at Yoshiko, "Your task is not yet completed."

She screamed, then fainted.

She awoke in bed, with Kenpachi brutally making love to her. Too drained to resist, Yoshiko attempted to close her mind to any emotion. She willed herself to think of Juro, of what Kenpachi had forced her to do to him. She tried to make her will deny herself any feelings of pleasure. And failed.

To her shame, her sexual response to Kenpachi began to grow. Her body remembered the gratification he provided and sought it once more. Against her will she abandoned herself to him, calling his name, begging him to do whatever he wanted.

In the morning, she lay in bed and told herself that last night had been a bad dream. But she saw her broken nails and the dirt on her body from the tunnel and knew that Juro had been walled up alive in the bowels of the castle. Kenpachi reminded her of the role she had played in the human-pillar ritual and in the death of her parents. Her choices now were silence, prison or death at Kenpachi's hands.

And then he told Yoshiko that she would have to leave Ikuba Castle.

Shocked, she could barely get out the word. "Why?"

"Because I am getting married."

She clutched his arm. "What will become of me? Where will I go?"

"I shall give you money. From time to time I shall, perhaps, find you a small film role. But do not return here unless I summon you. Is that understood?"

"I am frightened. Please do not send me away. How shall I survive?"

"If the need is strong enough, you will find a way."

* * *

SHE SURVIVED THROUGH her beauty and cunning. There
were jobs in a fried-fish and rice shop, in a souvenir shop, and
for a time she teamed with a lover to work as a *chindonya*, a
street musician hired to lure customers to the opening of new
bars and restaurants. When Yoshiko left him she stole money
and jewelry left to him by a dead wife. Friends found her work
as a club hostess, a masseuse in a turkish bath and in nude
shows, all prostitution fronts.

She appeared in *sutorippu*, strip shows, pornographic films
and posed for erotic magazines. There were affairs with
women, including an Australian stewardess who committed
suicide when the relationship ended. Another relationship
finished when a dance-hall bouncer, with whom she was living, was beheaded during a gang war between rival *yakuza*
mobs. Sex was her only concept of power but it was a concept
which had to be paid for.

She lacked acting talent, but because of her beauty Kenpachi was able to find bit roles for her in legitimate films, with
Bunraku, the puppet theater, and with a small Kabuki company. He also placed her with dance companies, first Kagura,
which performed festival dances at Shinto shrines, then with a
Bugaku group. Here, masked and costumed in red, with a
silver rod in her hand, she learned the bold and stately dances
which sometimes lasted for hours. While Yoshiko performed
adequately, she was late for performances, was caught stealing
and had to be let go.

Kenpachi never left her life. An American, whose sports car
she had stolen, was persuaded by Kenpachi not to have her arrested. And when Yoshiko stole the wallet of a nightclub
owner with underworld ties, it was Kenpachi who talked the
yakuza out of killing her. She attended parties at Ikuba Castle,
in Kenpachi's Tokyo duplex and in Kamakura, the seaside
town where he owned a beach house within sight of the Great
Buddha. He invited her on film locations, slept with her and
gave her money. Yoshiko never stopped loving him. But she
knew that everything he gave her only prevented her from
being free of him.

She was twenty-one when he told her that until further notice she was to work for Zenzo Nosaka.

"What does such an important man want with me?" Yoshiko asked.

"In the West it is called industrial espionage," said Kenpachi. "However, Japanese laws do not recognize such a thing. We think of it as gathering intelligence, nothing more. Nosaka-san has constructed his own intelligence network, one which functions through a bank owned by him. You will do exactly what Nosaka-san tells you, is that clear?"

"*Hai.*"

"You will be well paid. Nosaka-san is to be your *daimyo*, your lord. Obey him without question. If you don't he will kill you. Do you understand this?"

"*Hai*, Kenpachi-san."

It was a satisfying job, one which allowed her to achieve much while earning excellent money. With information provided by Nosaka's bank, Eastern Pacific Chartered Limited, she sought out Japanese businessmen who either willingly sold company secrets or who were targets for potential blackmail. She traveled to London, Paris, Geneva and Rome, sometimes as a courier transporting cash or information, sometimes as a "model" or "fashion designer" who quickly made friends with executives and engineers able to provide company information. And with Eastern Pacific furnishing background data on each assignment, the advantage was Yoshiko's.

In San Francisco, she convinced an executive with a microchip company to sell a piece of property to Eastern Pacific, which paid him four times its worth in exchange for valuable information. She traveled with Japanese research teams, who aggressively gathered information, then reported back to the government and to big business. She attended conferences and conventions in Japan and abroad, where she met managers, engineers, sales chiefs and executives and told Nosaka what she had learned.

Through him she received invitations to parties and press conferences, meeting politicians and journalists whose conversations and casual remarks became part of Nosaka's intelligence files. When ordered to, she spied on his employees. Once she learned of an executive's plans to release damaging information to the press on the company's industrial waste disposal program. Shortly after she informed Nosaka, the executive died of what was diagnosed as heart failure.

When a Russian pilot defected and landed at an American air base in Japan with a highly advanced fighter plane, only American military personnel were allowed to examine it. Yoshiko, however, obtained a copy of the file, which contained a detailed analysis of the aircraft, which Nosaka then passed on to Japanese intelligence in exchange for future favors.

If Nosaka was intimidating, he could also be generous. For the first time Yoshiko had everything she wanted. Prostitution and petty thievery were no longer necessary. She could afford clothes by the finest Japanese and foreign designers, as well as an American car. She purchased an expensive flat on Omote-Sando Boulevard not far from the holy Meiji Shrine, where the entrance to the gates were made of seventeen-hundred-year-old Japanese cypress. Omote-Sando, with shops that sold foreign fashions and ultramodern clothing, was a favorite with Japan's smart set and Yoshiko could not take her place with the best of them. Above all she could indulge her passion for antique jewelry. As for lovers, Yoshiko no longer went with them for money, but for pleasure.

There was a price for this luxury and comfort. She came to fear Nosaka as she had never feared Kenpachi. She knew of the Blood Oath League; on Nosaka's orders she had joined the league's secret training sessions in the martial arts. Yoshiko was a modern *ninja*; she had to be prepared to fight and, if necessary, die. Like it or not, she had chosen the way of the warrior, which was death.

Some part of her wondered if Kenpachi could bring himself to actually kill her. After all, there was a bond between them, a past with which neither wanted to lose contact. Yoshiko had no such doubts about Nosaka. If need be, he could have her killed without a moment's regret.

Which was why she had not hesitated when he had ordered her to murder the Hansards and bring their son back to Tokyo. The boy, Todd Hansard, was important to Kenpachi. Why, Yoshiko did not know, nor was it necessary that she know. Her duty, *giri*, was unquestioning obedience to Nosaka. Her fear of the old man made her feel ugly and lose her power of reasoning. That fear had also made her cruel and murderously effective in her work.

* * *

IN HER HONG KONG hotel room, Yoshiko put on a
Norma Kamali dress of white cotton, with wide, thickly
padded shoulders and full, flared calf-length skirt. Her small
waist was accented by a four-inch-wide belt of black patent
leather with tiny leather buttons. She wore sheer white stock-
ings and black-and-white slingback sandals with high heels
and the toes cut out. In addition to hoop earrings of white
gold, she had chosen two favorite pieces of antique jewelry—a
Victorian bracelet of gold leaves in enamel, set with blue sapphires, and a gold-and-enamel pendant by Giuliano, the great
Italian jeweler who had worked in nineteenth-century London. Her watch from Harry Winston in New York cost more
than she had earned in her entire life until going to work for
Nosaka.

Yoshiko packed her luggage but decided not to summon a
porter until after she heard from the Chinese couple hired to
pose as Todd Hansard's relatives. They were due to telephone
from the lobby any minute, letting Yoshiko know that the boy
was downstairs in a waiting car. Then it would be time to have
the luggage taken downstairs, pay the couple and take the car
to Kai Tak Airport. Here a private plane would fly her and
Todd back to Tokyo, where he would be taken off her hands.

Kenpachi had insisted that Yoshiko telephone before leaving Hong Kong. He had to know that the boy was in her
possession. The highly strung Wakaba was waiting by the
mobile telephone on location in Wanchai.

Did Kenpachi intend to use the boy as a human pillar or in
some equally frightening ritual? Such a man was capable of
anything. There was a concealed side to him, something that
Yoshiko found beyond her comprehension. It had to do with
violence, but not the cold-blooded, calculated kind she could
expect from Nosaka. Kenpachi's veneer of talent and good
looks hid something animalistic and demonic.

Some in the Blood Oath League knew why Kenpachi wanted
the boy, but no one would tell Yoshiko. She might have
pressed Kenpachi for an answer, but Nosaka was also involved
and it was wiser not to ask questions at this time. If they
wanted Yoshiko to know, they would tell her. If not, then the
matter was best forgotten.

Nosaka. He had warned her to be careful, to leave nothing incriminating behind in a hotel. Yoshiko had almost finished inspecting the bathroom when she heard a soft knock at the door. She closed the medicine chest and listened. She was not expecting anyone and she had no friends in Hong Kong.

Caution. She walked into the bedroom, reached in her shoulder bag and removed the fan Nosaka had given her from his collection of ancient weapons. It was efficient and deadly and she had spent hours learning to use it. A second knock brought her to the door. She said in English, "Who is it?"

"Soon." The Chinese man and his wife, who were to bring the boy to Yoshiko.

Yoshiko touched the knob but did not open the door. "You were to telephone me from downstairs."

"I tried to call you, but your telephone is out of order."

"Just a minute." She crossed the room, picked up the telephone receiver and held it to her ear. The line was dead. She relaxed. The fan was in her hand when she opened the door.

"Miss Mara? Yoshiko Mara? I'm Captain Fuller, Royal Hong Kong Police. This is Inspector Jenkins. Sorry to bother you like this, but may we come in." He turned to a Chinese policeman in the hall. "That will be all, Deng. Please escort Mr. and Mrs. Soon downstairs, if you will."

Shocked, Yoshiko placed both hands behind her and backed into the room. She had been tricked. How much did they know?

The English officers, both in plain clothes, stepped forward, followed by a single uniformed Chinese policeman and someone else, a large gray-haired American who watched Yoshiko with eyes that reminded her of the cobra that had sunk its fangs into Ian Hansard. He closed the door with his walking stick, but not before she saw the Soons being escorted toward the elevator by a Chinese officer. *Something was wrong. Had Yoshiko made a mistake or had she just been betrayed?*

Captain Fuller, the officer in charge, was fortyish, tall and stoop-shouldered, with a triangle of a mustache under a flat nose, and a determination to be discreet and helpful. He could have been a school principal offering Yoshiko amnesty if she would admit her part in a girlish prank. The second Englishman, Jenkins, combed his thick red mustache with his fingers and eyed her with undisguised lust. The Chinese officer maintained the attitude of a servant who knew his place, remaining a respectful step behind the Englishman.

The American with the walking stick had positioned himself against the door, his half-closed eyes following her every move. The sense of danger coming from him was strong enough to make Yoshiko blink.

Fuller said, "We were wondering if you could aid us in our inquiries. It concerns the deaths of Mr. and Mrs. Ian Hansard and a claim by the Soons to be Mrs. Hansard's only relatives and therefore entitled to the custody of the Hansards' only son."

To save themselves, they have led the police to me.

She smiled at the policemen, who had formed a semicircle around her, and brought the fan from behind her back. A flick of her wrist and the fan, made of ivory, silver, gold and iron, snapped open. She fanned herself with it slowly. "I am sorry, but I cannot help you. I have never seen Mr. and Mrs. Soon in my life."

"That wasn't the impression I got out in the hall," said the American.

Fuller sighed and his nostrils flared in disgust. The introduction was made reluctantly. "Forgive me. This is Mr. Frank DiPalma from America. We are told that he is Todd Hansard's natural father."

Yoshiko brought the fan up, hiding most of her face. *Hai*, she knew this one. He and Kenpachi-san were enemies, rivals in the way of the sword and now rivals for the boy. Yoshiko's eyes brightened above the fan. Did Kenpachi-san want the boy in order to revenge himself upon the hated American?

"Originally," said Fuller, "the Soons presented themselves as Katharine Hansard's relatives. But at Mr. DiPalma's request, we questioned them and now it seems they no longer make such a claim. At the same time, they did mention something about turning the boy over to you."

He smiled to show her that he, too, found such an idea to be contrary to reason and absurd.

Jenkins, still resentful of DiPalma, said, "Maybe we should mention that Mr. DiPalma has friends in high places. We've received telephone calls on his behalf from Peking, London and even our very own governor. Everyone asks that we cooperate with him to the fullest extent, which we'll bloody well do if we know what's good for us. Mr. DiPalma is here to show us that power can be a serious fact. Has some fanciful theories, he does. Thinks a beautiful woman like yourself murdered the Hansards.''

DiPalma's husky voice made Yoshiko uneasy. "Ask her how she came to know the Soons," he said.

"She's answered that," said Jenkins. "She said she'd never seen them in her life. You weren't listening."

DiPalma rubbed his unshaven jaw with the silver head of his cane. "Oh, I was listening, all right. Heard every word. You'll probably tell me that at the door she thought she was talking to the bellboy."

Yoshiko bowed her head. "As you say, the bellboy."

DiPalma's smile was edged and abrupt. "Nice move. I feed you the straight line and you follow through with the punch line. Maybe we ought to work up a little act. Well, let's see how you handle this. Somebody saw you beat Katharine Hansard to death, then set fire to her bungalow."

"DiPalma, really." Jenkins looked at DiPalma and raised his eyebrows. "Keeping secrets, are we? And why haven't you shared this little bit of news with us before now?"

"*Kunoichi.*" DiPalma drew the word out, turning it into a hoarse and jarring accusation. Yoshiko, caught unprepared, was left shaken and uncontrolled. *How could the American know about her unless there was the spirit of evil in him.* She had to escape from this room, from this demon.

The fan in her hand was a *tessen*, a war fan with a razor-sharp iron tip hidden beneath gold paint. It was not merely a woman's weapon; centuries old, it had been carried into battle by two feudal generals.

Yoshiko turned first to Captain Fuller. Her nervous smile appealed for sympathy and concern, a silent plea which found him off guard. His hands were at his side and he was defenseless when she backhanded the fan's cutting edge across his throat, tearing loose the cartilage. He spun around, spraying Yoshiko and the Chinese policeman with blood.

As Fuller crashed into a writing table, Yoshiko kicked the Chinese officer in the groin, then quickly drove her heel down hard on Jenkins's right ankle. Both Jenkins and the Chinese officer doubled over, and as Jenkins bent down, Yoshiko slashed at his eye with the fan. His hands came up too late to protect his face. Leaving the Welshman screaming behind her, she leaped over the prone Chinese at her feet and sprang at Frank DiPalma.

When she was almost on him, Yoshiko spun around and with her back to him lashed out with her right leg, kicking at his groin. DiPalma stepped to his left and deflected the kick with a quick, whiplike blow of his cane to Yoshiko's calf. She went down with her leg beneath her. Then, on the floor, she reached out and backhanded the fan at Frank's right knee.

Take the fang from the snake and the snake is harmless, said the stick fighters. The war fan was Yoshiko's fang. DiPalma went after it. Her backhand attack was met with one of his own; he swung the cane down in a short, powerful arc, putting his bulk into the blow, smashing into her wrist and breaking it. Yoshiko fell backward, clutching her useless wrist. Awkwardly she tried to scramble to her feet.

Gripping the cane with the silver knob exposed, DiPalma stepped forward and in the same motion brought up his right fist in an uppercut, driving the knob under Yoshiko's jaw. She landed on her back, then rolled over. She tried to rise to her knees, then fell back as the first bullet tore into her side.

DiPalma screamed "No!" but Jenkins, a two-handed grip on his revolver, continued firing until the weapon was empty. Two more shots entered Yoshiko's chest, sending red stains across the white dress. Another shot missed and hit the television set, causing it to explode. A fifth shot hit Yoshiko high in the shoulder and the final shot entered a sofa.

Jenkins, face covered in blood, moaned, "Bitch! Fucking bitch! Fucking, fucking bitch!"

DiPalma ran to him. "You didn't have to do that. The fight was over."

Jenkins kept his face turned toward Yoshiko. "My eye. You bloody bitch."

It was his right eye. There was too much blood for DiPalma to see the damage, but the eye didn't look good.

"Oh, God, the pain," said Jenkins. "Can't see. Can't . . ."

Jenkins fell back against DiPalma, who helped him onto the bed.

The police were banging on the door with their gun butts.

He let them in, two Chinese officers with drawn guns who shoved him inside and ran toward the bodies.

"Call an ambulance," said DiPalma. "I think Fuller's dead and so's the woman. Jenkins and the man on the floor can use some help. What about the phone?"

"It is working again, sir," one of Chinese officers said. "We have reconnected the line. The break we caused was merely temporary, as you suggested."

DiPalma stared down at Yoshiko's body. "Yeah. As I suggested." He had wanted her alive. She was only a mule, a courier who was carrying Todd somewhere else, to someone else. She was a link in a chain which DiPalma had wanted to follow to its source. Jenkins's anger was understandable, but by blowing her away he had slammed the door in Frank DiPalma's face.

In death Yoshiko's wig had fallen off. DiPalma crouched over the corpse. He stared at the face, then at the Adam's apple. Jesus, was it possible?

As the Chinese policeman tended to Jenkins and the other officer, DiPalma looked under Yoshiko's dress.

He stood up. A Chinese came over to stand beside him. "Captain Fuller is dead and Inspector Jenkins may have lost the sight of his right eye. Chang will be all right."

"The guy who got kicked in the balls?"

"Yes. Inspector Jenkins said the woman did this. Do you know who she was?"

DiPalma shook his head. "No idea. Tell you this much. Captain Fuller's not the only dead man in this room. Yoshiko Mara's not a female. She is a man. One very dead man."

11

IN WANCHAI, a restless Kon Kenpachi walked across the aged stone floor of the temple, leaving his crew to light the next scene. At the entrance he leaned against the pillar and stared at the crowd which had lined the street to watch the filming. He was inside Chai Kung Woot Fat, the Temple of the Living Buddha, where the interior was covered with thousands of mirrors. According to local custom, the Chinese recovering from an illness left a mirror here bearing a lucky inscription. Kenpachi wanted to be sure the camera lights did not reflect in the mirrors nor cause distracting brightness. Satisfying that demand took time, and Kenpachi was not a man who liked waiting. Especially now, when his mind was on Yoshiko and the boy.

Another local custom had delayed the afternoon's filming even longer, costing Kenpachi time needed to shoot on the temple steps in available sunlight. A Chinese funeral procession had marched in front of the temple, with musicians playing oboes and cymbals, mourners in white hoods and relatives of the deceased bearing roast pigs as gifts for the gods. A furious Kenpachi had pushed his way through spectators, then locked himself in his limousine until the procession passed.

To Jan Golden, the funeral cortege meant overtime costs. "This is going to run into money, said the monkey as he peed into the cash register."

At the temple entrance Kenpachi fingered the viewfinder

hanging from his neck and watched the Chinese onlookers applaud Tom Gennaro, who had just left the limousine which doubled as his dressing room. Gennaro, with a Chinese girl friend, had a scene in which he left a mirror inside the temple, in gratitude for having survived a grenade attack in Vietnam.

Kenpachi looked past the crowd to his own limousine parked in front of a furniture-making shop. No signal from Wakaba. Which meant no telephone call from Yoshiko. Damn her. It was late afternoon and still no news of the boy. Kenpachi found Sakon, Yoshiko's male name, to be thoughtless, forgetful and unsure of himself. Worse, the male side, despite Sakon's physical beauty, was dull and as common as dirt. Only as Yoshiko, complete with women's clothes and makeup, did Sakon become spontaneous, defiant, sensual. His female side was his greatest talent.

If the relationship between Nosaka and Yoshiko would never be other than master and servant, the relationship between her and Kenpachi was less easy to classify. Sakon had always loved Kenpachi. It was Sakon's only humanity. But Kenpachi had freed himself of love by concentrating on his own problems. Still, Sakon was more than a source of pleasure. He was a passion which Kenpachi had never been cured of, a beautiful object and pleasing delusion to which Kenpachi had permanent title. But deep in his heart Kenpachi knew the real reason why he needed him. It was only with Sakon that he truly felt himself to be loved.

At the temple entrance Kenpachi heard Jan Golden call his name. But before he could turn to answer her, blaring automobile horns cleared the street and two police cars pulled up in front of the temple steps. Three policemen walked up the steps and stopped in front of Kenpachi.

"Mr. Kon Kenpachi?" The officer was British and middle-aged, a small, hairy man with a tanned, wizened face and an air of troubled nobility.

"I am, yes."

"We would like you to accompany us to police headquarters. We think you might be able to help us with our inquiries."

"I do not understand."

"It will be explained to you when you get there. One of our officers was murdered. Two others were hurt, one rather badly."

"What's this got to do with Mr. Kenpachi?" Jan Golden stood beside the Japanese film director. She was vigilant, protective.

"Our business is with Mr. Kenpachi, if you don't mind."

Kenpachi willed himself to stay calm. "I must tell my crew—"

"Sorry, but there's no time for that. The killing of a police captain is a serious matter. We would very much like to get to the bottom of it. The *individual* who did it is dead. Bit of confusion there, especially about gender. Seems you and this individual were acquainted and that's what we'd like to talk to you about."

It was several seconds before Kenpachi realized that the "individual" was Sakon. Numbed, the Japanese let the policeman guide him by the elbow down the temple steps and into his car. In the back seat, between two Chinese officers, Kenpachi showed no sign that the news of Sakon's death had been a staggering blow. He closed his eyes, placed his hands palms up on his thighs and went into *zazen*, meditation. With the strength from Bushido, he resisted his attachment to the memory of Sakon and struggled to free his mind-spirit from sorrow and fear.

With the cast and crew Jan watched the car with Kenpachi pull away. Directly behind it was a second car, which slowly made its way past the Chinese lining both sides of the narrow street. And then the crowds filled the street behind the second car, blocking Jan's view. But not before she had seen Frank DiPalma sitting alone in the back seat.

12

DiPalma handed his black oak cane to Todd, who sat across from him in a restaurant located in the Landmark, a trendy new building whose five floors were filled with banks, boutiques, jewelers, restaurants and airline offices. They had just finished dinner on a suspended balcony overlooking a giant indoor plaza, where a circular pool-fountain contained water which shot up when the noise level around it increased. The restaurant, Todd said, had been a favorite of Katharine's. It was decorated to resemble a seventeenth-century pub, with flintlock pistols and pictures of highwaymen on the walls and Chinese waitresses in knee britches and three-cornered hats.

DiPalma and Katharine had come here together eleven years ago. Then the Landmark had been the site of a hotel, with a quiet bar and a Filipino pianist who sang only Broadway show tunes written before 1945. In those eleven years Hong Kong had lost so much of its past to the real estate developer and the wrecking ball.

As DiPalma watched, Todd gripped the cane as though it were a *shinai*. Silver knob resting in the palm of his left hand, the last three fingers squeezing while forefinger and thumb gripped the stick loosely. Right hand exactly one fist away, last three fingers holding the *shinai* tightly, forefinger and thumb relaxed. Both thumbs pointing downward.

Nice grip, DiPalma thought. Strong enough to withstand the weapon being knocked out his hand, yet flexible enough to give slightly when struck. Katharine had said Todd was an ex-

traordinary kendoist for his age. DiPalma wanted to see just
how good the kid was.

A waitress cleared the table, leaving behind a fresh pot of
tea. When she had left, DiPalma poured tea into small pewter cups, cooling his by filling half of the cup with milk. His
stomach couldn't stand anything too hot or too cold. Todd
raised the cane overhead, then slowly brought it down until it
almost touched the table. He did this several times, smiled at
DiPalma, then placed the cane on an empty chair.

DiPalma returned the smile. "Very good. *Jodan*, wasn't
it?" *Jodan* was the upper-level stance, fists in front of the
forehead before attacking or defending. It was one of the five
basic postures in kendo, though not the most commonly used.

"It's not for everyone," said Todd. "But it suits me quite
well. Sometimes in a match, I feel as though my *shinai* is a real
sword. So I draw it from an imaginary scabbard in the Katori
style and the *jodan* stance seems to blend in of its own ac-
cord."

DiPalma was familiar with the Katori method of drawing a
real sword. Thumb and forefinger pulling against the outside
edges of the handguard in a screwing forward action, making
the sword leap from its scabbard and stop in an overhead position. The draw, a quick one, was hard to block and achieved a
longer reach than other styles. Holding the sword overhead
also meant less distance between the blade and target, making
the Katori overhead cutting stroke one of the swiftest in
kendo. It was a style of swordsmanship which had flourished
during the sixteenth and seventeenth centuries and was
scarcely practiced today.

"Why does *nito*, the use of two swords at once, appeal to
you?" Todd asked.

DiPalma stirred his tea. "Most people won't fight with two
shinais at once. Too hard to control. Me, I enjoy it. The short
one lets me control the opponent's weapon and when I've
blocked it or knocked it aside, he's got nothing to use against
my long weapon. If you know how to use it, a short *shinai* is a
good defense. Still, you score with the longer weapon. It's got
the reach."

"But there is a time for the use of the short sword. When
your opponent is close and there is no room to use the long

sword. Or when you are fighting in a confined space. Also it is good to have both a short and long sword when fighting several opponents at once. Kenpachi-san says I must start to practice with two *Shinais*."

Kenpachi-san says. DiPalma caught it at once: defiance under Todd's politeness. A potential for insolence which didn't go with the boy's well-bred exterior. Todd's attitude toward Kenpachi was just as inconsistent. The boy appeared to fear him, while at the same time deferring to him as though he were his commander in chief. Or *daimyo*. DiPalma didn't want Kenpachi in Todd's life for any reason. Kenpachi had all the courage necessary to become corrupt and corruption was contagious.

DiPalma had told Todd about the confrontation at Yoshiko Mara's hotel but not about Yoshiko's connection to Kenpachi. He didn't want to make Kenpachi look bad in the boy's eyes. Putting his foot down to soon on Todd would only make DiPalma look the fool. Was this really the first day he and Todd had spent together?

There was no one with whom DiPalma could fully discuss Katharine's murder and that included the Hong Kong police. DiPalma's sole eyewitness to her death was Todd, who had seen the killing through his extrasensory perception. Frank believed him. But the police wouldn't and in their place neither would he. In a cop's world only facts mattered.

When the police had questioned him about what had happened at Yoshiko Mara's hotel, DiPalma had kept his explanation to a minimum. "I ran a bluff and it worked. Nothing more, nothing less."

"Forgive me if I fail to view the matter quite so simplistically," said the questioning officer, a round-faced superintendent with pebble glasses, wavy hair and a tendency to speak to his folded hands, which rested on his desk. "One of our officers has been butchered by a female impersonator. Another has been blinded in one eye and currently lies in hospital in a state of shock. 'Nothing more, nothing less,' you say. I say there's more. For example, what made you 'run a bluff', as you put it, on someone you had never met and ostensibly knew nothing about?"

"To begin with, Yoshiko Mara or Sakon Chiba, as we now

know him to be, lied about knowing the Soons. I was in the hall and heard him speak to Mr. Soon. Chiba knew him, all right. And was expecting him. Your men believed her lie. They wanted to believe."

The superintendent raised his eyes from his hands to Di-Palma. "And why would they want to do that?"

"Because they didn't like being forced to cooperate with me. Because they wanted to show me who's boss. It was an ego thing. Made them feel better. Fuller was polite, but he was only going through the motions. Anything to keep me quiet. In his own little way, he made sure I knew it. Jenkins? As far as he was concerned, Chiba or Yoshiko had just won the 'Miss World' contest. Jenkins's tongue was hanging out. He had found his dream girl. All he saw was a beautiful woman, not somebody who could kill two people."

"If you don't mind, I would rather be spared any criticism of my men at this time, thank you. I suppose we'll just have to work on being more distrustful in future."

In his polite way the man's throwing stones, thought Di-Palma. "I think a smart cop distrusts everybody he doesn't know."

"All well and good, but we had no hard evidence linking Chiba to the deaths of the Hansards."

"Katharine Hansard told me she feared for her life and Todd's."

The superintendent nodded. "That telephone call is on record, yes."

"Around that same time, Chiba shows up in Hong Kong dressed as a woman and using the name Yoshiko Mara."

"We found the different passports in his hotel room. Go on."

"Katharine's frightened. Chiba's in Hong Kong. Katharine and her husband die. And Chiba hires the Soons to bring Todd to him. You have the Soons' confession. I think that links Chiba to the death of the Hansards."

Without lifting his eyes from the desk, the superintendent steepled his fingers under his chin. "Suppose, just suppose, someone else and not Chiba disposed of the Hansards. Theoretically speaking, of course."

"Chiba had the stomach to do his own killing. He proved

that in his hotel room. I saw him do it and so did two of your
men.''

"Hmmm, quite. Anything else?"

"Ian Hansard and Chiba were seen together. At Hansard's
bank, at a restaurant, by Hansard's chauffeur. And Hansard's servants knew what was going on.''

"He did have a reputation for womanizing," said the superintendent.

"Not just women," said DiPalma. "Oriental women. Made
Chiba's job a lot easier.''

The superintendent looked up. "I assume it's Mrs. Hansard
you are most concerned about?''

"And Todd."

"That would explain your 'running a bluff' regarding *her*
death, as opposed to that of her husband.''

The superintendent wore his mask well, DiPalma thought.
A clever man who didn't appear clever. Choosing his words
carefully DiPalma said, "I came to Hong Kong at Mrs. Hansard's request, so I guess you're right. Her death is the one
which concerns me.''

"Yes, I suppose it would be. After all, you did father a child
by her. Seems odd that Chiba would kill to secure the boy.
Why not kidnap him instead?''

"Katharine loved Todd. If someone had snatched him, she
would have stopped at nothing to get him back. Dead parents
can't come looking for a missing child.''

"Good a theory as any. Odd sort of chap, our Mr. Chiba.
Telex from the Tokyo police said he had been an *onnagata*, a
male actor who played women's roles in Kabuki theater. Also
performed female roles in Noh plays and in Japanese dance
companies. Lives as a woman most of the time.''

"A woman with the fighting skills of a well-trained man,"
said DiPalma.

"A *ninja*, I believe you said. *Kunoichi*.''

DiPalma leaned back in his chair. There was no hesitation;
he made up his mind immediately. No mention of Todd's
mystic visions or nightmares. To do so would make him and
Todd appear to be fools twice over; once for believing in those
visions and twice for having said they did.

DiPalma said, "For the sake of argument, let's say Chiba or
Yoshiko Mara eliminated the Hansards. It means he had to

know a few things about them. About Ian Hansard's interest in Oriental women, about the best way to use that information. He had to know when and where to strike at Katharine Hansard. And he had to have people here who could help him with Ian Hansard's murder."

"And how do you know Chiba had help in killing Ian Hansard?"

"Because Hansard was killed by a cobra and I don't think Chiba came through customs with a cobra in his purse."

The superintendent permitted himself a smile. "Fair enough assumption. So Chiba had friends in Hong Kong."

DiPalma leaned forward. "He had more than that. It appears that he arrived here and was handed all the information he needed, all the intelligence, all the background, all the contacts. Chiba not only fought like a *ninja*, he also dealt with the Hansards as a *ninja* would. Get the information first, then make your move. He wasn't here long enough to get that smart on his own."

"Chiba did seem to move about Hong Kong in an efficient manner. If what you say is true, he managed to amass quite an amount of data on extremely short notice."

DiPalma shook his head. "No way. The telex you received from the Tokyo police department and the one Roger Tan got from DEA's Tokyo office both say the same thing. On his own, Sakon Chiba did not have the brains to walk into a strange city and take out two people he never saw before."

"Unless someone else was doing his thinking for him, as you seem to imply."

"The telexes say that Chiba had a police record. Petty crime. Porn actor, male hustler, petty thievery, ripping off tourists. Minor drug dealing. Car theft's the heaviest thing on his sheet. The man didn't touch anything that involved a lot of thought and planning. He was a loser until four years ago."

"And what do you suppose turned him around?"

DiPalma looked at the ceiling. "I wish I knew. All of a sudden, no more stealing wallets from johns, no more hot-wiring cars, no more shoplifting. Enter prosperity. Chiba suddenly buys a flat in a very expensive Tokyo neighborhood. He acquires a half interest in a Tokyo boutique. And he wears designer dresses with expensive-looking jewelry. No more arrests, no more trouble with the police."

The superintendent's fingers drummed on the desk. The conversation was becoming interesting. "Born again, as you Americans might say. And with a frightfully large amount of American dollars in his or her possession. Ten thousand was the amount, I believe."

"And four passports," said DiPalma. "Each with a different name, each a first-class piece of work. And none of them stolen, I bet. That would be sloppy and nothing about the born-again Sakon Chiba is sloppy. Loser into prosperous citizen. Somebody took over his life and turned it around. Nothing in Chiba's past indicates he would do this well on his own. Something else: I saw him fight. He took on three men. Killed one, crippled two. Whoever trained him trained him well."

"That alone would seem to confirm your suspicions of his being a *ninja*. Or does it?"

"Superintendent, I've made several trips to Japan and I've seen most of the martial arts in action. I've been taken around by some important people, but not once did I see a *dojo* where they taught the use of a war fan. If it's taught these days, it's taught in secret. I never saw fan fighting, I never even heard rumors about it. It was part of past history."

"Until now."

The superintendent removed a large brown envelope from a desk drawer. After looking inside, he held it out to DiPalma, who took it and turned it upside down. The folded war fan slid into his hand.

"Anything you can tell me about it would be of interest."

DiPalma turned the fan around in his fingers, slowly opened it and when it had reached its full length he examined it again, fingers brushing the handle and both sides. The fan was made of a thin but strong metal and was silver coated, with a cutting edge hidden beneath gold paint. A gold ring hung from an ivory handle inlaid with gold and silver. One side was painted with lilies, orchids and azaleas; the other was decorated with a snow-covered landscape and a hillside temple red with the setting sun.

"It's called a *tessen*," said DiPalma. "Japanese for war fan. Or iron fan. Samurai used it as protection when entering the home of someone they didn't trust. Catching a man's neck between sliding doors was an old trick. To avoid that, you held the open fan in front of your head. Kept the doors from closing on you. Good weapon in its own right. Could be used against knives, swords, sticks.''

He placed the fan landscape-side up on the superintendent's desk and with his forefinger tapped the hillside temple. "Those markings on the front. Hard to make them out. Here, just under the roof."

"What are they?"

"Markings from Kuan Yue, the Chinese god of the martial arts. The god of war."

The superintendent allowed himself a tiny congratulatory smile. "I bloody well know who he is myself. Favorite god of the Chinese underworld. And you'll find a statue of him in every police station in the colony, including this one. Always struck me as peculiar, policemen and criminals praying to the same god to protect them from each other. Why should Kuan Yue be appearing on a Japanese war fan?"

DiPalma picked up his cane and sat down. "Because Japan built its civilization on what it took from China."

"The Chinese never let us or the Japs forget it," said the superintendent. "It's one reason, among many, which makes the Chinese rather arrogant, not to mention insufferable. If rumors are to be believed Japan's still going in for 'borrowing' these days. Only it's called industrial espionage. No law against that in this part of the world, unfortunately. Done in Hong Kong all the time as well. You were saying?"

"Those markings probably mean a military man commissioned this fan. Kuan Yue's name was added for good luck. All Japanese military strategy for hundreds of years was based on the Chinese *Book of Changes*, on Chinese theories of yin and yang, on the ideas of Chinese generals and philosophers. The spear, the bow, the sword, they all came to Japan from China."

"I see. Where would one go about securing a fan like this today?"

"You couldn't. It's a museum piece, a collector's item. Almost four hundred years old. Probably late sixteenth century. The sort of piece even a top antique dealer would have a hard time coming up with."

The superintendent wriggled his small mouth before answering. "Could Chiba have stolen it, perhaps?"

You're coming around, DiPalma thought. Slowly but surely you're coming around. "You're saying somebody with Chiba's record wouldn't ordinarily own something like this."

"I suppose that is what I'm saying, yes."

DiPalma stood up. "Might be a good idea to telex Tokyo again. See if a fan matching this description has been stolen from a museum or a private collection."

The superintendent rose. "You've been most helpful. I regret the relationship between you and my department got off on the wrong foot. Difficult situation, being forced to obey an outsider. But you're really not that much of an outsider, are you?"

"I've walked your road, if that's what you mean. I didn't throw my weight around because I enjoy seeing people jump. My son was involved. You probably know about Katharine and me, about what happened eleven years ago."

"I do, yes."

"I owe her."

"The debt you owe to the past can be discharged by assuming custody of the boy, I grant you. But then there is Ling Shen. Your only chance against him is to take the boy and leave Hong Kong now, this minute."

"Katharine's funeral is three days from now. Peking's making the arrangements. I promised Todd I'd be there with him. I don't have to tell you that the most important thing in life to the Chinese is to be buried in the right way."

The policeman nodded. "I quite understand. Unfortunately, the Triads hold power in Hong Kong second only to that of Peking and the bankers. I will assist you in any way I can, but Shen is an implacable foe and I'm afraid that once his heart is set on revenge he cannot be dissuaded."

He patted his wavy hair and, being a pragmatic man, mentally began to steel himself for the furor certain to erupt from America and points elsewhere when Mr. DiPalma was dispatched by Shen, as would inevitably happen. DiPalma's concern for his child and his sense of obligation to the late Mrs. Hansard were both admirable. Very human. But being human was no solution.

DiPalma said, "I can give you a few places in Japan to start asking about the fan."

The superintendent folded the fan and returned it to the envelope. "In exchange for what?"

"For tying Kon Kenpachi to Katharine Hansard's murder."

"Mr. Kenpachi is not a murder suspect at this time. Which is why we released him after getting his statement."

"The telexes—"

"Said that Mr. Kenpachi had aided Chiba regarding past arrests, nothing more. Kenpachi's presence in Hong Kong during Chiba's stay appears to have been a coincidence, not a conspiracy. As far as we can determine the two did not meet during their respective stays here. You seem inclined to believe the worst of Kenpachi, which is your prerogative. But there is no evidence to indicate that he had any reason to want the Hansards dead. For that matter we've having trouble establishing a motive for Chiba. The only thing anyone appears to have wanted out of this is your son and with all due respect, I, for one, cannot see why."

"Chiba had the number of Kenpachi's mobile phone—"

"Which was the main reason we brought Mr. Kenpachi here for questioning. He had an explanation for that. There was to be some discussion of Chiba playing a role in Kenpachi's new film. They'd already spoken once on the phone and were to speak once more. No face to face meeting, said Kenpachi. Strictly business, strictly over the telephone."

"In Japan, Kenpachi bailed Chiba out of trouble more than once. Tokyo police also said that the two lived together and had been seen in each other's company off and on for a long time. There's a good chance they could have been more than just strange bedfellows."

The superintendent dropped the fan into his desk drawer and pushed it shut. "We have gossip columns in this part of the world and we are well aware of Mr. Kenpachi's sexual proclivities. Here in the East such practices are not looked upon as they are in the West. Sensuality, in all its aspects, is simply considered a matter of the flesh. To quibble about the form it may take, say the Orientals, is to condemn a man for eating with his left hand instead of his right. In any case, given the state of the world these days, it would seem that chastity's the only perversion."

DiPalma brought the silver head of his cane up to eye level and studied it. "Ask yourself why Chiba went crazy when we came for him in his hotel room. Ask yourself why the word *ninja* set him off and made him want to kill every one of us."

The superintendent was a long time answering. "Judging by his reaction, it would appear he was afraid. Afraid for himself, perhaps. Afraid of someone other than the police. It could well be that you were correct, that he had been trained and financed by someone whose identity he couldn't possibly reveal. His actions did appear to be those of a wild man."

"Chiba was scared shitless. I've seen that look before."

"Could he have been frightened of you?"

"Like I said, his money, his life-style and martial-arts training came from somewhere."

"Your bluff successfully spooked Chiba, but it also closed the door to further questioning. Or I should say Jenkins did, speaking of the actions of a wild man. So now Chiba's dead and Kenpachi's free to return to the glamorous world of films."

He extended his hand to DiPalma, who took it. "I won't insult your intelligence by suggesting you change your mind regarding the funeral. But do take care. Shen is ruthless. Things haven't gone well with him of late and more than ever he is determined to save face. He will not appear at his daughter's funeral. In eleven years he has had no contact with her whatsoever. That should give you an idea of his determination. She must have loved you quite dearly to do what she did, knowing what her father's reaction would be."

They parted in silence as the superintendent recalled the death of his own wife and remembered that to love well meant forgetting slowly.

* * *

IN THE LANDMARK'S balcony restaurant Frank DiPalma sipped lukewarm tea and said to Todd, "You're right. Benkai was very good with two swords. Where did you learn about him?"

"I have read about the great swordsmen. Hayashizaki, Ittosai, Shimpachi Nikai, Bokuden, Musashi and Benkai. Kenpachi-san has given me a book on the life of Benkai. Benkai once lived in Kenpachi-san's castle as bodyguard to

Lord Saburo who built the castle.''

"Is the book in English or in Japanese?"

"Japanese."

"When did you learn to speak Japanese?"

Todd looked embarrassed. "It would seem I have a knack for it. I began picking up words and phrases from my kendo instructor and when he noticed my interest, he insisted on our conversing in it. I suppose it's come easy for me. I don't know quite why."

Japanese hadn't come easy to DiPalma, who had spent years learning a language once described as making Chinese appear to be a puzzle for retarded children. Japanese was one of the world's most difficult languages; it was imprecise, with a massive vocabulary and a system of writing DiPalma still hadn't mastered. Yet his eleven-year-old son could speak Japanese and God knew how many Chinese dialects.

DiPalma thought of Sakon Chiba and his ties to Kon Kenpachi. "Kenpachi mentioned something about your visiting Ikuba Castle."

"We talked about kendo. At Ikuba Castle there is still the original *dojo* where Benkai trained and taught swordsmanship. It is something Kenpachi-san feels I must see. And there is the room where Lord Saburo and Benkai committed *seppuku*. I must go there. I must . . ."

His eyes widened and he held his breath. And just as suddenly, he relaxed and turned to DiPalma. "Benkai was *kaishaku* to Lord Saburo."

"Do you know what *kaishaku* means?"

Todd nodded gravely. "A *kaishaku* acts as second to one committing *seppuku*. It is his duty to end the pain of the one taking his own life. A *kaishaku* must be of strong character and a very good swordsman."

DiPalma was impressed. "Katharine said you knew a lot about the martial arts. And about Japan. *Seppuku* goes back a long way. No one knows for sure how long."

Todd stared down into his untouched cup of tea. "At least fifteen hundred years. It began with warriors who would strangle themselves because they could not live with the shame of defeat. Other warriors burned themselves to death by setting fire to their own homes."

"Does this mean they will live forever?"

"The soul cannot die. We are born again and again until we free ourselves from the wheel of birth and death to become one with the Ultimate Reality."

DiPalma smiled. "Your mother and I talked about this a few times. Like you, she believed in reincarnation. In karma. I don't mean to challenge you or anything, but I find it hard to accept that. Seems to me that when you're dead, you're dead. A door shuts behind you. The book's closed."

"You can never die," said Todd with cool certainty. "You cannot even imagine your own death. You can imagine anything else, but not your own death."

"Oh, I can do a pretty good job of imagining my death. I see myself lying in an expensive coffin, silk lined, hands folded across my chest and me in a neat black suit. I see flowers, maybe a few beautiful women sniffling in the front row and a fat, bald-headed man playing the organ."

Todd, half-smiling, leaned back in his chair. "But there it is. The truth. You see yourself lying in the coffin. You are the witness, the onlooker. You cannot be dead and be the witness as well."

"Hey," said a grinning Frank DiPalma, "you are sharp. Let me play with that one for a while."

"I'd like to talk to you."

DiPalma turned to see Jan Golden standing by the table, taking long, angry drags on a cigarette.

"Jan. You know Todd." The boy stood up. "Miss Golden," he said politely.

Jan ignored him. "We have to talk, Frank. Now."

"This is my first day with Todd. Maybe you and I can get together tomorrow. A lot of things happened today and—"

She removed DiPalma's cane from a chair, and sat down. "That's what I'd like to talk to you about. What the hell are you trying to do to me?"

"I don't understand."

"I'm talking about your having Kon arrested for no reason. I'm talking about you delaying my movie and costing me a damned fortune."

"And how did I manage to do that?"

"Kon's disappeared."

DiPalma looked at Todd, who sat quietly watching them. The boy's composure was impressive.

"I spoke to him at the police station," Jan said. "Right after that he left. I thought he was returning to the shoot, but he never showed up and nobody knows where the hell he is. A day's shooting, fifty thousand dollars, down the tubes." She slumped in her chair, a hand covering her eyes. "A drink, please."

DiPalma summoned a waitress and ordered a Rob Roy. Jan dropped her hand from her face. "He said it goes back to this rivalry you two have in kendo. Says you don't miss a chance to drag his name through the mud."

"He's a liar," DiPalma said. He felt Todd's eyes on him, but did not turn to look at his son.

Jan fumbled in her purse for her cigarettes. "Frank, I know you. You're Sicilian. You don't forget. You told me that, remember? Something else you told me, too. You said more than once that you wished you could go back in your life and change a few things. Make them right, you said."

"I wasn't thinking of Kenpachi when I said that. I was thinking of my wife and daughter. I was thinking of the partners I lost." He looked down at the table. "I was thinking of Katharine."

He lit her cigarette and watched her drag deeply on it. "Frank, all I know is I saw you with the police when they came for Kon. And down at the police station they think you're hot shit. Strictly heavy duty. Somebody to be scared of. You made a telephone call, to Senator Joseph Quarequio and everybody in Hong Kong sat up straight in their chairs. Or they're lying on their backs with their paws in the air and it's all because of you. That's a lot of power, my friend. It's the kind of power that usually ends up hurting other people."

"Jan, Kenpachi wasn't arrested on my say-so. He wasn't arrested at all. He was brought in for questioning, that's all. And only because a friend of his killed one police officer and blinded another in one eye. The man who did it—"

"A transvestite. I know."

"He had the number of Kenpachi's mobile phone."

She stubbed out her cigarette and reached for another. "And that's enough to involve Kon?"

"Kenpachi and the killer were tight for almost fifteen years. Yeah, I'd say that's enough to pull Kenpachi in for questioning ten times over. Especially when the two are in the same city at the same time."

She used her thumb and pinky to remove a tobacco strand from her tongue. "He knows we were supposed to get married and that it didn't work out. He thinks you're jealous of me and him working together, that you might make trouble for us."

"Do you really believe that?"

She looked away. "I told him about us. I felt he should know. Especially with this business of"—she stared across the table at Todd—"this business of what happened to your son's mother. Kon swears he had nothing to do with it."

The drink arrived. Jan snatched it from the tray and drained half of it at a gulp. Her lush, autumn red hair hung free and Frank was drawn to it. She said, "This has not been the best day of my life. This is serious. Delay, delay, delay. Then Kon goes up in a puff of smoke and a half hour ago I get a cable from Tokyo saying our permission to film in the Bank of Tokyo and the Mitsukoshi department store has been withdrawn. The bank doesn't think the film would be good for its image and the store, which gets three hundred thousand customers a day, says we would interfere with business. We need substitute locations in a hurry, not to mention rewrites. And the hurricane season's on the way. Might strike Japan this month, maybe sometime next month. It's going to hurt any exteriors we've got planned, especially some shooting Kon wants to do on the coast."

She held up a finger. "Now get this. I had the perfect *mix* on this film. The right American and Japanese actors, a great script, the director I wanted. Sometime this afternoon my production manager gets a cable from New York. An actor who's due to show up in Tokyo next week for filming has changed his mind. Seems he's been offered the lead in a new Arthur Miller play and is determined to do it even if it means breaking his contract with me. John Ford was right. Actors are crap."

She emptied her glass, set it down and stared at it.

It was Todd who broke the silence. "I am sorry about your father, Miss Golden."

Her head jerked up. She stared at him, then at DiPalma. "How did he know about my father? Did you tell him? Frank, are you spying on me?"

DiPalma forced himself not to look at Todd. He had never discussed Jan's father with the boy.

Tears formed in her eyes. "God, I really need this on top of everything else. He's back in the hospital again. Something wrong with his pacemaker. Frank, I'm sorry I ran out on you. It was wrong, I know it and I'm sorry. Nothing I can do about it now. For the time being this movie is my life. What I'm saying is this is my chance to be somebody, do something besides grow old. You and Kon, well, what I'm saying is, please don't spoil it for me. If there's something between you and him, I'd appreciate it if you'd let it go until the movie's done. That's all I'm saying."

Her hand reached across the table for his. He took it because he was dog tired, ready to drop and because he didn't have the energy to explain that despite what he still felt for her he didn't trust her. Frank DiPalma had loved Jan and so it had been easy for her to deceive him. It wasn't anything he cared to go through again.

In believing Kenpachi she was deceiving herself. Taking out her frustrations on DiPalma was part of that deception. If she failed to deliver a good film on time and within budget, her career as a producer would suffer, perhaps permanently. In Hollywood, where failure was a crime, few people got a second chance. She needed Kenpachi. She was also attracted to him, or she would not have tracked DiPalma down. Anytime Jan fell in love, it was a love that knew no limits and could not be controlled. The hurt and disillusion would follow, but for now she would fight for Kon Kenpachi even if it meant fighting against Frank DiPalma.

He remembered what his father had said, that in love you never got to choose.

"I didn't know you and Kenpachi were here in Hong Kong," DiPalma said. "I came here because Katharine asked me to. After her funeral I'll be leaving for New York. Believe what you want to believe, but I think you know me well enough to know I wouldn't lie to you."

She stubbed out another cigarette. "I'm sorry. I'm upset

and I just felt like bitching, that's all. As if we don't have enough problems, we sent prints of some of Kon's past films to New York for his retrospective at Lincoln Center next month and they haven't arrived. Kon's earned that showing and I'd hate to see anything go wrong with it."

She stood up as did Frank. "Hell of a way for us to meet after all this time," she said. "I didn't tell you how well you look."

"You too."

"I hear a lot of good things about what you're doing. They say you'll win another Emmy this year for sure. What will that be, your fourth?"

"Third, if it happens. Good luck with the movie."

Jan smiled at Todd, who rose and shook her hand. Then she kissed DiPalma on the cheek and left the restaurant. Frank's eyes followed her down the balcony stairs and across the plaza. *In love you never get to choose.* When she had left the building he turned around to ask Todd how he know about Jan's father's illness.

But the boy had disappeared.

13

IT WAS DARK when Kon Kenpachi knelt in front of a low table in the small room, struck a match and lit the four white candles. The flames sent long shadows across the low ceiling of the snake restaurant, the site of Ian Hansard's murder. Except for Kenpachi and his bodyguard, Wakaba, the restaurant was now empty. Wakaba locked the front door, then closed the thick wooden shutters over the two windows which faced the street. After peeking through a crack in the shutter, the bodyguard returned to the door and stood with his back against it.

At the table Kenpachi regarded the candles, which were surrounded by incense sticks and flowers—lilies, blue orchids and chrysanthemums—Buddhist ceremonial offerings to the dead. The ceremony was for Sakon, who was represented by an empty coffin, the head of which pointed north and touched the table. Sakon's body was still in police custody; there would be an autopsy the following morning. Kenpachi could not claim it without calling more attention to himself. He would have to perform the ceremony without Sakon's corpse.

Kenpachi's favorite photograph of Sakon stood in the coffin, resting on a white silk handkerchief. It had been taken at the top of Mount Fuji over ten years ago, when Sakon had been a teenager with an unspoiled and vulnerable beauty.

Assisted by Japanese from Nosaka's Eastern Bank, Kenpachi had hastily arranged the death rites to honor Sakon and to let his spirit know that it would be revenged. For the policeman who had done the killing there would be no pardon, no forgiveness. The murder of Sakon would be repaid with samurai justice; Sakon had died a warrior's death in service to Nosaka and Kenpachi. His death now made him a *kami*, a god, whom Kenpachi would soon meet in the next world. The filmmaker did not want to encounter Sakon without first observing the code of Bushido.

The death rites.

Because he now purified himself for his forthcoming *seppuku*, Kenpachi, using Buddhist rituals, acted as his own priest. Before entering the restaurant he had pasted a piece of paper with the words *mo-shu*, in mourning, on the front door. Now, at the table, he picked up a pen and pulled a blank sheet of white paper toward him. He dipped the pen into a bottle of black ink, then drew a circle in one continuous stroke, filling the entire page with its outline. Within the circle he drew three large comma-like shapes, each chasing the tail of the next.

As Wakaba watched, Kenpachi patiently filled in one comma, then drew a stork and a turtle inside the others. The stork and the turtle were both symbols of eternal life. Finished, he rose and carried the design, a *mitsutomoe*, over to the coffin and laid it near a photograph of Sakon. A *mitsutomoe*, with its three commas, represented the three treasures of Buddha— Buddha himself, his teachings and those who followed them.

Another table near the coffin held fruits, sweets, vegetables and tea, as well as a pair of sandals, a pearl necklace, a jeweled brooch and a kimono. As prescribed by ritual, Kenpachi, as Sakon's only survivor, had paid for these himself.

Publicly he had shown no grief. Now sorrow fell on him and for the first time since learning of Sakon's death there were tears in Kenpachi's eyes.

He knelt at the second table and began to wrap the gifts in white paper, strong, beautiful and handmade. Following tradition, he used one sheet of paper, working precisely and seeing that the last fold came out on top of the package and extended all the way around. He wrapped the sandals, the kimono, tea and *manju*, bean-jam buns. Then he rose and presented the wrapped packages to Wakaba, who accepted them and bowed from the waist.

Kenpachi now stood at the coffin and chanted Buddhist incantations he had learned from his mother. Then he closed his eyes and performed *kuji-kiri*, the magical signs made by *ninjas* to gain self-confidence and to strengthen the spirit in times of danger. Frank DiPalma was the danger facing Kenpachi; he had led the police to Sakon. Ling Shen would dispose of DiPalma within hours. But if Shen should fail. . . .

Kenpachi linked his fingers together in one of the eighty-one ways known only to a *ninja* and recited a Buddhist sutra used by *ninjas* for over a thousand years. As he recited he alternately made five horizontal then vertical lines in the air with his knitted fingers. *Kuji-kiri* increased a *ninja*'s perception; it allowed him to read the thoughts of others, to see into the future and to predict death. Through *kuji-kiri* a warrior achieved "the eyes of God," becoming all-knowing, all-seeing, all wise.

Eyes closed, Kenpachi spoke the mystic words. Arms extended, fingers linked, he envisioned *jigoku*, the Buddhist's hell, for the policeman who had shot Sakon . . . and he saw something else.

Opening his eyes, he reached into the coffin and took out the two weapons, Bankai's long sword and Saburo's *seppuku* knife. He whirled around, weapons held high overhead, and whispered to Wakaba, "Open the window on your left, then stand aside."

Wakaba pulled the shutters open, then stepped out of Kenpachi's line of vision.

On the darkened street, Todd stood and stared into the restaurant. He saw the sword and the *seppuku* knife held by Kenpachi. In the candlelight the two blades shimmered and glowed. Todd began to shake, his eyes riveted on the blades. Kenpachi made no move toward him, but held the weapons aloft and stared at Todd until the boy jerked his head away and was gone.

Jubilantly Kenpachi turned to face the coffin. In death Sakon had still managed to bring the boy to him.

* * *

FRANK DiPALMA lay still in bed and listened. He had been awakened by a knock on the door of his hotel suite. In the darkness he reached for his cane, then sat up and turned on the night light. His watch read 11:10 P.M. The knocking continued, soft, but insistent.

He got out of bed, put on his robe, then walked into the sitting room and paused at the door before opening it. "Hello, Todd."

"Forgive me for disturbing you, sir. May I come in?"

"Sure."

DiPalma stepped aside, flicked the light switch and closed the door behind his son. The boy looked as if he had been rolling around in a coal bin. His hands and clothing were smudged and there were scratches on both arms. A package which he clutched to his chest was streaked with black marks. It was the size of an attaché case and was wrapped in yellow oilcloth.

DiPalma sat down in an imitation Hepplewhite chair, shoved both hands in the pockets of his robe and waited. Todd was an unusual boy, with a touch of the unreal about him. He had been surprised when his son had walked away from the restaurant without warning, but for some reason he hadn't worried. Todd could take care of himself.

What bothered Frank DiPalma was Todd's self-control. His parents were killed violently and an attempt had been made to kidnap him. Yet the boy maintained the calm of a neurosurgeon. Or a samurai warrior. Either the kid had ice water in his veins or he had managed to bury the hurt deep inside.

Todd held out the package. "Please. It is what you want."

"It is?"

"The papers from my stepfather's bank. The files you were supposed to bring back to New York."

Frank DiPalma sat in his chair and didn't move a muscle. He had been caught unawares before in his life, but never like this. It was time to start asking questions. "Where did you find them?"

"They were hidden beneath an iron door in the floor of my mother's studio."

"Explains why you're dirty."

"Yes, sir. The man who originally built the main house used the bungalow as an ice house and to store his opium. He was an opium trader, you see. The iron door in the floor protected the files from burning. Everything is here in the attaché case.

I'm afraid it's locked. Only my stepfather had the key."

Frank DiPalma took the package from Todd. "In a world of paper clips and letter openers," he said, "there is no such thing as a locked attaché case."

He peeled off the soiled oilcloth, dropped it into a waste basket and reached for a brass letter opener. "How did you know I wanted these files? I never mentioned it to Katharine."

There was a moment of silence. He turned to look at his son, whose head hung as though he had done something shameful.

"Bothers you, having this thing," DiPalma said. "This telepathy business. This extrasensory perception."

"My mother called it second sight or thought transference. She said it is both a gift and a curse. It comes to me without warning. Sometimes I see frightening things. At the restaurant I saw something bad about Miss Golden's father. He will soon die."

"His heart is bad."

"He will not die that way."

"How will he die?"

"*Ninja.*"

Frank's eyes narrowed. "Is his name in these files? Is that why you ran away from the restaurant?"

"His name is here, yes. And it is on the list given to you by your friend, Roger Tan."

The list. He could have kicked himself. He had forgotten all about it. Back at the Hansard home, Roger had given him the names of Eastern Pacific's directors and Frank, busy with the call to Senator Joseph Quarequio, had never even glanced at it. He placed the unopened attaché case on the desk and walked to the bedroom closet. The list was where he'd left it, inside his jacket. Two pages of notebook paper in Roger's handwriting.

Jude Leonard Golden, Jan's father, was the fifth name from the top. Salvatore Verna and Duncan Ivy were there too, along with retired military officers from America, England, Europe and Japan. If Sally Verna was telling the truth, the men on this list were a part of Nosaka's industrial-espionage network and were also involved in his murky financial transactions.

Frank, with Todd looking on, studied the list further. Jude Golden had to be Mr. O., the organizer who Sally Verna claimed had worldwide contacts in the intelligence and law-enforcement communities. And he was Sally's partner in a bid to buy the late Ian Hansard's hidden banking files. This was not an educated guess. Jan had given him the proof, her birth in Japan a few years after her father's tour of duty as a war-crimes prosecutor. She had also told him of her father's life-long love of the Far East, of his business dealings throughout the Pacific, of the lavish Japanese-style home and gardens Jude Golden owned in Connecticut, complete with Japanese serving girls. And like Duncan Ivy, Jude Golden was a banker.

After the three of us convicted Nosaka, he vowed to kill us, said Sally Verna. Me, Ivy, Mr. O.

No doubt about it, thought Frank. The third man, Mr. O., is Jude Golden. Money had brought the Americans and Nosaka together; money had also made the Americans forget that Nosaka was the fox and they were the chickens. Nosaka, however, had a long memory; he would keep the vow he made forty years ago, because it was the only way he could die with honor. At his age, an honorable death had to be something he thought about often.

Nosaka's calling the shots on the new Blood Oath League same as he did on the old, said Sally Verna. He wants to build a new Japan by killing people.

Jan could be one of those people. All she had to do is be in the wrong place at the wrong time, like Duncan Ivy's lawyer, and she's cut to pieces by a samurai sword. Just let her be caught with her father when the Blood Oath League comes for him and she'd dead. Frank crushed Roger's list in his fist. Damn Kenpachi for bringing Jan this close to Nosaka.

Kenpachi, the superpatriot, the would-be samurai. The Blood Oath League would certainly get his vote. He believed in violence, flag-waving. He had been one of the first to come out in favor of the controversial new history textbooks, which gave a watered-down account of Japan's aggression during World War II. He had demanded a resurgent Japanese militarism, calling the war his country's days of glory. Kenpachi had ended one speech by cutting his arm and using his blood to draw a Japanese flag on a white handkerchief; when he held

it up to a group of Japanese war veterans they cheered him to
the skies.

He favored those films which showed the Japanese military
as peaceloving, the Allied forces as brutal and treacherous.
And in typical Kenpachi fashion, the filmmaker had produced, directed and written a documentary showing wartime
prime minister General Hideki Tojo not as sadistic and power
hungry, but as a gentle and scholarly father figure. It was like
claiming Charles Manson was a lovable camp counselor whose
charges sometimes got out of hand.

If Nosaka was behind the Blood Oath League, Kenpachi
knew about it, and approved. Jan was definitely in over her
head. She was holding a wolf by the ears.

But Todd . . . Todd was a different story. He believed
Todd's powers and yet he didn't believe. He believed because
Katharine had believed, because his instinct said the boy was
not a liar.

"You didn't eat at the restaurant," he said. "Are you
hungry?"

The boy grinned. He was going to break a few hearts when
he grew older. "I could eat, sir. If you please."

"Well, we've got twenty-four-hour room service, they tell
me. What'll it be? Hamburger, ice cream, french fries, milk,
soft drink. You name it."

"All of that sounds good, sir."

"All of it. Hey, why not. Your engine can't run on empty.
I'll order, then we'll see what's in this attaché case."

He telephoned the order then turned to the locks. No problem there. Both locks quickly yielded to a letter opener.

The leather case, new and unmarked, was packed with
folders. There were folders for memos, correspondence and
bank records. There were folders for records of conversations,
for dummy corporations, for customs personnel on the take.
It was the history of Zenzo Nosaka's industrial-espionage network, enough to place him under investigation in the Far East,
Europe and the United States. The lawyers at DiPalma's network would stay up nights checking every line. He would put
his own investigative team on the file to verify as much as
possible. He had more than enough to go on. When his team
finished, they would have a story hot enough to guarantee

Frank more than two minutes and twenty seconds on the eleven o'clock news.

Shieh Lei, Sally Verna had called it. Bribes. Ian Hansard had made an impressive case for Zenzo Nosaka as an industrial spymaster without equal. Nor were Hansard's hands clean. He was the one who had set up charities, ecology groups and wildlife organizations in America, England and Europe, fronts for dispersing payoffs to industrial spies on Nosaka's payroll. Hansard had been a bagman for Nosaka, carrying large sums of money from Hong Kong to foreign countries when the information and the person selling it were important enough.

There was more, showing Hansard's direct involvement in Nosaka's spy network. Bank information on loan applications, credit checks, business mergers, business expansions, money for research and development. All the transactions involved people in a position to pass on information about their companies, people who could be bought or blackmailed. Hansard had had a sense of humor. Beside one name the banker had written, "seeks the cure for poverty at our expense."

The former military men on Eastern's board had close contacts in defense and nondefense industries and Hansard had used them to gather information for Nosaka. They also had their fingers in secret arms deals, which involved laundering millions through Eastern Pacific Amalgamated. Naturally the bank took its commission on these details.

One page of names caused Frank's eyebrows to rise. We meet again, he thought. In his hand were the names and account numbers of several class-A narcotics traffickers, men whose annual volume of business topped that of most companies listed on the stock exchange. Frank recognized each name and knew its history. There was the Bolivian cocaine dealer he had failed to make a case against some years ago, a man who paid his country's generals fifty million dollars in protection every six months. And it didn't surprise Frank that a Mexican heroin dealer, whose beautiful twenty-five-year-old daughter was his mistress and second in command, had washed over six hundred million dollars in Nosaka's bank in nine months. The bank's fee, three percent, came to $18 million.

Not only was the bank delivering intelligence, it was also making windfall profit.

The file was worth millions. Hansard dealt in big bucks and wouldn't have sold information like this for peanuts. As to why Hansard suddenly decided to go into business for himself, the answer was in the attaché case. Bank books and false passports. The bank books showed hefty deposits in numbered accounts or under dummy corporate names in banks around the world. They belonged to Ian Hansard; Frank knew a hustle when he saw one.

The passports made it official. There were six, three for Hansard, three for Katharine. Three false names each, all passports officially stamped and with recent dates. There were no passports for Todd.

Was it the Blood Oath League that had made Hansard decide to take the money and run?

Frank flipped through some of the other pages. Nothing on the league. Which didn't mean it wasn't there. In any case, Sally Verna would help him with that, in exchange for the file and for keeping him and Jude Golden out of any story. Frank would look at the file again tomorrow and this time he wouldn't miss a page. Hansard the great record keeper was sure to have something on Nosaka and the Blood Oath League.

He would have to move fast. The sooner the word got out on Nosaka, his industrial-espionage network and the Blood Oath League, the better it would be for the former prosecutors, Sally Verna and Jude Golden. The glare of publicity might save their lives. On the other hand, it might not. Nosaka could decide to carry out his vow in any case.

Whatever happened, Frank stood to gain. This story would blow away every reporter in the business, not to mention the network libel lawyers, who would go over it with a fine-tooth comb. From any angle, the story was dynamite. A major war criminal who should have been hanged forty years ago would be hanged now. Not with a rope, but by the media. Nosaka was nothing more than a hood involved in the legalized thievery that was business. He deserved to go down, to be shamed before the world, to be dragged through the courts in countries where he had stolen business secrets. The disgrace would weigh heavily on the proud Nosaka. I love it, Frank thought. I fucking love it.

Then he remembered Katharine. Finding her killer mattered more than dumping on Nosaka. Sakon Chiba had been the instrument; somebody else had pulled the strings. Frank was going to let his investigative team run with Hansard's files while he looked into Katharine's death. It would gnaw at him until he found the answer.

There was a knock at the door. He put the files back into the case and closed it. "Feeding time," he said to Todd. "Let them in and have them put it down on the coffee table. You should be comfortable on the couch. Tomorrow I'll give these files one hell of a toss. Go through them from beginning to end."

"Yes, sir."

"Hey, Todd, no more of that sir stuff, remember? I know they brought you up to say it and it's great, but there's no reason for you to call me that. I hear sir and I look around to see who you're talking about."

"I understand . . . Frank."

My son. The words were strange, a foreign language. They would take some getting used to.

Todd opened the door, then leaned back to protect himself. Frank was out of his chair and rushing toward him, but it was too late. Three armed men pushed into the room and slammed the door behind them. One grabbed Todd from behind, an arm around his neck, and pressed a Colt .45 to the boy's temple. Frank froze in the center of the room. Ling Shen, he thought. I'm going to die a long way from home.

The other two men moved quickly. They separated, keeping distance between them, then stopped and crouched, guns in a combat grip and trained on Frank. One had a Walther PPK; the other held a .357 Magnum revolver fitted with a laser-targeting device which threw a brilliant beam of red light on the spot the bullet would hit. The beam was aimed at Frank's throat.

Frank's stomach reacted first, rumbling as though he hadn't eaten in a long time. Then knotted. Under his robe the perspiration dripped from his back. His eyes were on the man with the magnum, but he also picked up the light coming from the top of the weapon. He had stared into the barrel of a gun before, but none held the terror of this one. Prison guards armed with laser-targeting rifles had put down riots without firing a shot. The sight of that red beam on his body unnerved the toughest convict.

The man holding the magnum was tanned and slight, with small plump hands, silver hair and cool gray eyes. He wore a three-piece pin-striped suit and wine-colored tie, and spoke with an Australian accent. *Australian*.

"Hands behind the neck, Mr. DiPalma. Good. Now kneel facing me. Splendid."

These were not Shen's men. They were Caucasians. But they were still dangerous, especially the Australian, who seemed to find a primitive pleasure in his work.

"We've come to relieve you of Mr. Hansard's case," said the Australian in a nasal twang. "Him havin' gone to Jesus and all, I doubt if he has much use for it. And you, boyo, are not the rightful owner, so you'll forgive us if we don't ask your permission to go dashin' off with it. By the way, the food in this establishment is as bad as I've ever tasted. We called downstairs and canceled your order, for which you should be thankin' us. Now we'll be gettin' to the heart of the matter and havin' the case." He jerked his head toward the desk and the man with the Walther placed the case under his arm.

"I take it every scrap of paper is in place," the Australian said. "You haven't had it long enough to hide anything, have you?"

"It's all there."

"I'll take your word for it, guv. You appear to be an honorable man, a rarity in this devious world of ours. Now listen and listen well, for I'll not be repeatin' what I'm about to say to you. We're leavin' here with the lad. And the case, of course. The lad's going on a trip, but a brief one. He'll ride downstairs with us in the lift, then in the lobby he'll be released to return to you. You don't have a say in the matter, so I hope you'll find these arrangements satisfactory."

"Whatever you say."

"Splendid. You are to wait here in this room until your son

returns. Any deviation from this plan could bring something terminal down upon you and the boy. Do we understand one another?''

"We do.''

"It pleases me that we do. Two lives depend upon you controlling your heroic impulses. Now one last item of business and this meeting will be adjourned.''

He nodded. A signal.

The man holding the attaché case crossed the room to the couch and picked up the phone from the coffee table. A sudden move and the cord was jerked clean from the wall. Then he went to the bedroom and yanked out the second telephone.

Then the three men and Todd were gone, leaving Frank DiPalma alone.

It was fifteen minutes before Todd returned to Frank's room to find him packing his one suitcase.

"I thought you were going to stay for my mother's funeral,'' Todd said.

Frank stopped. "I am.''

"But you're packing.''

"We're going downstairs to reception. I want another room.'' He pointed to an ashtray sitting on the edge of his bed. "Bugs,'' he said.

Todd picked up one of the small metal disks in the ashtray.

"There was one in each of the phones,'' said Frank. "One behind the bed, one under the couch, one in a lamp near the desk. No way of knowing if I got them all.''

"How did you know they were here?''

"Our Australian friend in the tailored suit told me. That crack of his about the food, about his canceling our room service. And his mentioning that we hadn't had the files long. Hell, there were ears all over this place. I'd feel better if I had a new room.''

Todd's eyes widened. "That was clever of you, sir. I mean, Frank.''

"Todd, anybody with the brains of a radish could figure that one out. What I can't figure out is who hired those shooters. They're high-priced talent. They're slick, they've got access to good equipment and damn good weapons. Hell,

they're pros. It was almost a pleasure to watch them work.
Almost.''

* * *

IN THE HOTEL BAR, DiPalma began dialing long distance. "Got to call Sally Verna first. Our new room can wait.
He was hoping that file would keep him alive. All I can do is
warn him that somebody else has it now. I owe him that much.
Why don't you find a waitress and order a sandwich or something.''

"I'll wait here for you, if you don't mind.''

Frank tried three times to reach Verna and failed to get
through each time. After the third attempt he dialed a tele-
phone-company supervisor, who put him in touch with two
other phone-company employees. It took fifteen minutes of
being shuffled around before he finally learned that the New
York area had been hit by a severe summer storm and
telephone lines were down.

DiPalma hung up. "That's that. OK, how about that sandwich.''

Todd was staring straight ahead. Frank followed his gaze,
but saw nothing special. Just a handful of Chinese and one or
two Europeans at the tables and at the bar. Then he realized
that Todd was not staring at anyone in the bar. He was staring
at something only he could see.

"*Yamabushi*,'' he whispered.

Mountain warriors. Another name for *ninja*, who had
always trained in secret mountain strongholds.

"The *yamabushi* have come for him,'' said Todd.

Frank looked at his son and grew alarmed. The boy was
sinking deeper into a trancelike state.

He grabbed Todd by the shoulders. "They've come for
who, Todd. Who have the *ninja* come for?''

But Todd did not answer. He kept staring into space and
Frank DiPalma was suddenly afraid.

14

Long Island, New York

THE JULY storm which struck the New York area brought with it warm, heavy rains, moisture-laden air and flash floods so severe that Manhattan police in rowboats had to rescue motorists trapped on deluged transverses in Central Park. The storm had formed over the Caribbean, started west, then changed direction and moved northeast. It traveled along the Atlantic Ocean, more than four hundred miles wide, and brought sixty-five-mile-an-hour winds.

Flash-flood warnings were posted for portions of New England, northern New Jersey suburbs and parts of Long Island, which was especially hard hit. Here the heavy downpour caused rivers to overflow and raised sea levels, threatening homes and halting train service to New York City. Schools and airports were closed and fishing fleets stayed tied up in port. Telephone lines were down and entire communities were without electricity.

It was not the driving rain or strong winds which left Sally Verna's oceanfront home isolated, without telephone or electricity. All power lines and burglar-alarm systems connected to the white marble mansion had been deliberately cut from outside by six black-clad figures, who made their way in the downpour and darkness down the hilly ridge, rain slicked and treacherous, then over sand dunes and sodden beaches until they reached the wall protecting the west side of the mansion. Tonight no one stood guard on the ridge or on the swaying

dock or on the beaches and lagoons. And no one stood guard
outside the walls.

Using ropes and grappling hooks, the *ninja* scaled the walls
and dropped down on the estate grounds. The house was well
lit by an emergency generator in the garage. Three *ninja* trotted to the topiary animals cut from the hedges and followed
them to the garage and the generator, their target. The other
three went for the second target, the guards patrolling the
grounds.

Dogs. Outside the garage. And barking. One of the *ninja*
crept forward until he could see the snarling dogs. German
shepherds, ears close to their skulls, fur darkened by the rain,
teeth bared. No handlers, just the dogs. Their barking could
not carry in the storm and wind. And they were indecisive
about attacking. Taking advantage of their hesitation, the
black-clad raider removed poisoned meat from his pocket and
tossed it to the animals.

The dogs sniffed the fresh beef, then wolfed it down.

The *ninja* watched, and waited.

When the dogs slumped to the ground, foaming at the
mouth, he ran forward, picked up one of the dying animals
and ran back to his companions. He tossed the dog to the
leader, then returned for the second animal, now dead. Seconds later the two men stood on the edge of the swimming
pool and heaved the animals into the wind-driven water. A
guard coming upon a drowned dog would not be as suspicious
as finding a dog with its throat cut.

At the garage a *ninja* with only his slanted eyes visible under
a hooded mask, peered through a window at two men strad-
dling opposite ends of a workbench and playing cards. He
turned to his companions and signaled with his index fingers.
Two guards inside with the generator. Each *ninja* carried a
sword across his back, but they would not be used until they
reached the main house. A blade left blood and blood would
alert a guard.

There were two entrances to the garage, a wide one for cars
and a door facing away from the mansion. Two *ninja* positioned themselves on either side and the third pounded the
door with a clenched fist.

From inside came an irate voice. "Yeah. All right, all right. Fuckin' crazy to come out in this shit's all I gotta say."

The door opened and a chunky man shaded his eyes against the rain. "You mind gettin' inside before we all drown—"

One man grabbed his shirtfront, yanked him out of the doorway, then rushed past him into the garage. Then another grabbed him from behind, yanking a forearm hard into his throat, and slipping his other arm under the man's left armpit and behind his neck until the palm of the left hand was pressed against the man's right ear, pushing his head into the forearm. Now he couldn't breathe.

Inside the garage the second guard was killed almost instantly. A *ninja* sneaked up behind him as the guard examined the ten cards in his hand and gave serious thought as to whether he should knock with eight points or try for gin and get off the schneid. He never saw the attacker reach out; he felt only his hands and by then it was too late. The *ninja*'s left hand cupped the guard's chin and the palm of his right hand was hard against the back of the guard's skull. The left hand pulled the chin, the right hand pushed the head. Quick. Strong. And the guard's neck snapped.

The dead guards were hidden inside the Rolls Royce. While one *ninja* crouched inside the doorway, the others disconnected the generator. The garage went dark. A grunt from the man in the doorway signaled that the mansion had also gone dark.

Static crackled on a hand radio lying on the work bench. A voice called the name of the dead men in the Rolls.

At the doorway the three Japanese waited, listening to the heavy downpour on the garage roof and the roar of the ocean and the shrieking winds. Then the leader heard the sound he was waiting for: a rock tossed against the side of the garage. A pause, then two more rocks hit the garage and the second team of *ninja* joined the others, reporting to the leader.

Four outside guards were now eliminated. Two dogs poisoned. The bodies of men and animals hidden to prevent discovery and alarm. On the bench the radio squawked and a man's voice came cursing through the static. Ignoring the radio the *ninja* leader stepped out into the storm, ran to a hedge and crouching low at its base followed its outline toward the house. The rest followed him in single file, protected by rain and darkness.

* * *

SALLY VERNA, a camping lantern in one hand, walked to the top of the grand staircase and looked down at Petey George, who was walking up the stairs toward him. A large handsome man in his forties, who kept in excellent shape by boxing regularly, Petey George was in charge of mansion security. He was carrying a valuable painting upstairs, away from the flooding first floor that was pissing Sally off no end. The painting, a thirtieth-anniversary gift from Verna to his wife, was a Caravaggio which the union leader had purchased in Florence and spent a fortune having restored in Milan.

Petey George walked past Verna's light and moved down the hall into darkness. Fucking Petey, thought Verna in admiration. Moves like a cat and makes his way around in the dark like an owl. Petey George didn't have an ounce of fat on him, and he had the hands of a classy welterweight, something you didn't find on big men. Petey could have gone far in the ring if the commission hadn't pulled his license for throwing two fights.

Verna hadn't seen a storm like this hit the island since Hurricane Agnes in 1972, which killed a few people, and caused three billion dollars worth of damage. Tonight's storm was a ball buster, too. Sally watched two men nail planks across the terrace doors to keep them from flying open. A third man, sawed-off shotgun in one hand, held up a camping lantern, giving them light to work by.

There was broken glass on the carpet. Minutes ago the terrace doors had burst open and the wind had knocked down a mounted, glass-enclosed papal guard uniform, blessed and personally given to Sally Verna by Pope John XXIII. The treasured blue-and-yellow uniform, designed by Michelangelo, was now upstairs in the bedroom with the Caravaggio painting and other expensive art treasures.

Fucking storm. It had hit Sally like a kick in the balls. His basement was flooded and in the patio one of the stone cherubs had been blown off his dolphin, losing its head. The roof was leaking in two places and he had enough broken windows to keep a glazier in champagne for a year. His boats were probably getting the shit knocked out of them, if they weren't already at the bottom of the ocean. And no electricity, no telephone.

His wife Chiara was in bed and not well, but she was cheerful and trying not to complain. *Arte di arrangiarsi*, she said. We make do. We survive with style. It was the saying Italians fell back on when things went wrong. Chiara, a round, energetic woman with eyes as blue as the waters of Capri, believed in surviving, in resisting, in never giving up. Which is why she was alive with a heart that was growing weaker after years of giving to Sally, to the three kids and to anyone else who appealed to her generous heart.

Sally could not imagine life without the Admiral, as he called her. She was a descendant of Admiral Andrea Doria, Genoa's most famous seafaring man after Christopher Columbus. Chiara's most prized possession was a gilded silver plate said to have belonged to Doria and used by him at a banquet honoring Emperor Charles V. To impress the holy Roman emperor, Doria had tossed the gilded silver tableware overboard as it became dirty. He had done this every day during a twelve-day feast.

Petey George joined Verna at the railing overlooking the staircase. Together they watched the men nail planks over the terrace doors. "Talk to me, Chootch," Verna said in Italian, using Petey George's nickname. "What's with them bastards in the garage? It's like the Cotton Club in here. Dark as a nigger wedding."

"Sent Enzo and Rummo out there to see what the fuck's going on."

Verna's hand was in the pocket of his robe, resting on a .38 Smith & Wesson. "And if they don't come back?"

"If they don't come back, I go out there myself."

"No, no, no. You send somebody else out there. I want you right here keeping an eye on things. What's happening with the rest of the people we got outside, for which I'm payin' through the ass."

"Wish I knew. Radios can't do shit in this weather. They get wet, that's it. *Finito*. You got the storm, the wind, this, that. If you ask me, I don't think they're walking around. The dogs might be out in this shit, but hell, a dog ain't all that smart or he wouldn't be a dog. No, I think we got people hiding out in the garage, maybe the pool house, maybe in a car. And they don't wanna answer. Long as they don't answer, they can say they tried but the storm, blah, blah, blah. I think they're nice and dry somewhere."

"So you think I'm worryin' 'bout nothing."

"Hey, who in his right fuckin' mind's coming out in this weather. Roads are a disaster and you can forget about getting a boat through those waves. You got power lines down and you're taking your life in your hands goin' near them."

Petey George patted his thick, gray hair. "Not to worry, goombah. We got a dozen guys all over the house. No pussies. We got shooters. We got guys in both rooms on either side of you and your wife. Just you two, them and the grandchildren up here, nobody else. First pair slanted eyes we see—" He cocked his index finger. "Boom. That's all she wrote."

Sally Verna clapped him on the shoulder. "Think I'll look in on the grandchildren, then maybe lie down awhile. Thank God Chiara's resting. Says the rain relaxes her. My daughter got through before the phone lines went down. Claims she and Jim got the last available room in Manhattan. Hotels are jammed. Says they'll try to get out here tomorrow, but I told her not to worry. The kids are safe with us. Told her to stay in the city and spend money. She says her motto is Buy 'Til You Die and Shop 'Til You Drop."

Petey George smiled. "Maybe I should get married. Kid I'm going around with now comes into one trust fund when she's eighteen, another when she's twenty-five. A cool million and a quarter. Smart girl. Says going around with me is 'perverse and corrosive,' whatever the fuck that's supposed to mean. Some kind of vocabulary this kid's got. Some kind of ass, too. Gave me this badge that says 'Mozart. 400 Years Old and Looking Good.' One time she—"

The shot came from downstairs, from the back of the mansion. One shot. A gun was in Petey George's hand and he was past Sally Verna and running down the stairs three at a time. "In your room, Sal, and stay there. Lock the door and don't open it for anybody but me. Go!"

* * *

IN THE KITCHEN a guard named Gino Riviere had gone in search of a cold beer. He placed his .38 on top of the refrigerator, opened the door and using the beam of his flashlight finally located a six-pack of what was still fairly chilled beer. Gino needed the brew. He was sweating buckets—no air conditioning, locked windows and doors, the heavy humidity. Right now he'd give his left ball for the beer and maybe a dip in the ocean. The ocean would have to wait. Tonight it was the end of the world out there. Gino would settle for the beer, then it was back to watching the back door like he was being paid to do.

He slipped the flashlight under his sweating armpit, popped the top of a Bud and tilted his head back to drink. He never saw a shadow slide from under the large kitchen counter. Getting a firm grip on Gino's ankles, the shadow yanked hard. For one second Gino was suspended in the air. He dropped the beer and reached out for the top of the fridge.

A hand came down on the .38, but the gun was knocked to the floor and went off, sending a bullet into a spice rack. A second later Gino was slammed into the red-tiled floor, his skull cracking. The shadows scrambled forward, lifted a fist shoulder high and drove the knuckles of a bonehard fist into Gino's temple three times, killing him.

Shouting men were drawing closer. Footsteps rushing toward the kitchen. The shadow stepped over Gino's body, hurried across the kitchen and opened the door leading to the flooded basement. Stepping down the stairs in the pitch dark the shadow, with his excellent night vision, pulled a foot-long bamboo tube from his belt and eased into the waters of the flooded basement. He swam around and behind the staircase, keeping close to the basement wall where the protruding tube could not be seen. His job was to create a diversion. The shot would do.

In the kitchen Petey George and a half a dozen men looked everywhere. Closets, freezers, cupboards. Under tables and counters. And found nothing.

"Got to be here," said Petey George. "Son of a bitch has got to be in here. Didn't come past us and the fucking door's locked from the inside. Take a look in the basement.''

Someone did, shining a flashlight down the smooth black surface of the water. "Zilch, Petey. Fucking basement's flooded all the way up to the stairs.''

Petey George pushed through and stared down into the basement. "Tear this whole fucking house apart. But find the bastard. We got a visitor. Maybe Gino's got drunk, maybe he slipped, but I don't believe it. I think somebody's in here who shouldn't be in here.''

"But how the fuck he get past us?''

"Just find him. He's here somewhere and his ass belongs to me. Find him.''

* * *

IN THE DOWNPOUR two guards in hooded ponchos huddled under an overhang above the front door. A shit job being out here, but you didn't argue with Petey George. Even with nothing moving in this storm he still wanted men outside. Two men at all times on the door, to be relieved every couple of hours. The two on guard now had stopped parading back and forth. Fuck it. The wind was strong enough to pick you up and carry you to New Jersey and the rain was so heavy that the feel of it on your body was like being struck with a stick. Up yours, Chootch. You come out here and drown for a change.

One of the guards pointed. Two more men in ponchos coming toward them. Enzo and Rummo, the luck bastards, back from the garage. Maybe there would be some light now. The guard called out, "What's happening with the lights? You guys shoulda stayed in the garage. What are you, schmucks?''

The men in hooded ponchos kept walking until they were almost on them and then they attacked.

* * *

THE LIVING ROOM was on fire. The second *ninja* diversion. Orange flames danced brightly against the blackness. Smoke floated up to the high ceilings, remaining trapped there. Petey George shouted, "Come on, come on, move your ass. We got fire extinguishers around here somewhere. Let's get on this thing, okay? Where the fuck is everybody? Where's Enzo and Rummo?''

"They're back."

"No shit. And how come I don't know they're back. How come they don't tell me what's happening with the generator?''

"Jesus, Petey, why you asking me? They come in 'round the same time this fire starts. I seen them go upstairs same time I'm calling you about the fire. Hey, I thought maybe they went to speak to Sal or change clothes or something."

Petey George looked toward the front door. "Who's out there? Who saw Enzo and Rummo come in?"

"Ivan. Richie."

"Get 'em. Bring them here."

"Now?"

"Hey assface, anytime I tell you something it's now. Don't worry about the fire. We got insurance."

"It's just that we ain't got that many guys on the fire and if it gets out of hand—"

"If it gets out of hand, we'll all line up and piss on it. Now you gonna move your ass or what. And check the kitchen. I left Paulie and Dee out there. Just see if everything's all right."

The guard left and Petey George watched the fire. He was getting some very bad vibes, the kind you got in the ring when you hit a guy with your best shot and he wouldn't go down; he smiled at you and told you to do it again and kept smiling, kept coming forward and taking your best, then he slipped a punch and hooked to your kidney and you knew it was going to be a long night.

Generator gone. No word from the garage. No radio contact with the outside guards. Gino dead. No marks on him, but stone dead. And now this fire.

The messenger returned. "Can't find them."

"The fuck you can't find them."

"I mean there's nobody out front, nobody in the kitchen."

Petey George looked up at the second floor, where Sally Verna was. Where Enzo and Rummo had gone.

He drew his .38. "Forget the fire. You, Tony and Abe, come with me. Upstairs."

* * *

IN THE MASTER BEDROOM Sally Verna sat up in bed. *Smoke.* At his side his wife slept peacefully. Verna slipped out of bed and into his robe. A smoke alarm went off. He didn't like it. There was Chiara to worry about and the grandchildren. Taking them outside in this storm wasn't anything he wanted to do. Maybe it was a false alarm. Probably somebody playing around with the electricity.

"Grandpa."

Verna's youngest grandchild, his favorite. Five-year-old Vanessa.

"Grandpa, please." Something was wrong. The kid sounded in pain. Maybe the fire was scaring her.

And then she screamed.

Petey George's warning was forgotten. Lantern in hand, Sally hurried to the bedroom door and yanked it open. The three grandchildren stood in their pajamas, weeping. There was a red welt on Vanessa's face. She had been struck. Hard.

Verna stepped into the hall and went down on one knee, arms extended, inviting Vanessa to run to him. But she didn't. Instead her eyes went to something behind him. Sally turned to follow her gaze and saw two men in ponchos who had been hiding on either side of the door, their faces hidden by hoods.

Each held a samurai sword high overhead. The one on the right struck first, bringing the blade down on Sally's neck. The second hacked at the union leader's shoulder, slicing through thick muscle and into bone, spraying the squealing children with blood. In the lantern's light both blades rose and fell several times.

When it was over the *ninja* fled down the hall, disappearing into the smoke pouring from rooms on either side.

Petey George and his men rounded the corner to see the screaming, blood-stained children and to see Chiara stagger to the door and look down at the bloodied remains of her husband. The gray-haired woman's eyes turned up in her sockets and then, moaning, she slid to the floor.

Petey George crouched over her, feeling for the neck pulse. The other men ran along the hall banging on doors, kicking at them, opening them. "Holy shit," said one. "They're all dead in here. Cut up. Jesus, they're dead.''

"They hit us," one of the weeping children said. "They hit us to make grandpa come out.''

But a numbed Petey George didn't hear a word. He held Chiara Verna in his arms and gently closed her eyes with his fingertips. His tears fell on her still warm flesh and he held her closer, tighter, and slowly rocked back and forth. Even with the fire so near Petey George had never felt so cold and alone in his life.

15

Hong Kong

DiPALMA, with Jan Golden at his side, climbed the
faded stone steps and entered Chai Kung Woot Fat Temple. It
was midday, lunch break for the production company, and except for a handful of American and British crew members
guarding the equipment, the temple was empty. The crew on
guard sat cross-legged on the floor near the entrance, eating
Chinese food from paper cartons and washing it down with
Coca-Cola. They were complaining about the temple rule pro-
hibiting beer and wine. DiPalma watched an Englishman
make the sign of the cross over a can of Coke. "Christ turned
water into wine, didn't he," said the Brit. "So why can't he do
the same with this, seeing as how we're on holy ground, or so
I'm told."

Inside DiPalma welcomed the peace of the cool, mirrored
temple. It was an escape from Hong Kong's heat, crowds and
noise. Noise. Jackhammers and construction cranes, the high-
pitched falsetto of Cantonese opera singers in a nearby re-
hearsal hall, the disco thud-thud-thud from round-the-clock
topless bars. Street vendors, attracted by crowds watching the
filming, loudly hawking bowls of noodles, oysters grilled in
their shells and chicken blood cooked and eaten as soup. You
don't live in a town like this, thought DiPalma. You only survive.

Jan led him past dolly, crane and tripod cameras; past
lights, cables, props and cans of raw stock, unexposed film. It
was DiPalma's first time in the Temple of the Living Buddha

and he was impressed. Thousands upon thousands of mirrors from grateful worshippers who had recovered from illnesses. Mirrors that by candlelight become lustrous stars and glorious jewels. DiPalma had stopped going to church long ago, but it bothered him to see the temple invaded by a film company. It was a thought he chose not to share with Jan.

Jan herself seemed to belong to the temple. Her reddish hair caught patches of candlelight and shimmered with a fiery radiance. By candlelight her face assumed a mysterious elegance and DiPalma could easily imagine her as a temple goddess, arms spread wide, blessing the harvest. Her clothes were Japanese designed; she had been wearing them long before they were seen on the mannequins in Henri Bendel's window or in West Broadway shops. Their original and oversized silhouettes managed to complement her figure, while looking both seductive and sophisticated.

She wore an Issy Miyake white linen jacket and skirt, with a Rei Kawakubo T-shirt of black cotton and carried a shoulder bag of deep red eelskin. The effect was one of confidence and relaxed assurance. Today she was all of these things. DiPalma had watched her finesse, then, stroke, finally crack the whip with cast and crew, selecting the right approach at the right time and improvising with the skill of a great jazz musician.

In a flurry of long-distance telephone calls Jan had refused to cave in to a bullying studio executive who demanded that the due date on *Ukiyo*'s answer print be moved up; insisted the studio marketing head clear any program for promoting the movie with her before implementing it; optioned a new book and two original screenplays; and confirmed the arrival of several Kon Kenpachi films in New York for his Lincoln Center retrospective. She also confirmed the rental of sound stages in London to be used for interiors, and wrote a check for the Knightsbridge penthouse she had rented.

On the set she confronted a Chinese actress who had wept uncontrollably when criticized by Kenpachi for fluffing her lines. She agreed to speak at the Hong Kong press club and suggested a cutaway to Kenpachi, a shot of a hairy-faced, toothless old Chinese woman in the crowd outside, to be inserted between segments of the temple scene. Kenpachi agreed. She impressed the Chinese extras by speaking a few lines of their language to them and applauded when they finished shooting, causing them to break into rare smiles.

They loved her. Cast, crew, extras. DiPalma could dig it.

At the back of the temple, away from the crew members, Jan removed a small mirror from her purse and placed it on a table among dozens of other mirrors. "For my father. You're only supposed to leave a mirror here when someone's gotten over an illness. I guess I'm jumping the gun. But he's gotten worse and I figure I have nothing to lose."

And it's me who has to tell her, thought DiPalma. About her father. About Todd.

Jan stared down at her mirror. "I thanked the gods in advance for keeping him alive for one more year. I thought, why be greedy. Just ask for a year, no more. Don't ask me what gods, because I don't know. Right now, I'm desperate enough to try anything. One of our interpreters did the Chinese inscription for me."

DiPalma said, "Jan, something happened in New York yesterday, something you should know about. That's why I phoned you this morning."

"And you couldn't talk about it over the phone, you said."

"No, not over the phone. Has to do with a man named Sally Verna. Salvatore Verna."

She looked at him out of the corner of her eye. "He's a friend of my father's."

"I know. Or rather I didn't know for sure until last night. He's dead, Verna. Slaughtered in front of his grandchildren. His wife died of a heart attack when she saw his body."

"You're joking." Her fists tightened on the strap of her shoulder bag. "Jesus, you're not joking. Not you. Oh, God. Poor Sal. And Chiara. Who would do a crazy thing like that. Do they know?"

"No," said DiPalma. "But I do."

She flinched. Her lips parted.

DiPalma said, "Before I left New York Sally told me that a group called the Blood Oath League was out to kill him."

"The what?"

"Blood Oath League. A second World War secret society. Japanese. They were into assassinations, head breaking, espionage. They were connected to some very rich, very right-wing

Japanese. And to the Kempei Tai, the Japanese gestapo.''

"My father told me about the Kempei Tai. First-class bastards.''

"According to Sally, the Blood Oath League's back in business and the man who ran it then is running it now. A man who was also in the Kempei Tai. A man who should have been hung as a war criminal, but who got lucky with a little help from his friends. Zenzo Nosaka.''

She nodded, sure of what he was going to say next. "You're going to tell me that Kon's mixed up in this somehow. That because Kon and Nosaka are close friends—''

"Jan, hear me out. I didn't come here to talk about Kon.''

"God, I wish I could believe that. No offense, Frank, but you do have a reputation of getting those who got you. I just somehow see you getting back at Kon for something that happened while the two of you were beating up on each other with bamboo sticks.''

"You're reaching, Jan, and you know it. Yeah, I got even with some people. Dealers trying to blow me away. Informants who jerked me around. The sleazeball who killed my partner and left me to break the news to his wife and four kids. And the guy who killed my wife and daughter.''

She took his arm. He tried not to smell her perfume. "Shitty thing for me to say,'' Jan said. "I'm sorry.''

DiPalma thought: Kenpachi. She's sleeping with him. DiPalma's stomach started to burn.

He said, "I came here to warn you about your father. I got it from Sally, and it's beginning to look like he was being straight with me. Just after the war Kenpachi's friend Nosaka vowed to kill three men, three Americans who got him convicted of war crimes, who worked like hell to get him hung. That would be Sally himself, Duncan Ivy—''

"And my father,'' said Jan.

"Sally's dead and so's Duncan Ivy.''

"I don't know about Sal, but Duncan and his wife were killed by some kind of California cult.''

DiPalma shook his head. "No way. Cops, the press, they were all guessing out there.''

She released his arm. "For your information, my father,

Sal, Duncan, Nosaka, they've all been doing business together for years. I don't know the details and I'm not really interested. Some of it has to do with banking and running interference for Nosaka in the States. What I do know is that my father and Nosaka are definitely not enemies and haven't been for a long time."

DiPalma remembered the secret bank records he had read last night, the records Sally Verna and Jude Golden had been prepared to use against Nosaka. "The honeymoon between your father and Nosaka is over." He told her about his talk with Sally Verna, about the secret bank records and about having them taken from him at gunpoint by a well-dressed, silver-haired Australian.

"Australian?"

"You know him?"

"I think so. Rolf Nullabor. He works for my father."

"Left-handed, gray eyes, the kind of guy who'd freeze a kitten in a block of ice and drop it in a punch bowl."

Jan sighed. "That's Rolfie. A regular mean machine."

"What's he do for your father?"

"In charge of security. Bodyguard. Courier. Nobody you'd want to meet in a dark alley, that's for sure. Sadistic son of a bitch. He caught some kid driving a snowmobile on our property once. Fifteen-year-old kid. Had a dog with him. Rolf the weird poured gasoline on the dog, then burned it alive. Then he broke the kid's back. Literally broke his back. A warning to trespassers. A rotten little shit, that Rolfie. A few years ago he came on to me. Made my skin crawl. I said. 'You like sex and travel?' He drooled, oh, how he drooled. 'Indeed I do,' he said. 'Then go fuck off,' I said. Frank, the man turned eight different colors and I knew right then and there I'd made a mistake. Not in turning him down. Oh, no. My mistake was in being a wiseass, but you know me. Anyway, he got back at me in his own little way. He started leaving notes in my apartment. They'd be in the fridge, in the drawer with my underwear, in the pockets of my clothes, in my purse and even on the pillow during the night while I slept."

She shivered, remembering. "He was coming into my apartment as if there were no front door, let alone three locks. Now here's the part that really freaked me out. He left a couple of nude photographs of me behind and man, that's when I really climbed the walls.''

DiPalma said, "How'd he get pictures like that?"

"How the hell would I know? I certainly didn't pose for them, if that's what you're thinking. Rolfie's an absolute nut on any new gadget or piece of machinery that comes on the market. I guess he had some kind of long-range camera.''

"Maybe a hidden camera with a timer, some place where you'd never think to look. A miniature camera. Maybe he followed you and took the pictures when you were in a health club, or with some boyfriend.''

"All I know is I practically went broke changing the locks on my apartment. Fat lot of good that did. Rolfie managed to find a way in any time he felt like it. I never caught him at it and yes, I did go to the police.''

"What happened?''

She looked at him as though he were naive. "You're a cop and you ask me what happened? Nothing happened, that's what. No fingerprints on the notes or on the photographs or in my apartment. Except mine and those belonging to the man of the hour. No witnesses, no proof. The only thing that came out of it was I guess the cops got off looking at the pictures. Eventually Rolfie got tired of playing games and the whole thing died down. Except ever since then he's been calling me 'Butch Cassidy, the daughter Hopalong never mentions.' ''

DiPalma tapped the worn stone floor with his cane. Why steal the files when they were being brought to you? "Weird Rolf. I wonder if even he's enough to stop the Blood Oath League. That's what I wanted to see you about. Pass the warning on to your father. The Blood Oath League plans to kill him.''

"Frank, listen. You say Sal's dead. Okay. But it's very hard for me to believe that my father's going to be killed by someone who's been his friend for almost forty years. I mean, I make my living in the world of make-believe, but I don't know if I can get behind what you just told me.''

"I might not have believed it either except for one thing. Todd.''

She looked around. "Where is he?''

"Across the street with Roger Tan. Gave him money and told him to pick out any stereo cassette he wanted. My treat."

Jan grinned. "I don't believe it. You mean he actually wants one of those box radios, those ghetto blasters?"

"Last thing in the world I would have thought he'd go for. Guess there's a part of him that's like any other kid."

"That's a strange thing to say. What do you mean a part of him? Why not all of him?"

DiPalma waited a moment before speaking. It was nitty-gritty time. "Todd's got colors of his own. I guess the word is unique. I'm still trying to get used to him, frankly. He told me who killed his mother. The police didn't know and there were no witnesses. And Todd was miles away when it happened. But he knew. Turned out he was right. *Ninja*, he said. He also said *ninja* would kill Sally Verna. Happened just that way."

Jan gave him a doubtful look. "Todd told you about Sal *before* the murder?"

"Before. I finally got through to New York this morning. Had trouble with the storm last night. Jesus, I could not believe it. The kid flat out hit it. Sally's grandchildren were witnesses. They couldn't make out the faces of the guys who did it, but they did say swords. They saw Sally killed with swords That's the way the Blood Oath League took care of business in the old days. That's what Todd says is going to happen to your father."

"I don't believe it."

"Jan, Todd told me that I was in Hong Kong to get his stepfather's secret bank records. I mean he told *me*. I never mentioned that to anybody, not even to Katharine when I spoke to her from the airport. And if you remember, last night he said he was sorry about your father's illness. Jan, I didn't tell him that. I didn't know about it."

"Kon did say that Todd's unusual. Said he's a true samurai. Said they have a special relationship. Came about awfully fast. They've only known each other a matter of days." She looked at DiPalma. "You're asking me to believe Todd's psychic, that he can read the future."

"Like I said, he's been right so far."

"Or very, very lucky. Look, how can I telephone my father, who's sick enough as it is, and tell him to be alert for something called the Blood Bath League—"

"Blood Oath League."

"Whatever. I mean what do I tell him, that some kid had a vision about an old friend doing him in?"

I tried, thought DiPalma. I opened the door; she has to walk through it. "All I can do is tell you. I can't make you believe. Truth is, it's not the kind of thing I believe in myself. But I can't ignore the kid's record. He's batting a thousand. On target every time. What's more he doesn't go around bragging about it. You want anything out of him, you drag it out."

Jan said, "Speaking of keeping things quiet, there's been nothing in the papers about what happened in the hotel yesterday. I mean you would think that a cop and a drag queen found dead in the same room might merit some attention from the press. And don't tell me nobody knows about it. There are no secrets in Hong Kong, which happens to have one hundred and twenty-five newspapers. Even my interpreters were able to describe to me the fan used for homicidal purposes by one Mr. or Ms. Chiba. Kon's not talking, but that's to be expected, of course."

"Of course," said DiPalma. "Why the sudden silence? The police are partially responsible. They don't want to call any more attention to me than necessary. It's one way of avoiding telephone calls from Peking, London, the States. Anything about what happened in the hotel would be linked to Katharine's death. And the death of Ian Hansard as well. Hong Kong banks don't like nasty stories about bank presidents. Tends to make customers nervous."

"And we can't have that, can we," said Jan. "Now why do I get the feeling you're not telling all?"

"I don't know. Why?"

"Come off it. Let's have the rest of it."

"The rest of it. Let's see. The rest of it is that the press is waiting for the rest of the story, or so a police superintendent told me this morning."

"I don't understand."

"Me and Ling Shen. That's what everybody's waiting for."

Jan chewed her bottom lip and shifted her weight from one foot to another. "You could leave Hong Kong. Now."

"I've been told that."

"I see. So I'm supposed to get spastic worrying about whether or not you're going to be killed anytime soon. Here we go again. Golden's Rule. Never face the facts."

"Katharine's funeral is day after tomorrow," said DiPalma. "Then I'm off to Tokyo, to find out who sent a Japanese drag queen to kill Katharine. And why."

He was going to mention Kenpachi's name when Jan stepped closer to him and the film director was forgotten. Keep walking and keep smiling, Tiny Tim always said. But DiPalma didn't move. He was thinking what it would be like to warm his hands in the fire that was Jan's hair. And he didn't move because he felt the heat of his own hidden fire, his craving for her. Desire and want. The father of all misery.

She touched his face. A tear crept from beneath her dark glasses. "Don't die. If that happens—"

She threw herself into his arms and clung to him, her nails digging into his back. DiPalma's heart leaped. Slowly his hands came up to touch her. But then she broke away and walked toward the temple entrance. She never looked back. But then she never did.

* * *

DIPALMA STOOD at the top of the temple stairs and watched Todd hand his new box radio to Kenpachi for his approval. They stood at the base of the stairs, together with Jan, Roger Tan and Wakaba, the chauffeur. Wakaba had his back to the group as though irritated by what was going on. Once he looked over his shoulder at Todd as though he could wring his neck, then turned back to stare at the crowd. To DiPalma the bearish and surly Wakaba appeared to be playing the role of a woman scorned. With a switch-hitter like Kenpachi in the picture anything was possible.

Kenpachi pressed a button on the big radio. Marvin Gaye sang about "Sexual Healing." Don't I wish, thought DiPalma, remembering the feel of Jan near him. He watched Kenpachi hand the radio back to a pleased Todd. He said something to the boy, who nodded in agreement. Now it was DiPalma's turn to be jealous. Suspicious. Guarded. Watchful. Twenty years as a cop told DiPalma that Kenpachi knew

more about Katharine's murder than what he told the Hong
Kong police. Kenpachi and Sakon Chiba in Hong Kong at the
same time. Chiba knowing Kenpachi's telephone number. Too
many coincidences. And what did Kon Kenpachi want with
DiPalma's son? Was he interested only in Todd's knowledge
of kendo and ancient swordsmen? Was he thinking of using
Todd in a movie? Was he planning to get back at DiPalma
through Todd?

The least you could say about Kenpachi was that he was unpredictable. DiPalma knew all about his mystical side. His
desire to be a samurai, his love of mysticism, blood rituals in
particular, and his infatuation with his own beauty. Kenpachi
also revered the memory of Yukio Mishima, Japan's interna-
tionally known author and, like Kenpachi, a superpatriot with
a longing for what Mishima called "restoring Nippon to its
true state."

In November 1970 Mishima had committed *seppuku* on a
Tokyo army base, an act which in Kenpachi's opinion made
the author nothing less than a god. Kenpachi's first book had
been a flattering biography of Mishima, after whom he had
named his first son. The director had called Mishima *kensei*,
sword saint, a tribute usually reserved for only one other,
Miyamoto Musashi, the legendary seventeenth-century samurai known for *Go Rin No Sho*, A Book of Five Rings. Dealing
with the practice and strategy of swordsmanship, the book
was one which DiPalma had read and reread and never
stopped learning from.

Calling Mishima "sword saint," DiPalma knew, was
merely more evidence of Kenpachi's love of excess. Musashi
was the greatest swordsman in a nation of outstanding swordsmen. After the forty-seven Ronin he was Japan's most popular hero. Mishima had never risen above mediocre in the
martial arts.

Something else DiPalma did not like about Kenpachi. Word
was he had killed people. No one knew for sure how many,
but DiPalma had heard that rumor more than once. Kenpachi
was beyond being flaky. DiPalma had to keep Todd away
from him.

Roger Tan, perspiring in the heat, waved to DiPalma, then
held up a hand to keep him in place. Something the DEA

agent wanted to say in private. Something he didn't want anyone to hear.

"Freaking heat. What's good for crotch itch? Checked in
with my office while you were inside. There's a message from
Geoffrey Laycock. Says he has to see you toot sweet."

"Did you tell him we're checking on Katharine's funeral arrangements?"

"Yah, I told him. He says not to worry, Peking does good
work. If they say do something, it's done. He wants to see you
anyway. It's about the fan, the one that faggot used to cut up
on the cops."

"What about it?"

"Gone, Jack. Disappeared. Walked right out of the police
station."

DiPalma angrily whacked the step with his cane. Todd and
Jan looked up at him, as did Kenpachi.

Roger Tan said, "Laycock says he'll bet you a new tiara the
fan's on its way back to Japan."

"Let's go talk to him."

Together they walked down the stairs. Todd turned off his
radio, then lifted a hand in farewell to Kenpachi and joined his
father. Kenpachi smiled pleasantly at the boy and ignored Di-
Palma. Jan lifted her dark glasses to peek at DiPalma. "Take
care, Frank."

He nodded and let it go at that. For some reason he didn't
like talking to her around Kenpachi. And since DiPalma was
walking away, he gave Jan a smile. Look at me, Tiny. Walking and smiling.

Then DiPalma stopped. He did not like the way Wakaba
was looking at Todd. There was nothing inscrutable about
Wakaba's face. He loathed the boy. Why? DiPalma took a
few steps toward Wakaba, coming between him and Todd,
then stopped. Now he and the chauffeur were eyeball to
eyeball. And it was DiPalma who was getting the dirty look.

Kenpachi barked a command in Japanese. Wakaba said,
"*Hai*," and stepped back as though obeying a military command. Then he spun on his heel and walked away to stand
behind Kenpachi, arms folded, eyes all but closed.

DiPalma knew the type. Short fuse, malignant, capable of
murderous hatred. Kenpachi was smirking and saying it all

without saying a word. *He can kill you. It is something I would very much like to watch.*

DiPalma played the game. He said nothing; they understood each other. He didn't like Kenpachi, Kenpachi loathed him. And that would never change. As for the chauffeur, guys like him either tried to punch your ticket or they ignored you. When they brought it to you, they brought it good. Cold-blooded, unfeeling, remorseless. Words didn't impress them.

He walked back to Todd, who looked up at him with pride. And gratitude.

"Thank you, Frank," he said.

There was more to it, much more. Only Todd and maybe Wakaba understood. Hearing his son thank him for what he had just done made DiPalma feel better than he had in a long time.

16

JUDE GOLDEN knew he would not win tonight.

Nijo, the youngest and prettiest of his three Japanese serving girls, had become a tough opponent. After weeks of coaching she had become more daring in her strategy, unpredictable in her moves, increasingly difficult to trap. Go, with its four-thousand-year history, its squared board and black-and-white stones, was one of the most demanding and engrossing games ever invented. Westerners played it poorly. Orientals alone could truly understand Go, whose rules were simple but whose variations exceeded the number of atoms in the universe.

Nijo, despite her lack of experience, had a feel for the game; she was a deliciously treacherous adversary.

Jude Golden's heart condition had forced him to live in the most comfortable of his homes, in a red brick Victorian mansion on the outskirts of Mystic Seaport, a restored nineteenth-century Connecticut whaling village of cobblestone streets and white clapboard houses. Each of the mansion's three stories reflected his wealth and love of ease and comfort, his love of New England and Japan.

The first floor was New England, with maple, walnut and mahogany furniture dating from the 1830s, blown glass, long-cased clocks with metal disks and seventeeth-century Dutch silver tankards, two-handled cups and beakers. The second and third floors, both closed to visitors, were Japanese, Golden's private sanctuary. One floor contained straw-matted rooms divided by sliding doors, folding screens and shoji, wooden frames covered with rice paper. Golden slept and ate here, attended only by Japanese serving girls.

The top floor was an Ali Baba's cave of straw-matted rooms filled with tea ceremony utensils, jewel boxes, samurai swords with elaborate scabbards, lacquered screens, porcelain, pottery and costumes and masks from Kabuki and Noh plays. If New England was Jude Golden's wife, Japan was his mistress.

He had been born and raised sixty miles west in New Haven, but a love of clipper ships, kept on display in the harbor for tourists, had always drawn him to Mystic. In New Haven, where he was chairman and the largest stockholder in one of New England's most successful banks, he owned an Italianate mansion with a landscaped garden on Hillhouse Avenue, the street Charles Dickens had called the most beautiful in America. And he owned a condominium within walking distance of the ivy-covered buildings and green courtyards of Yale.

But his heart was in Mystic, where from his Victorian mansion he could smell the salt air from Long Island Sound and be alone with his Japanese artifacts. He loved to roam the cobbled streets lined with quaint nineteenth-century seaport homes, rigging shops, sailmaking studios, and talk with coopers, who made barrels and tubs by hand as their ancestors had done a hundred years ago for whaling expeditions. There was always something new to discover at the Mystic Marine Life Aquarium with its two thousand varieties of fish. But best of all were the tall ships in Mystic harbor.

Jude Golden owned the most beautiful of the old clipper ships. It had cost him three-quarters of a million dollars to restore the *Jan Amy*, a former China clipper named for his daughter and only child. The ship had once carried on a flourishing China trade in tea and opium, and before that had run slaves and sailed from the Atlantic coast around Cape Horn to the California gold fields. Now she rode proudly at anchor, first among equals, long, narrow and built for speed, and with a cloud of sails—skysails and moonrakers, topgallant and royal sails. She was his proudest possession.

In a straw-matted room on the mansion's second floor Jude Golden watched Nijo move to capture another of his stones. If she succeeded she would have three. Tonight's game was her best. But Golden was determined to end up the winner, to put up a real fight. For the first time he noticed that Nijo, who was seventeen, wore different color nail polish on each finger. A far cry from her namesake, a thirteenth-century Kyoto noblewoman who copied pages of Buddhist scriptures as an offering to Shinto shrines.

Nail polish and Buddhist scriptures. To Jude Golden Japan was incongruous, cultured yet crude, a mixture of mysticism and technology. In Japan illusion and reality were indistinguishable; everything meant more than it appeared to mean. The Japanese way of life was at once sophisticated and simple, immensely appealing, and Jude Golden was caught in its maze of hidden meanings.

He could not live in Japan; he was tied to America by family and career. But he could not erase from his mind the best of Japan, its mysterious past and elegant eroticism. He would have them both, the money to be made in America, the satisfaction of immersing himself in things Japanese.

Jude Golden had gone after money by fair means or foul, with an insatiable hunger. Now, on the edge of death, he saw that he had really been driven by fear. Fear of failure, fear of anti-Semitism, fear of his father. Too late he realized what he had had to do to acquire his great wealth. There was no crueler joke in life than getting what you wanted. And the cruel joke in his case was Zenzo Nosaka. Because of Nosaka, Jude Golden's past had become his present, bringing with it shadows and pain.

Jude Howard Golden was in his early sixties, a tall, square-faced descendant of Russian Jews, with graying, thinning hair and a whining cordiality which often hid the fraudulent man behind it. He headed the third largest bank in the East, founded by his father. Until his recent heart attacks, Golden had traveled thousands of miles on bank business each year, adding new names to his file of over ten thousand foreign politicians and businessmen whom he knew personally.

Under his leadership the bank's overseas branches increased, its stock doubled in value from 1970 to 1980 and its credit-card and traveler's-check operations had become one of the most successful in America. His father and other Jewish immigrants had started the bank in 1920, the year Jude

Golden was born. It was their answer to the snobbish anti-Semitism of the New England corporations and commercial banks of that time.

"A long time ago," his father once said to him, "I believed that money was the only thing in life that mattered. Then I was right. And now I am just as correct. With it we Jews create our own golden age. With money we bring order to our lives. I tell you something: when it comes to money we share the same religion with the goyim, except they are too stupid to realize it."

His father, a hard-driving man who had arrived in America penniless, never forgave an insult. Jude Golden grew up watching him make the WASP banking world pay for its snobbery and discrimination. Under the elder Golden, the fledgling New Haven bank aggressively sought out mergers during the Depression, bought shares in foreign banks, built the tallest building in New Haven and was one of the first banks to make loans to multinational corporations.

Jude Golden's father lived long enough to become one of the most influential bankers in the East and to savor the WASPs' sending their Ivy League-educated sons to him to learn banking. But Jude was not as strong or as uncompromising as his father. He was a man of fragile health, insubstantial character, sly and secretive.

He was also calculating and shrewd, with an excellent memory and a talent for gathering useful information. With a law degree from Yale and his father's influence he went into World War II with a lieutenant's commission and was assigned to the Judge Advocate General's Office. He was stationed first in Hawaii; then when the war ended he was sent to Japan to try war criminals.

Jude Golden would always look upon that time as the happiest of his life. To convict the Japanese warlords, generals and admirals who had once terrorized the world, was so exhilarating that he ignored his health and worked harder than he ever had in his life. Zenzo Nosaka was one of the biggest convictions Golden worked on, a man almost in a class with Himmler and Martin Bormann. On the day Nosaka received his death sentence Golden and the other members of his team celebrated with sake until they passed out in a geisha house.

But Nosaka didn't hang. The United States needed him to fight a new war, the cold war.

"How the world turns," said Salvatore Verna. "We team up with Uncle Joe to kill the Japs and now we're teaming up with the Japs to go bang-bang at Uncle Joe. Somebody tell me if I'm crazy or what."

"Life is licking sugar off broken glass," said Duncan Ivy.

"Hey Dunk, I think maybe you been in this here fuckin' country too long. Either that or somebody told you you were profound when you were a kid and you ain't been able to let go the idea."

"Salvatore, my friend, I was merely pointing out that in life things go right and they go wrong. Up and down, the waxing and the waning. Sun and shadow. Constant change, with uncertainty as the only certainty."

"Your ass. How's that. In any case Nosaka goes back to his cell to beat his meat for the next twenty years when all he should be doing is hangin' by his nuts for what he's done to people."

Jude Golden said, "Nosaka will go free."

"You're crazy," said Verna. "They ain't hangin' the bastard, that's all. He's still gonna be inside looking out for a long time."

"The word is *free*," said Jude Golden. "Mark my words. It's the old story of the camel. You let him put his nose in your tent so he can keep it warm. Then his head's in. Next comes his front paws. Then one hump, followed by the other hump. Before you know it, the camel's inside and you're out in the cold. Nosaka has his nose in the tent. Watch what happens next."

Jude Golden's father had told him how the medieval Jews had come to control banking. All other occupations had been closed to them and there were laws preventing Christians from earning interest. The Jews had no armies, but they had their brains and knew that to protect their banking business they would have to know all about the goyim. So with banking came one of the first and most efficient spy systems. Even the goyim came to learn that ignorant bankers did not survive and that a banker without means of espionage was a banker doomed to failure. Knowing a single important fact

and knowing it in time offered a banker more protection than
he could receive from a battalion.

Realizing the importance of Nosaka's information, Jude
Golden knew that the Japanese would not hang. American intelligence agencies had to keep him alive because they were
hungry for anything they could get on Russia, the new enemy.
Golden also knew that Nosaka could eventually talk himself
out of prison. Once free, in the pragmatic tradition of Japan,
he would turn for help to those who had tried to kill him.

Little favors at first. Then larger favors and each time there
was a payment in exchange for services rendered. The camel
now came bearing gifts. But as Jude Golden came to see, Nosaka was still a camel intent on having his own way. Golden,
Verna and Ivy's association with him was so prosperous that
the Americans were blinded to the knowledge that one day
there would be a big bill due.

It was Jude Golden's father who told him that he was committing his worst sin for a man he should have despised.

"He was with them, the Nazis," said the elder Golden.
"That makes him *dreck*. There are some things a man should
not do even for money."

"Nosaka's breaking no law in his own country."

"You think that means you're breaking the law?" The old
man touched his chest. "You are breaking the law in here.
Here. From the army you know people in the spy business all
over the world and you use them to help this Jap bastard and
make yourself rich."

"I do it for the bank. Your bank."

"You don't fool me, sonny boy. You do it for yourself.
Commitment you don't got. Except maybe to yourself, to
your Japanese girl friends. You think because you are involved with the bank, you care. Well, I tell you what is commitment. You take a plate of ham and eggs, excuse the expression. The chicken lays the eggs and that makes him involved.
The pig he furnishes the ham. That makes him committed to
something. When you get like that pig, then you are committed to something. Now you ain't."

"If I'm not committed to the bank, why is it making more
money than ever?"

"I tell you why. Because you like to plan, to scheme, to set a thing in motion, then sit back and watch what happens. Mr. Organizer. You are on the sidelines watching us poor bastards fight in the pit, which is a bad something to say about your own son, but I'm too old to lie. Lie down with dogs, you get up with fleas. That Jap is worse than a dog and he does not change. I tell you, he is the same man he always was. And don't tell me about legal in Japan. Some things just are not right. Not right.''

Jude Golden could have told his father that times had changed, that things were different now and the idea of right had changed. But he said nothing. Even his father knew Jude Golden had been born weak and that weakness intensified during the years with Nosaka. After the death of Jan's mother, it was Nosaka who had sent the first of the young Japanese "comfort girls." She was replaced by others, girls recommended by Japanese business associates, girls selected by Golden himself during his trips to Japan. During their stay with the American banker they were treated well, given cash and gifts, and served him with the submissiveness due a Japanese man. The girls were the same, none older than twenty-four, attractive, able to sing, dance and play Japanese musical instruments.

It was a comfortable, well-ordered world. Golden had money, a touch of Japan in his Connecticut mansion and his beloved clipper ship within walking distance of his home. Nosaka's vow to kill him was meaningless. Until a bad heart, the worst of Golden's many illnesses, all but gave out. The sharp pain in the left arm, a terrifying tightness in his chest, the difficulty in breathing. He knew without question what it was and that it was serious.

Two heart attacks within months. The best heart specialists held out no hope; it was only a question of when. His eyes were going to close in death and all of his treasures would be lost to him forever. Approaching death forced him to see his life for what it was, a house built on quicksand, a series of shortcuts. He had allowed Nosaka's manipulations to become his curse.

Commitment. Too late for that now. He was committed to Jan, but she no longer needed him. She was on her own, a successful television producer who was determined to make it in movies. He had written the obligatory checks to Israel, hired minorities to work in his bank and allowed his employees to buy stock. What else could he do? He thought of his father, of what he might say, and that was when Jude Golden decided that before he died he would destroy Nosaka.

Once committed to the idea, help came. Private reports from Japan included information on the murders of two Japanese businessmen. The murderers could have been terrorists, but the use of swords or knives reminded Golden of the Blood Oath League. When other businessmen were hacked to death in Rome, São Paolo and Buenos Aires, Golden checked with Japanese sources and learned that the Blood Oath League was indeed operating again. At least two people told him that Zenzo Nosaka, if not the leader of the new league, was a financial backer. But Nosaka was too important to challenge without overwhelming proof, and so far Jude Golden didn't have it.

Golden the organizer fitted the pieces together. Nosaka was old and, like Golden, facing death. It was time for both men to put their houses in order, to prepare for that journey to an unknown place. The Japanese industrialist was a descendant of samurai, an ultranationalist, and the spilling of blood for Japan's greater glory was nothing new to him. Then and now the purpose of the Blood Oath League was the same. In Japan the past and the present, as always, was one.

Which also meant that if Golden and his fellow war-crimes prosecutors had forgotten the promise made to kill them, Nosaka had not. The industrialist had now decided to act on that promise.

Golden had to act, too, but how? How could he effectively destroy the man who was Japan's most effective spymaster since the legendary Hideyoshi? This became the commitment Golden's father had always wanted him to make.

Ian Hansard, the English banker in charge of the Hong Kong branch of Nosaka's bank, came up with the answer. Golden had helped form the bank, had sat on the board with Verna and Ivy and had drawn in other prominent Americans, men with information and connections for sale.

At Golden's last meeting with Hansard, the Englishman had complained bitterly about Nosaka, giving Golden the weapon he needed to fulfill his commitment.

"I didn't think he'd actually go through with it," said Hansard. "Letting me go and all. But he's certainly planning to do it. Already the bastard's ordered a few of my duties transferred to some Japanese in the bank and he's given me vice-presidents, two to be exact, that I neither requested or need."

"That's the Japanese way," Golden said. "You're a *gaijin*, a westerner, an outsider. The Japanese pick your brains, then do it their way. As soon as they learn all you have to offer, the game's over. You're gone."

"I'm beginning to get the picture. Don't like it one little bit. It's me who's made this bank successful, not bloody high-and-mighty Nosaka. My brains, my sweat, my hard work. And what thanks do I get? Out on my arse with nothing to show for it."

Jude Golden said, "Oh, please, let's not be dramatic. You'll have plenty to show for it. Like those numbered accounts in Panama, Zurich and Amsterdam."

Hansard puckered his small mouth. "I don't know what you're talking about."

"The hell you don't. We're all victims in this life, but you really don't have to overdo it. I've always lived with the thought that to believe is to believe the worst, so I've made a point of knowing everything there is to know about people I do business with. And wouldn't you know it? Most of what I learn comes under the heading of the worst. Take you, for example. Those numbered accounts I mentioned. Even Nosaka doesn't know about them. If he did, you might have a problem."

Hansard chewed on a thumbnail. "Fascinating. Absolutely fascinating."

"You've been playing fast and loose with Nosaka's money. I could say stealing, but that's a strong word. Working your magic, shall we say, in such out of the way places as South America, Africa and the Arab world. Oh you're smart. You don't do a thing here in Hong Kong or anywhere in the Pacific where Nosaka spends most of his time. You're wheeling and dealing where he can't see you, where the lines of communication are stretched pretty thin."

Hansard said, "You do have a long nose. But that's an af-

fliction with your people, isn't it? Hell hath no fury like a Jew
who's been outfoxed by a wog." He lifted his drink. "I give
you Zenzo Nosaka, who's bloody well put the sharp end to us
all, you included. So what do we do now? May I inquire how
you got on to me?"

"You mean how did I come upon your creative accounting?
First let me say you're very good with computers and yes, I
know you erased all the tapes. And the phony companies you
formed to do business with your own bank are dissolved immediately after serving your purpose. And that business of
going after unclaimed bank funds in those out of the way
branches. Clever. You always manage to hire the most believ-
able false claimants. Though in the matter of certain loans to
companies which have no intention of repaying, companies in
which you have a hidden interest, well, I'd go a little slow in
that department in the future if I were you. But that's just my
opinion."

"You've made your point. Now what do you intend doing
about it?"

"Surprise. Nothing."

Hansard waited.

Golden said, "*You're* going to do something about it. Oh,
in answer to your question about how I came to know. Bekaa
Valley. Lebanon."

Hansard looked shaken. "How in God's name did you
learn about *that*?"

"As you might put it, us Yids stick together."

Hansard frowned and then the answer came to him. "Mos-
sad. You've got the bloody Israeli secret service working for
you. Christ, I should have known."

"The PLO makes millions off the marijuana it grows
there," said Golden. "You launder their money. Quietly. For
twice the going rate. And not through Eastern Pacific, which
costs Nosaka a pretty penny. You're supposed to do everything through him while in his employ. I believe that's one of
his rules. You know how the Japanese believe in teamwork
and toiling for the greater good."

"What is it I'm going to do regarding your newfound
knowledge of my activities?"

"Get me everything you know about Eastern Pacific, about

Nosaka's industrial spying, bribery, payoffs, blackmail. Anything that's damaging."

"That's all? Why don't I stick my head in a cannon or try wing walking on a cross-Atlantic flight. Are you mad? On second thought, I can't bloody well say no, can I?"

Golden said, "Our arrangement won't work if I attempt to blackmail you. I don't want that. I've learned one thing from Nosaka: make the game worth the candle. I want the best job you can do, nothing less. My health's bad and that's a major problem, one I don't care to go into right now. Before I go, I want to get Nosaka. I have reason to believe he's out to kill me."

Hansard smiled. "Is he, now. Pity."

"You don't seem surprised."

"You haven't exactly endeared yourself to me these past few minutes."

"That could change," Golden said.

"Oh?"

"When you have all of the information you think could ruin Nosaka, information that could bring him to trial in a dozen countries, then contact me. Don't write or telephone me about this until you have it all. There's a chance Nosaka might be bugging my phones or watching me. When you have what you think I want, let me know and we'll do a deal."

"Will we now. What to your mind constitutes a deal under these circumstances?"

"Three million dollars for you. Cash on delivery."

Hansard blinked.

"Take it or leave it," said Golden. "One way or another you're finished with Nosaka."

Hansard leaned back in his chair. He cleared his throat and swallowed hard. Three million dollars. Just like that. And Golden could easily afford it. Ian Hansard, he said to himself, you may just be in luck, in real luck.

* * *

IN THE STRAW-MATTED ROOM Jude Golden removed the oxygen mask from his face and turned off the tank. He breathed easier; the slight constriction in his chest was gone and his face felt less heated. He glanced at his watch, then back at the Go board, where he had surrounded one of the few white stones left to Nijo. 11:15. Almost time for the nurse to buzz him on the intercom with her annoying reminder that bedtime was twelve midnight sharp.

The midnight bedtime was the only compromise he and the implacable nurse had been able to work out. Golden, a life-long insomniac, rarely went to bed before four or five in the morning, preferring to nap during the day. The nurse, black Irish and hard as nails, had insisted he turn in no later than nine. To make sure, she had injected him at 8:55 with what she called a "sleepy-weepy." With that safely in his bloodstream, she then smugly dismissed him for the night.

Golden defeated her easily. Even with the injection he slept no more than three hours, then immediately buzzed the nurse and woke her up. A few nights of this warfare and a midnight bedtime was agreed upon, provided he had napped previously. Thereafter he rarely disturbed the nurse before her normal wakeup time of 6:30 A.M.

On a corner of the go board nearest her, Nijo fought capture and defeat. Rigid with concentration, she sat with both hands in her lap, focused on the cluster of small black and white stones. Two more moves and Golden would close the trap. In true Japanese fashion she would not give up without an intense struggle. Surrender was out of the question; Golden would have to defeat her decisively. To do otherwise was to risk losing her respect and what Nijo did not respect she ignored.

There was a dignity and grandeur about her that could have kept Golden watching the beautiful girl for hours. He was drawn by her perseverance, by her belief in herself. She had the courage for action and to be near her made Golden regret that he had not taken a more active part in life. There was something healthy and invigorating about Nijo. Even the other girls were drawn to her; despite being the newest and youngest, Nijo had quickly become their leader, the one who insisted they try new foods, visit new shopping malls, imitate the new dance steps seen on television and risk the new fashions, American or Japanese. In a dark and dead world Nijo was vital and garden fresh and Golden, who usually tired of girls after a few months, was infatuated with her.

The telephone rang. It was a private phone, kept locked in a honey-colored box and carried with Golden wherever he went in the mansion. The unlisted number was changed frequently, and the lock combination only Golden knew. As Nijo watched, Golden drew the box to him and began spinning the lock. Seconds later he lifted the top of the box and reached inside for the telephone receiver.

"Dad? It's Jan. Hello?"

"Gyp, how are you? What are you doing calling me on this line?" Gyp was short for Gypsy, a nickname given to Jan because of a teenage addiction to wildly colored shirts, head scarves and hoop earrings.

She sounded worried. "Are you all right?"

"As all right as can be expected. We've had a big storm here. Did some damage to the ship, but nothing that can't be repaired. Why? Do you know something I don't know?" He smiled at Nijo and mouthed *my daughter*. Nijo bowed and returned his smile.

Jan said, "Yesterday when we talked there was some trouble with your pacemaker. I tried the hospital, but they said you had checked yourself out."

"False alarm, Gyp. Not to worry. Sounds worse than it was. Had a few anxious moments, but it seems my pacemaker's functioning as it ought to. Right now I'm relaxing with one of the girls and enjoying a fast game of Go. You know me. The original night owl. What time is it there?"

"A little after one in the afternoon. Dad, let me ask you something. Where is Rolf Nullabor right now, this moment?"

Golden toyed with his obi, the sash he wore around his summer kimono. "I had the impression you weren't too fond of Rolf. Why the sudden interest?"

"I don't give a damn if he lives or dies, if you want to know the truth. Just tell me if he's in Hong Kong or not."

Golden looked at Nijo. Should he send her from the room? And then she slowly pulled her kimono down from her shoulders, baring her breasts. Lovely. Small, firm breasts. Grecian in proportion. Totally unlike the udders which passed for breasts in America.

Golden watched as Nijo took a vial of oil from the pocket of her kimono. She poured some into the palm of one hand and slowly oiled her breasts. Golden's throat went dry.

"Dad? Are you there?"

Golden watched Nijo squeeze her right breast, now shiny with oil, and stroke the nipple with a lavender-tipped thumb. "Here, Gyp. Right here. You mentioned Rolf. Yes, he's in Hong Kong."

"Oh, God. He was right."

Something in her voice jerked his thoughts away from Nijo. "Who was right? Have you talked with Rolf?"

"You've got to be kidding. I wouldn't go near that ding-a-ling with a whip and a chair. Someone I know claims Rolf robbed him last night at gunpoint. It has something to do with a group called the Blood Oath League and with your friend Nosaka."

Golden picked up a black stone from the Go board and began kneading it between thumb and forefinger. "Who are we talking about?"

"Frank DiPalma. He's in Hong Kong. He says you and Sal know why he's here. I heard about Sal and Chiara, by the way. Frank says the Blood Oath League killed them, that Nosaka was behind it and that you're next."

"DiPalma, DiPalma. That would be the television news guy. Crime reporter. Big fellow, gray hair, raspy voice."

"Daddy, no games, please. You know damn well who Frank DiPalma is. I've told you about him, you've seen him on the tube, so let's stop the bullshit."

"Never did get to meet him."

"Let's not go into that," said Jan. "I didn't want to discuss my family with Frank. He's a reporter and will bird-dog a story until he gets what he wants. I ended up playing dumb, rather than hurt you."

"Hurt me? How?"

Jan said, "Dad, before grandpa died I remember you and him arguing about Nosaka. I wasn't that interested, but I do recall one thing. Grandpa thought Nosaka was a shit. But you said business was business and that Nosaka was no worse than anybody else. Maybe so, maybe not. I really don't have all the facts, but Fran did tell me that Nosaka planned to kill you, Duncan and Sal. You've probably forgotten that you told me the same thing a long time ago. I didn't tell Frank because I don't want him coming after you. Also, I have a movie to make. It's my first and if I don't do it right there won't be a second. I don't want Frank complicating my life at the moment."

"But you called me," said Golden.

"You're my father. You're damn right I called you. Daddy, Sal and Duncan are dead. You're the only one left and I'm worried. And for God's sake don't talk to me about coincidence. I'm getting bad vibes from all of this."

Nijo pushed her breasts together, bowed her head and touched the nipples with the tip of her tongue. Golden closed his eyes in order to concentrate. He wanted desperately to keep Jan away from anything to do with Nosaka. When she had hired Kenpachi to direct her first film there had been no thought of Golden going after Nosaka, his longtime business partner. That came later, after the murders of Duncan Ivy and the others, after learning that the Blood Oath League had been resurrected with Nosaka behind it. Kenpachi, unfortunately, was too close to Nosaka; the two shared right-wing political views; for all Golden knew, Kenpachi, too, could be involved with the Blood Oath League. The film director intended to go overboard for his beliefs.

But for Golden to talk his daughter out of working with Kenpachi meant telling her things Golden didn't want her to know. Things about himself and the way he ran his business life. Things about himself and Nosaka.

Time enough to tell her when he had the files, when he knew exactly what he had to use against Nosaka. It was unlikely that anyone as stubborn as Jan could be convinced to fire Kenpachi, unless she herself caught him with the smoking gun. Jan was stubborn, ambitious, determined to succeed and unwilling to be controlled by her father or any other man.

Her life was movement and freedom; she scorned indecision, inactivity. It was more prudent to let her finish the film and get rid of Kenpachi, leaving Golden free to go after Nosaka. Jan would have the career she wanted. And Golden could fulfill a commitment his father would have been proud of.

Golden said to his daughter, "Rolf was in Hong Kong to get certain bank records for me."

"With a gun. Why send Rolf for those records when according to Frank he was bringing them back for you and Sal?''

Golden closed his fist around the black stone. "Sal only wanted to use the records to blackmail Nosaka, to make him back off and leave us alone. I want to finish Nosaka permanently. There's a difference. In any case, I saw no reason to argue the point with Sal. I mean why cause *tsuris* if you don't have to.''

"Let me get this straight. You let Sal think the two of you were partners, in agreement on whatever it is you're planning, when all along you had your own ideas of how to go about it.''

"Jan, please.''

"Always turning it to your advantage, aren't you. Everybody's some kind of commodity to you, nothing more. Sal was your friend and you strung him along. Daddy, that sucks.''

Japanese history and Hideyoshi taught me well, he thought. Send two teams of spies after information, with one team assigned to watch the other. Yes, Golden and Sal had agreed on the value of Hansard's records. The difference lay in how each proposed to use them. Golden wanted to draw blood. Sal would never have agreed. But, then, his opinion no longer mattered.

Golden said, "Jan, if Nosaka's after me—I say if—then nothing's going to stop him. I know the man. Sal's way would not have worked, believe me. With Nosaka it's hardball, or you don't play.''

"So Frank's right about Rolf. And you're saying he's right about Nosaka. What about Kon Kenpachi. Is he involved in any of this?''

"Far as I know, Kenpachi's not involved. And yes, Rolf is bringing the bank records to me. I don't want you to worry about Nosaka and me. One way or another, it'll work itself out.''

As he spoke Nijo moved the Go board aside, then leaned over and oiled the soles of his feet. The effect was soothing; the tension of thinking about Nosaka slackened. Then Nijo lay down at his feet and took his big toe in her mouth. The effect was galvanizing; a pleasurable jolt sped up his leg to his brain, invigorating him in seconds.

Nijo removed the toe from her mouth, blew on it, filling Golden's body with an exquisite chill. He trembled as she rubbed the oiled sole of his foot against her oiled breast in slow circles. It was a delectable sensation.

With an effort he forced himself to speak to his daughter. "Jan, the man who gathered those bank records for me was Ian Hansard. But he died just before DiPalma arrived. How did DiPalma come up with those records?"

"Through his son, who by the way predicted Sal's murder and also predicted you'd be in trouble with the league. Seems the boy has ESP or something like it."

Nijo, now lying on her back, closed her eyes and pushed off her kimono. Naked, she used one hand to rub Golden's left foot against her breasts. With the other hand she began to masturbate.

Golden opened his kimono and cupped his hardening penis.

"Psychic powers," he said. "I didn't know DiPalma was married."

"He's not. He fathered the boy, Todd, by a Chinese girl."

"Ah yes. Katharine Hansard. Who also died recently."

Jan said, "She was killed by some Japanese transvestite, who was shot to death by a policeman. Apparently Todd helped Frank find this transvestite. Frank says there might be something to the boy's predictions. Dad, I want you to take care of yourself. Just be on guard, okay?"

"That department's well taken care of. I have alarms, closed-circuit television, armed guards, you name it."

Ninjo fingered herself faster. Golden's penis was hard and warm in his hand. He couldn't stop looking at her.

"Gyp, I've got to run. Some hag of a nurse is hovering over me with my medicine and I can't get out of it. I'll be fine, believe me. Rolf will see to that. You just hurry up and finish that film of yours so I can see it before I die."

"Dad, you know I will."

"One other thing I want you to do, Gyp. If this boy of DiPalma's comes up with any predictions you think I ought to know about, get on the horn, will you?"

When he had hung up, the nurse Southy buzzed him on the intercom. "Twenty minutes, Mrs. Lyons. Then come upstairs."

And then Nijo, her face contorted, climaxed, pulling his
foot into her breasts, pushing her pelvis off the floor, the
thumb and forefinger of her right hand pinching her clitoris.
Then she fell back against the floor and rolled over to embrace
Golden's feet and ankles. Submissive. *Hai. And he was her
lord.*

Golden took her in his arms, pulled her on top of him and
fell back to the mat, mouth on hers, loving her, loving her.

No bad memories, no thought of death, no reality. Only
Nijo, who was in his life so that he did not have to deal with
himself, and who was in his arms and was all he wanted to
know.

* * *

NIJO LAY AWAKE, her back to Jude Golden, who was
snoring slightly. Both lay on the floor, on the comfortable
Japanese futon. She stretched out patiently. The injections
given by the nurse had now taken effect, and he slept deeply.

Shortly before 1:00 A.M. she sat up, looked down at Jude
Golden with loathing and wiped her mouth with the back of
her hand, wiping away the taste of him. Nude, she rolled away
from the bedding and sat up, her arms wrapped tightly around
her knees.

Nijo stared at Golden's form in the darkness. She hated the
touch of him, hated the medicine smells and the old-man odor
which clung to him, his sickly white flesh, his pretense of
knowing Japan and the Japanese. He was a *gaijin*, an outsider, a Westerner, a barbarian. He would never know Japan
nor understand its people, not if he lived to be a hundred.

She wept and thought of the day when she would return to
Japan. She no longer lived in the present; her life was a future
shaped by dreams of what Nosaka-san would do for her after
the hated *gaijin* was destroyed. Squeezing herself more tightly,
she rocked back and forth, back and forth, and did her best to
stop thinking about home.

17

Hong Kong

FRANK DIPALMA, amused, watched the two Chinese policemen, seated on the far side of the crowded tearoom, busy themselves with a fan-tan game and pretend not to be interested in him. Both wore light green summer uniforms with red tabs on the shoulders, indicating they spoke English. Neither was a good actor. DiPalma knew their game the second he walked through the door. He had seen customers near the entrance glance at the cops, then at him and back at the cops. No secrets in Hong Kong, paisan.

In fan-tan an unknown number of buttons are placed under an inverted cup, then counted out in groups of four. The players then bet on how many buttons are left in the last group to be removed, a number always between one and four. A lack of interest in their game indicated the cops were in the tearoom to sit on DiPalma. The younger of the cops would lift up the cup, slide out his buttons, then look at DiPalma out of one eye as if to say *hey was that a smart move or what?*

It was the older one who finally stopped pretending. He shifted in his seat until his back was against a marble-backed bench and drank his tea looking directly at DiPalma. DiPalma grinned and showed a palm in greeting; the cop looked through him as though he were invisible. DiPalma liked that. A real professional.

The same, however, could not be said for Geoffrey Laycock. From the moment DiPalma, Todd and Roger Tan had entered the small tearoom on Pottinger Street, a ladder street because of its vertical steps, the British journalist had been restless. He had been sitting alone, shifting around teacups, saucers and teapots, nervously drumming his fingers on the table. Even after they sat down with him he continued to toy with cups and saucers, eventually snapping at a waiter in perfect Cantonese to bring new cups and saucers, and be quick about it.

Surrounded by whirling ceiling fans, potted palms, black-wood tables and brass spittoons, Laycock in his white linen suit reminded DiPalma of an island colonial official gone native. The jittery Brit seemed to belong in the tearoom, with its Chinese menu in characters and traditional Chinese teacups with small lids instead of handles. Laycock was a reminder that at the beginning of this century his country had ruled a fourth of the world's area and population.

The waiter returned with the fresh cups and saucers. Laycock said, "I'll be mother, shall I?" and began to pour.

In deference to DiPalma's stomach, Laycock had ordered green or fermented tea, slightly scented and taken hot and straight—no lemon, sugar or milk. The lid on the cup was adjusted so that only the liquid passed into one's mouth.

Laycock sipped his tea and sighed. "Orgasmic. Positively orgasmic." He glanced around the packed tearoom before concentrating on DiPalma and Todd. The boy, wearing a connected headset, had given his full attention to the new radio on his lap.

Laycock whispered, "A contact in the police station told me about the fan this morning. Apparently it disappeared during the night. Of course no one has the slightest idea how this came about."

"Of course," said DiPalma. He wasn't surprised. Hong Kong was Hong Kong. Almost everything here was for sale, including the police. A war fan like the one used by Sakon Chiba could easily have been traced to its owner. DiPalma scratched an eyebrow. Hell, it still could be traced. He knew what it looked like. All he had to do was get out of Hong Kong alive, go to Tokyo and start asking questions. But he wasn't going until after Katharine's funeral two days from now. Fuck Ling Shen. DiPalma owed Katharine. And he owed Todd. He would have to take his chances for the next two days and hope that bird dogs like the two cops sitting by the front door would discourage Shen or at least slow him down. Even as the words flashed into his mind DiPalma knew that it wasn't true. Shen was going to have to make a move or lose face. And maybe lose his life for no longer acting like a true leader.

Laycock jerked his head toward the entrance. "You have company, old sock. Albert and Victoria are pretending to be caught up in the mysteries of fan-tan while contorting themselves into permanent paralysis by sneaking a peek at you. Rather transparent, wouldn't you say?"

"It would warm everybody's heart if I got dusted somewhere besides Hong Kong. Frick and Frack are sitting on me in the hope of discouraging Shen."

"Vain hope, wouldn't you say?"

"Fucking optimist we got here," said Roger Tan. "Is that why you're acting strung out? Nervous Nelly afraid she'll get caught in the cross fire?"

The Englishman fingered his bow tie and slowly turned toward Tan. "Oh dear. Vexed and cheesed off, are we? I'll wager it has something to do with requesting a transfer out of Hong Kong and having it denied."

"That's how you get shit on your mustache," said Tan. "You're looking for love in all the wrong places. But you're still smiling. Nobody happier than a golden-shower queen who's made it to the store in time for the one-cent beer sale."

Whoa, thought DiPalma. He watched Laycock's face redden, then saw something else, a look Laycock had never shown before. Eyes narrowed into a steely gaze. Face an unyielding mask. DiPalma had seen that look before, on men who were stone killers. Like the Cuban in Washington Heights who had killed his mother, then cooked pieces of her flesh and fed them to his dogs.

The look passed from Laycock's face. He relaxed, laying a small, damp hand on Roger Tan's forearm. "I do apologize, dear boy, for telling tales out of school. My problem, you see, is that I'm never at my best from sunrise to sunset."

He turned to DiPalma. "I'm also in a flap over you, dear heart. I do so want to be the first to get your complete story, which includes Shen. We're all waiting for the other shoe to fall. Have a vested interest in it, you might say."

"What's a vested interest?" asked DiPalma.

"Various and sundry wagers. Bets have been placed as to how long you'll manage to stay alive in Hong Kong. There were some who bet you'll live no longer than one hour. Forgive the pun, but they were dead wrong. Those who wagered you'd go to Jesus yesterday are also out of the running."

"How did you bet?"

"*Moi?*" Laycock's hand was over his heart.

"How much?"

The journalist looked at the ceiling. "How much." He gave DiPalma a thoughtful look. "A strong show of faith on my part, actually. Two thousand Hong Kong dollars at ten to one that you would live until Saturday."

"The day after Katharine's funeral. Yeah, that's a show of faith, all right." He sipped his tea. "So tell me about the fan."

"Nothing to tell, old boy. Gone, vanished, missing. No one seems to know a thing about it. Chiba's remains are still in custody, however. No one's come forward to claim them."

"Not even Kenpachi?"

"Not even Kenpachi. Oh, I did hear something about Chiba. Seems he did quite a bit of traveling. Europe, California, the Middle East and even throughout Japan. No one seems to know why."

"With the Japanese nothing is what it seems to be. For all we know, Chiba could have been an Avon lady or a Bible salesman. Something else for me to check out when I get to Tokyo."

"I'll give you something to check out in Tokyo," Roger Tan said. "Check out Japanese influence with Chinese Triads."

"What for?"

"Because nothing happens in Hong Kong without the Triads being in on it. Because a Japanese fan walked out of police headquarters with the help of one of the Triads in this town."

DiPalma leaned forward.

Tan said, "Triads own this town, Jack. And they own the cops or enough of them. You got cops who are in the Triads. I hear tell that one or two high-ranking cops are *Cho-kuns*,

Triad subchiefs. You want to reach the cops for something that isn't kosher, you have to deal with the Triads or you don't deal at all.''

Roger Tan stood up and stretched. "Better get my ass down to the office and show my face. If I stay out too long my supervisor gets antsy and starts checking my expenses too closely. Man's got it in for me. Sooner I get out of this shit hole, the better. Frank, check with you later.'' He tapped Todd on the shoulder. The boy looked up from his radio and smiled.

When Roger Tan had gone Laycock said, "Getting to be rather testy, our Roger. Still, he could well have a point. About the Triads and that fan.''

DiPalma finished his tea and put the cup down. A hand went up in refusal, halting Laycock's attempt to refill the empty cup. "Roger's sharp. Good head for collecting intelligence, but not the most diplomatic guy around. Frustrated over not being promoted. But he does know his stuff. Time for Todd and me to get rolling, too. Got to finish checking on Katharine's funeral arrangements. Chinese funerals are hell to arrange. Christ, I hate to think what it would be like having to do all this without Peking's help.''

Laycock said, "Delightful thing, power. Both a means and an end. Sometimes I think it exists only in its perception or in the opinion of others. Sometimes I wonder if it really does corrupt. Well, dear boy, do keep in touch. And do your best to stay alive at least until Saturday.''

He poured more tea for himself. "They say gambling causes you to lose your money or your character. At this stage of my life I so much want to hold on to what little I possess of both.''

* * *

DIPALMA LEANED FORWARD in the taxi and threw up. Then, breathless and shivering, he fell back against the seat and forced his eyes open as wide as possible. His eyelids weighed a ton; he stared through slits, barely able to see as far as his knees. His ears rang and with the ringing came a whistling sound which reminded him of a boiling teakettle. He felt chilled, as though he were sitting naked in snow. Seconds ago he had been perspiring, his shirt drenched and leaving a wet imprint on the leather seat. He willed himself to move his hand, lifting it from his thigh and placing it on his stomach. No feeling in the hand. Not a goddamn bit of feeling in either hand.

He hadn't felt this sick in a long time. Not since the shooting eleven years ago in Hong Kong.

From miles away he heard the Chinese driver curse him in very obscene Cantonese. And he heard a worried Todd, seated beside him, call his name and lay a hand on his cheek. Todd then said something in Cantonese to the driver, who angrily waved him away. It was late afternoon and the driver, who had yet to be paid after driving DiPalma and Todd around for hours, was losing patience in the heat and traffic.

Having driven several places to confirm Katharine's funeral arrangements, DiPalma and Todd were now returning to the hotel. From the tea shop they had gone to see the Fung Shui man, the diviner selected by Peking, who after consulting the spirits of nature and animals, had selected the auspicious date and time for the funeral rites. Then there had been a forty-five-minute drive south to Stanley Village, the coastal fishing community which was one of Hong Kong's oldest settlements. Here, where Japanese had interned their British prisoners during World War II, DiPalma and Todd had visited the monks in the two-hundred-year-old Tin Hau Temple, dedicated to the colony's popular goddess of the sea.

The unpretentious temple, whose main hall contained three walls with black-and-gold statues of gods, had been Katharine's favorite. She had come here to pray for DiPalma's recovery eleven years ago and had returned every year since then. This was Hong Kong's miracle temple; during World War II bombs had landed directly on top of the temple but did not explode.

And here, under a canopied shrine, was a statue of the god Wong Tai Sin, who generously granted his followers' wishes and was one of Hong Kong's most popular deities. Wong Tai Sin cured illnesses and also gave his devotees advice on horse races.

This is where Katharine wanted her services held, Todd said. And she wanted to be buried in China, just across the border in Shenzhen, in a special cemetery for Hong Kong residents who preferred to be buried on the mainland.

"To be buried in her ancestral homeland means favorable Fung Shui for my mother," said Todd. "This must be done according to the spiritual laws she lived by. Elements of heaven, ocean, fire, wind and earth have been consulted by the Fung Shui man. He has used *ch'i*, the breath of yin and yang, to decide upon the day and upon the place she will occupy in the cemetery."

"It'll be done her way," said DiPalma, understanding none of it.

The temple reminded him of that day in the Kowloon hospital when he had tried to get out of bed for the first time since he had almost been shot to death. Katharine had watched him as he hopelessly tried to stand up on crutches. Not once did she make a move to help him.

Then DiPalma had attempted to walk. A child could have done better. Three very awkward steps, agonizing steps, followed by disaster. One crutch slipped from under his arm and when he tried to cling to the other with both hands he lost his balance and dropped to one knee. It hurt like a son of a bitch. That was it. No more. He was giving up. He turned toward the bed.

Katharine blocked his way. "Crawl toward the window. Don't go near the bed."

DiPalma needed someone to be angry with and she was it. "Get the hell out of my way."

"Knock me out of the way. Because I'm not moving. Crawl, fly or roll on the floor. But get to that window any way you can, because you're not coming back to this bed."

He could have hit her with a crutch. Gone for her head and enjoyed doing it. "You get off watching people crawl? Well, I ain't a comedian. No laughs from this boy. Not today. For the last time, get out of my way. I'm not ready to walk to that window or any other fucking window and maybe I'll never be ready. Come back tomorrow. I always limp on Thursdays."

"I'd rather see you limp today." She folded her arms across her chest. "Because if you limp, Mr. Comedian, you're walking."

He clung to the one crutch and stared at her for long sec-

onds. Then he pulled the other crutch toward him and gave
her a hateful look, hating her yet knowing she had done more
for him than anyone else in his life. He turned his back on her
and began to limp toward the window. Ten feet between his
bed and the window. The longest ten feet of DiPalma's life.

There was pain every inch of the way and more than once he
wanted to quit, fall down and rest, but she was watching and
he kept going until he made it. He saw the sun, the gray water
of the harbor and a black, ugly freighter about to overtake a
sailboat. He was exhausted, drained. And ready to cry, because there were no words for what he had just done, for what
she had made him do. He looked over his shoulder at her.
Another time he might have been ashamed for a woman to see
him weep. Not now. She was weeping, too.

In DiPalma's mind there was no doubt that if he had stayed
on the floor that day or gone back to bed he would never have
walked again. Nor would he ever have loved again.

* * *

IN THE TAXI DiPalma sucked in air through his open
mouth. His head had split into fragments and his legs and
arms had lost all feeling. The terrible thirst which had plagued
him since early afternoon had returned. He had blamed that
on the heat. It couldn't be his diet. Since the shooting his diet
had been fairly bland; heavy on dairy products, boiled vegetables. A wild time at the dinner table was two pieces of fruit
with his meal.

Something else had caused this terrible thirst. Since leaving
the tearoom DiPalma had gone through half a dozen glasses
of milk, a couple of bottles of Perrier, club soda. No ice. And
still the thirst would not go away.

When the cab stopped for a red light DiPalma stiffened with
cramps and doubled over. *Jesus.* He heard Todd yell and
DiPalma forced his eyes open. Had he passed out or just come
close? Todd wasn't calling him; he was arguing with the
driver, who kept shaking his head. Now Todd held up his
radio so that the driver could see it in the rearview mirror.
Silence. A few words in Cantonese and the driver nodded. A
bargain had been struck. The cab speeded up, then the driver

made a U-turn away from the hotel, back the way they had come.

DiPalma, fighting for breath, looked at his son. "Hos-hospital."

"You are dying," said Todd. "Ling Shen has poisoned you."

"Hos, hos . . ." DiPalma couldn't form the word.

"No," said Todd. The boy's eyes bore into DiPalma, who wanted to scream. But his eyes closed and he climbed toward a starless and grotesque night.

18

GEOFFREY LAYCOCK had spent a pleasant evening in his kitchen preparing himself a first-class Chinese meal.

Because Chinese cuisine was the greatest the world had ever known, he had trained to become a superb chef, specializing in Cantonese cooking which called for food to be cooked quickly and lightly, preserving the flavor and original taste. By 10:00 P.M., after four hours of cooking, Laycock was ready to dine on food that would have pleased the notoriously finicky empress dowager of the Ching dynasty, who before she was deposed in 1912 enjoyed a daily meal of one hundred dishes, all of which her eunuchs first tested for poison.

Laycock had brought a plastic bag of live frogs from a Hong Kong market, sliced off their legs and deep fried them in a crunchy batter mixed with crushed almonds. After dipping them in sweet-and-sour sauce he munched on the legs while preparing the rest of the meal in his large, well-equipped kitchen. Working to cassette tapes of Placido Domingo, Mozart and Willie Nelson, Laycock boned and sliced small eels, then braised them in wine and garlic. This was a Shanghainese dish, the only diversion from his Cantonese menu. Next he prepared shark's fin soup, to be eaten with onion cakes.

For the main course he prepared Hakka-style stuffed duck. He deboned the duck through a hole in the neck, then stuffed it with lotus seeds, chopped meat, rice and pigs' brains stewed in wine. Dessert was to be a sea-swallow's nest, whose dried saliva lining was said to have rejuvenating powers. The nest, while tasteless, would be flavored with coconut milk, honey and almonds.

Cooking finished, Laycock showered, shaved his legs, then slipped into a red-and-gold gown and gold slippers, gifts from Hong Kong's most popular opera singer, a charming woman with whom he often smoked opium.

In the living room he set a service for one on a small table by the window. From here he would dine and look down on Murray Barracks, which the occupying Japanese used as their headquarters during World War II. For a few seconds Laycock stared at the timber-and-stone building with its deep verandas and allowed the memories to wash over him.

The smell of the meal he had cooked intruded on the hazy dream that was his past. He clapped his hands together. Time to enjoy a well-earned repast, his reward for a job well done. Was he not a good cook, and was not cookery an art, a noble science, and were not cooks gentlemen? Laycock lit incense sticks, which jutted from a tiny sandbox on the window sill, then lit two lavender candles on the table. From a teakwood cabinet he selected tapes by Mozart, Aznavour and the Clash. Music. The pleasing melancholy. The speech of angels.

When the doorbell rang, it made a most unmusical sound. An exasperated Laycock slammed the tapes down on the top of the cabinet. Who had the nerve to call at this hour, unannounced and uninvited. He had well and truly earned this meal, especially after all he had gone through in the past twenty-four hours. Whoever it was put a finger on the doorbell and kept it there. Bloody cheek.

Laycock crossed the living room and squinted through the peephole. He caught himself frowning, which he knew wasn't good for the face. He stopped and smoothed the skin between his eyebrows with the heel of his hand. He opened the door.

Roger Tan took his thumb off the bell.

"Your timing is foul," said Laycock. "Be brief, then be gone."

The drug agent's eyes took in the red-and-gold robe and the gold slippers. "Shit, I wouldn't have missed seeing this for anything. You wear that when you go to get your Pap test?"

"That's the trouble with masculinity. You must prove it over and over again. We are all as God made us, only worse. Speak your piece, Roger, though I fail to see why this couldn't wait until tomorrow. You could even have tried telephoning. But then stupidity is such an elemental force, isn't it?"

"Well, it is a bitch being butch sometimes. I just dropped by to tell you that you fucked up. Blew it."

Laycock folded his arms across his chest. "Your vanity is insufferable at times. Such as now. Just what is it you know and I don't?"

"Frank DiPalma's still alive. You didn't kill him. Came close. Real fucking close. But Frank . . . well, he is a cat with nine lives."

Laycock pressed his lips together and hugged himself. He took deep breaths, then clenched his teeth and fought to keep himself from trembling. Without being aware of it he backed into the living room. All thought of food was forgotten.

Tan entered the apartment and kicked the front door closed behind him. He stopped and sniffed the air. "Smells good. Private party?"

Laycock cleared his throat. "I happen to be alone."

"Well, if you're celebrating, you jumped the gun. Frank's still with us. Barely alive. There's a chance he might not make it, but if he does, well, you know where that leaves you and Ling Shen. Up shit's creek, the both of you."

"I'd like to sit down."

"Hey, why not. We'll both sit down." Laycock sat down on a black metal chair near the kitchen. Roger Tan sat down on a brown leather couch, then removed a Beretta from his jacket pocket and casually placed it on the coffee table in front of him.

There was amused contempt in the drug-agent's voice when he said, "You're not going to give me any trouble, Miss Priss, are you?"

Laycock, head down, mumbled, "No."

Tan leaned back, hands behind his neck. "Worst you can do is hit me with your purse or give me a hickey."

He stared at the ceiling and did not see the Englishman look up. Laycock's face held the same hard look he had worn when insulted by Roger Tan in the tearoom. Then he smiled. "So you think I tried to kill Frank DiPalma."

"Know you did, Miss Priss."

"And what put you on to me?"

Tan kept his eyes on the ceiling. "Teacups, saucers and teapots." He looked at Laycock. "You were playing around with them when we walked in the tearoom this afternoon. You were signaling somebody. You were telling whoever was watching you from Ling Shen's Triad that you felt it was all right to proceed with killing Frank.''

Laycock folded his hands under his chin. "*Moi*, the golden-shower queen, a taker of life? Surely you jest."

"Hey queenie, you're a member of Shen's Triad and we both know it.''

"Now how can that be, dear boy, when Triads are Chinese only. No *gweilos* need apply.''

"Wrong. That's what Triads like the world to think. Oh, I admit not many Europeans get past the membership committee. Damn few, in fact. But you did.''

Laycock said, "For your information, Triads were founded in seventeenth-century China by Buddhist monks to fight Manchu invaders. Early freedom fighters, you might say. Patriots risking their lives for the greater good. Since then—''

"Since then they've become hoods. Dope, whores, extortion, counterfeiting, pornography. And political corruption. There was a time they practically ran China. If you weren't in a Triad or a secret society you damn sure had no chance of ever being a successful politician. You like my gun? You keep staring at it.''

"Makes me nervous. What is it with you Americans and your guns? A penis substitute?''

"Yeah, well don't worry about my dick, Miss Priss. Worry about yours, because it is definitely caught in the wringer. You were supposed to burn Frank and you didn't. You know what that means. Means your ass is grass and Ling Shen's the lawn-mower. Means you're dead. Am I getting through to you?''

Laycock said, "I sit here enthralled by your rhetoric. Could it be that I underestimated you after all?''

"My specialty is intelligence and if I say so myself, I am fucking good at it. There's a book, not many people know about it, called *Zhong-guo Bi-mi*. Written in the last century by a Japanese secret agent named Hiraya Amane. Amane was the first Jap to really get on to the Triads. See, Japan's been spying on China for years. Knowing Japan, they're probably still doing it. China's a lot bigger than Japan. Potentially a hell of a lot more dangerous, too.''

"You know, of course," said Laycock, "that China has dominated this part of the world for hundreds of years and that Japan's military and economic success of the twentieth century are looked upon as nothing more than a blink of the eye insofar as time is concerned. That Japan's moment in the sun will pass and China will again rule the East as she always has."

Tan continued as if Laycock had said nothing. "China's always been fucked up. Warlord against warlord. Emperor against prime minister. Dynasty against dynasty. Intrigue up the ass. No end to it. Japan wanted a united China under its control. How do you bring that about? You spy. You work your way into the secret societies, into the Triads."

"Fascinating. Do go on."

"You take Chinese immigrants who come to Japan and you turn those suckers. Make them your agents and send them back to China to collect information and pass it on."

Laycock said slyly, "Don't forget the Chinese politicians, rebels and generals who wanted power. They came to Japan for tea and sympathy, not to mention money and bullets. And received a helping hand, did they not, albeit for future considerations."

Roger Tan missed the dig. He was too interested in the sound of his own voice. "All this shit went down before World War II started. By the time the war was on, Japan had so many agents in the Triads, in Hong Kong and all over China, that it was a fucking joke."

"May I correct you on one point," said Laycock. "The full name of the Amane book is *Zhong-guo-Bi-mi She-hui Shi*. Still being used as a source for intelligence in China, by the way. And yes, he was the first to discover the secret language and rituals used in restaurants and other public places by Triads all over the world. If you don't mind, dear boy, I would like to enjoy my food before it gets cold. And you can tell me more about secret societies and Americans being poisoned in Hong Kong in July."

Tan stood up. "I'll bring the food. You keep your tail glued to that chair." He pocketed the Beretta. "One dish at a time. What do you want to start with?"

"Let's have the soup for starters. First pot on your right facing the stove. Should be a low flame under it, which you can turn out. Place it in one of the puce-colored bowls you'll find on the cooking table."

"Puce?"

"The moronic know it as light purple. I'll need a spoon and napkin, please. And kindly refrain from picking your nose while your are serving me. I suppose it's too much to ask you to wash your hands. And you say Frank DiPalma is still alive."

Tan walked into the kitchen. "Barely. His kid saved him. Kid knew they'd never make the hospital in time, so he had the driver turn back to Causeway where they'd just come from. Stopped at an herbalist, who made a special tea. Todd forced that into Frank, made him vomit some more to get rid of most of the poison."

Laycock, who had not moved from the chair, nodded. "Clever. A bright lad, our Toddie. Should go far."

Roger Tan returned from the kitchen with a bowl of soup in one hand. "Keep the bowl in your hand and walk over to the table. Bring back one spoon. Make sure I can see both hands at all times."

He walked to the couch and sat down, his eyes on Laycock. When the Englishman returned to his chair with the spoon, Tan took his hand out of his pocket. "Twenty-four flavored tea. That's what they called it. Fungi, roots, stems, seeds, different kinds of grass. Todd mixed it by himself. Didn't need the herbalist. Poured it into Frank. Then called a police car. Wasn't for the kid Frank would never have lived to see the hospital. As it is now, Frank's in deep shit."

Laycock blew into a spoon of shark's fin soup to cool it. "If you don't mind my asking, how did I poison DiPalma? Certainly the tea wasn't poisoned. We all drank it and by his own admission DiPalma had to make several stops after leaving the tearoom. He could have been poisoned anywhere. Perhaps it happened when he took a cold drink from a food stall."

"We didn't use the same teacup," said Tan. "You used one set of cups to signal whoever was watching. Told them it was a green light. You got Frank to come to the tearoom, which is probably a Triad front, and you made sure he got a certain cup to drink from. A cup from a new set, a cup which was coated with poison before you filled it with tea. Whatever they gave Frank had no odor, no taste and worked like a time-release cold capsule."

Laycock patted his lips with a napkin. "There are many

such poisons in China. They say there's one which creates a monstrous thirst in the victim. Seems the more liquid he drinks the more effective the poison becomes. I'd like my eels, please. They're in a covered dish in the oven. Just bring the dish. I'll eat from that. Have you figured out why I would want to kill DiPalma? He and I are supposed to be friends, after all.''

"Bullshit. You're in a Triad and they've got first call on whatever loyalty you may have. Truth is, you're not even that loyal to them. You're doing what one man tells you to do and you've been doing that for a long time.''

"The eels. Who might this supreme authority be whom I serve with such slavish devotion?''

Roger Tan stood up. "You said it, I didn't. You've got your nose so far up this guy's ass, if he farts he'll blow your brains out. Nosaka. Zenzo Nosaka. Still want those eels?''

Laycock said, "Yes, please.'' He watched Roger Tan back into the kitchen, keeping his eye on Laycock all the time. Mr. Tan was quite full of himself at the moment.

Laycock ate the eels with his fingers, an ignominious approach to a superb dish. The more he thought about having the meal interrupted, the more he began to dislike Mr. Tan.

Tan said, "The teacups got me started. Not every day you see a white man go through that ritual the way you did. Not one mistake. When I got back to the office, I went to work with computers, printouts, telephone hookups. Know what I found out? You were a British prisoner of war here during the Japanese occupation. You went over to the other side. Betrayed your people. Naughty, naughty, Miss Priss.''

Laycock licked his fingers. "I wanted to survive. It was that simple, yet not so simple. I was quite impressed with Colonel Nosaka. He can be most persuasive. The Far East has always appealed to me. Always felt comfortable here.''

"Exotic Orient and all that shit. So you stayed alive during your internment by sucking Nosaka's cock.''

Laycock raised his eyebrows. "You do have a way with a phrase. We were lovers, yes. I did truly love him. Actually when I was young I did have a certain pristine beauty. You could say that I was crystal.''

Roger Tan chuckled. "Fucking unreal. Crystal. Anyway you couldn't go home after what you did, so you stayed right here in Hong Kong and became Nosaka's man inside Ling Shen's Triad.''

Laycock drank wine sauce from the eel pan. "Seemed like a good idea at the time. Would have been the height of folly to present myself in Britain, considering my past behavior. Parents had disowned me. And my native land had always been rather hard on us fairies. Blackmail, imprisonment, social disgrace. That sort of rot. All in all, it seemed wiser to stay here.''

He placed the eel pan on the rug beside his chair. "There were three kinds of Triads during the war years. One was more or less loyal to Chiang Kai-shek. A right old sod he was. Devious, obstinate, corrupt. Startlingly uneducated. Egotistical and vindictive. But an expert at manipulating the secret societies for his own purposes. The secret societies, with their mystic mumbo-jumbo and ties to Confucius, just about controlled China. They were rather dangerous to play around with but Chiang played and won.''

Laycock crossed his legs. "There is a heavenly duck in the kitchen. I would like that served now. The wine with it, of course. You'll find a bottle uncorked on top of the fridge. A delicate little Beaujolais, since Chinese wines leave something to be desired. In the light of recent events, I shall refrain from offering you a glass.''

When the duck arrived the Englishman sat cross-legged on the floor and ate it from the pan. Roger Tan allowed him a fork, but no knife. "Now the second type of Triad," said Laycock, "did not allow the war to interfere with business-as-usual. They remained committed to their usual illicit enterprises and prospered. To do so meant coming to an arrangement with the Japanese. You know, espionage, handing over wanted men and women to the Japanese military police, eliminating anyone who was a bother to the Japanese, that sort of thing.''

He pointed his fork at Roger Tan. "Which brings us to the third type of Triad. One hundred percent loyal to the Japanese, they were. They, too, made a profit here and there. But in effect, they were an arm of the Japanese military police. There is one thing that bothers me. How did you learn about my association with Nosaka?''

Roger Tan said, "Made a phone call."

"To whom?"

"Jude Golden."

"Ah."

"Computer coughed up a lot of shit on Nosaka, including his war-crimes trial and the names of the guys who prosecuted him. Two of those guys are dead, by the way. Frank thinks Nosaka's behind it. But that's another story. Golden's the last one. He told me about that trial, about a certain British POW who had turned traitor and should have been hung. But he lucked out, this English guy. Nosaka made him part of his deal. If the Americans wanted his cooperation, they had to make sure this English guy got off. British high command was pissed, but what could they do? In those days America had the Marshall Plan and if you wanted money it was the only game in town."

Laycock pulled a crisp bit of skin from the duck. "Quite. I remember America's generosity to what was called 'war-torn lands.' But in the process your country did throw its weight around. Fortunately, it was to my benefit."

"It was that, all right, Mr. Phillip Tibber."

Laycock froze, his greasy fingers over the duck. Then, "I see. You have been busy, haven't you?"

"Golden's a smart dude. Knows a lot of stuff. His daughter's here in Hong Kong doing a movie. Frank used to bang her. Anyway, her old man says you ain't who you claim to be. Says you took the name Geoffrey Laycock from a dead two-year-old child who's buried in a little English town called Chalfont St. Giles."

Laycock held his wine glass up to the light. "I do wish you'd learn how to handle one of these. You hold them by the stem when presenting it to whoever is to drink out of it. Spares them the hideous sight of your fingerprints. Chalfont St. Giles, is it. Must remember to send flowers. I wasn't aware Mr. Golden was in possession of so much information about me."

"Standard procedure for spies. Use the name of a dead kid, somebody who can't be traced. Have phony papers made up with that name and you're home free. Golden says you've had plastic surgery."

"Is nothing sacred? Very well, yes. A nip and a tuck in Morocco. More than a nip and a tuck, actually."

"Golden told me something else. Said Nosaka's got this fantastic collection of old Japanese weapons. Stuff even a museum doesn't have. See, I'd mentioned that you'd got us over to this tearoom to talk about a certain missing war fan. Well, one thing led to another and he tells me about Nosaka's collection."

Laycock giggled. "Very well, you have me. The fan does belong to Nosaka. And I helped him to retrieve it from police headquarters. There, are you satisfied?"

"You and a certain cop, whoever he might be. You didn't walk into police headquarters to get it. Somebody brought it out to you."

Laycock staggered to his feet, glass in one hand, wine bottle in the other. He giggled again. "Best police money can buy. Right here in old Hong Kong. Nosaka tells me, I tell Ling Shen, Ling Shen tells the constable who shall remain nameless and *voila!* the war fan tiptoes out the door."

Tan shook his head sadly. The faggot was getting looped and talking good noise. "Why did that drag queen kill Katharine Hansard?"

Laycock gulped wine and rocked back on his heels. "But you see, dear boy, he killed them both."

The drug agent blinked. "Both?"

"Little Toddie had to become an orphan and that's all there was to it."

"Why?"

Laycock waved him away. "It's all so beyond you, dear boy, but briefly, Kenpachi wants the boy for some little ceremony he's planning. *Seppuku*, it's called. The lad is to be a participant."

Tan scratched his chin. He didn't like what he was hearing. This was weird shit.

"A minor correction," said Laycock. "Ian Hansard went to his reward for another reason as well. He was planning a bit of blackmail aimed at Nosaka and involving certain bank records. Even if Kenpachi had no use for the boy, Ian Hansard would have ended up a lump of lead. Mustn't cross Nosaka, you see."

He sipped more wine. "My turn. Obviously, with DiPalma lying at death's door, you've had no opportunity to discuss any of this with him. And you've come here alone. Why is that, pray tell?" He rocked back and forth on his heels, but did not go down.

"Simple," said Tan. "I want out of Hong Kong and you, my man, are my ticket to ride. I've got a statement typed up right here in my pocket. Don't have everything in it. You've just added a few things, but we'll get around to including them. Ain't sharing the glory with nobody. Not the cops, not the agency. This dumb chink is bringing you in alone. Only I ain't so dumb."

"You are sadly Americanized, old boy. You lack the subtlety and restraint traditional with your people. Pity."

"I got your pity, sweet meat. I plan to tie you into the murders of the Hansards, tie you into Ling Shen's drug trafficking, tie you into Nosaka's stealing business secrets. You are also gonna tell me what you know about whatever the fuck it is Kenpachi's planning to do with Frank's kid. If Frank ever gets onto that, oh boy."

Laycock looked down at his robe. "Blast. Grease spot on my sleeve. I do wish someone would tell DiPalma that the past is irrevocable. He seems to be consumed by thoughts of two dead women, the late Mrs. Hansard and his own departed wife. It does make him something of a bother."

"He feels he owes them. That's Frank's style."

"I'm sure he's sincere, but sincerity has its limits. Bury the past. Look to the future, I always say."

"Couldn't agree with you more. Your future lies in cutting a deal with me. You show your face on the street right now and Shen's liable to blow it off. You ain't got but one choice and that's to 'turn'. Sooner we get out of here and down to DEA headquarters, the better your chances of living to get that robe cleaned."

"Having no wish to become a dead queen, I submit myself to your tender mercies."

"You can start by turning around so I can cuff your hands. Behave yourself. I don't want to work up a sweat kicking your ass."

Laycock set the wine bottle and glass down on the metal

chair, sighed and turned his back to Tan. "Godawful, it is. Here am I, Mrs. Tibber's little boy, about to be paraded through the streets looking as colorful as a tropical parrot. Most regrettable. Oh well, just another shitty day in paradise."

He glanced over his shoulder. Roger Tan was almost on him, the cuffs in his right hand, his left hand empty. Laycock looked ahead and smiled.

And lashed back with his right leg, driving his heel into Tan's right shin. The drug agent dropped the cuffs and clawed at his jacket for the Beretta.

Laycock spun around with astonishing speed and in the same motion jabbed the stiffened fingers of one hand into Tan's right eye. When the drug agent brought both hands up to the pained eye, the Englishman kicked him in the testicles, folding him in half. A straight punch from Laycock crushed Tan's nose. A right uppercut to the cheekbone, followed by a vicious left hook to the right temple, and the drug agent spun round and dropped like a stone.

Laycock removed the Beretta from Tan's pocket, released the clip and the single bullet in the chamber and put them into the deep pockets of his robe. He picked up the platter containing the remains of the duck and carried it into the kitchen. Returning to the living room he poured himself a glass of wine, then sat down in the metal chair and watched Tan roll over onto his back and moan.

Laycock said, "And what do you think of the old queen now. Interesting style of combat, wing chun. Never ceases to amaze me even after all these years. Doesn't have the force-against-force style of the Japanese forms. Lacks the pyrotechnical displays of the Korean fighters, with their spinning and leaping kicks. Wing chun is simpler, quicker. No brute strength. Low kicks, straight punches and always immediate counterattacks. Never block. Just counterattack."

A glassy-eyed and slack-jawed Tan attempted to sit up.

Laycock sipped more wine. "Did you know that wing chun is said to have been invented by a Buddhist nun? Imagine that. A second woman came along and refined it. Marvelous origins, wouldn't you say? One of the deadliest fighting forms ever to come out of China and it was born of two women.

Bruce Lee trained in wing chun, you know. That should tell
you something. But I suppose it doesn't, you being so virile
and masculine.''

Tan fought for breath. "Ling Shen. Gonna kill . . . kill
you.''

Laycock stood up. "Which reminds me. Must make a telephone call. You stay there on the floor and try not to throw up
on the rug. Leaves a smell no matter how many times it's
cleaned. Shame your computers didn't warn you about us old
queens. You'd be surprised, dear boy, how violent some of us
Nellies can be. I do my wing chun in places not open to the
general public, not even to most Chinese. Believe me when I
tell you I've run across gays who could tear masculine fellows
like yourself apart with ease.''

Laycock sat on the couch behind Tan and made his call. He
spoke in Cantonese and the call was a brief one. When Laycock hung up, he looked down at Roger Tan. "Well, I suppose you understood what was being discussed.''

"Shen told you to finish it, to go to the hospital tonight
and—''

"Finish DiPalma. Quite. Seems if DiPalma is around to see
the sunrise, Ling Shen's life is forfeit. And so is mine. Di-
Palma must not be allowed to leave the hospital alive. Simple
enough, isn't it? I see by your eyes that you would like to prevent this from happening. Don't see how, dear boy.''

"Guards, guards on DiPalma's door.''

"Been taken care of. Starting''—Laycock looked at his
wristwatch—"five minutes from now, DiPalma's hospital
room will be unguarded. I'm afraid you won't win your
laurels tonight after all.''

Laycock leaned over the coffee table and pulled a dark
wooden box toward him. He lifted the top and took out
Nosaka's war fan. A snap of his wrist and the fan was open.
Its metal cutting edge glittered.

Laycock, the fan held coquettishly in front of his face,
stood up and walked over to Roger Tan. "The paths of glory
lead but to the grave, dear boy.''

19

NUDE, KENPACHI crossed the room and switched off the light shortly before midnight. Except for two candles burning in the living room the director's suite was totally dark. In the living room Kenpachi had placed a thick red rug four feet square and enclosed it on three sides with a white screen. The candles in front of the screen were each four feet high, wrapped in white silk and resting on bamboo stands.

Benkai's long sword, the Muramasa, still in its scabbard, rested on a low wooden stand, the jeweled hilt wrapped in a white silk cloth. To the right of the sword was a small table holding a bowl of rice wine, Saburo's unsheathed *seppuku* knife and the black lacquer box finished in Benkai's ashes and containing the *Hotoke-San*, the bone taken from Bankai's throat after his cremation.

It was time for *zazen*, the daily meditation that was to prepare Kenpachi for his own *seppuku*.

He stepped on the rug, knelt facing Benkai's sword and bowed, his forehead touching the floor. Then he sat back on his heels, eyes closed, back straight and palms on his thighs. He was alone. Wabaka was on guard in the hall and the hotel switchboard had been ordered to hold all calls until further notice.

Zazen.

Surrounded by objects which had been used in Saburo's *seppuku*, Kenpachi sought to unfasten the ties that bound him to life and to increase his growing contempt for death. Nosaka's instructions came to mind. *Look into your soul. Explore death. Become truly fearless. Above all, find a way to touch the universal mind, the one mind to which we all belong. From there you will be able to find him who would be your* kaishaku. *You must go beyond your limits.*

Kenpachi thought of the boy who was to be his *kaishaku.* Todd was not only the epitome of youthful beauty but a reminder of the ugliness of the old. The young were free, strong, warm. The old were decrepit, remote, subdued. Had not Bushido, the warrior's code, taken much from Buddha, and had not Buddha's three warnings spoken of death and old age?

* * *

> *Did you ever see in the world a man or woman eighty or ninety years old, frail, crooked as a gable roof, bent down, resting on crutches, with tottering steps, youth long since fled, with broken teeth, gray and scanty hair or bald-headed, wrinkled, with blotched limbs?*
>
> *And did the thought never come to you that you are also subject to decay, that you also cannot escape it?*
>
> *Did you never see in the world a man or a woman who, being sick, afflicted and grievously ill, and wallowing in his or her own filth, was lifted up by some people, and put to bed by others?*
>
> *And did the thought never come to you, that you also are subject to disease, that you also cannot escape it?*
>
> *Did you see in the world the corpse of a man or a woman, one or two days after death, swollen, blue black in color and full of corruption?*
>
> *And did the thought never come to you that you also are subject to death, that you cannot escape it?*

* * *

UNLIKE HIS BELOVED MOTHER, who had wasted away of

cancer, Kenpachi would escape disease and decay. As for death, most people died too soon or too late. He would die at a time of his own choosing, raising himself to glory and immortality, and his voice would be heard in Japan forever.

Kenpachi shared Nosaka's belief in the *Hotoke-San*. The sight of the ugly and shapeless bone had caused the boy Todd to become temporarily possessed by a samurai warrior who had been dead four hundred years. It had forced the boy to acknowledge Kenpachi as his master, and it had brought out in Todd the fear of being enslaved by the demon *Iki-ryō*.

Tonight Kenpachi sensed the presence of the *Iki-ryō* in the bone, though not as strongly as had the boy. Born of evil thoughts, the *Iki-ryō* was a ghost which now sought a home in something as deadly as itself. Kenpachi's practice of *zazen* had enabled him to sense the demon's desire to leave the bone and come to life fully, to rejoin the soul and mind of Benkai.

The boy, more sensitive than Kenpachi, had known this instantly. Which was why he recoiled when Kenpachi had held out the box to him. Todd had resisted the *Iki-ryō*'s claim on him. But the boy was *bushi*, a warrior; he must be made one with his ghost, and then he would become the implacable Benkai, pledged to obey his master.

For a few seconds there was resistance in Kenpachi's mind. He feared the *Iki-ryō*. Could he control the boy after he had become possessed?

Only five or six weeks of scheduled work remained on the film. Kenpachi had not changed his mind about committing *seppuku* when the film was done. For maximum impact, his work and his life must end at the same time; that was how his mother had died. He would issue a *zankanjo*, a death statement explaining his disgust with modern Japan and his sincere hopes for the return of Imperial Nippon. The *zankanjo* would be delivered to the emperor, with copies to the press. Such a courageous death would mark Kenpachi's last film as art of the highest order. And the film itself would forever remind Japan that it was Kenpachi who had forced it to seek out its past greatness.

The right *kaishaku* was essential. Kenpachi needed someone other than the brutish Wakaba or the maniacs of the Blood Oath League. They idolized Kenpachi enough to behead him.

But they were also proof that in life too much was often not enough. Wakaba, jealous of all who came near Kenpachi, desperately wanted the honor of being his second. He had even begged to be allowed to commit *seppuku* with the film director.

Wakaba, high-strung and loyal, would give his life for Kenpachi tomorrow. His love for the film director bordered on idolatry. Wakaba could easily kill the boy, believing that in doing so he was saving the director from being defiled by a *gaijin*.

But it was Benkai, who lived in Todd, whom Kenpachi wanted for his *kaishaku*. And so there could be no fear of the *Iki-ryō*, Wakaba or anyone else. Including DiPalma, who was either dead or dying. A samurai must not be a coward; he must bear all calamities and never flee.

Zazen.

Kenpachi concentrated his mind on the *Hotoke-San*, closing out all thoughts of family, career, life and death. For him there was only the small, hideous bone. And the demon within it.

In front of the tall white candles a perspiring Kenpachi lost all sense of his body and began slipping in and out of consciousness. Then he began to grow alarmed; he sensed he was no longer alone in his suite. He heard a noise, a screeching that was neither animal nor human. It began softly, slowly, then gained power until it filled the room with such a grating noise that Kenpachi began to shudder. The suite's windows and doors were locked, but an icy gust blew out both candles, leaving Kenpachi in frozen darkness.

Eeeeeeeiiiiii. The screeching stabbed his ears. There was the smell of burning flesh and Kenpachi grew sick.

Then, suddenly, the screeching sound stopped. But the room remained cold and there was that nauseating odor. The silence in the room was one of imminent horror.

Exhausted, Kenpachi slumped on the floor and passed out, but not before he realized that he had succeeded in driving the *Iki-ryō* from the bone and had sent the demon in search of Benkai.

* * *

WHEN GEOFFREY LAYCOCK stepped from the elevator into a sixth-floor corridor of the Connaught Road hospital it was five minutes past midnight. He was dressed rather smartly, he thought, in the khaki uniform of a police lieutenant, complete with swagger stick and holstered pistol on a lanyard. Completing the disguise were a false mustache, dark glasses and a cap pulled so low it pushed his glasses painfully into the bridge of his nose. Despite a slight case of nerves he found the playacting exciting. He saw himself with the military bearing of the young officer he had been during the war. He was Jack Hawkins in *The Cruel Sea*. British pluck personified.

On the other hand it was doubtful if Hawkins had ever sneaked into a hospital with the intention of sending someone on to a better world, which is what Laycock intended doing to Frank DiPalma. It was DiPalma's life or Laycock's. Ling Shen had little tolerance for failure.

In the corridor Laycock encountered two Chinese nurses. As he passed them he brought a folded newspaper to his face, but they ignored him, chattering away. Halfway down the corridor the Englishman stopped in front of the EXIT door leading to a staircase. After making certain he was unobserved he pushed through the door and closed it behind him. Then, fanning himself with the folded newspaper he began walking up the stairs. On the eighth-floor landing he stopped in front of the door leading to the corridor and cracked it.

The corridor was empty. There was the smell of medicine and sickness, which Laycock despised, and there were empty wheelchairs and a walker here and there. The receptionist was around the corner and out of sight. Even if he was spotted, who would give a second thought to a policeman on the floor, given the precarious state of DiPalma's health. Most important of all, DiPalma's room, three doors away, was unguarded. As Ling Shen had ordered it to be.

Laycock closed the door and leaned back against it. He unfolded the newspaper and regarded the small black box containing the hypodermic needle. The needle was filled with the same poison that had been smeared on DiPalma's cup at the tearoom. Except this time there was more, much more. Not to worry. Laycock would do his deed and be gone. Needle at the base of the skull. Thumb on the plunger and Mr. DiPalma was off to join the angels.

Laycock removed his cap and massaged his forehead with his fingertips. Patience. The art of hoping. Of course everything would proceed as planned. No reason for it not to. Hadn't he shown patience back at the flat, when he had forced himself to eat in order to catch Roger Tan off guard? And being alone in the flat with Tan's corpse until Ling Shen's men arrived had required patience as well. And a strong stomach. Laycock was not keen on keeping company with the dead.

A bit of White Dragon Pearl to soothe the nerves would be most welcome. The chalky white heroin, mixed with a barbiturate called barbitone, was ground into powder, then mixed with regular tobacco. It was by far the colony's most popular brand of heroin, more popular than opium and produced a better high. Laycock was not addicted to heroin, as were many in the colony. Ninety percent of Hong Kong's prison population were heroin addicts.

The Englishman was twirling his cap on his forefinger when he froze. He cocked his head and sniffed the air. And smiled.

He put the cap back on his head, turned and cracked the door. There were rushing footsteps at the far end of the hall. Someone yelled *fire*. Laycock stepped into the hall, pulling the door closed behind him. The smell of smoke was stronger out here, as it was supposed to be.

Laycock walked to DiPalma's room and with his hand on the knob looked left, then right. No one was nearby, no one was watching him. And no one saw him enter the room, close the door behind him and walk toward an unconscious Frank DiPalma.

* * *

JAN GOLDEN switched on the small lamp beside her bed, sat up and screwed her cigarette into an ashtray. Then she shook another loose from the pack, lit it and inhaled. She put on her glasses and picked up her wristwatch. A little after midnight. She dropped the watch back on the table, stood up and drew her robe tighter around her. It was going to be a long night. Especially if Frank DiPalma died.

She had the room next to his, with a creaky air conditioner that furnished little in the way of cool air. The sealed windows hadn't been washed in months. There was a private bath, but the toilet was sluggish and the wash basin had permanent stains. The bathroom mirror was cracked and a tiny waste-basket under the basin was overflowing with mildewed rags. It was the tackiest place Jan had slept in since her affair with the Yugoslavian conceptual artist who lived in an unfurnished railroad flat on Manhattan's Ninth Avenue and kept a gerbil named Dali. Love, or something like it, had allowed her to tolerate several weekends in that roach farm. Love now had her pacing the floor of a Hong Kong hospital room; in her own way she loved Frank DiPalma. And the thought of a world without him was terrifying.

Todd was in the room next to hers. Where else could either of them spend the night except here? Waiting. Jan remembered Frank's face when he had been wheeled back to his room after the doctors were through with him. Unconscious, with a dark purple discoloration of the skin due to poor circulation. Cyanosis, a doctor had said. Also caused by a shortage of oxygen in the bloodstream. Narcosis had been another effect of the poison, a stupor so deep that no one knew for sure when Frank would regain consciousness. If it hadn't been for Todd . . .

Goddamn Ling Shen.

She walked to the window and looked down at the parking lot. In the scanty light she watched two white-clad interns leave the building then climb on bicycles and pedal off the parking lot. She had sent her own driver home, with instructions to call for her at 7:00 A.M. and take her to the set. But if Frank died or didn't come around . . . Jan closed her eyes. Right now the film was the last thing on her mind. Frank dead. She leaned forward, her forehead pressed against the cool glass.

Which was worse—not loving, or loving and not telling. He mustn't die before she spoke to him again. She thought of what he had done for her. Dealing with Ray when he had attempted to blackmail her. Dealing with the network executive who had tried to rape her. The award-winning documentary she had done on prostitution, with his help. And the chance to go into films. Frank had been supportive and protective, never asking questions, never accusing. In return she had hurt him.

She was sleeping with Kon now. It had happened the night she had angrily sought out Frank in the restaurant, the night Kon had appeared at her hotel room after having disappeared from the police station. Jan had gotten what she wanted, a great fuck, but something had been missing. It was as if Kon had been standing outside of himself watching himself perform. And as physically satisfying as it had been, Jan, when it was over, felt even farther away from ever possessing him.

That's me, she thought. Run away from the ones who want you and run after those who don't and hate yourself for it. Love only had one great enemy and that was life itself. Jan's sensible and farsighted side told her that Frank DiPalma was best for her, that she could be with him without being known only through him. That wasn't possible with Kon. Everything about Kon was erotic. His talent, his unpredictability, his unwillingness to be cured of his passions. Sooner or later, Jan said for herself, this bastard is going to destroy me. Just like the other bastards did. But the wildness in him drew her like a moth to flame.

Both men, she suspected, knew her secret, that when Jan fell in love she would submit to anything, endure anything. Frank would never use that knowledge against her. Kon would. Would he ever. And if she were in trouble, who could she depend on? The Sicilian, who else. Kenpachi's concern was only for himself. A classic case of a man whose love for himself came first.

But why fool herself? That was Kon's appeal. He was as dangerous as a Grand Prix racecourse; he was an irresistible challenge to women drawn to the exotic, the outrageous, the unexpected, and there were enough of them to keep men like Kon busy for months. Why hadn't she married Frank? Because it would have meant demanding more from herself than she had up until now.

She walked into the bathroom and looked into the mirror. Christ, did that face belong to her? She needed sleep, lots and lots of sleep. And when had she last eaten? A fish dinner in the room had gone untouched. Just coffee and cigarettes. No wonder she looked like a frog in a blender, red and green and going through life at a hundred miles an hour.

She touched her nose. Jewish girls were supposed to do something about long noses. Jan hadn't. She and Streisand. This is it, folks. Take it or leave it. You look like Wayne Gretzky the hockey player. Frank had said. Meryl Streep, Jan had said. She looks like Gretzky too, said Frank.

I need Frank, I want Kon. Didn't some actor once tell her that being drunk or on location never counts. Maybe when the movie was finished she and Kon would be finished. Maybe it would be a good idea to finish with Kon sooner than that. He was into some off-the-wall shit, talking about black magic, ghosts, reincarnation and the beauty of death. Jan saw nothing beautiful about Frank dying.

She ran cold water in the basin, cupped her hands and splashed water on her face. She dried her face and had reached for a jar of cold cream when she heard the sound of breaking glass coming from Todd's room. Then a thud. Had he fallen out of bed and hurt himself?

"No! No!" shouted a frightened Todd.

Jan heard him whimper. She ran from the bathroom, stopped a moment to belt her robe, then stepped into the hall. She never noticed that there were no guards at Frank's door.

At Todd's door she hesitated, fist poised to knock, then turned the knob and pushed. The door was stuck. She gripped the knob with both hands, threw her body against the door, then stumbled into the room as the door flew open. She turned on the light and rushed to the boy.

Todd lay on the floor, backed into a corner and trembling. The night table was turned over. Lamp, dishes and drinking glasses were scattered on the floor. Avoiding broken glass, Jan crouched barefoot beside the boy and reached to take him in her arms. He was terrified, completely unnerved.

Nightmare. Of course. First his mother dies, then his stepfather and now his natural father is critically ill from being poisoned. Jan's heart went out to him.

A cringing Todd, knees drawn up protectively, edged as far away from her as possible. "*Iki-ryō*," he said.

"What?"

There was no warning. He shoved her aside violently, sending Jan flying back against the bed. She struck her elbow painfully. Todd scrambled past her and raced to the door. Angry, yet concerned for him, Jan pushed herself off the floor. Todd was pulling at the doorknob. Stuck.

She stepped on a pice of glass, cut her bare foot and cried out. But she reached Todd, pulled at him and was thrown off. Jesus, the little bastard was strong. Now he had the door open, pulling it so hard that it banged into the wall. Jan ran after him.

In the hall she watched him push Frank's door open, then lean back, hands covering his face. There was something in the room Todd didn't want to see.

Jan, limping, came up behind the boy. She placed her hands on his shoulders, preparing to turn him around and read the riot act. He wasn't helping Frank by bursting into his room like a wild man. That was when Jan felt the icy air. The cold was a shock. It jolted her and she staggered a few steps back into the hall.

It reminded her of the worst of the New England winters she had endured, when twenty-six inches of snow and winds strong enough to overturn cars piled up drifts twenty feet high and the mercury dropped below zero. Frank's air conditioner must have gone insane.

And there was something else. A smell that the incredible cold could not hide. A burning smell, so nauseating and repellent that it made Jan sick to her stomach. Eyes closed, she backed away from the room, hands cupped over her nose and mouth. Then she stopped, opened her eyes and looked into the room.

And screamed.

* * *

Was he awake or sleeping? Todd no longer knew. But his skin was dark and hairy, his forearms rock hard with muscle and the Muramasa, gripped in both hands, was held high overhead. He was in a man's body. A Japanese man. He was squat, bearded, powerfully built and poised to strike, to bring the sword down on the bared neck of a man bending over Frank DiPalma, who lay unconscious in a hospital bed. Todd's father was in danger. Seconds away from death. Todd had to save him.

But the sword would not come down. Todd's arms remained inflexible, unyielding. None of his great strength could bring the awesome weapon into play.

He grew fearful. It was not right that he should feel fear. He must conquer it.

And then he felt the presence of the Iki-ryō, felt it probe him, felt its baseness and unspeakable hatred. Frightened, he resisted. Fought with his mind. Tried to will it back into the past. Were he to accept the Iki-ryō he would become the instrument of its depravity. But he would also possess a power that would allow him to grasp the world.

The Iki-ryō spoke. "Accept me. I am the ghost of the living and I alone can save your father. I will keep him away from shi, from death. But first you must accept me."

At the side of his father's bed Todd saw the stranger take a small black box from inside a folded newspaper, open it and remove a hypodermic needle. He held the needle to the light and pushed the plunger, sending a thin stream of clear liquid across the room. He turned back to Todd's father.

"Yes," said Todd. "Save him. I accept you, but save my father."

A searing heat enveloped the boy's body and he screamed. For an instant he saw himself as iron hardened in fire, a blade thrust into flame to create a classic weapon worthy of a samurai. Then the heat vanished, leaving behind a great cold. He saw his past lives, and all time came to stand as one within him. The unknown that was the past and the unknown that was the future became known to him. His name was not Todd. He was Benkai. He was samurai.

* * *

THUMB ON THE PLUNGER and DiPalma would be with

the angels. Laycock, hypodermic held high in his right hand, reached down with his left to turn DiPalma over on his side. Had to get to the base of the skull. Hide the needle hole in the hairline. But turning this walrus over was no easy task. Laycock would have to use two hands.

The cold. The overpowering stench. Where on earth did they come from? Laycock felt himself being squeezed in an iron grip and opened his mouth to cry out, but no sound came from his lips. Terrified, he looked over his shoulder and saw no one. But if there was no one behind him, then who was squeezing the very breath of life from him?

He was being pulled across the room, toward the window. An irresistible pull, growing stronger, faster, and suddenly he was jerked across the room as though on wires, leaving his feet like an adagio dancer. He was spun around in midair. He witnessed himself flying, *flying* toward the window, and he screamed. A woman screamed, too. And then Laycock was driven through the glass, feeling excruciating pain as shards of thick, broken glass tore at his flesh. For a second he hung suspended eight stories above the ground, then fell still screaming toward the parking lot, feeling and hearing the rushing wind, feeling himself being suffocated by the wind pouring in his face, and then came a great pain that filled his mind and body as he felt nothing more.

He hit the top of the metal flagpole, which passed through his back then emerged from his stomach. The Englishman slid down the pole, coming to rest in the center. His bleeding body hung on the bent flagpole, arms and feet dangling, and his lifeless eyes opened and focused on a hazy moon.

20

Tokyo

IT WAS DAWN when Frank DiPalma and Obata Shuko, a Tokyo police captain, walked side by side along a quiet alley in Rokubancho, one of dozens of small, quiet communities hidden away behind Tokyo's noisy main thoroughfares. Like other villages in the heart of the city, Rokubancho maintained its separate identity with lanes too narrow for cars and an almost total absence of street names. While this was discouraging for visitors, it gave those who lived there a sense of secure isolation.

At this hour DiPalma and Shuko were alone on a winding street of temples, low houses, shops and villas whose walled gardens were topped by trees thick with leaves. The flapping of birds' wings caused DiPalma to look up at the gray sky. Wood pigeons. Nearby the Imperial Enclosure, a parklike island of three hundred acres, surrounded the Imperial Palace.

He had seen photographs of this secret valley of willow groves, pine trees, brooks, ponds, wild birds and rustic paths, all of it solely for the pleasure of the imperial family. But neither he nor anyone else, Japanese or westerners, were allowed inside. For that matter, few Japanese or westerners were allowed where Suko was now taking DiPalma. DiPalma was on his way to a swordsmith, to participate in the forging of a blade, an honor he had dreamed of for years but had never imagined would be granted him.

There were elements of a religious ceremony in the swordsmith's task: he purified himself, wore special robes, prayed to the gods before he began, then cut himself off from the outside world until he had finished.

From the beginning of sword making in Japan, each school attempted to keep its manufacturing techniques secret. Few written records existed; instructions were passed from father to son, from master to disciple, and men had been killed for attempting to steal information. Poets, emperors, shoguns and warriors all praised the sword maker.

While DiPalma was well aware of the sword's mystique among Japanese, he insisted on remaining a realist. There was no magic in the sword. And what magic there was in the swordsman was nothing more or less than a skill honed by thousands of hours of practice. The sword was a well-crafted weapon; it came alive only in the hands of a trained warrior. Nothing supernatural about that. The cryptic approach to *ken*, the sword, struck him as pretentious, verging on superstition. He could tolerate that attitude in the Japanese. In westerners it was presumptuous.

The attempt in Hong Kong five days ago to kill him had done more than leave him physically weak. It had done something to his head, to his mind, and DiPalma didn't like it. At night he shivered and dreaded falling asleep, fearing he would die when he closed his eyes. He had lost weight and had trouble digesting his food. Was it his imagination or had there really been changes in Todd? He seemed to have grown more surly since they had left Hong Kong.

DiPalma owed his life to his son. Todd had given his new radio to the Hong Kong cab driver in exchange for driving to the herbalist. The boy had forced the tea down DiPalma's throat, making him puke his guts out, saving his skin. Maybe the kid was just having a delayed reaction to his dead parents.

Dai-sho, Shuko called the two of them. Big sword and little sword. Shuko was looking forward to seeing Todd fence. So was DiPalma.

The poison which almost took him out had not yet been identified by the hospital; it probably never would be. There were poisons used in China that went back a thousand years and the people who knew the ingredients weren't telling. Bruce Lee was rumored to have died from such a poison administered by Hong Kong gangsters when he had refused to make films for them. There were as many rumors about Lee's death as there were Chinese in Hong Kong. One thing was sure: no poison was found in Lee's system.

The poison had affected DiPalma mentally more than physically. It had left him feeling depressed, without mental energy or spiritual fire, the things that had made him a good cop. Instead of going after Nosaka, he had to force himself to start contacting people and asking questions. He had ignored the Hong Kong reporters who had called to tell him that Ling Shen was dead. The Triad leader had been found floating in Victoria Harbor with over fifty stab wounds in his body.

DiPalma had only spoken to his network once, taking the first call when he arrived in Tokyo, then ignoring the rest. He had taken only one call from his TV investigative team; they had been worried sick, especially after hearing about the poisoning. They were digging into Nosaka, as DiPalma had requested, and getting some good dirt. He was only half-glad to hear from them, politely listened, then said he'd call back and hung up. Only Roger Tan hadn't called.

Shuko had given DiPalma a juicy piece of news. Sakon Chiba, the transvestite, had not only been a close friend of Kenpachi's. He had also been an industrial spy for Zenzo Nosaka. Chiba, Kenpachi, Nosaka and the Blood Oath League were now linked together. DiPalma should have been jumping for joy. He should have been out pounding the bricks and going for Nosaka's jugular. Instead he was going through the motions and trying not to be scared shitless when the sun went down and he had to go to sleep.

Jan was due to arrive in Tokyo the following day. Filming was shifting to Tokyo for the next four or five weeks. She had stood beside him during the funeral ceremonies, had held his hand in the car when he couldn't stop shaking. He needed her now, but she belonged to Kenpachi. He desperately wanted a drink.

Three days in Japan and he had yet to practice kendo, yet to see any of his Japanese friends except Shuko. DiPalma had met him years ago at a law enforcement conference in Hawaii and the two had hit it off immediately. Both were kendoists and shared a passion for Duke Ellington. Among Shuko's huge Ellington collection was the piano used by the Duke when he began his career as a jazz musician in 1916.

The two men kept up their friendship through letters, telephone calls and visits. For Shuko the relationship proved invaluable when his sister Nori was kidnapped. Nori was the wife of a Japanese importing executive assigned by his company to New York. Thye lived in New Jersey with other Japanese who had moved to the suburbs to escape New York's crime. Crime, however, found Nori in a shopping mall not far from her home. She was kidnapped and held for ransom. Shuko, devoted to his sister, asked for DiPalma's help.

DiPalma met him at Kennedy Airport, drove him to New Jersey and acted as interpreter for Shuko with the FBI and local police. At the request of Shuko and his brother-in-law's company, DiPalma was allowed to act as go-between, contacting the kidnappers and arranging for the delivery of the ransom. Nori was returned safely and the kidnappers captured twenty-four hours later. It was a favor neither Shuko nor his brother-in-law would ever forget. DiPalma also received a letter of gratitude from the Japanese ambassador in Washington. He had made some very useful friends.

This morning Shuko was about to repay the favor.

The two made a comical-looking duo walking along Roku-bancho's walled streets—DiPalma, large, gray-haired, strained but still forceful looking with his hooded eyes and flat, ugly-handsome face, moving in long strides; the small, bandy-legged Shuko, with jet black hair and unlined face, almost trotting to keep up with his companion.

DiPalma stopped. He was having second thoughts. "I appreciate what you're trying to do, Shuko-san, but I'm not sure it's going to work. What can I get out of watching the making of a new blade?"

"Not watch. You do. You clean your soul. You wash the poison from your mind. You become *bushi* again."

He walked away from DiPalma and never looked back to see if he was following. DiPalma caught up to him. "Such things exist for others. They do not exist for me."

Shuko said, "Duke Ellington said that a problem was a chance for you to do your best."

"Duke Ellington never drank tea in Hong Kong. At least not where I did."

"There are things about the sword you do not understand. You have much information, but you have little knowledge."

"Shuko-san, there are things about my own son I don't understand. He saved my life because he knows more about herbs than an herbalist. Where did he learn that? He and San told police they saw Laycock throw himself out of the window. If they hadn't, I'd be in jail accused of murder. As it was, the police had a hard time believing that anyone had the strength, not to mention the insanity, to throw himself through glass half an inch thick."

Shuko looked at him. "Ah, but he did. Or so it would appear."

"It's as if Laycock was possessed. The man just went crazy. And speaking of possessed, my son's nightmares are getting worse. Same dreams. Either he thinks he's Benkai or Benkai's after him. We can't seem to get that straight."

"You know, of course, that Benkai was said to have been possessed by what we call a ghost of the living."

"*Iki-ryō.* Yes, I know it. Someone's secret thoughts, evil thoughts, leave him and go out and make trouble."

"You do not believe?"

"No." And that's all there is to it. Nothing logical about a thing like that. Just part of the local mythology. But DiPalma wasn't buying it.

DiPalma said, "Something else I do not believe and that's reincarnation. Would you tell me how someone can be alive forever and not know it?"

They passed burlap-wrapped bales of rice stacked in front of a restaurant. "Reincarnation is accepted by many," said Shuko. "India, China, Japan. Africans. Sufi mystics. It appears in Persian philosophy, in Greek philosophy. Once it was a part of early Christianity, but the Christian fathers eliminated it from the teachings."

"Why?"

"Too rational, my friend. Reincarnation meant that you alone were responsible for your fate. This gave the church less authority. To keep its power, the church dispensed with karma and reincarnation."

Shuko gave him a shrewd look. "As for why we do not remember our past lives, may I say that your existence does not depend on your memory. You cannot remember your childhood. Does this mean you did not exist as a child? Do you remember the details of your life as a very young man? Can you remember all that you did last year?"

DiPalma smiled. "You have a point, Shuko-san."

"It is a blessing that you do not remember, my friend. It would disturb us, make pretenders of us, be the cause of great foolishness and much harm."

DiPalma thought of Todd, who could remember his past lives and suffered for it.

He said, "How much farther?" His limp was beginning to bother him.

"Soon. The walk is part of the preparation. It allows you to compose your mind, to subdue impulses. Too often the mind is resistant to all supervision. We say it is as wild as a monkey who has been stung by a scorpion."

"At the moment I don't feel in charge of my own monkey. Shuko-san, may I ask a favor of you? While I am with the swordsmith will you please take Todd to your *dojo* and ask permission of the *sensei* for him to fence? It might help the boy while I am away."

"It will be done, my friend."

"Thank you. How long will I be with the swordsmith?"

"We have arrived, DiPalma-san."

The American stopped and looked around. They were in a narrow street of walled houses, a street without a name. A street of hidden houses without numbers. Without Shuko, DiPalma was lost. One door was ajar. There was no need to ring the old-fashioned brass bell hanging beside it. He was expected. Through the open door DiPalma saw bonsai, dwarf trees, and twisted pines and a small pond. From the other side of the wall came the faint sound of someone chanting. DiPalma had to walk through that door. And didn't want to.

He waited for Shuko to urge him forward, to tell him that there was magic in the sword, that he could find his soul in the blade. DiPalma turned around. Shuko was gone.

DiPalma looked at the door. It slowly opened wider until he could see the entire garden. He limped toward the empty doorway, the tapping of his cane the only sound in the narrow street.

* * *

THERE WERE THREE PROCESSES in producing a blade:
forging the steel, then tempering and sharpening it. DiPalma
was to assist only in the forging, the first and most difficult
step. The rest would be done over a period of weeks by the
smith, his assistants, and by professional sword polishers.
After that came the mounting of the blade, which meant adding the guard, hilt, collar, ornaments and decorated scabbard.
The finished weapon would be a highly prized *daito*, a long
sword with a two-foot blade.

Inside the forge, a small two-room house in the middle of
the garden, DiPalma stared at a single blade hanging on the
wall beside the deity shelf. It told him which school of sword
making was practiced here and also gave the blade's history,
all in characters eight hundred years old and written in gold inlay on the tang.

*December 2, 1192. Sukesada, sixty-three years old, smith
of the Sagami Province. Made for Minamoto Yoritome. The
tester was Tenno Nitta. Three bodies with one stroke.*

DiPalma took a deep breath. To call this blade rare was an
understatement. It was matchless, unparalleled in its work-
manship and place in Japanese history. From such blades
Japan drew its feeling of moral strength and oneness with the
past. DiPalma stepped closer. Courage, integrity of heart and
spirit, self-control and honor. All in this one blade. The vir-
tues which made up the moral code of Bushido. And it was important to remember that the strength of those who carried
this sword lay in their contempt for death.

Minamoto, for whom the sword was made, was Japan's
first shogun, the military strong men who ruled the empire and
the emperor for over seven hundred years. Tenno belonged to
a professional group who tested a sword's sharpness by slicing
metal, wood, clumps of straw and human flesh. Records were
kept of each test, noting witnesses, date, tester's name and
how many bodies were cut with a single stroke. The blade on
the wall had been tested by cutting through three corpses or
three condemned criminals.

A dejected DiPalma had not asked the name of the smith he
was to meet. Why bother when nothing was going to come of

it. He had agreed to the visit only to avoid offending Shuko. The honor which had been granted the American was lost on him until now, until he came face to face with the swordsmith in the forge. That was when DiPalma's cane slipped from his hand and his jaw dropped. He was visibly shaken. He was in the presence of a living immortal.

In Japan the swordsmith enjoyed a status above all craftsmen. The country possessed only a handful of men with this skill that was so much a part of its history. Standing above them all was the legendary Tendrai, whose blades were said to rival those of his twelfth-century ancestor, the great Sukesada. Tendrai was never seen, refusing all requests to be interviewed, photographed or observed at his ancient task. Ten years ago, when the emperor had declared him a living treasure, an honor given to few, Tendrai had consented to come to the Imperial Palace. But the palace photographer took his orders that day from the smith, not the emperor. One photograph, no more. DiPalma recognized Tendrai from Shuko's copy of that rare photograph.

In recent years Tendrai's health and sanity were the subject of wild rumors. He was said to be blind, dying of cancer, the victim of a severe burning accident which had webbed the fingers of one hand together, preventing him from ever forging another blade. Old age and the loss of his skill were said to have caused him to commit suicide. Both hands were supposed to have been cut off by a wealthy man who became enraged when Tendrai refused to make a sword for him.

DiPalma now stood before this man who was a link between the Nippon of the past and the Japan of today, tomorrow, the future. Tendrai was the heart of Japan, a reminder of *giri*, eternal duty, of self-discipline, of all that was worth preserving from the old Japan. DiPalma felt lightheaded, aware that he stood in the presence of someone very special.

Tendrai was imposing, a big man in his late seventies, white-haired and heavily jowled, with large gnarled hands and the air of a man whose authority was seldom resisted. He took a long hard look at DiPalma, examining him with eyes that bored holes in him. The ex-cop was used to people trying to stare him down on the streets and he usually won the game. Not this time.

It was DiPalma's place to bow first and he did so, bending from the waist. "*Sensei.*" He did not trust himself to say more.

Tendrai's face remained impenetrable, as though nothing had been said. Then he looked at his *sakite*, his two assistants, and left the forge. He and DiPalma were to speak to each other only once. Instructions came from the *sakite* and were to be obeyed instantly and without question. The atmosphere in the forge was one of strict religious ritual and DiPalma soon understood that talk was neither welcomed nor necessary. He was in a place where all that mattered was thought and action.

They began immediately.

DiPalma followed the *sakite* to the main house, a two-story wooden building near the forge. Here, in a large room covered with mats, all four men stripped nude, then purified themselves by pouring cold water over their bodies. Next they put on orange robes, black conical hats tied under the chin and *tabi*, white split-toed socks and clogs. Everything was done in silence, including the walk from the house back to the forge.

Inside the forge Tendrai led the way to the room with the deity shelf, a collection of small statues, vases, teakwood box, scroll, fresh flowers and amulets, all dedicated to the god of Tendrai's forge. In front of the shelf the three Japanese bowed from the waist and remained in that position. DiPalma thought, why not? and bowed, feeling hypocritical, yet not knowing what else to do. This was not the time to say that he believed in only one world and one life with nothing beyond.

Tendrai stood up, inhaled and exhaled. It was time to go to work.

The object was to weave numerous fine threads of steel into one perfect unit. DiPalma watched as a melon-sized chunk of steel was heated in an open furnace, then removed to be flattened. Tendrai wielded a large hammer with a thick, wooden head, pounding the reddened metal in huge, powerful strokes. Minutes later he was relieved by one of his assistants. DiPalma swung the hammer last. It was heavier than it looked. After only three strokes his shoulders ached and he knew there were going to be blisters on his hands.

He was relieved when one of the assistants tapped him on the shoulder. The steel was flat enough. Using tongs, Tendrai

picked up the steel and thrust it into a bucket of cold water.
DiPalma was kneading a sore bicep when he felt a sharp pain
in his ribs. One of the *sakite* had jabbed him with an elbow
and was glaring at him. DiPalma recognized that look from
his early days of kendo practice. His instructors would glare at
him when he made too much of an injury. Reacting to pain in
front of an opponent would only make him attack you more.
DiPalma let his hands fall to his sides.

The assistant then looked at Tendrai, who nodded. The
assistant then pointed to the hammer. Instead of resting Di-
Palma would now go first. Silently he picked up the hammer.

He pounded the quenched steel, bringing the hammer down
with all his strength, ignoring the three Japanese watching
him. DiPalma, the steel, the hammer. That was his world. It
took his mind off the edginess he felt in Tendra's presence.
Besides, he began to enjoy the glow and the warmth coming
from the furnace.

Stop.

It was a command from one of the assistants. DiPalma was
so consumed by his hammering that he failed to notice he had
broken the steel into pieces. Now the exhaustion hit him and
his lungs burned and he couldn't stop his stomach from rising
and falling. Someone pried the hammer from his hands, which
were bleeding. He had broken the steel, had done it by himself. He looked over at Tendrai. Still the stone face, but the
eyes didn't seem as hard now. Or was it his imagination?

DiPalma watched one of the *sakite* place the pieces on a
steel spatula, which Tendrai picked up and carried to the fire.
The smith's face was red from the flames, but his eyes never
blinked and he looked into the fire as though seeing something. In a while an assistant went to the smith, who handed
the spatula to him without a word. DiPalma noticed all communication was in silence and that the Japanese did everything
without any wasted effort. The second assistant took his turn
holding the spatula in the flames, and after a time he simply
looked at DiPalma, who had had the sense to do what the
rest were doing, which was to watch what was going on. He
stepped forward, crouched and was handed the spatula.

At first the fire was painful. It was blisteringly hot on his
face and the warm spatula handle was hell on his bleeding

hands. But he wasn't going to walk away. It became important to do all that was expected of him, to see it through to the end. In his whole life it had always been balls forward. Even if the poison had done a number on his head, he wasn't going to shame himself in front of Tendrai.

That was when the fire became hypnotic. DiPalma stopped thinking about the heat and his hands. The problem now was to avoid falling asleep. To keep awake he recalled the names of the great swordsmiths of the past. Enshin, Chikamura, Arikuni, Iesuke, Jumyô, Hideyoshi, Gisuke, Kanehira, Kanetomo. Muramasa, the Emperor Go-toba. Daruma, Naotane.

Someone tapped him on the shoulder. He looked up to see an assistant point to the spatula, then to the hammer. Time to pound the pieces again.

DiPalma brought the spatula over to an anvil resting on the earthen floor. Neither of the assistants moved, so he guessed he was still on. Tendrai stood to one side of the anvil and motioned for DiPalma to squat across from him and hold the spatula on the anvil. Both men were now fitted with thick eyeglasses, a protection against flying sparks; the steel was white hot and at its most dangerous. DiPalma's glasses were all but opaque; it was the world as viewed through egg white.

Tendrai's pounding of the steel shook DiPalma's arms, forcing him to tense his muscles and grip the spatula harder. Sparks flew and struck his face, his hands and arms. Through his thick glasses he watched them flit and take off like miniature comets. It was a beautiful chaos and he wondered if the creation of the universe had been anything like this.

An assistant took the spatula from him, while another hammered the steel. Then it was DiPalma's turn to swing the hammer and by noon the steel, reheated and pounded over and over, had become a solid piece, six inches long, two inches wide and a little over half an inch thick. At this point work stopped and the two men ate a lunch of cold vegetables, noodles and hot tea brought to them by servants. DiPalma and the Japanese ate in the forge, in silence. When Tendrai finished, he stood up. The *sakite* set their food aside, as did DiPalma, who had had an appetite for the first time since the poisoning. It was back to work.

The flat rectangle of steel was heated, cut in the middle,

then once more folded and pounded into a rectangle. At the same time a second chunk of steel was being prepared in the same fashion. Heated, broken into pieces, then pounded into a small, flat rectangle. Toward late afternoon both rectangles were heated and joined together, then cut, folded and pounded. DiPalma had sweated buckets; his robe and the light garment under it were drenched. There was blood on the robe from his hands.

When had he made such good use of his time? When had he been so fulfilled and satisfied? The effort was everything; the struggle had never been so pleasing. It was as if Hong Kong had never happened. He could do anything.

When he saw the metal take the shape of a stick, DiPalma was as keyed up as when he had joined the police academy. Tendrai had shaped it, using a metal hammer and lighter strokes. After a while he stopped and held out the hammer to DiPalma. When the smith stood up and stepped aside, DiPalma hunkered down over the blade and hesitated. He felt a heat that had nothing to do with the burning furnace. He felt exhilarated, yet calm. Confident, yet humble. He wondered if it were true that in Japan man had no need to pray, for the soil itself was divine.

In a trancelike state he pounded the stick-shaped metal. The blade had become DiPalma's life and the hammer in his bleeding hand was an extension of his body. He was experiencing truths that could not be expressed in words, could not be felt anywhere except in this forge. See with your heart. Feel fully. Believe in what you feel.

DiPalma brought the hammer down on the blade until someone shook him and he opened his eyes. It was night and the door to the forge was open. He was lying on the floor in the room with the deity shelf. One of the *sakite* had come to wake him. A shocked DiPalma sat up quickly. What in hell had happened? He scrambled to his feet and rushed to the room where the furnace still burned, where Tendrai sat at the anvil shaping the metal into a rough blade. The smith used a *sen*, an ancient form of shaver, which he gripped by two handles. Occasionally he paused to use a file, then returned to using the shaver.

DiPalma rubbed his eyes. How could he have been so stupid

as to have fallen asleep? Was he still that weak from the poisoning? More important, what did Tendrai think of him? DiPalma wanted to run and hide. Physically he felt like his old self. And the embarrassment was going away. He was starting to feel confident. Strong. Strong in body and mind. Maybe he could explain to Tendrai about Hong Kong.

DiPalma entered the room as Tendrai dipped a hand into a pot, then brought it out and smeared clay on the blade. The smith looked up and stopped. Here it comes, thought DiPalma. Tendrai beckoned him closer, pointed to the blade and stood up. What the hell? He wasn't going to kick DiPalma's ass after all. And it hit the ex-cop. They knew he was sick. Sleep had been as much a part of the cure as helping to forge the blade.

Sleep. *He had not worried about dying.* He had closed his eyes, had not thought of poison, of Ling Shen, of the hospital. It was an effort for DiPalma now to remain composed. He squatted down behind the crude-looking blade, dipped his hand in the dark, thin mud, a special mixture of Tendrai's, and smoothed it along the blade. The clay would be allowed to dry, then scraped off by Tendrai so as to give the blade the desired tempered pattern. After that, the blade would be heated once more, the curvature corrected. The polishing was the last step.

An assistant stood in front of DiPalma and bowed. There was something final in the gesture. DiPalma got to his feet. Fatigue was forgotten. His fear of dying was gone. He wanted to stay in the forge until the blade was finished and mounted, until the task was complete. He did not want to leave. But his part in the making of the *daito* was over.

Saddened, he bowed to the assistants. He walked past them, through the forge and out into the night where Tendrai waited for him. The smith said, "That which touched you when you lay dying has been driven away."

DiPalma thought of what Jan had told him at Katharine's funeral. *Icy cold. And a stench that went beyond putrid. And if I didn't know better, I'd swear something invisible yanked Laycock through that window. Through plate glass that's supposed to be unbreakable.*

DiPalma bowed. How could someone have gone through a

window like that on his own? He said, "*Domo arigato gozai-mashita, Sensei.*"

Tendrai said, "It now lives within him in whom it once lived." He gave a slight nod, then turned and stepped into the forge. A servant led DiPalma to the bath. When DiPalma had bathed, he returned to the room and found his clothes. Cold water was waiting for him in the same wooden buckets which he had used to purify himself hours ago. He poured water over his aching body, dried himself and dressed. And thought about Tendrai's words.

A servant led him from the house and through the garden. DiPalma stopped to stare at the forge and to listen to the sound of the hammer on the crude blade. Then he followed the servant to the garden door leading to the street.

Outside, Shuko stepped from the shadows and bowed. Di-Palma returned the bow and then they smiled at each other. The American looked over his shoulder at the smoke rising above the wall behind him. Then in silence the two men began walking along the narrow street.

21

JAN GOLDEN stood on the ramparts of Ikuba Castle and looked down on the cars pulling into the cobbled courtyard for the party. A Cadillac Eldorado caught her eye. As it rolled to a stop the driver put his hand on the horn and kept it there, playing the first few bars of "The Yellow Rose of Texas." Jan swallowed the last of her Campari and soda. There were times when the Japanese *gaijin compurekksu*, western complex—the feeling that anything Western was better—was a real pain.

She watched two Japanese couples leave the Eldorado. Exactly what Kon would have on his guest list. The men were *yakuza*, straight from Warner Brothers casting in their pinstriped suits, spats, dark shirts, white ties and slouched fedoras. This was everyday wear for them, as well as an expression of their admiration for American movie gangsters. Their women, slim and pretty and neo-punk: spiky hairdos streaked with pink and green, leather jackets, stiletto high heels and designer jeans. Straight from downtown L.A., thought Jan. Or the Mudd Club in Manhattan.

She was alone on the ramparts, relieved to be outside and away from the castle which was mobbed with Kenpachi's friends, acquaintances and admirers. Originally the party had been planned only for the film's cast and crew. A casual buffet dinner, followed by a tour of the castle for those who had never been inside. It had been a typical Kenpachi impulse; as a rule Japanese rarely invited foreigners into their homes. There was always the fear that the home might prove too humble or Japanese customs appear bizarre.

Then Kon had changed his mind and the casual dinner became a party celebrating his Lincoln Center tribute in three weeks. Typical Kenpachi. Impulsive, self-centered, unpredictable. In minutes the guest list expanded to include Japanese and foreign press, members of the Japanese film community, Japanese and foreign models, sumo wrestlers, baseball players, gays, *yakuza*, Kabuki performers and several tough-looking young men with hard eyes and short haircuts. Members of Kenpachi's kendo club, Jan was told.

This last group kept to themselves, giving the impression of being an elite, men of high mark. They didn't smile and scarcely spoke to anyone. Jan put them down as goons when one shoved a waiter to the floor for no apparent reason, then kicked him in the side before being pulled away. Kon's reaction had been to curse the waiter. That was when an angry Jan had walked outside. She had had enough of Kon's gross behavior for one night.

On the ramparts she drew her shawl around her shoulders, placed her empty glass on top of the wall and began to walk. She felt like a fly on the wall; she could see the grounds, the arriving guests and the white wooden castle, but no one looked up at her. A handful of people strolled on the grounds, but most were inside, in the matted rooms with the original gilded ceilings and their sunken panels of waterfalls and seashores.

Jan had been impressed with the care that Kon had lavished on the castle. Its cast corridors were highly polished and the rooms, separated by sliding doors, had been redone to gleam with the gloss of lacquer and gold as it might have been in Lord Saburo's time. Golden brassware, Edo period sculptures and colored paintings completed the *daimyo* effect that Kenpachi sought. Was Kon's career really on the downswing, as Jan had heard? If so, it was going down in style.

But there were times when his style was hard to swallow. Tonight, for example, Kon had decided to show off his skill as an *onnagata* and attend the party dressed as a woman. Jan had thought he was kidding until she watched him put on the makeup and assume the role. She watched fascinated as he sat in front of the mirror and began coating his eyebrows with softened wax, then covered his face and neck with white pigment.

Then he brushed on blue eye shadow, powdered his face and drew in thick, dark eyebrows. After he had brushed on eye liner he drew a small red mouth and leaned back to admire his beauty. And he was beautiful. Jan found herself wondering what it would be like to make love to him *now*, then closed her eyes. It was wrong, or was it? Japan could really turn your head around.

She opened her eyes to see Kon being helped into a dazzling kimono by a servant. The kimono was made of red, black, blue and white silk, with designs of birds, flowers and deer sewn into the fabric. Jan couldn't take her eyes off the garment, which was belted at the waist by a wide gold sash with a tiny, round-faced doll attached just over the heart. For Jan to speak would have broken the spell. She still had not accepted the idea that Kenpachi would go through with it, that he would appear in front of his guests in full drag.

But was it full drag? Wasn't she viewing his world through her own mind? When men did that to her she became angry. Did she have the right to judge Kenpachi by her standards?

The wig was the last piece of apparel. It was heavy and elaborate, covering his forehead and reaching down to his shoulders. It was topped by a diadem of blue sapphires and blue silk flowers. When it was in place Kenpachi covered his forearms and hands with white pigment, then took a fan from a drawer and snapped it open. He stood up, fanned himself and looked down at a stunned Jan.

Then he began to walk. Not like a man, but as a woman. Knees close together, feet slightly pigeon-toed. Body swaying, head moving gently from side to side and elbows at the hips. The effect was staggering. Kon Kenpachi had disappeared, to be replaced by a woman so feminine that Jan, who knew the truth, now began to doubt her eyes. It left her ill at ease. The degree of Kon's sexuality never failed to surprise her. If it is physically possible, he had said to her, it is not unnatural.

But in the end it was more than Jan could handle. That and Kon's flirting with several of the men at the party and his cruel attitude toward the servant who had been kicked by his friends. So she had taken her drink and gone outside to stare at the stars and think of Frank DiPalma. She had to laugh at the thought of Frank in a dress. And as tough as he was,

Frank would never push an old man to the floor and use him for a football.

Most of the men closest to Kon impressed Jan as on the edge, barely keeping their violence in check. Head cases like Wakaba. Wakaba hadn't been on the plane when it left Hong Kong. He's delivering a message for me, Kon had said in a way that closed the subject. Jan hadn't been interested enough to pursue it. If she didn't see Wakaba again in this life it was fine with her.

She remembered the scene at the temple between Wakaba and Frank, who had delivered a message of his own. Don't bother my son. Why did Wakaba hate the boy? Jan shuddered to think of what might happen to Todd if Wakaba ever caught him alone.

Jan owed Todd a great deal. He had saved Frank's life, first by forcing him to drink the herbal tea, then by entering his hospital room in time to stop Laycock from poisoning him a second time. Again and again Jan had asked herself what had happened in that room, and had failed to come up with a reasonable answer. She remembered the incredible cold, the horrendous smell. And she could never forget Laycock's throwing himself through the window. But the glass had been so thick that the police had failed to break it with a hammer.

Had Todd really saved his father a second time or had something occurred which couldn't be put into words? It really doesn't matter, Jan thought. Frank is alive. I'll take that and be happy.

From the ramparts she looked down at Kenpachi's gardens, swimming pool, guest cottages and private theater. Kenpachi's wife and children rarely came here and then never without an invitation. He talked about them quite freely, boasting of the children's scholastic achievements, praising his wife for being a good mother.

"But you see," he said to Jan, "my choice was to be faithful to others or to myself."

Jan was about to ask if it mattered whom he hurt by such a choice when she remembered that she had done the same thing all her life. It was a shock to find out how much she and Kenpachi had in common.

Near a stairway leading from the ramparts down to the

courtyard she stopped to light a cigarette and then looked
back at the castle. Kon had stepped into the courtyard. Still
looking like a beautiful woman, moving as though he had been
a woman all his life. She watched him greet newly arrived
friends, saw them accept him as though a feminine Kenpachi
was nothing extraordinary; then he walked across the courtyard toward Jan. She dropped her cigarette on the wooden
walk, stepped on it and moved back deeper into the darkness.
She didn't want Kon to see her.

She watched him pause before the fencing hall, just below
her, then look around before entering. Jan relaxed. He hadn't
seen her. Lights went on inside the *dojo*, paper lanterns which
cast a soft orange glow on the window facing Jan. She could
see that someone else was in there.

Todd.

Jan stepped forward. What was the boy doing here? And
why was he hiding where he couldn't be seen? Kenpachi and
Todd stood facing each other, and Kon was doing all the talking. She couldn't hear a word, but she saw Todd nod in agreement.

A taxi crossed the drawbridge, then glided into the courtyard, catching the party guests in the glare of its headlights.
Jan ignored it; her mind was on Kon and Todd. Why was the
boy at Ikuba Castle without Frank? Had Kon brought the boy
here on his own? For what reason? An angry Frank could
easily send Kon Kenpachi to the hospital and Jan's film right
into the toilet. Why couldn't Kon stay away from the boy?

The taxi made a U-turn and stopped, motor running, headlights still on. A man left the back seat and slammed the
door hard enough for the sound to carry up to the ramparts
and draw Jan's attention. She looked at him and flinched.
Wakaba.

He set a suitcase down on the cobblestones, paid the driver
and turned around to look up to where Jan had hidden in the
darkness. She cringed against the stone wall and pulled her
shawl tighter. *Don't let him see me*.

Wakaba's left hand was bandaged and there was a white
patch on his forehead. Did the bandages have anything to do
with the message he had delivered in Hong Kong? And Todd.
What if Wakaba saw him? Jan remembered how Wakaba had

glared at the boy in Hong Kong. What if Kon's chauffeur came across the boy alone tonight on the castle grounds? Todd would be safer away from Ikuba Castle.

She saw Kenpachi's hardnoses, led by the man who had kicked the waiter, step into the courtyard and noisily greet Wakaba. There were smiles all around as Wakaba and the hardnoses shook hands and slapped each other on the shoulder. She felt her skin crawl; they were scary.

The light in the *dojo* suddenly went out. Todd was a child; he had no business being with a grown man who hosted parties dressed like a woman. Maybe it was time she barged into the *dojo* and broke up whatever was going on. Kon wouldn't like it, but to hell with him. Jan owed it to Todd. And to Frank.

She had her foot on the top of the stairs leading down to the courtyard when the door to the *dojo* opened. Jan froze. Kon stepped out alone. Wakaba greeted him, shoved a bandaged fist in the air and smiled. Kon, still a woman, minced over to his bodyguard, who bowed from the waist as the hardnoses watched in respectful silence. Jan felt as if she were witnessing some secret ritual.

Kon and Wakaba began talking quietly in Japanese. Wakaba did most of the talking, the messenger boy making his report. Kon reached out and touched Wakaba's bandaged forehead, then asked a question. Wakaba clenched his bandaged fist and seemed to talk tough. The hardnoses listened and nodded as Wakaba delivered his report. Jan wondered if Wakaba had delivered Kon's message wrapped around a brick.

Two photographers stepped from the castle doorway, followed by a mannish-looking Japanese woman wearing a fedora and tuxedo. The woman called to Kenpachi, who raised his fan in acknowledgement. He looked back at Wakaba, tapped him on the shoulder with the fan, then began his swaying, knees-together, toes-in walk to the castle. One of the photographers looked around, said something in Japanese and the other photographer nodded in agreement. Jan guessed that it was too dark outside even for a flash camera. Or maybe they wanted pictures posed against an indoor backdrop. Whatever the reason, Kon, the mannish-looking woman and the cameraman disappeared inside the castle.

Most of the hardnoses strolled after Kenpachi, but two remained behind to talk with Wakaba. Jan began to tiptoe down the stairs. Wakaba hadn't yet spotted her. He was staring at the *dojo*, at Todd. The boy stood in the doorway, thin, vulnerable and Jan, now at the bottom of the stairs, looked at him, then at Wakaba, and opened her mouth to cry out. At that moment two leather-jacketed bikers roared into the courtyard on powerful Hondas, and there was no way Jan could be heard over the rumble of those ear-shattering machines.

She ran toward the *dojo* as Wakaba started toward Todd.

* * *

DiPALMA WALKED QUICKLY along the narrow Rokuban-cho lane, staying behind Shuko, who suddenly stopped and flattened himself against a low stone wall. DiPalma, cane held high, did the same. Seconds later came a white-shirted delivery boy on a bicycle, a tray of covered metal dishes balanced on the palm of his right hand. Without looking back, Shuko stepped into the lane and DiPalma followed. At the corner they again backed into a wall, this time making way for an old man pushing a cart of steaming roasted sweet potatoes, a favorite Japanese delicacy.

Now the two men walked slower, peering into the windows of a pachinko parlor, a coffee bar, a Korean restaurant. They were searching for Todd, who had disappeared from Shuko's home.

As they searched, Shuko continued to tell DiPalma the story of his ties to Tendrai and the swordsmith's ties to Nosaka and the Muramasa long sword which had once belonged to Benkai.

Earlier Shuko had taken Todd to his kendo club, then after practice brought the boy home. Leaving Todd with his wife and two sons, Shuko then made the long walk through the winding streets of the village to Tendrai's forge, where he picked up DiPalma. At 10:00 P.M., when the two men returned to Shuko's home, Todd was gone. No one had seen him leave. The boy could easily get lost in an area without street signs, house numbers and with few streetlights. An embarrassed

Shuko had accepted full responsibility for Todd's disappearance. For the first time DiPalma felt a wave of panic.

DiPalma had telephoned their hotel, the New Otani, the largest in Asia, with a ten-acre Japanese garden dating back to the seventeenth century. There was no answer in the room.

Shuko had sent out his teenage sons to look for Todd, before teaming with DiPalma to search in a different direction. DiPalma had needed something to take his mind off Todd; in the dark and deserted streets he had asked Shuko about Tendrai. How did the police captain know a man who had gone to great lengths to hide himself and his work? Shuko had never spoken of this relationship and might not want to speak of it now. A conversation with a Japanese often found him parrying, modest, evasive, silent and, when need be, a liar. Lying was not only accepted but was considered a social grace! It was often used to save face and spare others' feelings.

"Tendrai-sensei is my uncle," said Shuko without breaking stride.

A surprised DiPalma stopped dead in his tracks, then rushed to catch up to the little man. "Then your sister is his niece."

"*Hai.*"

Jesus, thought DiPalma. All these years and not one word about being related to the greatest living swordsmith in Japan. Typically Japanese to be so damned closemouthed. Yet neither Shuko nor Tendrai had forgotten what DiPalma had done for the niece. Today that favor had been repaid. Forging the blade had brought out DiPalma's true strength, his inner fire, and given him back his confidence. Now he couldn't wait to go after Nosaka, and Katharine's killer.

Shuko said, "Tendrai-sensei knows of your interest in the sword. He knows of your writings and your research. And he is also aware of your conflict with Kenpachi. I am to ask you to do a service for sensei."

"Tell Tendrai-sensei it will be my honor."

Shuko stopped. There was a force behind his words which had not been present until now. "He asks that you destroy the Muramasa blade belonging to Benkai."

DiPalma shook his head. "That sword doesn't exist anymore. It was destroyed in the great earthquake of 1923."

Superstition said that a giant catfish lived beneath Japan

and when he lost patience with the sins and stupidity of human beings, he would rear up in righteous anger, causing earthquakes and tremors. The quake which struck Tokyo on September 1, 1923, was a calamity. More than half of the city was destroyed and over one hundred thousand people died. It was the son of Emperor Taisho, Hirohito, who supervised Tokyo's reconstruction.

Shuko said, "Benkai's Muramasa was never destroyed. It is now in the hands of Kenpachi."

"Are you sure?"

"Tendrai-sensei told me and I do not question how he came to know. The way of the sword is his life. It has made him exceptionally perceptive."

"I won't question that. Tell sensei he has my word. I will destroy the Muramasa. How did Kenpachi come to own it?"

For a long time Shuko didn't answer. They passed a movie theater, a library, their eyes searching in every dim alley for Todd. Then Shuko spoke with surprising emotion.

"At midnight on August fourteenth, 1945, the Emperor Hirohito recorded a message announcing Japan's surrender to the Allies. The message, which was to be broadcast the following day, would end World War two for Japan. Atom bombs had been dropped on Hiroshima and Nagasaki, killing over one hundred thousand people. This was the weapon which your President Truman called 'the source from which the sun draws its power.' It could, of course, destroy my country, the land born of the rising sun.

"Shortly after the emperor finished the recording, a group of fanatical officers decided to kidnap him, destroy the record and break off all negotiations with the Allies. They wanted the war to continue until the last Japanese was dead. For them destruction was better than surrender. Nosaka was one of those officers, these military gangsters, who lacked all common sense.

"Of course, those plotters needed the support of others and desperately tried to convince their fellow officers to join them. But one young officer, let us call him Gappo, resisted Nosaka and told others to do so. Obey the emperor, said Gappo, and consider the living. This angered Nosaka, who decided Gappo must be taught a lesson.

"In feudal wars, a samurai knowing he faced a difficult battle would sometimes kill his wife and children. This prevented him from thinking of the three things no warrior should remember in battle: those whom he loved, his home and his body. With all that he cherished gone, the warrior was prepared for *shini-mono-gurui*, the hour of the death fury. From this point on he would neither ask nor give any quarter.

"Nosaka waited until Gappo had left his family unguarded. He then entered their home and, using Benkai's Muramasa, slaughtered Gappo's wife, mother and eldest son. Two children escaped because Gappo's wife gave her life to gain time. Nosaka then told Gappo he had killed his entire family, that Gappo now had nothing to lose and was free to join the plot against the emperor. Gappo, however, could think of nothing but revenge. He drew his sword, but Nosaka struck first and beheaded him with the Muramasa."

Shuko stopped walking and continued to stare straight ahead. "Gappo was my father and the brother of Tendrai-sensei. Sensei, like his brother, also wanted revenge. The emperor, however, made him vow never to harm Nosaka. All members of our family were bound by that vow, for Nosaka became important to Japan's survival. The plot to kidnap the emperor and stop the surrender failed, but the situation was still quite dangerous and the emperor knew it. Should Nosaka be murdered he could easily become a martyr to the rebels, who might redouble their efforts to keep Japan fighting. The emperor did not want this to happen.

"When the war ended Nosaka immediately began helping the Americans. In return the Americans aided Japan and protected her from Russia. In the last few days of the war, Russia was ready to invade our country and eliminate the monarchy. Without the monarchy our country cannot survive. America, backed by the atom bomb, ordered Russia to keep away from us and it did. Any occupation of Japan by Russia would have been permanent and unbearable. America, once our enemy, suddenly became our most needed ally. And the emperor, who had rebuilt Japan after the earthquake, knew that to rebuild Japan after the war meant securing the aid of men like Nosaka, men on whom the Americans depended.

"I cannot tell you how difficult it was for Tendrai to turn his back on vengeance. It took all of his strength to do this. He was asked to place Japan and the emperor first and he did so. But it meant that he must retire from public view, to stay within his forge and draw his strength from it. I suspect that he must also have remained there in order to hide his shame. And in the forge he knew he would never run into Nosaka and be tempted to kill him.''

The two men resumed walking. Shuko said softly, ''My sister and I owe our lives to our mother's sacrifice. Tendrai-sensei, perhaps, made an ever greater sacrifice.''

DiPalma said, ''He gained more. Blows bring out the fire in a piece of flint. And I have seen how blows shape steel into a sword. The deaths of those he loved and his vow to the emperor were blows which shaped Tendrai-sensei and brought out his greatness. By keeping his vow he has become Japan's finest swordsmith. Which is the most glorious achievement, to have killed Nosaka or to have become Tendrai-sensei?''

Shuko smiled. ''You have learned much in the forge.''

''I *feel* more, but I cannot put it into words. Perhaps feeling is enough. I'm calmer, more relaxed. Shuko-san, something has just occurred to me. When the Muramasa is destroyed, does this mean Nosaka will be destroyed as well?''

Shuko avoided a direct answer. Instead he said, ''The evil you suffered from has gone. Sensei knew of it merely by conversing with me. He had told me that you will be confronted by the Muramasa and if you do not destroy it, it will destroy you. Such an evil sword always finds its way back to its original master, for like is drawn to like and—''

In the darkness ahead a woman screamed in English, ''Run! Get out of here!''

DiPalma stepped forward past Shuko and listened. He knew that voice.

''Run, Todd, run!''

The woman was Jan and she was terrified.

DiPalma, the black oak cane in his right hand, ran toward her.

22

FROM THE TOP of a broad flight of stone steps Wakaba looked down into the blind alley where Todd and the woman now stood trapped.

In his hand was a *balisong*, the Filipino "butterfly knife" that was his favorite weapon. His little finger undid the hinged lock at the hilt; freed, the blade's cutting edge was face down. With his knife arm dangling at his side, Wakaba slowly descended the stairs into the alley, a deserted cul-de-sac of shuttered shops, turkish baths and snack bars. His shadow, cast by a single streetlight, reached out for the woman, whose frightened face was colored silver by moonlight.

Wakaba grinned as she put an arm around the boy and drew him close, then edged toward the darkened window of a silk shop. It was pointless for them to run; both were trapped in a dead end and the only escape was past Wakaba. He felt no pity for either one. They threatened his dreams and his life with Kenpachi in this world and the next.

The woman began to beg. "Don't do this. Please don't do this." She brushed tears from her eyes and looked wildly around.

Baka, thought Wakaba. Fool. Rokubancho's shops had been closed four hours and would attract no pedestrians. There were no private homes here, no nightclubs; the street was not a thoroughfare. The only passersby were drunkards, who tumbled down the stone stairs to lie unconscious on the pavement until kicked awake in the morning by an angry shopkeeper. A human scavenger might join filthy long-tailed cats in prowling through plastic trash cans lined up at the bottom of the stairs. None of these intruders would be of much help to the boy and the woman.

The sight of Todd and Kenpachi together in the doorway of the castle *dojo* had made Wakaba almost physically ill. He had vowed never to allow a *gaijin* to take part in the suicide of any Japanese as great as his master. Why couldn't Kenpachi-san understand that using a foreigner, a mere boy, as his second would only corrupt the most honorable act of his life?

Fiercely jealous of all who came near Kenpachi, Wakaba saw himself as the only one who deserved to behead him. He loved Kenpachi violently; he was even willing to commit *seppuku* with him, to open his own *hara* so that the world could see the strength of his soul center. Only Wakaba had served the film director with honor and unswerving devotion, even when it was dangerous to do so. Love, a selfless and pure love, made the bodyguard determined to spare his master the disgrace of being beheaded by *gaijin*.

Before Kenpachi had befriended him, Wakaba's life had been dark and empty. The bodyguard's mother had been a prostitute, his father one of her customers. At thirteen Wakaba was on his own, a boy whose great strength and psychotic behavior made him uncontrollable. He suffered headaches, epileptic seizures and had a reputation for random sadism which made him feared even among Tokyo's most violent men.

From their first meeting in a Ginza nightclub, Wakaba had never stopped worshipping Kenpachi. By putting Kenpachi on a pedestal, Wakaba had lifted himself up higher than he had ever been. The film director was beautiful, world famous, brilliant and a samurai, all that the burly bodyguard admired. What drew the two men together was cruelty; neither restrained that impulse, drawing from it a savage and necessary satisfaction.

Once connected to Kenpachi's power, Wakaba vowed to live through him until one or both of them died. For the bodyguard there was no greater joy than to be consumed in Kenpachi's fire. The director's hypnotic voice, the drugs he fed him, the touch of his hands eased Wakaba's terrible headaches. The epileptic fits became fewer and less severe. Under Kenpachi's direction Wakaba improved his reading and writing and developed his martial-arts skills with Tokyo's finest instructors.

Nor did the film director ridicule him when the hulking Wakaba confessed that he had always wanted to do something gentle and beautiful with his hands, that he had always yearned to carve delicate combs out of aged, fragrant wood. Kenpachi had sent him to the workshop of a man who was the eighteenth generation of his family to fashion such combs. Under his instruction Wakaba produced beautifully crafted combs from sweet-smelling wood, often spending hours on a single piece carved in an extraordinary shape of his own design. Kenpachi set up a workshop for him in the castle dungeon and arranged for Wakaba to sell dozens of pieces of his striking work to Japan's most famous people.

This grateful bodyguard gave the filmmaker unqualified obedience even when it meant risking his life, as in Hong Kong, where Wakaba had brutally dealt with the British policeman who had killed Yoshiko. Only Wakaba's martial-arts skills and the *balisong* prevented him from becoming the policemen's second victim. Instead, Kenpachi's curse of *ji-goku*, the Buddhist hell, had been realized. Yoshiko had been avenged.

Tonight Wakaba had decided to kill the boy without further delay.

The bodyguard had borrowed a car from the Blood Oath League members who had greeted him in the courtyard, then followed the woman's limousine to Rokubancho. Here the gods smiled on Wakaba; the narrow streets forced the woman and the boy to leave their vehicle and walk. Here there were no hotels or elaborate Western-style guest lodges, with their well-lit lobbies, security guards and crowds of tourists. At night, in Rokubancho's cramped and dark streets, the woman and the boy would be easy to kill. *Hai*, the gods intended for Wakaba to get rid of the two *gaijin* and spare Kenpachi-san a dishonorable death.

The driver of the limousine remained behind the wheel, unwilling to get lost in Rokubancho's meandering and signless streets. Besides, the boy had claimed to know the way to the house belonging to his father's friend. Let the foreign child and the redheaded woman wander around in darkness, in an

area of Tokyo known only to those who were born there. The
driver pulled his cap over his eyes and slumped down in his
seat. He never saw Wakaba leave his car and jog noiselessly
into Rokubancho.

In the Rokubancho alley Wakaba, the long-bladed knife
hidden behind his thigh, stalked Jan and Todd. The sight of
the boy not only angered Wakaba but made him feel alone and
want to destroy everything around him.

As for the woman, Kenpachi had planned to kill her; Wakaba would now do it for him. She, too, was an enemy, the
reincarnation of Saga, who four hundred years ago had betrayed the lord of Ikuba Castle.

Wakaba heard running footsteps and spun around in a
crouch. He held the knife in front, thumb on the blade, and
waited. Seconds later DiPalma and Shuko turned the corner,
saw Wakaba, Jan and Todd, and slowed down. DiPalma motioned Shuko to hang back.

"He has a knife," the American whispered.

Wakaba looked over his shoulder at the woman. The American had heard her screams but he could not save her or the
boy; Wakaba would kill them both, even at the cost of his life.
Their death would be his final gift to Kenpachi.

But Wakaba did not expect to die. There was nothing to
fear from either the woman or the boy. He had only contempt
for the big American, the *gaijin* who played at being a swordsman and who had once defeated Kenpachi in a kendo match.
Kenpachi fenced with enthusiasm and practiced karate dili-
gently, but his skills did not approach those of Wakaba. The
bodyguard was a born fighter who had never learned to fear.

He found Western men inferior; they were unwilling to fight
to the death and believed that a foe should be shown mercy. A
gaijin was a coward and a weakling. Wakaba spat in the direction of the big American and waited.

DiPalma, cane at his side, slowly descended the stairs. He
had been physically drained, played out from the long hours in
the forge and from walking Rokubancho's serpentine streets.
The feeling was gone now; he felt relaxed, calm. The gut feeling that Todd was in trouble had been proven true, but the
tension was gone. Something like the heat felt in Tendrai's
forge passed over him, then disappeared.

As DiPalma walked down the staircase he kept his eyes on Wakaba's face. He saw neither fear nor indecision in the bodyguard, only a determination to kill, a conviction that nothing could stop him.

At the bottom of the staircase DiPalma, holding the cane away from his body, circled to his right. Wakaba, scornful, scarcely moved. He looked with contempt at the American's cane; the *balisong* had opposed tougher weapons. The *gaijin* had only seconds to live.

Wakaba tossed the knife from hand to hand, changing grips, blade up, blade down. Then he sandwiched the knife between his palms and went down in a crouch.

The attack was swift, unexpected. Jan cried, "Oh God!"

Wakaba leaped forward and swung the knife low, slashing at DiPalma's left knee. The American moved without thinking; he stepped to his right and quickly backhanded Wakaba across the face with the cane, crushing his nose. Bleeding heavily, the enraged Japanese hesitated briefly, then charged, thrusting his knife at DiPalma's heart.

DiPalma stepped aside and cracked Wakaba on the right knee. The Japanese grunted, stumbled forward and spun around to face the American, who had backed out of range.

DiPalma remembered his training. See through the opponent. Look strongly into his mind. See his fears, his doubts, his weaknesses. Pay only passing attention to the opponent's size and physical skills; to observe them too clearly was to be beaten before the fight began.

He looked into Wakaba's mind, saw the anger which prevented him from concentrating properly, saw the overconfidence which told him his opponent was of little consequence. He saw Wakaba's chief weakness, his inability to think. The bodyguard relied on his immense strength, his technique, the pleasure he received from hating.

Wakaba tossed the knife from hand to hand as he inched toward DiPalma. His right leg dragged slightly. He had been hurt and wanted revenge. His plan was to take the *gaijin's* cane, then slice his throat and genitals. Wakaba bent his knees, ready to spring forward.

In kendo the three best opportunities to attack came when the opponent was about to make a move, after he had made the move and when the opponent was waiting.

The three methods of attack were to go for the opponent's weapon, his technique or his spirit.

DiPalma decided to do what Wakaba least expected—attack first and break the bodyguard's seemingly unbreakable spirit. He saw Wakaba's knees bend, his nostrils flare and his knife hand start to come up. Preparation.

Screaming at the top of his voice DiPalma charged and brought the cane down on the bodyguard's bandaged hand, once, twice, shattering the hand. Before Wakaba could withdraw DiPalma struck him on the elbow, faked another attack on the ruined hand, then unleased a vicious head strike. The head strike never landed; the boydguard, to protect his tortured left hand, leaned back and out of range.

Wakaba continued backing up toward the trash cans near the stairs. With his sleeve he wiped blood from his fractured nose and face. His left arm was useless. His right knee throbbed and had begun to swell; his damaged nose now forced him to breathe through his mouth. Inside he could feel the power gained through his anger begin to ebb. The *gaijin* had left him confused and frustrated. Wakaba no longer faced a weak enemy, but one who attacked with murderous precision, with a spirit strong enough to force a retreat. But the bodyguard would die before he surrendered.

The tiger of wrath raged within Wakaba; to feed his anger he had only to look at the American's son. Suddenly, he conceived an idea which so possessed him that it blotted out the pain. There was one sure way of defeating the American, one which would break his spirit and leave him too shaken to continue fighting.

Wakaba would kill the American's son before his eyes.

The *gaijin*'s will was not free; it was strongly attached to his son, something Wakaba had seen in Hong Kong and again here in the alley. The pain of witnessing his son's death would be a suffering the American could not overcome. But to get to the foreign boy, who stood at the opposite end of the alley, Wakaba would first have to deal with the American.

His leg brushed one of the plastic trash cans. *Hai.* There was a way to take care of the American.

DiPalma advanced slowly toward the bodyguard, the black oak cane held shoulder high in a two-handed grip. He had learned to end a fight quickly, to put an end to it before the uncertain occurred. Wakaba was hurting, dragging his right leg, making no attempt to use his left arm. He's still dangerous, thought DiPalma. He's too stubborn and stupid not to be.

DiPalma was inching closer when Wakaba suddenly dropped his knife and in a single motion grabbed a trash can by the handle and flung it across the alley at him. Trailing garbage, the container hit DiPalma in the hip, knocking him off balance. A second trash can crashed into his chest and arm. The cane was sent flying across the alley and landed in a shop doorway. DiPalma, fighting panic, turned to run after it as a third can hit him between the shoulder blades, sending him stumbling to finally fall on his hands and knees.

The American looked over his shoulder as still another trash can was flung at him. He rolled over, the concrete painfully scraping his face and hip; the container sprayed him with broken glass and empty beer bottles. On his back DiPalma watched as Shuko reached the bottom of the stairs, leaped forward and attempted a roundhouse kick to Wakaba's rib cage.

Obsessed with destroying the boy, the bodyguard threw himself to the pavement, landing on his right side. At the same time he kicked up with his left leg, driving deep into Shuko's stomach. The policeman was lifted off his feet, then dropped to the ground, the wind knocked out of him.

Wakaba scrambled toward his knife, scooped it up, then pushed himself off the pavement. Looking neither at Shuko or DiPalma, he half-limped, half-ran toward the closed end of the alley, toward Todd.

DiPalma was on his feet, frightened and frustrated almost to tears. He glanced away from Wakaba, to the oak cane lying only a few steps away. Todd was doomed. He and DiPalma were at opposite ends of the alley. With or without the cane DiPalma would never reach his son before the bodyguard. Todd was going to die and there was no way to stop it. Unless—

DiPalma ran to the shop doorway. "Todd!" he yelled.

With all his strength DiPalma hurled the silver-knobbed cane toward the boy, arching it high enough to fly over Wakaba's head.

As soon as the cane was in the air DiPalma's heart sank. It

was a poor throw, off line, too far away from Todd. It floated softly, turned twice in midair, then began its descent. As the boy ran to catch it, Wakaba angled toward him, ignoring Jan, who backed along the windows of the darkened shops. Once behind Wakaba, she bolted toward DiPalma.

The cane hit the ground, bounced twice, then rolled away from Todd.

Wakaba shouted, "I will not let you be *kaishaku* to Ken-pachi-san! You will never violate his *seppuku*!"

He was almost close enough to touch when the boy dived for the cane. He landed on his stomach and stretched his arm until his fingers closed around the silver knob.

Wakaba, leaning forward, slashed down at Todd's back.

But the boy, cane clutched to his chest, quickly rolled a few feet away and sprang to his feet. He was now between Wakaba and DiPalma and could have run. Instead he stood his ground and with both hands held the cane near the knob, the tip aimed at Wakaba's stomach. "Goddamn it, run!" yelled DiPalma. "Get out of here!"

But a fearful DiPalma could only clutch Jan and watch as the bodyguard, slowed by his injured knee, turned to face Todd. Wakaba limped closer, and, incredibly, the boy inched forward to meet him.

DiPalma shoved Jan aside. "Back off, Todd! Stay away from him!"

The boy did not answer nor did he turn around. Instead he continued to stare at Wakaba. And continued to move forward.

Wakaba had the distance he wanted. He slashed at Todd's neck with all his strength. As Jan screamed, Todd stepped left and crouched. The knife passed over his head. At the same moment he backhanded the cane against Wakaba's damaged knee, causing it to buckle.

With one knee on the ground, Wakaba, off balance, braced himself against the alley floor with his knife hand. He and Todd now faced each other, their heads at the same height.

As though he had done it hundreds of times before, Todd jammed his foot down on Wakaba's knife hand, pinning it to the ground. Then, with his hands wide apart on the cane—right hand on the knob, left hand near the tip—the boy gave a

savage yell that paralyzed DiPalma and drove the cane length-
wise into Wakaba's throat.

The bodyguard dropped like a stone. He twisted and
turned, his eyes bulging.

"Oh, my God," whispered Jan, hands clutching her own
throat.

Stunned, DiPalma ran to his son, who gazed down at Wakaba with cold satisfaction. The boy's eyes were half-shut and
the ghost of a smile played on his mouth. He stood supremely
confident, a war lord who had pronounced judgment and
meted out punishment.

DiPalma reached for the cane, but Todd clung to it with
surprising strength and glared at his father. Then the boy
relaxed and removed his hands from the cane. A second later
his eyes turned up in his head and he collapsed in DiPalma's
arms.

DiPalma knelt, eased his son to the ground, then felt the
boy's neck for a pulse. It was erratic but strong. He wiped
sweat from his temple, then smoothed the boy's damp hair.
Katharine had understood their son in a way he never would.

He looked up to find Jan and an unsteady Shuko standing
behind him. But before he could speak Wakaba rolled over on
his side to face Todd. Only minutes ago he had shouted at
Todd: *I will not let you be* kaishaku *to Kenpachi-san. You will
never violate his* seppuku.

DiPalma looked at the bodyguard and in that instant he
understood and knew. The horror of it chilled his blood. Kenpachi was planning to commit suicide and wanted Todd to
behead him. DiPalma's son was to be the film director's *kaishaku.* Wakaba had to answer some questions and answer
them now.

But the bodyguard was dying. His eyes had an unnatural
brightness and his face was dark from lack of oxygen. Todd
had crushed Wakaba's larynx and now he was drowning in his
own blood.

The bodyguard reached for Todd with a trembling hand and
willed himself to form a single word.

"Benkai," he rasped. Then his hand flopped to the ground
and he was silent.

23

Zurich

KEN SHIRATORI stepped from his chauffeured Mercedes and stopped to listen to the bells of the Grossmünster, the eight-hundred-year-old cathedral whose Gothic twin towers were the symbol of the Swiss city. He was late for an 8:00 A.M. breakfast meeting. The bells, however, reminded him that there was no escape from memory. For a moment the Japanese businessman stared into the past, then shook his head and dismissed the memory. He had no time for dead and dying things. He belonged to the future.

When the bells finished striking, Shiratori, flanked by two Swiss bodyguards, walked into the office building he owned on Bahnhofstrasse, Zurich's elegant avenue of banks, deluxe stores, high-rises and cafés. Until recently he had traveled with at least one security man. But the recent murders of Japanese and western industrialists had convinced Shiratori to keep a minimum of two guards with him at all times. He wasn't sure if he believed in the existence of the Blood Oath League, the group which rumor had credited with the killings. But he knew that to ignore danger was to increase it.

This morning a cold wind blew off the elongated lake from which the city took its name. Shiratori wore neither a topcoat nor a sweater. And he had refused to use the car heater during the drive from the Dolder Grand, the fairytale castle of a hotel located on a wooded hill which looked down on the city. He had also denied a request of his bodyguards to close the car windows. The muscular Swiss could only turn up their coat collars, blow into their cupped hands and softly curse in Romansh, a language spoken by only one percent of the Swiss. The bodyguards had a name for Shiratori. "Old Split Foot." The devil. What else could you call such a warm-blooded prick.

Before any major business deal, Shiratori always suffered a chemical imbalance; his skin reddened, his body temperature shot up, and he perspired so heavily that he was often forced to leave the conference table and change into a dry shirt and clean underwear. His increased body warmth neither made him physically ill nor affected his judgment. He had been master of himself since boyhood; he had learned long ago that what lay in his power to do also lay in his power not to do.

This morning he was to meet with a consortium of Italians and French who had agreed to invest two hundred million dollars in Shiratori's most ambitious project, a $500-million Tokyo theme park that would include Japan's most modern golf course. He had all the money he needed, money, in fact, that had been easy to come by. Shiratori's toughest problem had been finding available land in Tokyo, where real estate prices topped those of Paris, Zurich and Manhattan. The Grossmünster bells reminded him that in acquiring the needed land he had also destroyed Japanese traditions and made enemies.

Ken Shiratori was in his early forties, a lean man with delicate features spoiled by a harelip which he attempted to hide with a mustache. He was the son of a Japanese airline pilot and a French actress; his response to his mixed parentage had been to develop a brutal instinct for making money and exercising it without passion or feeling. He owned Japan's largest chain of hotels, held large blocks of stock in a well-known beer company and was a partner in a baseball team. He also controlled a real-estate corporation which bought vast parcels of land throughout Japan, then built *danchi*, cheap apartment houses.

To do this, Shiratori uprooted thousands of poor and lower-class families, leveled hills and destroyed sacred trees and small parks. He had little reverence for tradition, seeing the old Japan as obsolete and outdated.

"Japan's obsession with its past is weakening," he had said in a speech to a group of admiring young Japanese businessmen. "Habit and custom should not be beyond criticism, nor should the dead rule the living."

Shiratori made no secret of his *gaijin kompurekksu*, his belief that western culture was superior to that of Japan. He spoke fluent English, wore his hair in a permanent, ordered his clothes from Rodeo Drive in Beverly Hills and Saville Row and had an American wife. He was a champion speedboat racer and had spent a small fortune outbidding other Japanese promoters for the right to import top American show-business talent.

To Shiratori, being first meant being faithful to his instincts; his life was dedicated to rising above the snobs who still looked down on him for not being "a true Japanese." He boasted that neither fire nor war could avenge him as well as he could avenge himself.

Apart from his lavish Tokyo homes, he kept a suite at New York's Hotel Carlyle and condominiums in Los Angeles, Acapulco and Honolulu. His favorite western city, however, was Zurich. He felt at home among its fabled "gnomes," the bankers who had made the city a world financial center and to whom money was the elixir of life. The Swiss were indifferent to Shiratori's mixed parentage, his ruthless business tactics, his determination to invest his own traditions.

Life in the bankers' town pleased Shiratori enough to spend four months of the year here. His French wife loved Zurich's medieval quarter, with its maze of narrow, sloping streets and old houses with wrought-iron signs. He preferred the new Zurich, especially the Bahnhofstrasse, the beautiful broad street which ran three quarters of a mile from the main railroad station to ice blue Lake Zurich, and which was one of the world's most expensive shopping avenues. Through the gnomes' influence, Shiratori had purchased an office building on Bahnhofstrasse, where vaults of gold were buried under the pavement and the summer air was sweet with the smell of linden trees.

Without consulting Shiratori, the gnomes inserted a clause in the purchase agreement, giving them the right to buy a twenty percent interest in the building, at a price to be set by them. He was forced to go along; nothing could be done in Zurich without the bankers' approval.

The gnomes earned their forced partnership by helping Shiratori to finance his ambitious amusement park. They found the last two hundred million dollars he needed and arranged dummy corporations so that European investors could remain anonymous. Accounts were then set up in Swiss banks and abroad and the money flowed back and forth until no French or Italian tax man could trace it.

The gnomes also found Shiratori a first-class law firm and acted as his financial advisers on the amusement park. Some Japanese saw the gnomes as cold-blooded and pitiless, obsessed with greed and gain. Shiratori saw them as brilliant and energetic, bold princes in rimless glasses and close haircuts. Willingly he paid their multimillion-dollar fee and gave them two percent of the amusement park's gross.

The park, called Cosmos, had a science-fiction theme. It was the world of the future, time unborn, the existence yet to come. It was Shiratori's world and he had planned it carefully, first consulting scientists in six countries, then turning to American and British film technicians who had worked on the most successful science-fiction films of the past ten years. Cosmos was going to be the finest park of its kind in the world. It was also going to be the biggest problem of Shiratori's life.

In gaining title to the land he had been as ruthless as the gnomes, using money, influence and perseverance, his own brand of courage. But land was scarce in Tokyo, where too many people were packed into too little space. The press, citizens' groups and politicians attacked Shiratori for "stealing" precious real estate and evicting families in the name of profit. Shiratori shrugged off the critics. He was building a new Japan, and only the ignorant would oppose that.

To drive home his point he selected a particular parcel of land to be leveled first. Besides cheap wooden houses, a beautiful pagoda and a small park, it also contained an ancient Buddhist temple, whose bell was said to have been blessed by Lord Buddha himself. Emperors and shoguns had worshipped here and some claimed to have witnessed miracles within its walls. Shiratori ignored all the pleas to save the temple.

Neither censure, threatening letters nor media criticism could change his mind.

Thousands of Japanese who lived near the temple signed a scroll asking that the temple be spared. A delegation of temple monks, accompanied by reporters, attempted to present the scroll to Shiratori at his office; he refused to see them. The land had been legally purchased and the proper authorities had given their approval to Cosmos, which could be expected to draw tourists from all over the world. As for the golf course, Shiratori was already in touch with golf associations in America and Europe about staging a tournament. The prize money would be double that of any current Western tournament. Like it or not, the land and anything on it belonged to him to do as he pleased.

Then Shiratori heard about the three monks. His Tokyo lawyer showed him the letter.

"I received it in the mail this morning," said the lawyer. "No return address. Postmarked yesterday. Not much to it. Three monks are going to set themselves on fire the day you begin demolition of the temple."

"I guess I should be grateful," said Shiratori. "This proves there are at least three men in the world dumber than me. A perfect example of conscientious stupidity. Don't bother me with this nonsense. Just wipe your ass with it and flush it down the toilet. Nothing's going to happen. I'm not about to help them get the publicity they're looking for. No comment. And that's official."

"What if they're serious? What if they carry out their threat to kill themselves?"

"God will forgive me. That's his business, isn't it?"

But on the morning of the demolition Shiratori arrived at the temple site feeling uneasy. His anxiety grew when he saw the thousands who had gathered along with extra police and the press. Outwardly he appeared detached, even amused. Nothing in the world was permanent. Nothing lasted forever. He had never shared the "true Japanese" idolatry of the past and never would. No one was going to stop that temple from coming down.

But he felt a foreboding which grew when the temple bells started to ring. The crowd, which had been restless, suddenly became silent and Shiratori, his engineer and construction foreman all turned to stare at the temple entrance. Half a dozen monks in saffron robes, their shaved heads bowed, stood chanting on the temple stairs. Several others now left the temple, playing flutes, drums and cymbals. The last to leave were three monks, holding prayer books and beads.

While the three monks knelt outside the entrance, the bells continued to ring and ring until Shiratori wanted to put his hands over his ears. Suddenly he hated that sound. To hell with the monks. He opened his mouth to give the order, to tell his engineer and foreman to proceed. That was when the crowd groaned. Several men and women cried out. Shiratori looked at the temple. And felt sick.

It happened too quickly for anyone to interfere. The three kneeling monks struck matches and touched them to their robes, which were already soaked in gasoline. All three were immediately engulfed in flames. A shocked Shiratori watched as many in the crowd prevented the police from going to the monks. People screamed, fistfights broke out and the three monks fell to the ground, wrapped in pale blue fire.

The bells continued to ring as the observing monks chanted louder, their droning voices ominous to a now frightened Shiratori. A rock grazed his cheek and a bottle sailed in front of him, cracking a tinted window of his limousine. Now rocks and bottles rained down on his crew, who backed away from their equipment and looked toward him with pleading eyes. The crowd surged toward Shiratori and the handful of employees around him. Without waiting to be told by the police, he fled the temple site in his limousine.

The burning monks stayed in his mind for days. As did the temple bells.

A week later, after an official investigation and dozens of negative press reports, the temple was destroyed. Shiratori, meanwhile, looked at what he had and wondered why he was not happy.

* * *

IN THE LOBBY of his Zurich office building Shiratori and his two bodyguards walked toward the private elevator that was held open by a uniformed Turk who spoke six languages and had been a university professor in his native Istanbul before fleeing a repressive Turkish government. The elevator was used only by Shiratori and kept locked when he was not in Zurich. The Turk held the keys and was so grateful to Shiratori for the job that he had vowed to die rather than surrender the keys to "improper authorities."

Shiratori felt perspiration run down his forehead and chin. His hands were damp and his skin heated as though he were standing in front of a roaring fire. He was also becoming sexually aroused. He smiled. His body was signaling him that he was ready to confront the gnomes, the Italians, the French and the dozen lawyers waiting in the conference room.

He stepped to the back of the carpeted, polished oak elevator as a bodyguard pressed a button. The door closed on the smiling Turk, who held up the keys. Shiratori ignored him. There were other things to focus on. He had to change into a fresh shirt before entering the conference room. The one he now wore was wringing wet. A good sign.

The elevator ride would be a swift one. Silent too. Thirty-three floors nonstop in seconds. Shiratori wished it was faster.

The elevator began its ascent, picked up speed, then slowed down and stopped.

Shiratori angrily pushed past a bodyguard and banged the starter button with his fist. Nothing. Again he pounded the button, then again. The elevator did not move.

"Shit," he said in English. "Get on the goddamn phone and call the Turk downstairs. He's supposed to make sure this fucking thing is working whenever I'm in Zurich. Tell that wog I want this elevator moving and I want it moving now."

Felix, the older bodyguard, slid back a stainless steel panel below the elevator buttons. For a few seconds he said nothing. Then, "Mr. Shiratori, we have a problem."

"I'm not interested in problems. I'm only interested in results."

"There's no telephone."

It had been removed, its wire neatly cut.

Felix and the other bodyguard, Stephan, exchanged looks. Felix tugged at his earlobe, a lifelong habit when bothered by anything suspicious.

Shiratori backed into a corner and rubbed his palms on his thighs. He was losing control. The perspiration had stopped. He looked at his watch. Eight-twenty. He had to get out of this damned elevator. He reached for his cigarettes.

Felix looked up at the ceiling. "I wouldn't do that, Mr. Shiratori. Smoking, I mean. Don't know how long we'll be trapped. Better to conserve what fresh air we have. There is a trapdoor on top. Maybe one of us can get out that way. Maybe see how close we are to one of the floors."

He turned to Stephan. "You're the gymnast around here. Or you used to be when you were a schoolboy."

Stephan smiled. "That was years ago. But I try."

Shiratori wrung his hands and nodded. His voice became soft. He knew he was on the edge of hysteria. "Do whatever you can to get us out. I do not like to be closed in. I must have air."

"We'll do our best," said Felix. "Stephan, time to make like a monkey or like you are escaping from a jealous husband."

Felix squatted and Stephan, in his stocking feet, sat on his shoulders. Felix then rose to his full height, pushing Stephan close to the ceiling. He reached overhead, unlatched the trapdoor and threw it back. The sound of the door hitting the top of the elevator echoed along the darkened shaft. Felix wobbled as Stephan, grunting, pulled himself through the opening and disappeared. Shiratori braced himself against a wall as the elevator rocked gently. Stephan was walking around on top.

Felix called out, "Hey Stephan, lose some weight while you're up there. You're heavy."

Stephan's voice had an echo. "Maybe I go jogging before I come back down. Very dark in this shaft. Let me get my cigarette lighter and I—"

Suddenly the car rocked so violently that Shiratori and Felix almost lost ther balance. It jerked on its cable and scraped the sides of the concrete shaft.

Felix cleared his throat. He didn't want to criticize Stephan in front of this Jap bastard, but what he was now doing on top of the elevator was dangerous. "Stephan, I think—"

Shiratori was raging. He shrieked at the ceiling. "Are you mad? I order you down from there this minute, or you're out of a job. And I'll see to it that you never—''

Something hard, wet and red flew through the trapdoor and bounced off Shiratori's shoulders, landing on the thick carpet.

Stephan's head. Eyes wide with disbelief. Neck and chin slick with warm blood.

Whimpering, Shiratori backed into a corner, hands over his ears. The bells. The bells. And death.

Retching, Felix stared down at Stephan's head. And when he heard the noise above him, he tried to do everything at once. Tried to remember his training.

Turn to face the enemy. Draw the PPK Walther. Thumb off the safety. Empty the gun into the bastard.

The *ninja* was faster and more cold-blooded. He dropped through the ceiling, landing on Felix's back with both knees. In pain and out of breath, the bodyguard fell forward, striking his head against the wall. He was on his knees, dazed, the PPK Walther still in his hand, when the black-clad figure slit his throat from behind in one smooth gesture.

Then the *ninja* leaped on a screaming Shiratori.

Moments later the *ninja* returned the knife to the small of his back, bent his knees and gracefully leaped toward the ceiling, where dangling arms caught his wrists and pulled him up. Then he disappeared through the opening, and the door closed.

In the darkened shaft three black-clad figures began to climb the elevator cable with the ease of acrobats.

24

Tokyo

THE SMELL MADE JAN sick to her stomach. Turning her back on the fire now burning in the temple courtyard, she removed a tissue from her shoulder bag and held it over her nose. A few seconds later she thought, to hell with it. Where is it written that I have to stand on top of my crew while they work. Shading her eyes against the blistering sun, she crossed the courtyard and stood near a pond filled with water lilies and shaded by yellowing gingko trees.

From here she watched the second unit film two Buddhist priests as they burned a collection of dolls in the center of the temple courtyard. Women and girls surrounded the priests as they fed dozens of damaged and worn dolls onto a large metal tray of hot coals. It was an ancient and moving ceremony, but the odor of burning plastic forced Jan to watch from a distance.

To the Japanese, dolls were not mere toys. They demanded love and consideration at all times. Childless women and spinsters kept dolls to alleviate their loneliness, treating them as babies. In time such affection was said to create a soul within the doll. That was why when a doll began to fall apart, it could not be treated like trash.

Proper respect called for destruction by purification through fire or water. Some women and girls floated old dolls on a river or allowed the tide to take them out to sea. Others, like those Jan now stood watching, brought their dolls to be purified in a temple fire. For a small donation Jan's crew had been allowed to film a doll-burning ceremony in a rundown neighborhood of flimsy wooden houses with sliding paper doors.

Because locks were useless on such doors, one member of the household stayed home at all times to guard against burglars. Today dozens of them leaned out of windows and stood in doorways watching the actors and crew. To win the neighborhood's cooperation, one Japanese crew member had gone out into a street near the temple and, as the local people gathered around him, acted out the entire film, even to the point of falling down when "shot."

At the moment Jan could easily have shot Kon Kenpachi. He had had an 8:00 A.M. appointment with the Tokyo police, the fifth straight day the police had talked to him about the late Wakaba. It was now past noon and no word from Kon. Not even a quick telephone call letting Jan know when he might return to the set. With production costs now running close to sixty thousand dollars a day, Jan's first movie could fall apart for lack of a director.

What had saved her so far was Sam, her efficient production manager, who had quickly shifted to the backup shot, the doll-burning scene in the temple courtyard. It was something a second unit could handle without Kenpachi. Under a first assistant director, a second unit shot exterior footage—crowd scenes, car chases, floods, avalanches—scenes which didn't need major stars or a director. The doll burning was to be used as a cutaway while Tom Gennaro and Kelly Keighley discussed the *yakuza* money stolen by Gennaro's Japanese girl friend.

Gennaro and Keighley were due to go before the cameras this morning. Instead they sat around bored, until both decided to go off and amuse themselves until Kon returned. Both actors had a star's ego; when they were ready to work, everyone else should be ready. By talking to each man, Jan had managed to cool them down, but they couldn't be controlled for long if they had nothing to do. Gennaro was off on a side street throwing a football with some of the American and British crew. Keighley, with his teenage Venezuelan mistress, was strolling under the weeping willows which lined the bank of the Sumida River.

Jan believed in keeping to a tight production schedule,

something she had learned in television, where there was no such thing as working too fast. A producer never allowed actors, especially expensive actors, to become bored. Bored actors gave boring performances. Without a strong director or producer, actors could easily lose interest in a film. Worse, they might attempt to take over a production.

But if God had wanted actors to direct themselves, he would have made them all fat and bald and named them Hitchcock.

In the week since Wakaba's death, Kon had spent so much time with the police that the crew had nicknamed him "Monopoly Man."

"'Cause he don't pass Go, he don't collect two hundred dollars, but he do go directly to jail."

Not funny. Without Kenpachi, Jan had no movie. She couldn't fail, not the first time out. In Hollywood, if you blew it there was no mercy. Failure was a contagious disease. Anyone who came down with it was ostracized.

"Don't you ever come up short out here, girl," a black casting director had told Jan on her first trip to Los Angeles. "That's the same as admitting your feet stink, your breath's bad and you don't love your Jesus."

Why were the police leaning on Kon? He hadn't killed Wakaba. Todd had. In self-defense and in front of witnesses. God knows he was a nice enough kid, but after what Jan had seen him do to Wakaba she suspected him of having more than a homicidal touch in his soul. In Hong Kong she had almost passed out at the sight of Geoffrey Laycock lying skewered in the middle of the hospital flagpole. But when Todd had looked out the window at the dead Englishman, Jan thought she had seen a smile on his face.

The Royal Hong Kong Police, who had seen everything in the way of violent crimes, had never seen a man die as Laycock had. And the hospital staff on duty that night had been horrified; some, like Jan, had to be sedated.

Todd had been unmoved. He had stood by Frank's bed and stared down at his unconscious father as though he, Todd, were the father, the protector, and Frank the child, the one in need of protection.

In Tokyo, this same boy kills a knife-wielding grown man

who outweighs him by over one hundred pounds. Also spooky. Jan had tried to tell herself that the boy had acted out of nerves, that his adrenaline had been pumping in the alley and he had just gotten lucky. But the more she thought about it, and connected it to the incident at the Hong Kong hospital, the more she believed that Todd had known exactly what he was doing.

Todd Hansard was beginning to look less cuddly and more creepy-crawly. Frank must have noticed. He never missed much.

What was behind Wakaba's incredible hatred of Todd? The two had never laid eyes on each other until a couple of weeks ago, when *Ukiyo* moved to Hong Kong for location shooting. When Jan asked Frank why Wakaba had hated his son, the only answer was, "The man was a wacko. Let it go at that."

Which immediately told her he was holding something back. His hooded eyes seemed more veiled than normal and he stared at Jan as though challenging her to doubt his answer.

Over drinks at Ikuba Castle she had asked Kon Kenpachi the same question. His answer had been more detailed, yet simple.

"Jealousy. The greatest of all punishments. I'd offered Todd a small part in *Ukiyo* and refused to do the same for Wakaba."

Jan didn't know whether to laugh or cry. "Kon, I've heard of people dying to get into show business. But *killing?* No offense, but it makes Wakaba sound as if he had the brain of a crouton."

"There is a little more to it than that."

She sipped an almond-flavored French liqueur. "With you there always is."

"I would very much like to star Todd in a film of his own."

"Are you serious?"

"It's not something I'm prepared to discuss for publication, but I do have a project in mind for the boy. I admire the way Steven Spielberg works with children. He has a very good way of telling a story from their point of view, while managing to retain the interest of adults. That's the sort of thing I have in mind for Todd. The boy has a certain magnetism, a brooding quality, which I feel could transfer quite well to the screen."

Jan said, "But he's never acted before. How do you know he can do it?"

"It is my business to know such things. Besides, most of my films depend on casting performers who have not lost their beauty, their vigor." His eyes glazed over and his voice grew soft. "Beauty, youth and death. So irresistible."

"You mean like James Dean, Valentino, Jean Harlow."

He nodded vigorously. "Yes. That is exactly what I mean. And now they are beautiful for all time. As is our own Yukio Mishima, whom some now consider a god. Through death one can live forever."

Jan hated this kind of talk. But Kon was a performer and performers all had a touch of the fanatic in them. She said, "I take it you haven't discussed Todd's movie career with Frank."

Kenpachi swallowed his drink, then refilled their glasses. "Mr. DiPalma's life and mine run counter to each other in every possible way. He does not like the idea of his son being in my company."

Jan reached over and touched Kenpachi's arm. "Baby-cakes, you have not exactly spent your life in mad pursuit of clean living."

"I can assure you I have no sexual interest in the boy, if that's what you are insinuating. Wakaba was jealous, yes. But no relationship I had with other men ever pleased him."

"Sexual or otherwise?"

"Sexual or otherwise."

"Were you and Wakaba ever lovers?"

A faint smile crossed Kenpachi's face, but it told her nothing. "Pleasure articulates itself," he said. "Pleasure finds its own voice. Then a day arrives when that voice becomes silent. Intoxication is temporary and inevitably fades. Wakaba found this part of our relationship difficult to accept."

"I see. Today a chicken, tomorrow a feather duster. Sooner or later everyone in Kenpachi's life has to get up and give his seat to someone else."

She swallowed more almond liqueur. She felt relaxed, daring, she wanted to challenge Kon. Why not? Why have an affair if you can't kick each other in the shins once in a while?

"From what I could see," Jan said, "Wakaba was very loyal to you. Yet you're treating his death as if it were nothing more serious than dropping a piece of toast on the floor. No tears, no long face. Is it because the show must go on or what?"

Kenpachi gave her an ugly look. For a second she feared he might strike her. Then he said smoothly, "Wakaba attempted to kill the boy. I shall never forgive him for that. Todd is of immense importance to me."

"Speaking of movies, ours is running behind schedule. You've been off to see the police every day since Wakaba's death. Meanwhile we're losing time and time is money."

"Perhaps this is something you should discuss with your friend, Mr. DiPalma."

"I don't get it. You're saying my movie's behind schedule because of Frank DiPalma?"

"Captain Shuko is his friend. And it is Shuko who insists on my appearing in his office whenever the mood strikes him."

"If I read you right you're saying Frank blames you for the attempt made by Wakaba to kill Todd. And that he's using Shuko to get back at you."

Kenpachi looked at Jan with contempt. "On the subject of DiPalma, your mind is not exactly possessed by wisdom. The day will soon arrive when you will be forced to concern yourself with those things you do not wish to know at present. Has it not occurred to you that DiPalma feels extremely guilty in the matter of Katharine Hansard's death?"

"He's told me so, yes."

"Then does it not make sense that this guilt may have settled his mind in the matter of the boy?"

"Anything's possible, I suppose."

"He would not be the first man who did not want to accept responsibility for his own actions. Why should you be surprised that he wishes to unload this guilt on others. You know why he's here in Tokyo."

Jan said, "He's investigating Katharine Hansard's death."

"For which he holds Nosaka-san responsible. And to get at Nosaka-san, DiPalma is having me harassed by Captain Shuko in the hope that I will soon tire of such treatment and help them to destroy a very great man. DiPalma is even going so far as to pry into Nosaka-san's business affairs."

"Frank says Nosaka's deep into industrial espionage—"

Kenpachi slammed his fist on the table, making Jan jump in her chair. "You are now in Japan. Here, industrial espionage does not exist. What information our government and businessmen gather is for the good of our country as a whole. Much of what we gather is public knowledge, available to anyone who will take the time to collect it. We do not spy. Do you hear me? *We do not spy.*"

Jan held up a hand in a stop signal. "If you don't mind, I'd appreciate not being yelled at. Call it what you want to over here. What Frank's concerned with is the effect of Nosaka's actions in America and maybe in a few other countries as well. He has a right to his opinion same as you. I'd rather not go into that at the moment. You said something about Shuko getting involved in all of this because Frank asked him to. Assuming Shuko's not a moron and he's not being paid off, why should a man in his position do something so dumb? You'd think he'd be the first to come out on Nosaka's side. Let's face it: Frank's a foreigner here, an outsider. Shuko and Nosaka are both Japanese, or they were the last time I looked."

Kenpachi rose and stood with his feet apart, hands folded across his chest. Just like Yul Brynner in *The King and I*, thought Jan. Except this time the king has only one subject to put in her place. Me.

"Shuko is scum," said Kenpachi. "He's looking out for himself, not for Japan. During World War II, his father was an army officer who brought disgrace upon himself at a time when his country needed him. Shuko's father betrayed Japan. For this he was executed by Nosaka-san. Shuko, who is not a man, has never stopped hating Nosaka-san for doing his duty. That is what Shuko and DiPalma have in common. Both are too weak to accept responsibility for their own karma. Both now seek to blame Nosaka-san for their own weaknesses."

"Frank never mentioned this to me."

"And if he had?"

She took her cigarettes from her purse, shook one loose and lit it. She blew smoke toward the lacquered ceiling. "I don't know. I really don't know."

"I understand that the women of your country think for themselves."

"I'm still working on the difference between reasons that sound good and good, sound reasoning. Get to the point."

"The point, my dear free-thinking American, is that you should reason for yourself and do so independently of Frank DiPalma. If you will investigate you will find that the emperor himself approved of Nosaka-san's killing of Shuko's father. The emperor placed Nosaka-san under his personal protection, where he still remains. Shuko and all members of his family are forbidden to harm Nosaka-san. This does not, however, prevent them from enlisting others to do their dirty work for them."

"You mean Frank?"

"He carries two dead women with him at all times, does he not? He even seeks to involve your father in this charade."

Jan lifted her chin. "My father *is* involved. I didn't need Frank to tell me that."

Kenpachi stepped closer. "Because your father and Nosaka-san are business associates does not involve them in a criminal conspiracy. Is it not possible that the files now in your father's possession are nothing more than forgeries?"

"And who would go to the trouble of forging files on Nosaka's bank and other businesses?"

He dropped to his knees beside her and grinned like a schoolboy. "Mr. DiPalma would. His is a nature which craves revenge."

Jan touched her forehead to his. "Passionate Sicilian nature and all that. Don't forget people like him love to wear bright colors and pointed shoes." She leaned back. "Now that we've disposed of the obvious, let me tell you that my father thinks the files are genuine. And it wasn't Frank who put the files together. It was Todd's stepfather. Meanwhile, dad's gone to a lot of trouble to protect those files."

"And what exactly has he done to protect them?"

Jan sighed and reached for her drink. "Checked himself into the hospital again. He says, or rather the weird little man who heads his security says, the hospital's the safest place. Easy to guard, that kind of nonsense. The weird little man, someone called Nullabor, feels he can better protect my father in the hospital than in either of dad's homes. From what I can gather, the files are within reach at all times.''

Kenpachi kissed the palm of her hand. "I assume when you say protect, you're referring to the Blood Oath League?"

Jan nodded. "I have to tell you, I really don't understand what's going on. Part of me says dad's getting paranoid in his old age. The other part says two of my father's friends are dead and they weren't tickled to death. Salvatore Verna and Duncan Ivy. Jesus, I'd known them all my life. So what do I do? Is my father right or not?"

"I can see the confusion in you. Your mind is a collection of shifting winds. Has DiPalma said anything more about your father?"

She finished her drink before speaking. "That's just it. Frank and I haven't seen each other or spoken since . . . since what happened to Wakaba. True, he's running all over Tokyo digging into Nosaka's life. But I feel a draft coming from Frank. A definite draft since that night. He doesn't seem to want to confide in me any more than he has to."

Kenpachi cupped her chin in his hand and gently turned her face toward him. "To confide in you is perhaps to confide in me. Or he could be jealous of our relationship. I think you still have an affection for DiPalma and find this difficult to accept. In any case, you cannot put him out of your mind."

Her smile was weak. "Moving right along, let's talk about the rains that are supposed to hit Tokyo next month. They could cause us more delay. You'll be taking time out to fly to New York for the Lincoln Center retrospective, which is going to be something. The Japanese ambassador's flying in from Washington and we've got requests from over three hundred press people who want to cover—"

Kenpachi, still on his knees, used his tongue to make circles in her palm. Jan shivered, remembering previously experienced pleasure with him. And humiliation. She cleared her throat. "We're putting together a collection of clips from your old films. I'd like to include a clip from *Ukiyo*. Did I tell you that the studio wants to rush *Ukiyo* into December release to qualify for the Academy Awards? They're talking about a formal dinner, a knockdown, drag-out bash at the Metropolitan

Museum of Art in New York after the world premiere—"

He silenced Jan with a kiss. There was nothing more for her
to say. What did they have in common? The movie, of course.
And a love of Japan. And a willingness to accept in themselves
what they would never tolerate in others. Both were too often
dominated by desire and when that desire was satisfied, both
believed they possessed everything.

Was there any answer to the question of desire? Or had Jan,
in walking away from Frank DiPalma, turned her back on the
answer? Since seeing him again she had recalled the time when
she had possessed his heart and had given him hers.

She dreaded going to bed with Kenpachi. And longed for it.
Was humiliation the pleasure she got from him, or the means
by which the pleasure was attained? One thing was certain:
Kenpachi's sexual mastery unnerved her, for with it came a
sense of shame.

In a drugged haze Jan was brought to the brink of orgasm
several times, only to have Kenpachi back off, deliberately to
deny Jan her climax. After the third or fourth time Jan did as
he ordered. She begged. And after she had done so, Kenpachi
lovingly kissed her eyes, her mouth and neck, her breasts, her
stomach. When his tongue found her clitoris, she closed her
eyes and clawed the sheets. But again he stopped, deliberately
preventing her orgasm.

This time, however, she did not have to beg. He inserted a
ri-no-tama, two small metal balls, into her vagina. He had
used them before. One ball contained a vibrating metal
tongue, the other a small amount of mercury. The slightest
movement sent sensual tremors through her and along her
spine. Without waiting for Kenpachi's orders, she drew her
legs toward herself slightly, then straightened them. She repeated this, slowly at first, then faster, thrashing about on the
bed until she arched her back with an orgasmic cry which went
on and on and on.

Then she collapsed back on the bed, drained and breathless.
Only when she opened her eyes did she realize that Kenpachi
had been watching her with casual disdain. But his attitude did
not register as distasteful, for the drugs they had both taken in
an ancient bowl of red wine had left her mind clouded and
uncertain.

Kenpachi now removed the metal balls and entered her, making love with an insistence and skill that brought her quickly to within reach of another climax, until he pulled out and began to kiss her thighs. Once more his tongue found her clitoris. Eyes closed, Jan stroked his hair and called his name over and over. The waves built up again, unstoppable. Kon's denial only increased her longing for him, for orgasm, for release, for Kon.

She opened her eyes to drink in his beauty, to feast on the sight of what he was doing to her, and in that instant the orgasm seized her and she called his name and with all her strength pressed his head between her legs.

She exploded, eyes closed, touching that thin line between ecstasy and death, and not caring if she died.

Kon called Jan's name. Slowly she opened her eyes to see him standing naked beside the bed while hands and tongues caressed her body. The drugs . . .

With an effort Jan forced her eyes away from Kon and looked down at the naked Japanese man and woman who were making love to her. She wanted to stop them, to cry out, to push them away. But then she felt warm with pleasure again and Kenpachi was forcing her to drink more wine, and soon she was slipping into a shadow world and there was nothing to feel anymore.

When Jan awoke in the morning, Kon and the man and the woman were gone. The shame of the previous night was too strong to believe it had never happened. For a few minutes she curled up in bed and wept. She had no idea who the other man and woman were and she dreaded the thought of seeing them again. She had never done this before. Never. She had fantasized about it, but had never done it. It was as though Kon had read her mind, discovered her secret thoughts and brought them to life. She had never made love to a woman before, had never gone to bed with a man whom she did not know.

But she had done so last night and enjoyed it. With an effort she made her way to the bathroom, turned on the hot water and stood under it for a long time. She shivered with fright, not at what had happened, but at its effect on her in the future. The night could not be undone.

* * *

IN THE TEMPLE COURTYARD Jan was joined by several
staff members. Together they watched a young Japanese
mother in fashionably baggy jeans and T-shirt lead her weeping daughter away from the crowd surrounding the bonfire.
Jan signaled her second-unit crew to film them against a temple wall where the woman knelt and hugged the tearful child.

The Japanese girl was adorable in pink kimono, gold sash
and clogs. She looked like a doll herself as the kneeling mother
softly spoke to her and pointed to the black smoke spiraling
above the courtyard. Was she telling her that the doll had gone
to heaven? The mother kissed her daughter's tears, then took
the child's left hand in hers and linked her left pinky finger
with her daughter's.

Jan's turn to cry. Smoke gets in your eyes, she said to no
one in particular, and reached into her bag for another tissue.
Yubi-kiri it was called. Linking your pinky fingers and making
a promise to be fulfilled in the future. A child's game. When
Jan was a child and living in Japan on an army base with her
father, they had played *yubi-kiri*. What had she wished for
then? Long life? To be forever happy? A date with the Everly
Brothers?

Time to take herself in hand. Link pinky fingers with Jan
Golden. No one else was going to save this movie.

She looked around and began to issue orders. Neil Weiner,
her personal assistant, was ordered to find Kenpachi. "Start
with the police station. If he isn't there, find him anyway.
Don't speak to me until you locate him. Time he and I had a
full and frank exchange."

Then she turned to Debbie Elise, her secretary. "Leave a
message for Frank DiPalma at the New Otani Hotel."

Debbie looked up from her note pad, then dropped her
eyes. Jesus, thought Jan, they're all so goddamn well informed around here about my personal life. Aloud she said,
"He's probably out. I hope he's out because I don't want him
to say no. Just leave a message. Say I want to have a drink
with him. Today if possible. Have him leave a message at my
hotel."

Jan was going to find out for herself if Frank was using the Tokyo police to dump on Kon. At sixty thou a day she was damned if that would go on.

Then it was her production manager's turn. "Is there any way we can set up another shot this afternoon, something which does not involve the active participation of Kon Kenpachi?"

"Tough one," said Sam Jonas. "Permits we need for the park scene tomorrow aren't due to come through until late this afternoon. Gennaro and Keighley are ready for the Ginza scene, but you can eighty-six that. They only agreed to do this picture for a chance to work with the Monopoly Man."

"Sam, do me a favor. As long as you're on this picture, kindly do not use that term around me, okay? I mean it's about as funny as AIDS."

"How's this for funny. Guy sees a sign on the Ginza says Karate-Judo. He says it's the name of that Mexican actress who used to be married to Ernest Borgnine."

"Sam, please?"

"Okay, okay. Look, I'll push for the permits today. No promises. I may have to grease a few palms."

"Grease, already. We can break for lunch, which gives you time to get lucky."

"Got lucky last night. Model from L.A. who's over here doing a cosmetic commercial for Japanese TV. She's getting five thousand dollars a day and I had to pay for dinner."

Neil Weiner trotted up to Jan. "Found him."

Jan turned her back on Sam Jonas. "Where?"

"I think I found him."

"Think?"

"Police station says he left there at ten-thirty."

Jan looked at Neil from the corner of her eye. "Ten-thirty, did you say?"

"Oh, shit. Messenger bearing bad news loses his head. You have to understand, I'm getting all of this through one of our interpreters. I did make her repeat it to me and I did write it down. The local law says Mr. Kenpachi departed their circle of warmth around ten-thirty and, wait for it, was returning to Ikuba Castle."

Jan brushed past him. "You come with me. I think it's time we kick ass before I lose control of this movie altogether. If I didn't know better I'd swear Mr. Kenpachi's retired on the job, for which I am paying him very big bucks."

At the cramped noodle shop which the production company had rented as a temporary headquarters Neil Weiner dialed Ikuba Castle. Jan dragged heavily on a cigarette and paced back and forth. What the hell had gotten in Kon? He was on a picture and couldn't afford to be away from the set for an hour. His appearances at the police station had cost her more time and money than she cared to think of. Her grandfather was right. Your friends come and go, but your enemies just keep on growing in numbers.

And don't forget the August rains. Or typhoon. She had hoped to be finished before they arrived. She desperately wanted *Ukiyo* ready by December, time enough to qualify for the Academy Awards. She felt good about this film. And in that case, why not go for it. Gennaro was acting his ass off and Keighley had never been better. If Jan got the New York critics to rave over *Ukiyo*, she'd have the studio by the balls. Then they would have to give her the promotion she wanted. Marketing, they called it these days. Whatever it was, it was the only game in town. Studios were so hung up on marketing that if the marketing boys didn't like a script, it wasn't made. Dumb? But Hollywood wasn't called fruit-and-nut city for nothing. As Jan's agent told her a long time ago, nobody in Hollywood ever gets fired for saying no.

Jan wanted a strong trade campaign geared strictly to the Academy Award nominations. Then she wanted gossip columns, still an effective way of creating want-to-see. But before she could get any of that she needed a finished movie. Edited, scored, dubbed, looped and printed before the third week in December. The more she thought about what she stood to lose, the more pissed she became at Kenpachi.

"No answer," said Neil, the receiver pressed to his ear.

"What the hell do you mean, no answer. He's there. The police said he's there."

Neil looked through the noodle-shop window. "Notice anything?"

"Yeah. I notice we have no fucking director."

"Monopoly Man's friends are among the missing. Everyone of those clowns has hauled ass away from here. Now why's that, I wonder?"

Neil was right. Some of the tough-looking characters Jan had seen at Kon's party the other night had been put on the film as extras, drivers, security. The Bananas, someone from L.A. had called them. Yellow and always hanging around in a bunch. Wakaba had been one of them. Gorillas with flattop haircuts. Even the other Japanese avoided them.

Kon practiced karate and kendo with them during film breaks. They were good. Almost too good. Watching them fight gave Jan the feeling that they really worked at it.

And now they were gone. Drifted away like the movie smoke now rising above the temple walls.

Jan said, "Kon's at the castle. And the Bananas have slithered off to join him. Get my driver."

"I'll go with you."

Her back was to Neil and he could not see her face. He could not see the fear. This morning the Bananas had leered at her when she arrived on the set. Burning with shame Jan had hurried by them and into the noodle shop. *One of them had been in bed with her last night.* That son of a bitch Kon. She decided right then to fire his friends, then thought better of it. If he wanted them on the picture, they were on and there was nothing she could do about it. Not at this stage of filming. She was stuck with them, she could only pretend that she didn't know what the hell they were carrying on about.

"Stay here," she said to Neil. "My driver knows the way. I'll be all right. Kon and I need to clear the air."

Neil looked down at the floor and scratched his head. So you know, she thought. So what. Fuck you very much for thinking of me.

She hurried to find her driver.

* * *

AT IKUBA CASTLE the drawbridge was down. Strange, thought Jan. Kon said he preferred to keep it up all the time to insure privacy. Not only was it down, but there were several cars on it that probably belonged to the Bananas. The castle gate, two huge steel doors, was closed against the outside world. In the center of one large door was a smaller one, also closed. Jan hesitated before leaving her limousine. Her nerves screamed cigarette. She lit one and smoked half of it before leaving the car.

She wished she had brought Neil with her. Better yet, she wished Frank was with her. He was in her thoughts more and more.

She walked across the drawbridge, carefully picking her way along the cars, wishing she had worn flats instead of heels. At the iron door she stamped out the cigarette and closed her eyes. If God had wanted us to be brave, why did he give us feet? She opened her eyes and pounded on the small door.

The sound echoed across a quiet courtyard. Jan looked behind her. All those cars and not a peep from inside. Weird. She was about to knock again when the grating of the handle on the other side of the door made her jump. The door opened wide, and what Jan saw in the courtyard made her jaw drop.

One of the Bananas glared at her as she looked past him in the courtyard. A naked Kon, his body glistening with oil and perspiration, knelt alone on a red carpet. A samurai sword, its blade polished to a jewellike perfection, lay in front of him on a small, low table.

He knelt in the center of a square formed by four bonfires. The Bananas stood outside the fires watching. Instinctively Jan knew she had seen something she was not supposed to see.

The man who had opened the door stepped through and angrily shooed her away. A second man joined him. Both looked as though they wanted to kill her.

Turning, she ran along the drawbridge toward her car and never looked back.

25

FROM THE FRONT SEAT of Shuko's parked Datsun, Di-
Palma and the Tokyo police captain looked across the traffic-
clogged street at the Takeshi Building, Zenzo Nosaka's corporate headquarters. The dark, bulky structure, its eight
stories looking more Victorian than Japanese, stood on the
corner of Marunouchi Square, Japan's industrial and banking
nerve center. There were other corporate high-rises near it and
the adjacent banks held deposits totaling billions of dollars.
But somehow the squat, funereal-looking Takeshi building
intimidated every structure within blocks. If the taller, more
graceful buildings were like flamingos, Nosaka's stronghold
was an alligator.

From where DiPalma and Shuko were parked it was possible to look past the Takeshi building and down a wide mall
leading to the Imperial Palace and lined with oddly shaped
pine trees propped up to withstand the autumn typhoons.
At one in the afternoon every foot of the mall was packed
bumper to bumper with cars, yellow taxis, buses and trucks.
The pollution was eye burning. According to Shuko, Tokyo
pollution was strong enough to corrode metal.

Sitting here reminded DiPalma of his days as a cop, when
he had pulled surveillance and lived on soda and pizza. He
smiled, remembering the first rule of the game. Make sure you
pee before it starts, because when surveillance starts you can't
move. You keep an empty milk carton on the floor of the car.

You'll learn to love it because it's your toilet.

In the back seat of the Datsun a Japanese cameraman aimed a handheld camera at the Takeshi Building. This was as close as DiPalma could get. Nosaka's corporate headquarters was off limits to both Japanese and western press. Nosaka himself hadn't given an interview since the end of the war. The only photographs of him had been taken with his permission at kendo matches. The Alligator was well guarded. Uniformed, armed men checked everyone who entered the lobby. If the guards knew DiPalma was filming the building there would be heavy trouble.

The cameraman was a twenty-one-year-old Tokyo film student who called himself Ford Higashi after John Ford, his favorite director. Ford spoke English, used dated American slang and worked with earphones turned up loud enough for DiPalma to hear every note of the score from Errol Flynn's *The Sea Hawk*. Ford did a lot of work for the Tokyo correspondent of DiPalma's network, a bone-thin, preppy-looking Canadian named Donald Turney. Turney, twenty-nine and ambitious, was the son of a Canadian diplomat who had played a role in the release of the American hostages from Iran. Young Turney had never stopped looking for a story to top the one his father had lived, which was why he had tried to force DiPalma to include him. The ex-cop wondered if things in Tokyo were really that slow.

"Ford says the shoot he's doing for you has something to do with Nosaka," said Turney. He tried to sound commanding.

DiPalma had been about to leave his hotel room when the phone rang. He didn't like Turney's tone. "I'm on my way out."

"DiPalma, I want in. You're on my turf."

"You're on my time."

"Hey, guy, don't hardball it here. You're a long way from home. Over here you're not destiny's child. You're just a wayfaring stranger who can very easily get caught in the crunch. Do I make myself clear?"

"Ain't this a bitch. Good-bye, Mr. Turney."

"Suit yourself, friend. But as soon as I hang up, I'm calling New York. And then we shall see what we shall see."

DiPalma, receiver in two fingers, extended his arm and let the receiver fall.

A day later Turney called again. He didn't sound so tough this time. "New York says we ought to try and work something out. Should be enough glory to go round. Might be good for the both of us. You scratch my back and I'll scratch yours kind of thing."

"New York told you to fuck off. They said if you've got any sense you'll keep away from me. I've got a team on this thing in New York, I've got friends here who are helping me. You're deadweight. And I don't need you."

"Mister, I can hurt you in this town."

"If you do, don't ever let me find you. Call New York and ask them if I mean it." He dropped the receiver again. Let Turney get his information from Ford. Such as it was.

Before the film student had arrived, DiPalma had sat in the car and told Shuko some of the results of a week's investigation. "Nosaka's not too popular here, though no one's willing to speak out publicly against him. I've got two people on film who agreed to talk if their identities were kept secret. We shot them sitting in darkness."

"I do not need to know their names, DiPalma-san. But I would be interested in what they had to say."

"Fine. I found them through a friend, Rakan Omura."

"*Hai*. He is the antique dealer for whom you have done certain investigations."

DiPalma nodded. "And from whom I have purchased swords. I checked out a couple of Madison Avenue antique dealers for him in the past. One was a thief, the other was okay. I also put him in touch with someone at the Metropolitan Museum in New York and he's gotten rich off that. Sells them thousands of dollars worth of stuff every year. Seems he sells to Japanese businessmen as well, including two who used to work for Nosaka. One, whom we'll call Joe, feels Nosaka's definitely behind the Blood Oath League. He says two of the men who were killed were business rivals of Nosaka's. Ken Shiratori was one."

"The man who was murdered in Zurich last week."

"*Hai*. Apparently Nosaka wanted a fifty-percent share in

Shiratori's amusement park. Shiratori turned him down and did it in a nasty way. Nosaka was very insulted because Shiratori did it in front of a roomful of people. What you have here is not just killing for a new Japan or an old Japan. What you have is killing for money, for good old-fashioned greed.''

"Did the second man also speak of Nosaka's greed?'' asked Shuko.

"*Hai*. But he had a personal story to tell me. The second man we will call John. John and I have practiced kendo together in Tokyo in the past, but we do not know one another outside of the *dojo*. He has read some of my writings on the sword. He agrees and disagrees, but this is his privilege. In the matter of *ken*, the sword, you Japanese are not easy to please. Anyway, John contacted Omura-san and asked to speak to me. However, I cannot reveal his name nor use his face in my film.

"John told me about Nosaka's bank, where he was once an executive. He says the bank gathers business intelligence and washes money. John sees no harm in any of this. Like most Japanese, he considers knowledge important to Japan's survival.''

Shuko said, "I do not understand. If John sees no harm in what Nosaka does, why then did he want to see you?''

"To tell me about his dead son. He blames Nosaka for the boy's death. The boy was an excellent fencer and a member of the Takeshi *dojo*. What attracted him to this club was the spirit of its fighters, their belief that Japan must again become a great military power.''

"Did Nosaka tell him this?''

DiPalma nodded. "According to John, his son heard patriotic speeches from both Nosaka and Kenpachi. Everyone connected with the Takeshi kendo club is superpatriotic. Very far right. Which was fine wtih John's father. He felt the same way. Then sometime this year the boy told his father that he had joined a secret nationalistic group which would revive Japan and make it first among nations once more. Kenpachi was involved, the boy said. And Nosaka was putting up the money. Other than that, everything had to remain a secret. The boy had taken an oath in blood to reveal nothing.''

"The Blood Oath League," said Shuko.

DiPalma loosened his tie and looked around for the tardy Ford Higashi. Shuko's Datsun had no air conditioning and the fumes from the traffic were stifling. He said, "At first, John was proud of his boy. This secret organization, whatever it was, seemed just the thing the country needed to get it back on course. Then came the killings. Suddenly John started to get nervous. Talking tough was one thing. Spilling other people's blood was another. But what could he do about it? He was scared of Nosaka and his own son was involved in whatever was going on. In the end John simply told himself to believe in Nosaka. Until his son died."

"When did this happen?" asked Shuko.

"Around the time Labouchere, the French businessman, was killed in Paris. The French police have an unclaimed body in their custody. A Japanese male. The head's missing and so are both hands. Neither the French nor Japanese police have been able to identify him. The boy, of course, is John's son. Since his death, the heart's gone out of John. He has retired, given up kendo and spends a lot of time saying prayers for the soul of his son."

"Did Nosaka contact his father?"

"*Hai*. The boy had told his father that the Takeshi fencing team was scheduled to give exhibitions in London and Brussels. From either city Paris is less than a hour's flight away. When the boy did not return from the tour, his father spoke to other members of the *dojo*. Their silence and press reports of the mutilated body confirmed his worst fears. Nosaka paid John a visit and forbade him to claim the body. Nosaka didn't say why. He didn't have to."

Shuko looked straight ahead. "And the father obeyed. Tell me, what is the religion of the dead boy's parents?"

"Shinto."

"They die each day that their son is denied the proper burial rites."

"*Hai*." DiPalma stared at the Takeshi Building. That was the son's karma. Just as it was the karma of the dead Wakaba to lead DiPalma and Shuko to this building. On Wakaba's corpse they had found a passport stamped with his arrival from Hong Kong less than two hours before his death. And an airline ticket to Geneva the following day, where he was to join the Takeshi team for a fencing match. Information in the ticket envelope indicated that Geneva was the first stop on a six-city European exhibition tour by the Takeshi kendo club, Japan's best.

Like many Japanese corporations, Takeshi encouraged its employees to practice the martial arts in order to strengthen their spirit and make them better workers. Outsiders were not allowed to join the team or observe its practice sessions. This rule, however, did not apply to Kon Kenpachi.

DiPalma's talk with "John" had convinced him of two things: the Takeshi team, backed by Nosaka's money, was the Blood Oath League. And Kenpachi was a member. It hadn't taken Shuko three seconds to draw the same conclusion.

The bandages on Wakaba's forehead and hand, along with his passport and its Hong Kong exit stamp, had bothered DiPalma. The bodyguard should have been with Kenpachi. Instead he had left Hong Kong *after* his boss. Why? And those wounds. Deep gouges made by a sharp instrument. The more DiPalma thought about it, the more his curiosity grew. From Shuko's office DiPalma telephoned the Hong Kong police superintendent.

"Jenkins attempted to fight off his attacker," said the superintendent, "but obviously he wasn't quite good enough. He'd been gardening at the time. Tried to fight the bastard with a hand gardening tool. We still have it. Bits of blood and flesh on the steel end."

"What happened to Jenkins?"

"Tongue cut out. Blinded in his remaining eye. Spinal cord slashed several times, leaving him paralyzed waist-down for life. He's alive, but that's all to be said for him. He's living in hell."

When DiPalma hung up, he said to Shuko, "I told him you would send blood and tissue samples from Wakaba. My guess is Wakaba was acting for Kenpachi, who wanted revenge. Jenkins did kill Sakon Chiba."

"*Hai.* I will question Kenpachi about this and send a report on to Hong Kong. I must also question Kenpachi about Wakaba and what occurred with your son in the alley."

In Shuko's parked Datsun, DiPalma thought of Todd, now

at the Tokyo police headquarters under the protection of Shu-ko's fellow officers. DiPalma had requested this favor; his excuse was that Wakaba's friends in the Takeshi kendo club might want revenge and try to harm the boy. That was a lie. An indispensable one but still a lie. Todd did not have to fear Wakaba's fencing companions. He had to fear Kenpachi.

To get his hands on Todd, Kenpachi had been willing to kill. That was why he had ordered Katharine's death.

I will not let you be *kaishaku* to Kenpachi. You will never violate his *seppuku*.

In the alley DiPalma had heard Wakaba make this threat. Jan had heard it but she didn't understand enough Japanese to get it. To her, his shouting had been the raving of a loonytune, nothing more. As for Shuko, he had been too far away to hear anything. He had been at the opposite end of the alley, recovering from the effects of a kick in the stomach.

DiPalma himself could hardly believe what he had heard, but he knew it was true. Every frightening word of it. It was true because Wakaba's last act on earth had been to point at Todd and call him Benkai. Benkai who had beheaded the first lord of Ikuba Castle four hundred years ago.

Shuko had remained silent. And when Jan asked DiPalma what it meant, he had ignored her and walked away with an unconscious Todd in his arms. Jan was now too close to Ken-pachi for DiPalma to confide in.

How could he tell her or Shuko that his son was quite possibly a reincarnation of an ancient samurai warrior? Would they believe this warrior was alive in the body of an eleven-year-old boy? And about to take part in another *seppuku* within the walls of Ikuba Castle? Would anyone believe this story? Shuko might, but he would be obligated to report it to his superiors.

Kenpachi would deny it, then select another time to come after Todd. The film director already had too many advantages. Todd was drawn to him and he had Jan.

DiPalma had come to Tokyo to find evidence linking No-saka to Katharine's murder. The evidence now pointed to Kenpachi, who would be more on guard than ever.

DiPalma saw no reason to tell Shuko of his conversation with Andy Pazadian, a Tokyo DEA agent he had worked with on past drug cases. The conversation with Pazadian might prove offensive to the police captain.

In Pazadian's office the two Americans had begun by talking about Roger Tan.

"Looks like he's dead," said Pazadian, a dark and stocky Greek in his mid-forties with pointed ears. "No trace of him. Gun he signed out for was found in the apartment of a Geoffrey Laycock."

"I knew Laycock."

"So I hear. Gun was in the pocket of one of Laycock's dressing gowns. Looks like Laycock's apartment was Roger's last stop."

"Any rumors floating around Hong Kong on Roger?"

Pazadian straightened a paper clip and used it to dig wax out of an ear. "We hear things. None of it's good. Triad's supposed to have done him in. We think it was Ling Shen's Triad, the same clowns who were supposed to whack you. Roger's log says he made long distance calls here to Mystic, Connecticut, to a Jude Golden. His daughter's here in town doing a movie."

DiPalma nodded and waited for the rest. Pazadian wasn't as bad as Roger Tan, but he did like gossip.

"She's a friend of yours?"

"Acquaintance would be more like it. What did Roger and Jude Golden talk about?"

"Roger's notes say they talked about Laycock's true ID. Turns out he was a prisoner of war in Hong Kong under another name. Speaking of names, guess who's name was also on Roger's desk?"

"I'll bite, who?"

"Mr. Zenzo Nosaka, who I hear you're in the process of checking out."

DiPalma said, "That's why I'm sitting here watching you scrape wax out of your ear." He told Pazadian about Nosaka's industrial-espionage network, its worldwide dirty tricks. He didn't mention Katharine, but he had a hunch Pazadian knew all about her.

Pazadian leaned back until the front legs of his chair were off the ground. "Industrial espionage is not, repeat, not a crime in this country. It's part of Japan's defense against

Russia and China, its two biggest potential enemies. That's
why it doesn't do you any good to knock this kind of spying to
a Japanese. To them knowledge is power and all knowledge
improves their country's chances of survival. Fucking Japanese are obsessed with knowledge. Any kind of knowledge.
Military intelligence or stealing silicon chips, it's all the same
to them. Japan can't survive without either one. You and me
may think something's wrong, but we don't count.''

DiPalma said, ''Nosaka's no one-hundred-percent patriot.
He's out for himself. Japan gets what's left over.''

''All well and good, paisan. But you ain't gonna get a living
soul in Japan to dump on the guy. Look, Japan lost the war,
remember? They don't like losing. So to make sure it doesn't
happen again, they're in the spy business up to their eyeballs.
Especially when it concerns Russia, who ain't but a hop, skip
and a jump away. Fact is, Japan's paranoid about Russia,
which has a lot more nuclear bombs and a helluva lot bigger
army than she does. There's a twenty-four-hour underwater
watch off the Japanese coast for Russian subs and who's to
say the Japs are wrong? They also keep an eye on China and
the Chinese spies in this country. Lots of them around.''

''So you're saying that espionage isn't a dirty word in Japan.''

''Not today, not yesterday, not tomorrow. Russia and
China are tough-ass neighbors. Wouldn't you keep an eye on
those fuckers if they were on your doorstep? Look, by law
Japan can't have a large army, nuclear weapons, a big navy,
none of that shit. Losing the war was a nightmare to these
people. They had never been conquered, never been occupied,
never had to surrender as a nation.''

''Surrender is not in the Japanese vocabulary,'' said Di
Palma.

''Not until Hiroshima and Nagasaki put it there. Anyway,
with no national defense to speak of, the best protection they
can have is espionage. Espionage equals national security.
You don't believe me? I'm telling you it does. That's why the
Japanese government is behind it, behind all of it. They don't
tell guys like Nosaka to go out and do piggy things, but you
can bet your ass they don't take it quite as hard as we would if
Nosaka gets caught with his hand in our cookie jar.''

"So that's why Japan has so many research institutes, think tanks, data bureaus, trade councils, business groups. All of them into industrial espionage, and if they come across anything the Japanese military might be interested in, they just pass it along."

"Hooray for the Italians. Now you want to hear what we get out of it?"

"We?"

"My country 'tis of thee."

DiPalma said, "Let me guess. Free espionage."

Pazadian pointed the wax-coated end of the paper clip at him. "You probably know the difference between pussy and parsley, you're so smart."

"Nobody eats parsley."

Pazadian grinned. "My wife thinks that joke is sexist. I fucking love it. Anyway, you're right the first time. We get a lot of information we might not come up with otherwise. Like information on drug smuggling in this part of the world. Like information on Arab terrorists and Latin American guerillas being trained in North Korea. Like stuff on various arms deals, gold smuggling. And we get a lot of shit on Russia and China. All from them spy-happy little Nips. It goes without saying you and me never had this little talk."

The little talk that DiPalma and Pazadian never had also revealed that ninety percent of all Japan's spying went to boost the economy. Gathering military intelligence was an afterthought. Information poured into the country from every corner of the globe on new technology, changing markets, trade unions, consumer demands, current and future research, ecology and politics.

How did the Japanese do it? DiPalma wondered.

"The most curious people on God's earth, bar none," said Pazadian. "They want to know everything and I do mean everything. And when they know it, first thing they do is sit down and improve on it. Show them a better way and they'll take it. None of this Let's do it this way, 'cause that's how it's been done all these years. Shit like that you get in the West, not here. And they work hard. I mean to the point of pissing blood. Always, always open to new ideas and they know how to read intelligence, how to use it. Patient like you wouldn't believe and they don't miss a fucking thing, no matter how small."

Pazadian laughed. "You know what's funny? They spend one-tenth of what we do on research and development. One-fucking tenth. And look how it pays off."

DiPalma said, "Military or industrial espionage. All the same, you say."

"Right you are. Japanese government treats it as one and the same. You got a lot of government agencies promoting this intelligence gathering. Ah, you're writing this down I see. Pearls of wisdom from my ruby lips."

"Not quite. Go on."

"Government agencies. Yeah, well there's M.I.T.I. Ministry of International Trade and Industry. Very heavy duty and they can play tough. They are not backed by the government. They *are* the government. Always sending research teams around the world, attending conferences, going over stuff that's public information, asking questions. They've got scientists and laboratories for them to work in and lotsa dudes who just sit around all day and analyze shit. That's M.I.T.I."

DiPalma looked up from his notes. "I hear there're schools here that train people to be corporate spies."

"You're telling me. How about more than four hundred detective agencies in Tokyo alone that stay in business by ripping off other people's business secrets. This does not include agencies in Osaka, Kyoto, Yokohama and God knows where else. Intelligence gathering of one kind or another is just about the most important thing you can do in Japan."

"And you say there's no law against it."

Pazadian waved him away. "None at all. They got a law that says if it involves copping other guys' patents, that's a no-no, though I wouldn't want to be hanging by my dork from a very tall building while they brought some guy up on this charge. If it's not copyrighted, Japanese law says it's up for grabs. Coke dealer once told me, 'If it's worth having, it's worth stealing.' "

"And it's official, I mean the government—"

"Will you come off this shit about the government? Hey, like they don't care. The end justifies the means. Get there any way you can and we'll worry about the details later. Only the

Japanese government doesn't worry. The guys who set up this operation in the first place, this research bureau so called, were top World War II spies. Patriots. You get where I'm coming from? They were patriots."

DiPalma closed his notebook. "So Nosaka's a hero."

Pazadian turned his hands palms up. "Nobody says you got to sit on the curb and clap as he goes by. That's just how it is. Just as I think it's gonna be a cold day in hell before anybody accepts what you told me earlier. It ain't gonna be what the Japanese *believe* about Nosaka killing people. It's gonna be what they do about it."

He leaned forward in his chair. "Winners don't get asked if they're telling the truth. And little old Nosaka is a winner, a very big winner."

* * *

IN THE FRONT SEAT of Shuko's Datsun, DiPalma turned around to look at Ford Higashi. The young cameraman had been late; he had gone to see a screening of *The Searchers*. This was the fifty-fourth time Higashi had seen the John Ford western, a favorite of American directors like Francis Ford Coppola, George Lucas and Steven Spielberg, themselves current favorites among Japanese film students. *The Sea Hawk* theme was still blasting on Higashi's earphones.

Higashi shot the Takeshi Building from top to bottom, shot people entering and leaving, shot the guards making scrupulous ID checks, shot limousines and Rolls-Royces pulling up and company executives getting out. When DiPalma returned to New York he would write copy to go with this footage. That copy would be more potent if he could only get his hands on the Hansard files now in Jude Golden's possession.

"*Daimyos* of the twentieth century," said Higashi in English, the camera still pressed to his eye. "Modern warlords, man. Groovy guys."

"Who?" asked DiPalma. Shuko, whose English was barely passable, turned to look at Higashi.

"Talking about cats like Nosaka," said Higashi. "Dudes like him have money, power, cars, women. Anything they want. Guys who work for him are like his samurai, dig?"

DiPalma quickly translated for Shuko, who nodded and
said in Japanese, "Such samurai now conquer the world with
attaché cases and expense accounts instead of swords."

Higashi nodded and continued to film the Alligator.
"That's why you got all them Datsuns, Sonys and Hondas in
the States." He took his eye away from the camera to look at
DiPalma. "Bet you didn't know that the first Tokyo businessman, I mean heavy businessman, was a samurai."

DiPalma smiled and translated for Shuko, who said, "Hai.
The oldest department store in Tokyo, Mitsukoshi, was
founded almost five hundred years ago by a samurai named
Hachirobei. One day he found himself destitute, so he pawned
his dai-sho, his two swords. He also sold candles, shoes, wom-
en's clothing, ribbons. Other samurai insulted him, spat on
him, until they saw how much money he made. Hachirobei's
family crest is today still used by the corporation which owns
that store and other businesses."

DiPalma said, " 'John' told me that Japanese business does
not use terms like manager, assistant manager, managing director like we do in the West. What they use are the same
ranks that samurai armies used a thousand years ago. It
amounts to a military chain of command in modern business."

"Efficient," snapped Shuko. He said the word with pride.
"Insures discipline. Sometimes a certain businessman can be a
Sa-konye or U-konye. General of the left or the right. Also
captain of the left or the right. And other military ranks, of
course. A simple system, yes, but an efficient one."

"Right on, my man," said Ford Higashi. Then, "Hey, hey.
Wow. Numero uno himself."

He looked at DiPalma. "The daimyo."

DiPalma swiveled in his seat to face the Takeshi building.

Nosaka. Stepping from a limousine. A little man in a derby,
dark suit, bow tie and walking stick. He stopped to say something to the chauffeur who had opened the door, then walked
toward the entrance. Two massive bodyguards dwarfed him.

The guards cleared the way, opening doors, shooing people
to one side. Some stepped aside without being asked and
stared at Nosaka as though he were royalty. As though he
were a daimyo. And then he disappeared inside.

"Wow," said Ford Higashi, collapsing back against the seat. "Far-fucking-out."

DiPalma had to fight from being impressed. It was in Nosaka's bearing, the way he walked, the way the guards and pedestrians had reacted to him. He was Japan's exotic past come to life. The empire builder. Surrounded not by human beings but by instruments to be discarded when they had served their purpose.

DiPalma looked at Shuko. The police captain, eyes narrowed and hands gripping the steering wheel, stared straight ahead. And also into the past. Not at Japan's past brought to life in a modern warlord, but at the man who had murdered his mother, his father and other members of his family. And who could not be touched because of a vow made to the emperor forty years ago.

* * *

FROM A FOURTH-FLOOR WINDOW facing the street, Nosaka and a male secretary watched the Datsun pull away from the curb and enter the heavy flow of traffic. The secretary held a telephone receiver in his ear and said in English, "Yes, Mr. Turney, I have passed on your request for an interview to Mr. Nosaka and he will consider it. He is most grateful for your call regarding your colleague, Mr. DiPalma. No, we have no statement to make at this time. Such things are handled through our public-relations counselor. His name?"

He looked at Nosaka, who nodded once.

"His name is Mr. Yoshinaka. His address—no. We prefer that all requests for interviews be submitted in writing, along with a list of prospective questions. Mr. Yoshinaka does not accept telephone requests for interviews."

After the secretary had hung up, he and Nosaka stood side by side and watched the Datsun until it disappeared into the shimmering heat waves rising above the frantic traffic in the mall.

26

NOSAKA LOOKED UP from his desk and out into the walled garden behind his villa. The sliding door to his weapons room was open, and an aroma came from a pine branch burning in a Korean stone lantern used as a censer. Near the lantern a servant tossed chunks of bread into a pool filled with carp. Nosaka believed that the huge fish, which the Japanese prized for their courage and determination, brought him luck. They made him feel bold and victorious.

He rose and stood in the open doorway, admiring the dwarf bamboo trees, peonies and camellias now blood red in the setting sun. When the world threatened to overpower him, the garden was his retreat. Surrrounded by its beauty, and stillness, all passions were forgotten and he found peace within himself. It was the one place on earth where he felt content, where he did not wish for more than he already had.

A hanging weight-driven pillar clock read 6:30 P.M. Kenpachi was thirty minutes late, not unusual for him. When would he learn that men counted up the faults of those who kept them waiting. Since possessing the Muramasa blade the film director had grown more arrogant, even disrespectful. Nosaka found Kenpachi's vanity increasingly difficult to stomach. Kenpachi was convinced that his *seppuku* would bring Japan to a standstill, that it would trigger an outburst of patriotism not seen since World War II.

"The emperor will be moved by my death," said Kenpachi. "He will declare me a hero. I will be buried in Yasukuni

Shrine with other warriors who have given their lives for Japan.''

Such arrogance made him charismatic to the Blood Oath League. Convinced that he was sincere in wanting to die for the glory of the nation, the members became even more willing to risk their lives for him and Japan. Nosaka, however, found Kenpachi none the wiser.

Nosaka returned to his desk to resume examining a saddle which, if purchased, would cost him more than most of the weapons in his collection. There were other saddles among the swords, daggers, armor, spears and bows in his weapons room. But none equaled the one he now peered at through a magnifying glass.

It was carved from dark wood and covered with rich gold lacquer. The pommel was ivory with silver inlay and there was blue velvet padding which prevented a horse from being chafed. The stirrups, shaped like half shoes with turned-up toes, were made of silver with gold inlay. More than four hundred years old, the saddle represented matchless craftsmanship and incomparable beauty. It was one of only three made by the great Muramasa.

Like his swords, spears and knives, Muramasa's saddles were also said to be possessed by the evil which haunted the brilliant but unbalanced swordsmith. During the year an antique dealer had owned it, his wife had been injured in a severe fall, he had suffered a serious automobile accident and a beloved granddaughter had died in her sleep of unknown causes. In a quivering voice, the dealer had confessed that, to him, the Muramasa curse was all too real.

Nosaka did not fear the evil in a Muramasa weapon nor in the exquisite saddle. Nosaka was samurai and he feared nothing. Fear was a source of superstition, born of uncertainty and he had never been less than absolutely certain of his own worth. He was immune to any form of dread or panic. His arms collection, much of which he had donated to Tokyo museums, contained many Muramasa weapons. Over the years they had given him the forcefulness and vitality which had made him one of Japan's wealthiest men. On his death the remainder of his collection would be distributed among the country's museums.

Meanwhile he kept the choicest weapons in his hilltop villa.
If he purchased the saddle he would keep it here too. He
stroked its pommel, then leaned closer with the magnifying
glass to focus on the left stirrup. *Hai*. He recognized the work-
manship and became excited. Such intricate, serpentine use of
silver, such complex, mystifying patterns no other sword
maker had been able to duplicate. Muramasa. Nosaka's heart
began to beat faster. He must have this saddle. He stroked it
with a shaking hand. Kenpachi was forgotten. With this saddle Nosaka would now own at least one sample of every creation by Muramasa. With this saddle the cycle of collection was
complete.

Kenpachi arrived ten minutes later dressed in a white Yves
St. Laurent suit and sunglasses with a tiny diamond in the corner of one lens. He made no apology for being late, nor did he
indicate a wish to change into a kimono, as was his usual custom when visiting Nosaka. When he bowed to the older man,
it was so casual as to be disrespectful. Nosaka's offer of tea
was refused.

They sat on the matted floor on opposite sides of a low
table. A restless Kenpachi fingered the viewfinder hanging
from his neck and looked past Nosaka into the garden. It was
clear that he felt himself now being summoned to Nosaka's
home.

As Kenpachi chewed a thumbnail, Nosaka pointed to a
small tape recorder on the table. "They met in the park near
Toshogu Shrine," he said. "One of my operatives, a woman
pretending to be a mother, brought her baby to the park for
fresh air and sat three benches away. She taped their conversation with this machine. Its microphone is powerful enough to
pick up any conversation two hundred yards away. With as-
tounding clarity, as you will hear."

He pressed a button on the machine then slid the recorder
toward Kenpachi.

* * *

*Sounds. Schoolboys playing baseball. Airplane over-
head. Barking dogs. Squealing girls awkwardly attempting to maintain their balance on roller skates.*

A cassette radio comes into range and Elton John singing "Rocket Man" drowns out all other sounds.

"—believe the walls have ears," said Frank Di-Palma. "Especially in Tokyo."

"You said something about maybe being followed. Are you serious?" It was Jan Golden.

"I'm kicking over rocks and peeking into Nosaka's life. Damn right, I'm serious. He's the twentieth-century spymaster. Hideyoshi come to life. He's a fool if he isn't spying on me. In his place I'd do the same. I don't mean to rush you, but I have to get to the police station and pick up Todd. We're having dinner with Shuko. It's our last night in Tokyo. Tomorrow we leave for New York."

Jan Golden said, "I didn't know. Well, I guess it's a good thing I called you. Especially since I'm not too sure you would have called me. I have to ask you something about Kon."

"You're asking me about Kon Kenpachi? Christ, the Japanese are right. They say the unexpected often happens."

"Frank, this picture's a bear. A ball breaker. We've got between three and four weeks' shooting left and I need my director. Trouble is he's spending so much time down at the police station, my crew calls him Monopoly Man. You know, do not pass Go, do not collect two hundred dollars—"

DiPalma chuckled. "Go directly to jail. Funny."

"Kon says you're behind it. He says you're doing a number on him through Captain Shuko."

"What do you say?"

"Didn't make sense to me, a foreigner coming to Japan and ordering the police around."

"Shuko's a good cop. Nobody tells him what to do. He's on Kenpachi's case for a reason. Wakaba tried to kill my son. And he was also tied into something very nasty. That's why Shuko's talking to Kenpachi."

"Does this nasty thing involve Kon?"

"Let's hear why you want to see me."

"Around noon today, when Kon still hadn't showed up, I dropped in at Ikuba Castle. I couldn't get him on the phone and anyway I felt it was time he and I had things out in the open. In private. At the castle I saw something I don't think I was supposed to see. I saw Kon naked, kneeling in the courtyard on a red rug—"

"In the center of four fires. Noon, you say. Makes sense. The ritual—"

"What ritual?"

Silence.

DiPalma said, "You saw a Buddhist austerity ritual, something Kenpachi probably learned from his mother, who was a Buddhist priestess. And you're right, you weren't supposed to see it. Kenpachi was making a deal with the gods for his next life."

"His what?"

"First he punishes himself. Fires, hot sun. He has to suffer. It's a trade-off. He suffers in exchange for what he hopes the gods will give him in his next life. It's literally a matter of life and death."

Jan said, "You're telling me Kon plans to die soon? That's ridiculous. The man has everything to live for. He wouldn't kill himself. That much I know."

Silence.

Then she said, "I need him, Frank."

"Everybody invents their own dreams, what can I tell you."

"I'm in trouble, aren't I? With Kon, I mean. That's why you've avoided me the past few days. That's why you brushed me off in the alley the night Wakaba was killed. You know something about Kon and you don't want to tell me."

Silence.

"Look, I can keep a secret," she said. "If you want me to say nothing, I'll say nothing. Just tell me. Please."

DiPalma said, "If I ask you to walk away from Kenpachi, leave Tokyo and come back to New York *with Todd and me, would you do it?"*

"Walking away from the movie?"

"And you'd never do that, right? Nobody walks away from a movie. Jesus, why am I wasting my time? You've spent your life doing exactly what you wanted. Just push the right or wrong of it aside and keep on trucking."

Jan said, *"I'm scared to death of one thing. And that's watching people only half as good as me come along and succeed in this business after I've failed. Look, if suffering were the answer, the world would have been a better place years ago. So don't ask me to suffer any more than I have to. A month. That's all I need. Maybe less, if Kon can get his act together. Just let me get the film in the can."*

She wept. *"Frank, I'm so close, so close. I can't walk away. Not now. Ask me anything else."*

"That's the only thing worth asking. You don't want me to understand, you want me to approve. Wakaba might have smoked you if he'd had the chance. And remember Kenpachi's fag friend, Sakon Chiba?"

"The drag queen who tried to kill you in Hong Kong."

"He managed to kill a cop before he got smoked by another cop named Jenkins. Jenkins isn't doing so well now after Wakaba paid him a visit. Did you notice Wakaba stayed behind in Hong Kong when the rest of your company left?"

Jan said, *"Kenpaci told me Wakaba had to deliver a message for him."*

"He definitely delivered. He cut out Jenkins's tongue."

"Are you serious?"

"He also gouged out Jenkins's one remaining eye, then cut his spinal cord. Jenkins is now paralyzed for life. And blind. And speechless."

"I think I'm going to be sick."

DiPalma said, *"There's no doubt Wakaba did it. His blood and tissue samples match those found on a garden tool near Jenkins. Wakaba was also a member of the same Blood Oath League which killed Sally Verna, Duncan Ivy and plans to kill your father."*

"How do you know this?"

"An airline ticket to Geneva was found on Wakaba's body, along with a schedule of kendo matches to be played in three European cities by the Takeshi kendo team. Nosaka's team. And the team Wakaba worked out with. At the same time the Takeshi team was putting on a show in Geneva, a Japanese businessman was killed in Zurich. The two cities aren't that far apart. There's a lot of violence around the late Mr. Wakaba and his friends. I think that's reason enough to request Kenpachi's presence down at police headquarters. Wakaba was his boy, remember?"

A nervous Jan said, "Slow down. You're saying that Kenpachi's involved in the Blood Oath League. What about Nosaka?"

"He's still on my list. Kenpachi and Wakaba both practiced kendo on Nosaka's team, the Takeshi team which is connected to the Blood Oath League. I think Kenpachi owes a few people some explanations. Jan, your father's in danger. And if you keep hanging around—"

"You're pushing me, damn you! I don't want to hear any more. I can't listen to you or anybody else. I have to do what I think is right. That's it. That's it."

* * *

NOSAKA SWITCHED OFF the machine. Interesting, he thought. Kenpachi had lost his arrogance. He stared at the machine and looked worried.

Nosaka said, "This was recorded less than two hours ago. Miss Golden ran weeping away from Mr. DiPalma, who did not follow her. As you can see, Mr. DiPalma is aware of your plan to commit *seppuku*. His awareness of the austerity ritual, his leaving the boy at the police station as he goes prying into my life. He knows. And I am sure you noticed how the woman led DiPalma closer to the Blood Oath League. Closer to us."

Kenpachi, frowning, hugged himself. "She knows nothing. How—"

"Think upon what you have just heard. Analyze what was said and not said. Miss Golden caused Wakaba's death. She interfered with his plans to kill the boy, then led him to the alley where he died. Wakaba in death is proving to be something of a liability. Why did you not ask my permission before revenging yourself on the policeman Jenkins?"

Kenpachi dropped his eyes.

"Insolence ill becomes a stupid man," said Nosaka. "Wakaba's wounds at the hands of Jenkins triggered DiPalma's inquiry. Suspicion causes a man to store facts and bits of information in his brain. DiPalma, a former policeman, easily becomes more suspicious than most. Especially when the woman reports to him what she has witnessed in your courtyard. What was your explanation to her of what you were doing?"

"I told her it was a religious ceremony for the soul of Wakaba."

"Obviously she does not trust you or she would not seek out DiPalma. He is strongly attracted to her. Even now he attempts to warn her. But she rejects his warnings. She is ambitious." Nosaka smiled. "He does not want her to die as did the other two women he loved. He is willing to risk his life for her. That is why the two of them are dangerous. Do you think you can make the film without her?"

Kenpachi shook his head. "No, *sensei*. All that is necessary for the film comes from her. Money, actors, the important American studio. I need her."

"And she needs you. Still I feel DiPalma will find a way to use her against you. He can ruin your plans for a glorious death and do harm to me."

Nosaka rose gracefully from the floor and turned his back to Kenpachi to look out at the garden. The light of a setting sun bronzed the businessman's small, catlike face, making it appear more timeless than old, more infinite than human. "Two men, one woman," he said. "Both cannot have her."

He looked over his shoulder at Kenpachi. "I will tell you why I have not harmed DiPalma while he is here in Japan. He is going to bring me the Hansard files. Security is very strong around Jude Golden and too many people know about the Blood Oath League—DiPalma, Shuko, Jude Golden, his daughter. I would rather not use the league now. You will convince the daughter that the files in her father's possession will be more effective if given to DiPalma who, after all, is a journalist."

Nosaka turned back to face the sun. "After we have taken the files from DiPalma, then you may kill him. In America. It is best that it be done as far away from us as possible. Since you now possess the power, I suggest that you have the son kill the father. The *Iki-ryō* came to you in Hong Kong where it killed Laycock. Now have it kill DiPalma."

Nosaka walked to a nearby wall, removed a *tessen* and began to fan himself. It was the same war fan that Yoshiko had used to kill a Hong Kong policeman.

27

Dawn, gray and muggy over Ikuba Castle. On the horizon a rising sun spread its fiery reflection across the top of the blue hills and the muddy Sumida River, now rain swollen and overflowing its banks. On all sides of the castle rice fields, roads, marshes and plains were black with Hideyoshi's cavalry and foot soldiers, an army made confident by an unbroken string of victories.

Like the ninja *who had preceded him, Hideyoshi, the Crowned Monkey, had used rain and darkness to "steal in." Ikuba Castle was surrounded, its garrison outnumbered and cut off from any escape.*

In the daimyo's *quarters Todd, who was Benkai, watched his lord prepare for seppuku. Stepping onto a thick red rug enclosed on three sides by a white screen, the lord dropped to his knees, pulled the kimono off his shoulders and bared his chest. Todd nodded at a steel-helmeted guard wearing leather armor, who stepped forward and removed the lord's sandals.*

The averted eyes of the guards told Todd how harrowing was his own appearance. There was the arrow in his left eye; his kimono was soaked with his own blood, and the woman's head hung from his sash by her long black hair. He was a terrifying sight, one to

be feared more than the attacking ninja or Hideyoshi. Fear had robbed the castle guards of all judgment. Nothing mattered except to obey Todd, who
was Benkai.

Smoke floated from beneath the barred oak door
to the daimyo's quarters. And smoke drifted down
from the gilded ceiling, from the burning rooms
above the daimyo's quarters and through the open
window above the courtyard; the ninja were attacking throughout the compound. The smoke did
not hide the dead ninja destroyed by Todd when
they had attempted to enter the daimyo's quarters
through the secret tunnel.

Other ninja kept trying to reach the daimyo from
in the tunnel and the hall, where the nightingale
floors "squeaked" under their sandals.

Suddenly the hall became silent and then came the
sound of racing men and the door shook under a
roar from many throats and from the thrust of a battering ram.

The daimyo was doomed. He could retain his
honor and avoid the shame of capture and disgrace
only through seppuku.

Todd, who was Benkai, said, "A samurai must
choose between disgrace and glory. Seppuku is the
way to glory."

"Hai!" shouted the guards.

Todd looked at his lord, who smiled at him and offered him a katana, a long sword with a white cloth
around its jeweled hilt. White, the color of death.

With both hands clasped tightly around the hilt,
Todd lifted the sword and gazed into the dazzling
light which enshrouded its razor-edged blade.

Bowing his head, the daimyo waited.

Todd looked at him, waited, then swiftly brought
the blade down on Kenpachi's neck.

* * *

New York

TODD OPENED HIS EYES. He was terrified, breathless, unable to see. He fought for air, breathing deeply through his mouth. Then light attacked his eyes and he raised his arms against the harsh brightness. *Did the brightness mean that the sword was near him once more?* He feared the sword. He wanted to hide before it found him. Before he had to kill.

"Easy," said DiPalma, who had turned on the light in Todd's room. "Another bad dream. Just relax. You're awake now. Just take it easy."

He crossed the room and sat down on the bed. He had almost said *Nothing to worry about. Those things are far behind you.* But he knew better and so did Todd. This was not the first nightmare the boy had suffered during his ten days in New York.

They were in DiPalma's comfortable Brooklyn Heights flat, among beautiful old brownstones and tree-lined streets overlooking New York Harbor and the southern tip of Manhattan. DiPalma had been born and raised in Brooklyn, had married and been a cop here. He preferred Brooklyn to Manhattan; it was more peaceful, less pretentious.

Todd said, "Perhaps it is better to accept what will happen."

No games, thought DiPalma. Not with this kid. He said, "Kenpachi?"

"For the first time in my dreams I held the sword. And I killed him. I was the *kaishaku*. I was Benkai. It was so real. The smells, the screams of dying men, the wounded horses. And the dampness from the rain, the perfume from the giant camellias."

DiPalma nodded, silently urging him on. "I saw armor, pieces of leather and iron held together by colored silk cords. I saw riderless horses in the courtyard with blood on their wooden saddles. Not horses. Ponies. *Hai.* Small, ugly ponies. I saw a general lying in the courtyard beneath the *daimyo's* window. He wore a *kabuto*, an iron helmet with horns on top. He had been carrying a *saihai*, a baton with blue paper streamers. The *ninja* had killed him in the first attack."

Sweat stood out on Todd's forehead. "I am being told to kill a second time."

DiPalma playfully rubbed his son's head. "Dreams are only true while they last. You're awake now. Sleep can't hold you forever. Sooner or later it has to let you go."

"It was so real tonight," said Todd. "For the first time I knew for certain that I was Benkai. I was myself, but I was him as well."

There must be something more I can do for him, thought DiPalma. *Something.*

He said, "How'd you like to go for a walk?"

Todd looked at the small clock on the night table. "Now?" It was 3:35 A.M.

DiPalma shrugged. "Why not? Might relax us both." He didn't add that it would also prevent Todd from doing what he had done in Hong Kong and Tokyo—leaving the apartment at night alone.

Todd grinned. He looked like a boy again. "I'd like that. I would enjoy that immensely. The night can be peaceful, you know. If it's not too much trouble, may we have some ice cream?"

"Now that's going to take some doing this hour of the morning, but we'll try. Give me a few minutes to throw on some clothes and we're on our way."

In his bedroom, where a balcony offered a stunning view of the Manhattan skyline, DiPalma stopped dressing to look at his cane, laid across the arms of a stuffed chair. An excellent weapon. But he thought about the .38 Smith & Wesson he was still licensed to carry. What was Kenpachi waiting for? Why hadn't he tried to take Todd away from DiPalma in New York? Why hadn't the Blood Oath League tried to kill him?

In his closet he rummaged around for a good pair of walking shoes. He didn't own jogging shoes or sneakers for the same reason he didn't own a single pair of jeans. He hated uniforms. Moccasins were just as comfortable and more stylish. Especially if they were handmade in Milan. He selected a brown pair and sat down to put them on.

Ten days ago, he had worn these shoes to his first network meeting since returning from Japan. At DiPalma's request a handful of network brass had sat in on the meeting, which had included his investigative team, producer, editor and the station manager. In a conference room overlooking Sixth Avenue, DiPalma had held his audience spellbound. He began with an explanation of why he had gone to Hong Kong and ended with a rundown on Nosaka's industrial-espionage network. He recounted the attempt on his life, the story of the Blood Oath League, of the file that could bring criminal charges against Nosaka.

He told them about Katharine and Todd.

But he said nothing about Todd's nightmares or that the boy might be the reincarnation of a four-hundred-year-old samurai. Or that he had killed a man. He mentioned Jude Golden, but said nothing about Jan. Or Kenpachi's planned *seppuku*.

When he finished, the room was silent.

Then Raffaela, his chief researcher, said, "Do you think this Blood Oath League or Kon Kenpachi will still try and kill you?"

"Yes."

"Because of the file?"

DiPalma nodded. "I think everyone here knows about Sally Verna and Duncan Ivy. That should give you an idea of just how the Blood Oath League plays the game. Which is why I'm the only one who's to go after those files or who's to contact Jude Golden. I want that understood."

A vice-president said, "Didn't you forget to mention that Jude Golden is Jan Golden's father?" He threw out the question as if to say "Gotcha."

DiPalma looked at him until even the men around the vice-president began to shift uncomfortably. When the vice-president turned his face toward the ceiling, DiPalma rasped, "I didn't forget. I *don't* forget."

He looked around the table. "My team's been on this thing the past three weeks. I'd like the rest of you to hear what we've come up with. I'd appreciate it, however, if you'd hear us out before asking questions."

"Question before we start," said another vice-president, looking down at his manicured nails. "Will you be on the air while you're preparing this one? When you were away we didn't get our usual numbers in your time period. Compliment to you, of course. But we prefer to be on top looking down, instead of on the ground and staring up at someone else's ass.''

DiPalma said, "I'll be on the air tonight. That's what you're paying me for."

The vice-president forced a smile. "No offense, Frank. We need you, that's all. Mind telling us what we can expect?"

"Something we were putting together before I left for Hong Kong. Piece on a teenage dope dealer."

The vice-president reached for a pencil and began to make small interlocking circles on a blank pad. He kept his eye on the pencil. "Teenage dope dealer. You've done one or two of these before, haven't you, Frank?" A quick smile at the pencil. "No offense."

"This dealer's seventeen and a Brazilian countess. She owns a penthouse in an East Side building full of rich Europeans and South Americans. Her drugs come into the country by diplomatic pouch and she only sells to the foreign jet-setters she meets at private clubs. She's been on the cover of Vogue and Harper's Bazaar, she's turned down two movie contracts and she clears over a million a year dealing. Her family's wealthy and she doesn't need the money. She does it for kicks, for the power. I'd say she's different from other teenage dealers I've done, wouldn't you?"

Those around the "suit" who had asked the question looked at him, then turned away. Someone said, "I think we got our numbers back. Welcome home, Frank."

Rafaella said, "We have her on film shooting a 'speedball'. That's coke and heroin combined. She's one of the most beautiful women I've ever seen in my life. And totally crazy. Completely out of her tree."

Someone else said, "She sounds fascinating. How did you happen to get her?"

DiPalma looked down at the table. That was the suits for you. Either at your throat or at your feet. "Let's get back to Nosaka and the Blood Oath League. We have a few things we'd like you to listen to. We'll try and make it as brief as we can because I have some film I'd like you to see."

Marshall Harris, DiPalma's producer, joined the team in presenting the facts collected on Nosaka's relations with congressmen, lobbyists, businessmen, journalists, and how he had used them to build an industrial empire. Newspaper clips told of past arrests of Nosaka's industrial spies in America and abroad. Each time the spies had pleaded guilty, avoiding a trial and further publicity. Fines had been imposed, but no one had gone to jail.

Then it was DiPalma's turn. He explained the role of the Japanese government in backing industrial espionage. He reported on Nosaka's role as a war criminal, how America had used him as a cold-war spy, how Nosaka had organized his bank as an espionage network. Then DiPalma showed film footage of Nosaka's corporate headquarters, factories, businesses and home. He showed them film clips of the Tokyo research bureaus, trade-commission headquarters, detective agencies and business institutes specializing in industrial espionage, many of them with government sanction and support.

There were interviews with "Joe" and "John." And footage of a Japanese management school for business trainees. "Nosaka has a secret interest in this school," said DiPalma. "As you can see, it's hidden in a wood north of Tokyo. Very private, very secluded. What the school does is turn Japanese businessmen and women into warriors. Twentieth-century samurai dedicated to keeping profits high and cutting costs to the bone. The training is brutal, a marine boot camp for executives who want to get ahead. They train in everything from English to the martial arts, to penmanship, speed-reading, positive thinking and how to get the most out of the people working under you.

"Japanese companies spend a lot of money to send their people here. Courses run ten days or two and a half weeks. The only thing you learn is how to make your company rich. You do that by letting the instructors humiliate you until you learn to obey without questioning. Either you pass the course or, in most cases, you lose your job. Give you an idea of how tough it is. Trainees sign insurance forms in case of accidents. An there are accidents.

"Everybody's tested twice a day. Builds character, they say. Food is putrid. Try doing a fifteen-mile forced march on a bitter rice soup and a potato. Anybody here want to put his or her career on the line with a seventeen-day stay in a joint like this?"

Jokes were made but they were all clearly impressed. Then the lawyers had their say. Like all cops DiPalma had no love for lawyers. He had spent enough time in courtrooms watching them distort and delay and fuck up the judicial system until it had become nothing more than their private money-making machine. How many times had DiPalma seen a case postponed because a lawyer was awaiting the arrival of "Mr. Green," a very important witness. Meaning the lawyer hadn't been paid and until he was there wasn't going to be any goddamn trial.

In the conference room, the lawyer who gave DiPalma the most trouble over the Nosaka story was a man named Kenner. He was the youngest network legal gun and therefore had the most to prove. Even though it was the last week in July, he wore a three-piece suit. Fingering a gold sovereign on his watch chain Kenner said, "Before we label this a go, I want to make sure we're not shooting ourselves in the foot. Especially with the big names involved. Nosaka, Kenpachi. Heavies. With all due respect, Frank, while you're saying this thing can fly, my job is to make sure it doesn't fly up and hit us in the face. Still, what I've seen and heard here is mucho effective. Mucho. Up to a point, that is."

He hooked his thumbs in his vest pockets. "Would you like to know what would soothe my troubled breast, Frank?"

He waited.

DiPalma didn't look up from the table.

Kenner cleared his throat and said, "I'd greenlight this sucker if we could do a criminal number on Nosaka which would stick. Get where I'm coming from? We need a jockstrap, Frank. Something to give it support."

DiPalma said, "The Hansard files support it. All the dirty tricks are spelled out there. Everything about the money, who got it and why."

"What about the Blood Oath League?"

"It's in there."

Kenner threw up his hands. "My point, you see. Corroboration. That's our jockstrap. Those files. If we're going to take on Congress and retired generals and maybe the CIA, we need a nice big pile of rocks to throw at them. Libel suits are hard on the blood pressure, Frank. Lay those files on us. If they're top shelf, state of the art, then it's green light."

* * *

IN HIS BEDROOM DiPalma unscrewed the top of a vacuum cleaner, then reached inside and pulled out the .38 in its ankle holster. A pair of handcuffs dangled between the trigger and the guard, making it impossible to fire the weapon. DiPalma took out his key ring, found the tiny key he was looking for and unlocked the cuffs. If the Blood Oath League decided to make a move while he and Todd were taking their early morning stroll, the gun could make a difference.

Todd was quite the little fighter himself. At DiPalma's kendo club the boy had shown that his skill was out of the ordinary, that what he had done to Wakaba was no fluke. Watching his son fight had left DiPalma both proud and uneasy. No eleven-year-old should be that good. His skill was uncanny, superior to all but two or three fencers in the *dojo*.

When he appeared for practice everyone slowed down or stopped fencing to watch him. Todd practiced tirelessly and with such solemn demeanor that the *dojo* nicknamed him Little Buddha. The more DiPalma watched him, the more ambivalent he became. Todd was a remarkable fencer and he was DiPalma's son. But he was *too* good.

When DiPalma fenced with Todd he felt uncomfortable, nervous. But then the boy's aggressive style and strong spirit forced him to concentrate on the match. Where did Todd get his strength from? And where did he learn to handle a *shinai* with such incredible agility? DiPalma used his long reach to keep the boy at bay, but Todd managed to score on him twice, to the applause of the *dojo*. And DiPalma was considered one of the top three fighters in the club.

Only old Hidiya-*sensei* was totally able to control Todd. Hidiya, who had run the *dojo* for over twenty years, had trained in Japan's top fencing schools and university clubs; he had served as a police instructor and competed in tournaments held in the presence of the emperor. Hidiya had twice fought his way to the finals of the all-Japan championships. He had also trained championship fencers and instructed all over the world.

Watched by the entire *dojo*, Hidiya and Todd fought an electrifying match. The silent men and women watched intently, then broke into loud applause again and again as the man and the boy brought to life the finest movements of medieval Japanese swordplay. Hidiya alone scored, but several times he was forced back by Todd's aggressive tactics.

When the match was over the applause erupted and went on for a long time. Hidiya removed his helmet and did something he had not done in a long time. He smiled. He looked at Todd as though seeing him for the first time. The applause, the cheers and whistles drowned out his words to Todd and the boy's reply. DiPalma, however, knew Hidiya did not consider this a routine match.

Hidiya said to DiPalma, "Your son speaks excellent Japanese. Whoever taught him also taught him a bit of old Japanese, words that are not used in daily conversation. They date from many, many years ago, from a form of Japanese which is not spoken anymore. One can easily see that he has practiced the sword in past lives."

DiPalma nodded and said nothing. He did not trust himself to speak. Benkai, Wakaba had said. Did men tell the truth when they knew they were dying?

DiPalma sat in the stuffed chair and took off a moccasin. He had almost fastened the wide leather strap containing the holstered gun around his ankle when Todd said, "You will not need that."

DiPalma looked up to see the boy standing in the doorway.

Todd said, "You are in no danger until she has given you the files."

"She?"

"Miss Golden. She will see that the files come to you."

DiPalma leaned back in the chair and eyed his son. Like it or not, fate led or dragged you along a prescribed path, forcing you by its terrible power to play the game. He wondered if his son saw death for him. It was a question the former cop did not have the courage to ask.

Reaching down he removed the ankle strap, attached the handcuffs to the trigger guard and returned the gun to the vacuum cleaner.

Then father and son walked silently out into the warm night.

28

Tokyo

THE SOUND OF THE RAIN had brought Jan out of a sleep so deep that it took all her strength to open her eyes. Slowly the room began to assume form. There was the ceiling with its sunken panels of painted waterfalls and seashores. And there were cedarwood folding screens inlaid with mother-of-pearl, bamboo screens, mats on the floor and the smell of burning incense sticks.

Across the room Kenpachi, nude, stood at a window looking down into the courtyard of Ikuba Castle. Until today he had been a miracle worker. They were now into August with only ten more shooting days to go and only one day behind schedule. Kon had cut scenes from the script, rewritten others and inspired the cast and crew members to work like demons.

The rushes were great. Jan knew they were great because the studio execs, who had not seen them, telephoned her long distance every day to tell her how great they were. The jungle drums were beating. Word was out that Jan had come up with a winner. A few weeks ago, when Kenpachi was spending hours at police headquarters, those same drums were pounding out the message *Don't dress*. Don't expect the Kenpachi project to happen. Now *Ukiyo* was chiseled in granite: it was absolutely going to happen.

A few execs were going to meet her in New York next week at the Kenpachi retrospective, where she would show them the rushes and talk about a new contract. No options. A firm three-picture deal. Play or pay. If the studio decided not to go ahead with the new deal after she signed it, they would still have to pay her the full amount. Based on what Kenpachi had done these past few weeks, Jan was now a heavyweight. And her first picture wasn't even in the can.

Her agent in New York had telephoned her to say he was being shown some outstanding new properties. Books, plays, original scripts. "No fingerprints on them either," he said. "You've got first look."

Kon, Kon, Kon, she said to herself. Make the fucking rain stop, why don't you?

Days before the rain arrived Tokyo had been covered by the *shitsuzetsu*, the wet tongue, the warm moist air from the tropics which preceded the August rainfall. The wet tongue had been hell; Jan had not stopped perspiring the whole time it had hung over the city. With the rain, which started the night before, had come predictions that it would last anywhere from three days to three weeks. With four more days of exterior shooting to do, the last thing Jan needed was a deluge.

She sat up in bed and lit a cigarette. Shouldn't smoke on an empty stomach, but what the hell. Her hand shook. She was doing too many drugs. With Frank she had rarely done more than an occasional joint. Why couldn't she just say no to Kon? Simple question, simple answer. She didn't want to.

Kon was the right temptation at the right time. He was all that was alluring and forbidden about Japan. To experience him was to experience this country in ways few people ever did. And yet . . .

When they had started filming she had been hungry for him. Now she was sick with the thought of what he made her do in bed. The excuse was, of course, the movie. She needed him. The truth was she wanted to stop sleeping with him, but she didn't know how. Pleasure was a sin and sin a pleasure and none of it came without remorse.

Her affair with Kenpachi was taking its toll. She felt ashamed, emotionally drained, helpless, dependent. And none of it could be undone. She worshipped Kon's talent and she found his beauty unspeakably desirable. There were times when she wished she didn't.

As the rain became torrential, she punched out her cigarette in an ashtray and put her hands over her eyes. Why did the rain have to happen now? Why did it have to prevent her from finishing the movie and getting out of Japan? Away from Kon.

"It will stop soon," he said.

She dropped her hands. He was smiling down at her. His hair was wet.

"Have you been out in that rain?" she asked.

"Yes. I went to the *dojo* to meditate."

"I wish you'd meditate this rain away."

"Get dressed," he said. "It will stop within the hour."

She shook her head. "No way. This is just the first day. According to the weather report, we're in for a few more days like this."

"It will stop. We can go to work on schedule today."

"Kon, I know you're into the occult and I know you meditate, but what makes you think the rain's going to stop?"

"I know. That is enough. Just as I know you are going to meet some important men next week in New York at my retrospective."

"Come on. You could have heard that from anyone on the picture."

He sat down on the edge of the bed and stared into her eyes. "Did you tell anyone?"

"No, I didn't. There're so many egos on a movie. The last thing you want is resentment or jealousy."

Damn him. Lately he knew too much. About the weather, the film. And her. But give him credit, he had come through for her when she needed him. A week from today she and Kon would break off filming to fly to New York for the restrospective; Jan would also make a quick side trip to see her father. Then back to Tokyo for three days' work, followed by a wrap party at Ikuba Castle, a party which Kon had promised cast and crew would remember as long as they lived.

Kon looked into her eyes, stroked her forehead with a soft hand, and Jan relaxed. Her fear of him was gone. "There is something I want to discuss with you," he said. "When I arrive in New York, DiPalma will be there and I think he will do his best to harm me."

Jan felt herself grow tense. It always came back to Frank.

"I have nothing to hide," said Kenpachi. "Nor does Nosaka-san. I think this can easily be proven with your help.''

"My help?"

"Your father has certain files, you told me. Suppose Di-Palma were to be given those files or allowed to examine them. Suppose he were to see for himself that Nosaka-san and I are innocent of all wrongdoing?''

The drugs. Lack of rest. In her weakened state Jan tried to look away from Kon's eyes. She couldn't help herself, however. He had mastered her.

Kenpachi leaned closer. "The files . . . your father . . . DiPalma . . .''

29

Mystic, Connecticut

DIPALMA STEPPED from the gangplank onto the deck of Jude Golden's clipper ship, the *Jan Amy*, where three men wearing baseball caps and cradling shotguns blocked his path. They were polite and impressed with his celebrity; DiPalma, after all, was a cop, a part of their world, and he was on the tube, which gave him status. But the guards had a job to do and Rolf Nullabor, who stood near one of the masts, was watching.

DiPalma had to undergo his second security check before being allowed to see Jude Golden. The first had occurred at the base of the gangplank. Here guards had relieved DiPalma of his .38 pistol and ankle holster and had gone over him with a metal detector. Such was television fame that other guards, who had been sitting in parked cars, had opened the doors to get a glimpse of DiPalma.

On board the *Jan Amy* he submitted to a second search with a metal detector, while his face was checked against two separate photographs. More stares, this time from guards scattered around the deck of the tall ship from bow to stern. Even a man at the top of the masthead trained his binoculars on DiPalma. Only Rolf Nullabor seemed unimpressed.

When a guard started to lead DiPalma to Jude Golden, Nullabor's Australian twang stopped him in his tracks. "Forgetting something, aren't you?"

The guard frowned.

"His cane, you stupid cunt!" shouted Nullabor.

"It stays with me," said DiPalma.

Nullabor shook his head. "Not on board my ship, mate. Oh, and one more thing. I'd like you to drop your pants and unbutton your shirt. I need to be satisfied that you're not wired for sound, as it were."

DiPalma gave him a long, hard look. Then he said, "Golden knows where to reach me."

He turned and walked toward the gangplank.

Nullabor pushed himself away from the mast. "And just where do you think you're going?"

DiPalma continued walking.

* * *

JUDE GOLDEN leaned forward in his chair, one arm extended. "May I?"

DiPalma handed him the cane.

The tall banker turned it around in his hands. "Well made. Strong. Silver knob, not silver plated. Nice. Katharine Hansard had excellent taste."

He returned the cane to DiPalma.

They were below deck in the captain's quarters, a dark wooden room with a low ceiling, two bunk beds and a rolltop desk bolted to the floor. DiPalma found the room depressing, reminiscent of a police holding cell. The stuffy air circulated by a small electric fan trained on Jude Golden. Golden had dismissed two pretty Japanese girls, sending them on deck, but DiPalma could still smell their perfume. And the marijuana. For a heart patient who needed a full-time nurse, Jude Golden still believed in unrestrained satisfaction.

"Sorry about Rolf," said Golden. "He's only doing his job."

"So was Martin Borman." DiPalma didn't care if Nullabor heard him. The Australian stood guard outside in the passageway, looking like a neatly pressed autumn leaf in maroon jacket, wine-colored shirt and slacks and tan suede shoes.

"And you would have walked away without seeing me rather than give up your cane," said Golden.

"In Hong Kong Nullabor got a kick using that laser gun of his. I walked away today rather than hurt him."

Golden studied DiPalma. "I believe you. Rolf just might push the wrong person one of these days." The banker popped several pills in his mouth, swallowed Perrier from a battered pewter mug and closed his eyes. He pinched the bridge of his nose. "My daughter's called me four times the past week. Wants me to turn the files over to you. Failing that, I'm to allow you to study them at your leisure. Says it's important to her, but won't say why."

He opened his eyes. "She sounds . . . I guess the word is *disconnected*. Not herself. Not the real Jan. Rather like someone standing on top of a tall building without quite knowing how she got there. I've turned down your requests to see me because I thought we had nothing to talk about. I know you want the files, but why should I waste your time and mine when I have no intention of giving them to you."

A helicopter swooped low over the tall ship, then banked right. Golden looked up at the ceiling.

"Mine. Rolf's idea. Eye in the sky, he calls it. Moving me hither, thither and yon, that's Rolf. The hospital, New Haven, here. Disconcerts the enemy, he says. Keeps the bastards off balance." Golden smiled, showing even, white dentures. "He's a shit, our Rolf, but he's my little shit. Let's talk about my daughter."

"Let's not," DiPalma said.

Golden frowned. "Didn't you have an interest in her once upon a time?"

"Once upon a time I had an interest in Gene Autry and Hoot Gibson. Times change. I want those files, Mr. Golden. It's the only reason I drove up here in this heat."

Golden leaned back in his chair, linked his fingers together and began to twirl his thumbs. "Frankie, I've played every game of intrigue that comes to mind and a few that haven't yet been labeled. In the process I've learned how to keep what was mine and acquire whatever else I needed that didn't belong to me. You haven't a prayer of separating me from anything I choose to hold on to. My daughter was intent on my seeing you. Why? That's the question I'd like answered, if you'd be so kind."

"She's there, I'm here. How would I know what's on her mind?"

"Ah, we've decided to stonewall the old gray fox. Mr. DiPalma, I detect a sense of the dramatic in you. Tell me, do you figure to strike some sort of defiant pose and so impress me with your fighting spirit that I will simply wilt and press those files upon you? Those files, Mr. DiPalma, give me strength. With them, I feel powerful. I can break Nosaka like that.'' He snapped his fingers.

"Why haven't you?"

"Reasons."

"If you're waiting until Jan's out of Japan and no longer involved with Kenpachi, it may be too late."

Golden aimed his chin at DiPalma. "Explain."

"She's attracted to Kenpachi. It's not that easy for her to break away."

"I'm aware of her personal life, thank you. It's something she and I do not discuss. She'll be here tomorrow, by the way. Something to do with a trip to New York for a tribute to Kenpachi. Maybe I can talk her out of returning to Tokyo. Maybe I can talk her into putting this Kenpachi business behind her."

DiPalma shook his head. "Jan can't be talked out of a damn thing and you know it. That's one reason why you haven't moved against Nosaka. She's in trouble until she gets out of Japan, away from Nosaka's friends. Also you don't want to look bad, so you've been trying to clean up those files so you don't look like a prick."

Golden sighed and adjusted a yachting cap on his large head. "I had no idea how many people were involved until I read those files. Not just me and Sal and Duncan. Nosaka's using quite a few people in this country, men of substance and stature. They not only take his money, but in some cases they've come to depend on his reports."

"People like the CIA?"

"Among others. Jan's bound to catch some of the fallout. I'd at least like her to have that one movie under her belt before I play God. There's another reason I haven't turned the files over to you and probably won't. Some of these organizations and individuals are presently investigating you, Mr. DiPalma. Did you know that?"

"No, I didn't."

"Rather important people, some of them. They're trying to

find something on you, something to discredit you just in case you do get your hands on those files. I don't know if you're the man to stand up to that kind of pressure. Some of them have already been in touch with your network. I see by your face you weren't aware of this. We live in a world, Mr. DiPalma, where there are fewer and fewer secrets. I promised Jan I'd see you. I didn't promise I would turn over the files to you. And now that I think about it, I don't exactly like your attitude regarding my daughter. It strikes me that you don't care as much about her as I thought. At least not as much as you care about the Hansard files."

"Doesn't it bother you that Jan sounded scared?"

"Scared? What the hell do you mean by that?"

"I don't work for you, Mr. Golden. I don't have to be nice to you. You know what I mean by scared."

Golden's nostrils flared. His face turned red. "I was right. You do know something you're not telling me. I could have Rolf beat it out of you."

DiPalma tilted his head back and looked at Golden from under his hooded eyes. He smiled.

The banker said, "She's all I care about. If it wasn't for her—"

"You wouldn't have seen me. I know." DiPalma leaned forward. "When did you say Jan was returning to Tokyo?"

"Day after the Kenpachi thing. You're right. She won't leave that film until it's finished. Christ, she's an obstinate bitch sometimes."

"Kenpachi's close to Nosaka. Would you say he knows about the Blood Oath League?"

Golden sat up in his chair.

"Kenpachi's planning to commit *seppuku*," said DiPalma. "Probably when he finishes the movie."

Golden moved his jaw. He rubbed the area over his heart and did not speak for a long time. Then, "How do you know?"

"His bodyguard told me before he died."

"The one your son killed. Where is your son?"

"At my *dojo* with friends."

"I hear tell he's a rather unusual boy."

"Kenpachi wants to use him as *kaishaku*. I'm sure you

know about his interest in Todd. You know so many things, Mr. Golden. Do you know that if Jan's anywhere near Kenpachi when he commits *seppuku* she could be killed? Do you know that Nosaka has never stopped hating you for forty years and that maybe he just might hate Jan, too?"

"You've told her this?"

DiPalma sighed. "Does it matter? Look, you say she sounded uncomfortable. She senses something's wrong about her relationship with Kenpachi and that's all she knows. In Japan, your mind plays tricks on you sometimes. Things are never what they seem there."

"Makes sense now," Golden said. "Kenpachi sending the *onnagata* to kill the Hansards." He studied the ex-cop. "They say your boy's special."

"So's Jan."

Golden kept quiet for a long time. "You still love her, don't you."

DiPalma did not leave the clipper ship for another hour. When he did, he carried the Hansard files with him.

30

New York

IN A CAFÉ at the corner of Broadway and Sixty-fourth
Street Jan walked to a row of telephone booths and entered
the one nearest the kitchen. On the metal shelf beneath the
phone was a glass of champagne, a bottle of Dom Perignon,
and a single rose in a thin, crystal vase. She took a card from
under the vase and sat down in the booth to read it. *Thanks.
Frank.* Removing a handkerchief from her bag, Jan blotted
the tears and waited for his call.

She remembered the champagne and sat up. As she sipped it
she looked across the street at the crowd milling around Lincoln Center, the performing-arts complex on Manhattan's
Upper West Side. Tonight the mob ignored the richly wrought
chandeliers and Marc Chagall murals, which could be seen
through the glass front of the Metropolitan Opera House.
Dozens of uniformed police prevented the hordes from pushing each other into the dancing waters of the Lincoln Center
fountain, glowing with blue and green lights.

For the hundreds gathered in front of Avery Fisher Hall,
tonight had nothing to do with culture. Their numbers swollen
by audiences leaving ballet, theater and concert performances,
the crowd was waiting for a glimpse of the celebrities attending the Kon Kenpachi retrospective. Jan wanted to tell
them they were in for a long wait. None of the stars, the beautiful people, Japanese dignitaries, politicians and film critics
would be leaving before midnight. The projector had broken
down, speeches were running long and after the tribute a

champagne buffet and press conference was scheduled to begin at 11:00 P.M.

The telephone rang as Jan was pouring herself a second glass of champagne. To calm down she drained half of it in a gulp, took a deep breath and felt her pounding heart before reaching for the phone.

"Jan?"

"Frank? Frank, is that you?" She was getting teary again without quite knowing why.

"I see you made it," he said. "How's the champagne?"

"State of the art. I love it."

"Wanted to thank you for the files."

She thought of Kenpachi. "If it helps you, why not? Dad says you promised to keep him out of it if you could."

"I'll do my best."

She fingered the rose. "Your best isn't too shabby. It's really good to be back in New York. Nice to see Blacks and Puerto Ricans on the street, to read a menu in English, even though I miss the Tokyo cabdrivers. They all wear white gloves, jackets and ties and are very, very polite."

"Wasn't sure you'd be here. Your father said this was a big night for you."

She shook her head. "Not for me, kiddo. Big night for Kon. We put together forty-five minutes of clips from his films, plus a rough cut of a scene from *Ukiyo*. Went over big. Meanwhile a bunch of actors, directors and film critics are onstage telling him how great he is."

"How'd you manage to get out?"

She laughed. " 'And with one leap she was free.' That's a line from a script. Seems a writer had his hero in trouble and couldn't get him out, so he simply typed 'and with one leap he was free' and turned the script in. No, what I did was wait until the lights went down, mumbled something about the little girl's room and off I went."

DiPalma said, "Sort of a coincidence my getting the files just about the time Kon bops into town."

She tugged on the telephone cord. "You got me there, paisan. Christ, I wish I could sit down and just talk over this thing between Kon and myself. I admire his talent, which I suppose makes me a star fucker of sorts. And I do need him for this movie, which mercifully is coming to an end in three days.''

Jan looked toward Lincoln Center. "It's just that lately . . . oh, God, I sound like something out of 'Twilight Zone.' He seems to have a force in him, something that draws you to his way of thinking, whether you feel like it or not. Sounds unreal, I know, but there it is.''

"I understand," said DiPalma. "Maybe I understand better than you know.''

"Know something? In New York he doesn't seem all that special to me. But in Japan, Jesus. Over there on his turf the man is definitely *extraordinaire*. Could be it's just Japan, I don't know.''

She looked at the rose. "Three days. Then it's a wrap, thank God. I'll spend time in London for the editing, music, looping. Then it's home, home, home. Speaking of home, where are you by the way? I mean, calling people in public telephone booths sounds like the sort of work you did before you sank to the level of television journalism.''

"I'm in a hotel. Why do you ask?''

"Because, Mr. DiPalma, you sound a bit edgy. Look, if you say so, I won't mention any of this to Kon. I'll just tell him you have the files—''

"Oh, he'll know soon enough, believe me. I just don't want anyone to know I have them until I have another chance to go over them. I've spent almost twenty-four hours going over every line. Don't think I've slept more than three hours during that time. Man, I could crash right now. Put my head down on the desk and not move for days.''

Jan frowned. "Why the big push? Don't you have an office and an apartment, a very nice apartment if I remember correctly?''

"According to your father, certain people are trying to cut a deal with my network about these files. At the moment I can't trust anybody. So before I turn them over to the lawyers, who are having shit fits about libel, I want to see just what I've got here. Todd doesn't mind the hotel. Hell, he's crazy about room service. Especially ice cream.''

"How is Todd? Is he still having those nightmares?''

"He'll be okay.''

She twisted the telephone cord around the fingers of her free hand. "Frank, I'd like to see you."

He didn't answer immediately. "When?"

"Tonight. It's the only time I've got, I'm afraid. I have a breakfast meeting with some studio people, then right after that Kon and I fly back to Tokyo."

"Movie's got to have an ending."

"I have done some crazy things in my time, as we all know. I'm thinking. Wouldn't it be nice if I didn't have to go back."

Silence. Then DiPalma said, "You don't have to go back. Why don't we both be crazy. You bring the champagne over to the hotel and we'll sit around and see if we can't come up with a reason for your not returning to Tokyo."

"Are you serious?"

"Italians are always serious about champagne."

"Do you know what you're saying?"

"Hotel Buckland. East Sixtieth off Park. Room 309. Ask for Harry Rigby. If anybody at the desk says anything, tell them you're in charge of pest control."

A tearful Jan hung up and clung to the receiver with both hands. She hadn't been this happy in a long, long time. She was free of Kenpachi. She had a first-class production manager in Sam Jonas; let him take charge of the last three days of filming. So what if she missed the wrap party at Ikuba Castle. She would lie. God knows lying was the indispensable part of making life endurable. Kenpachi's contract called for final cut, so let him edit the film without her.

Tonight, boys and girls, Jan Amy Golden was going over the wall. As of now she was free of Kon. And whatever kind of number he was doing on her head.

Frank.

Jan picked up the champagne, turned and dropped the bottle. Shocked, she collapsed back into the telephone booth. Kenpachi, backed by two squat, muscular Japanese, reached into the booth and took the yellow rose from the vase. After he inhaled its fragrance, he smiled at Jan. And crushed the rose.

* * *

TODD PLACED THE FILE folders in the attaché case that had once belonged to his stepfather, closed it and looked at Frank DiPalma. The ex-cop had fallen asleep face down on his desk. The boy's unnaturally bright eyes burned into his father's back. There was a .38 on the desk near the ex-cop's right hand and his black oak cane rested on top of a nearby wastebasket.

Todd cocked his head and listened to the voices which urged him to kill his father, to let the *Iky-ryō* come forth as it had in Hong Kong. The boy suddenly stood rigid, eyes closed, and began to perspire heavily.

The room grew frigid and icy winds pulled at the drapes and fluttered the pages of a newspaper on the desk near DiPalma's head.

Minutes later Todd left the hotel carrying the attaché case. He walked to the corner of Sixtieth Street and Park Avenue, where he stood waiting in the August night. A bus stopped in front of him and a passenger got off. When the bus pulled away, a limousine glided to a halt at the bus stop and the rear door opened. Todd stepped into the car, which headed downtown, then turned right on Fifty-seventh Street and sped downtown on Seventh Avenue.

At Forty-second Street, the limousine turned right and slowly cruised toward Eighth Avenue. Todd shuddered at the sights—porn movie houses and bookstores, street peddlers selling stolen jewelry, blood banks, video-game arcades, junkies and prostitutes. At the corner of Forty-second Street and Eighth Avenue the limousine stopped and a squat, muscular Japanese in a tuxedo and wearing dark glasses got out and began to walk back toward Seventh Avenue.

In the middle of the block he stopped in front of a young Puerto Rican boy lounging in front of a record shop whose windows were covered with steel shutters. The boy was slim and dark-eyed and wore a tank top with the word Menudo spelled out in rhinestones. Beneath that were photographs of the five Puerto Ricans who made up the wildly popular rock group. After a few words the boy followed the Japanese back to the limousine.

With the Puerto Rican boy now inside, the limousine pulled

away from the corner, turned right and headed north on Eighth Avenue.

* * *

THE TELEPHONE JARRED DiPalma awake. He sat up quickly and looked around for Todd. The boy was probably asleep in the next room. It was probably Jan calling to tell him she'd changed her mind and wasn't coming over. Jan Amy Golden. Last of the free spirits. When it comes to her, he thought, I got it bad and that ain't good. The first one to get over a love affair is the luckiest.

Still groggy, he crossed the room and snatched at the receiver.

"Frank?" A male voice, familiar.

"Charlie Griffith. They asked me to call you."

An alarm went off in DiPalma's head. Griffith was a fireman he'd known for years, an old friend who had finally gotten the captain's rank he deserved.

"There's been a fire over at your kendo club," Griffith said. "We found a body. Just a kid. Burned pretty badly. Looks like it was your boy. I'm sorry. I'm really sorry."

DiPalma looked toward the bedroom. "Griff, hang on a minute, will you?"

He stood up and walked to the bedroom. At the door the hairs on the back of his neck stood up. He opened the door and looked inside the room. Twin beds. Both unslept in.

DiPalma tore himself away from the room and picked up the phone. "Yeah Griff, I'm listening."

"Kid had ID on him. And a Buckland hotel key in his pants pocket. Note had your name and this room number. I was hoping he had no connection to you. Some of the kendo people came down here the minute they heard about the fire. They said only one kid had a key to the *dojo*. Only one kid had the instructor's permission to come in here and practice anytime he wanted to."

DiPalma's voice was husky. "Be right down. Thanks for calling."

He hung up and stared at the bedroom, then covered his eyes with one hand and wept.

31

Tokyo

AT MIDNIGHT, in the *dojo* of Ikuba Castle, Nosaka stepped away from a bare wall and walked to the center of the matted floor where Todd stood alone, naked except for a *fundoshi*, a white loincloth. The boy wore his hair in ancient samurai fashion, the back braided, then oiled and pulled forward across the top of his shaven skull. There was a wolflike brightness to his eyes and a sense of power emanated from him that filled the room.

Outside, a strong southern wind drove the heavy rain against the castle buildings. Water poured from the castle roofs down onto sand and rock gardens, turning them into black whirlpools. Pine trees ringing an ornamental pool bent beneath howling gusts that drove sheets of water across the cobblestones and onto the parked cars. The drawbridge was up and the huge iron gates were locked, isolating the walled castle from Tokyo. Within the compound every building was dark, except the *dojo*, where two men stood guard at the entrance.

Inside Kenpachi and half a dozen members of the Blood Oath League stood in the shadows cast by paper lanterns and watched Nosaka complete the ritual which would signify Todd's emergence as a samurai. Nosaka had been selected as the boy's sponsor, an honor comparable to that of godfather or guardian.

Dressed in the traditional gray kimono of his clan and wearing a *hachimaki* tied around his forehead, the industrialist handed Todd a *hakama*, the loose black trousers worn by

feudal samurai. After Todd had put them on, Nosaka handed
him a green ceremonial gown embroidered with storks and
tortoises, symbols of longevity. The stork was said to live a
thousand years, the tortoise ten thousand. Nosaka then lifted
a hand and an earthenware cup of rice wine was brought to
him on a tray.

Nosaka took three stips, then handed it to Todd, who did
the same. Nosaka then took another three sips and returned
the cup to the tray. Lightning flashed brightly, and the courtyard lit up as though it were day. Then came thunder, an ear-
shattering crack.

Nosaka clenched his fists and attempted to stay calm. The
thunder and lightning triggered a storm of wind and waves in
his mind, leaving him again restive and unsteady. He had
begun to feel this way with the purchase of the Muramasa saddle. But just as quickly he had rejected the idea that the saddle
had anything to do with his distress.

In buying the saddle he knew that some would say he had
completed a cycle of evil, that he was now surrounded by base
objects which could produce only suffering. But he remembered the power he had drawn from Muramasa's weapons
over the years. Especially from Benkai's sword. For the past
three days Nosaka had lived in Ikuba Castle, watching Kenpachi draw that same power from the sword and from the
bone which had once been in Benkai's throat. This was the
power Kenpachi had used to control and manipulate the boy's
mind until the fearsome Benkai, long buried in his soul, had
emerged.

There had been no resisting Kenpachi. He had convinced
the American woman to return to Japan against her will.
Nosaka had only contempt for her weakness. She was easily
manipulated, she with the untrained western mind found in
fools who lived to serve their own feelings. She was not like
Nosaka, who had always been master of himself.

Yet tonight he was in danger of yielding to a fear of evil. For
the first time in many months he felt his age; exhaustion
weighed so heavily upon him that it seemed to be pushing him
into the grave. He shivered in the warm *dojo*. Everyone else,
even the boy, was perspiring; the tropical August storm had
brought with it steamy, dank air, more uncomfortable than
the hottest summer heat.

Nosaka felt a coldness that brought to his mind the *Iki-ryō* and the reason it had not killed DiPalma despite Kenpachi's control of the boy.

Nosaka had said, "The *Iki-ryō* saved DiPalma's life in Hong Kong because the boy felt a loyalty to his father. Having given life the *Iki-ryō* cannot take it back. It can never be used to kill whom it has saved."

Kenpachi angrily turned his back on Nosaka. "Then DiPalma is invincible."

"No. He can be killed. Remember, the boy was not then Benkai. His sense of loyalty to his lord was not as intense as it is now. True, if the *Iki-ryō* refuses to kill, it will not recant. It is also possible that DiPalma has been purified in Tendrai's forge. The power of the sword can manifest itself in many ways. The American, however, is mortal. Never forget that he can be killed."

In the *dojo* a clap of thunder startled Nosaka and he shivered again. Others in the ancient fencing hall threw each other quick, nervous glances. Only the boy stood calmly, impassively waiting for the ritual to conclude. When it was over he would be Benkai.

Even now his swordsmanship surpassed that of anyone else in the Blood Oath League. Only Nosaka and Kenpachi had not been shocked. By drawing blood from three opponents, Todd had also won the respect of league members. The purification rituals of the past three days had included fencing with actual swords. Now no one wished to spar with Todd; even to fight him with wooden swords could mean death. He had knocked two men unconscious and had to be forcibly prevented from clubbing a third to death.

The following afternoon Kenpachi would complete the film for the American woman, who now slept drugged in his bed. Hours later he would host a party in the castle for the actors and crew. There would be other guests, including Nosaka. All would be held hostage until Kenpachi had completed his *seppuku* and a film of it shown on Japanese and American television.

All in the Blood Oath League had taken a vow neither to surrender nor bargain for amnesty. Fear of disgrace, Nosaka knew, would make them keep that vow at the cost of their lives. This was the league's strength and its greatness. This is

why it would live long after Kenpachi's *seppuku*. Just as
Benkai had lived for hundreds of years.

The lightning flashed, followed by thunder. And by something else. Alarmed, Nosaka looked around the *dojo*. No one
else seemed to have heard it.

It was a harsh whisper, a ghostly utterance which made
Nosaka's flesh crawl.

"*Shini-mono-gurui.*" The hour of the death fury. Giving
and taking no quarter. The deepest commitment a samurai
could make before going into battle. Killing those closest to
him to free himself for a fight to the death.

The words made Nosaka sick to his stomach. With an effort
he faced Kenpachi, who held out the Muramasa blade in its
scabbard to him. The final part of the ritual. As sponsor
Nosaka was to hand it to the boy, thus officially designating
him samurai.

Suddenly Nosaka backed away. Everything in him said reject the sword, flee. Kenpachi was speechless. Everyone
watched Nosaka back to the door and open it, letting in the
wind and rain. Paper lanterns fluttered and one tore loose to
bounce across the matted floor. Todd's robe billowed and his
face became wet and slick with rain. While others around him
cringed before the terrible storm that had invaded the *dojo*, he
stood firmly in place, arms folded, his eyes riveted on the
Muramasa held by Kenpachi.

Nosaka staggered out into the warm, heavy rain. He smelled
the stench of the *Iki-ryō* and felt its icy chill and heard Kenpachi call his name. Nosaka was supposed to witness his
zankanjo, a written vindication of Kenpachi's suicide and the
murders by the Blood Oath League. He was also to serve as
witness when Kenpachi signed his will.

But white faced with cold, Nosaka now stumbled through
the downpour to his limousine, where a bodyguard quickly
opened a back door.

The car horn blared and the huge iron gates slowly swung
open. The heavy drawbridge dropped. Lightning illuminated
the courtyard as the car swung around in a half circle, sped
past the *dojo* and rumbled across the bridge before disappearing in the darkness and rain.

32

New York

WHEN DIPALMA opened his eyes it was almost dawn. He lay motionless, still hearing Todd's voice. For the third consecutive night he had dreamed about his son. Tonight's dream, however, had been the most vivid of all. Todd had pleaded with his father to come to Japan and save him.

DiPalma sat up, turned on the bedside lamp and looked at the digital clock-radio. Almost 4:30 A.M. He slipped into a robe, then walked out to the balcony to stare at New York harbor. From the darkened waters came the sound of a tugboat's horn as it guided a freighter out to sea. A chain of barges, looking like a string of giant black pearls, floated across the horizon. A single gull spread its wings against a pale sky before squealing and dropping to skim the water for food.

DiPalma looked east toward a rising sun. Toward Japan. Toward Todd.

* * *

The greased braid of hair had been pulled across the top of the boy's shaven skull. His outstretched hands held a sword whose jeweled hilt was wrapped in white silk.

Todd wept and begged his father to come to Ikuba Castle before it was too late.

Then Kenpachi entered the dream. The film director knelt before the boy and smiled. As though on command, Todd gripped the sword, lifted it high in

*the air and brought it down on Kenpachi's bared
neck.*

*Blood spurted and covered the boy's face. As the
blood cleared it washed away his skin, leaving the
skull bare. DiPalma heard Katharine's voice behind
him, but when he turned, he saw only fire. He looked
back at Todd, who was now a skeleton.*

*The skeleton spoke. "There is a way, my father.
Steal in as did the yamabushi. Steal in." And then
the dream was over.*

* * *

ON THE BALCONY DiPalma closed his eyes and tried to
concentrate. In each dream the boy had been in Ikuba Castle.
But there was something about the last dream which bothered
DiPalma.

Then he remembered. *Todd had once told him about this
dream.* There were slight differences between his version and
DiPalma's, but basically both were the same. Until now he
had believed his son was dead. But with the final dream he
knew Todd was alive, reaching out for him with a will almost
as powerful as that of the great swordmaker Tendrai.

DiPalma opened his eyes and began to pace. The dead boy
found in the burned out *dojo* was not his son. Now it made
sense. Todd's missing dental records in Hong Kong. The delay
in forwarding his medical history. Someone didn't want Di-
Palma to have those records. Todd was alive and DiPalma
knew where to find him.

He raced from the balcony into the bedroom. Fumbling
through a drawer in the night table he found his address book,
then sat on the bed. When he had the name he wanted, he
pulled the telephone toward him and dialed Tokyo.

* * *

Mystic, Connecticut

ROLF NULLABOR looked at his wristwatch, then at Jude
Golden's nurse. They stood outside the sliding door to Gol-

den's room on the second floor of his Victorian mansion. Golden had overslept, which annoyed the nurse, a stickler for punctuality. He was due to get his first shot of the day and she was not about to let him avoid it. Nullabor had been summoned to help her.

Nullabor loathed her as he loathed most black Irish. She was too authoritarian for his taste, and, besides, much taller than he. Hell-bent on giving Golden his injection, she might enter when he and Nijo were doing the old in-and-out. Better to warn Golden first, just in case the little Jap beauty was sitting on his face while saying her morning prayers.

Nullabor removed his shoes. The nurse did the same, though it was a custom she found pagan, as she did Jude Golden's penchant for collecting Oriental concubines.

Nullabor knocked on the wooden frame. "Mr. Golden? Nursie's here. Wakey, wakey."

He grinned at her. "Could be he and his friend are locked in a convoluted discussion concerning the adverse effects of thermonuclear warfare on plant life."

She folded her arms across her ample bosom and eyed him with loathing.

Nullabor knocked on the frame again.

"Well?" the nurse said, thrusting her head back and forth.

"Well, me bleedin' arse," said Nullabor as he slid back the door. Across the room Jude Golden lay on his side, his back to the door.

"Mr. Golden, Princess Di is here with her magic wand. Time—"

The looseness of the banker's body, the stillness surrounding him. Nullabor had seen it before. It meant only one thing.

He crouched down and turned Golden over on his back. The banker's lips were blue, his face discolored. Poison. He had not died an easy death.

A search of the house failed to turn up Nijo.

Nullabor did find the other two Japanese girls, but they could tell him nothing. They too had been poisoned. Nijo had covered her tracks well.

33

Tokyo, Evening

DiPALMA WAS SILENT as Suko drove fast over the rain-slicked roads leading from New Tokyo International Airport into the city. Even without the rain and heavy traffic the trip would take over an hour. The U-shaped, ultramodern airport was forty miles outside of Tokyo in Narita, a town built around a tenth-century temple dedicated to Fudo, god of fire. Airport traffic on this road was bad enough. The eight million pilgrims who came yearly to worship Fudo made it worse.

Rain slapped the hood and windshield like waves from an angry sea, and gusts rattled the car. It skidded several times, causing DiPalma to push his feet against the floorboard and stiffen his arms against the dash. Off to one side he saw an overturned truck, its cartons spread out along the highway as though being offered for sale. In a lane leading back to the airport a car had been blown into the path of an oncoming bus, halting traffic. DiPalma could not recall a worse storm in his life.

On the phone from New York he had told Shuko everything. Todd's reincarnation. Kenpachi's planned *seppuku*. And DiPalma's dreams.

"The circle is complete," Shuko had said.

"I don't understand."

"Tomorrow Kenpachi finishes the movie. And tomorrow is the day when Lord Saburo committed *seppuku* over four hundred years ago with Benkai as his *kaishaku*. Karma, DiPalma-san. What is, was. What was will always be. Past, present and future. The same."

DiPalma rubbed the back of his neck. The fourteen-hour nonstop flight had been rough. But there had been no more dreams. This meant Todd was dead or no longer wanted to contact him. One thing was certain; belief in the unknown, which DiPalma had begun to accept in Tendrai's forge, was now stronger than ever. There was a Japan which could not be seen, which could only be felt, which could only be experienced.

When Shuko braked behind a truck load of pigs, DiPalma said, "What would happen if Kenpachi's death were not honorable, if he were to die at the hands of someone not worthy to be his second?"

"It would be bad karma. It would be the judgment of the gods condemning him to an unhappy life in the next world. His death would be useless and of no value. Even Mishima is not a hero to everyone."

The truck pulled away and the pigs began thrashing about. Shuko said, "And you know a way into the castle?"

DiPalma hesitated. "I think so. There is only the dream to go on. And what Todd told me weeks ago about the tunnel."

"The tunnel is supposed to have been destroyed in the great earthquake. If it has been rebuilt, it has been done so in secret. And most illegally."

"Kenpachi would do it and not think twice."

Steal in. Was the dream real or just wishful thinking? DiPalma leaned forward and wiped steam from the windshield. The heavy rain prevented him from opening the windows, turning the car into a sauna on wheels. He leaned back in his seat. *Was the dream real?*

Shuko said, "After your telephone call I spoke to Tendrai-*sensei*. I told him of our conversation. About the dream."

DiPalma waited.

"Tendrai-*sensei* told me to do as you ask. Without question."

"Did he say anything else?"

"He did not have to."

DiPalma rolled down his window and let the rain hit him in the face. He had his answer. "How long has the party been on?"

"It was scheduled to begin thirty minutes ago. Most of the

people attending worked with Kenpachi on the film. Othe
are friends."

"They won't stay when he starts to kill himself."

"He will keep them hostage. Kenpachi needs an audience."

DiPalma nodded. "When we go in we'll have to be car
ful."

"I will have six men. They will be armed with automat
weapons and sidearms. Unfortunately, I am not allowed
give you a gun, DiPalma-san. You know our laws."

"Strict as hell. Wish we had laws like that. I'll take n
chances with this." He held up the cane. "Did you tell the
what we were going to do?"

Shuko smiled. "No. It was not necessary. They will obey n
without question. I also did not tell them that a *gaijin* will l
our leader."

DiPalma grinned. "Can't wait to see how they'll take that.

"They have a duty to me. Just as you have a duty to yo
son."

And to Jan, thought DiPalma. She had not come to t
hotel after the Kenpachi tribute, nor had she called. Was it Ja
acting up again or had Kenpachi taken her over as he ha
Todd? Kenpachi had to be responsible for her recent behavio
DiPalma tried not to think that Kenpachi intended to kill Jan

The car came to a halt in a sea of traffic. DiPalma gre
alarmed. "We're not going to arrive in time."

"Karma will bring us to the castle or keep us away," sa
Shuko.

He closed his eyes.

After a few seconds DiPalma did the same.

* * *

HAND IN HAND WITH Kenpachi, Jan walked down tl
long polished corridor toward light softened by a sliding ric
paper door. The corridor was lit by pine torches hanging fro
walls decorated in ancient handscrolls, colored silk drawing
of horses, landscapes and flying geese. They walked in silenc
as did the men who followed them. Instead of shoes all, ii
cluding Jan, wore *tabi*, the split-toed white ankle socks. Ja
also wore a golden kimono with a brilliant red sash and h
hair had been done in the ancient fashion, an elaborate stylir

of cascades and cocoons containing fragile oyster shells. Her face was coated in white makeup, leaving a small red mouth.

She had been dressed by Kenpachi, who had also done her makeup.

"Tonight you must look the role of the *daimyo*'s mistress," he had said.

She was in a daze, hypnotized by the pounding rain, by the drugged wine she had drunk from an earthen cup, by Kenpachi's words. She had reached the point where she believed he could speak to her without words as he had done in New York. Then he had simply stared at her as she cringed in the telephone booth, dreading his touch and wanting to cry out for Frank.

But no sound had come from her. Kenpachi's piercing eyes were all she remembered until Japan, where she woke up one morning in his bed and suddenly realized that New York, Lincoln Center and Frank had happened three days ago. Depressed and frightened, she had searched the castle for a telephone. She had to speak to Frank. But when she found an empty room and a phone, she was unable to make the call. She was too guilty, too ashamed, too weak.

Something in her cried out for Frank, but she had betrayed him once more and had to be punished. So she punished herself by walking away from the phone and by doing as Kon ordered.

Now, in the corridor, she forced herself to gather up the pieces of her life. The film was over, in the can. But where was the satisfaction she should have felt? There was a party in the castle. Yes. That's where Kon was taking her now. To the party.

She slowed down. Her steps faltered, but Kon's strong grip pulled her along the corridor. She had slowed down out of panic; she wondered if she could ever leave Kon. Would he let her go? *Frank*. A tear slid from a corner of Jan's eye to become a pearl on her white-coated face. The worse thing, she knew, was being unable to forgive herself.

When they reached the sliding door at the end of the corridor, someone behind them stepped forward and opened it. Jan tensed. There were dozens of men and women attending the wrap party. Several decorated, sliding doors leading to other rooms had been pulled back to create one large room whose low ceiling was sectioned off by dark wooden beams; the only light came from paper lanterns and tall candles in bamboo stands.

As the conversation suddenly stopped, Jan tried to concentrate her mind, to think clearly. The silence was all wrong. And why were people staring at her and Kenpachi? What was wrong with her? She looked at Kenpachi. He was dressed oddly. White kimono and matching headband. And behind them were a dozen men dressed in white kimonos and armed with samurai swords. Some had a short sword tucked in their sashes. She remembered that Kon's parties were bizarre affairs, but tonight's was even more weird. *Why?*

Kenpachi and his men pushed guests back from the entrance. Those who did move fast enough were slapped, kicked, threatened with the swords. Jan saw it all through a haze. A woman shoved; the man beside her stepped forward and was kicked in the stomach. A guest who was trying to reason with Kon's friends was punched in the mouth. Two women were struck with the flat of a sword.

The guests, holding drinks and plates of food, now ceased to eat and drink.

Kon released Jan's hand and stepped inside the room. Someone else took one step forward to stand at his side. *Todd.* What was he doing here? Why was he dressed in a black kimono with the top of his head shaved? And carrying a sword. He looked bizarre, a miniature version of an ancient samurai on one of the hanging scrolls in the corridor. He gave off an air of being too formidable to oppose. Even the hard-looking men around Kenpachi, men older and bigger and armed with swords, seemed to be afraid of Todd. Why were they afraid of a boy?

Kenpachi folded his arms across his chest and coolly surveyed the room. "Listen carefully and do not speak. From this moment on, all of you are my hostages."

There was mumbling from the guests. Kenpachi waited. The mumbling faded.

"You are my hostages and will remain so until my purpose has been realized. I will retire to my bedroom to await the arrival of a television crew who will film the reading of my *zankanjo.*" He hesitated. "And my *seppuku.*"

"My *seppuku,*" he repeated. "I—"

An American stunt man, high on pills and Cognac and bored with Japan after weeks of filming, staggered toward Kenpachi. Several Blood Oath League members rushed toward him, but Kenpachi's command stopped them.

The stunt man stood in place and weaved. Pointing at Todd he said, "Fuck you suppose to be, something from *Fantasy Island*?" He giggled. "The plane has landed, boss."

He threw his arms wide. "Fuckin' wild party, right? Shit, I'm ready for that." He charged Kenpachi, who took one step back. Todd stepped forward. He wielded the sword in its scabbard, like a club, bringing it up hard between the stunt man's legs.

The big, blond American doubled over, and Todd delivered a series of blows so quickly that the horror of it shocked Jan into consciousness. The boy struck the blond man across the face, then in the right temple, spinning him around and dropping him unconscious to the mat.

The silence in the room deepened to grim helplessness.

Kenpachi smiled. "You have seen what my *kaishaku* can do. Had he taken the blade from the scabbard, the fool on the floor would have died, for a bared blade has the right to blood. Actually I am happy that his blade was not soiled by this man's blood. Benkai, my *kaishaku*, has been purified for me and by me. But I see an object lesson is in order."

He nodded at a guard, who stepped forward and cleanly hacked off the stunt man's head. Women screamed and Jan almost fainted. She was now propped up by two of Kenpachi's men.

Kenpachi clapped his hands once. Todd stepped forward, picked up the head by its long, blond hair and held it high in one hand. His sword was held high in the other. Slowly the boy walked back and forth in front of the guests.

Kenpachi said, "Look at it! Look at it or I will have another killed until the rest do as I say. Take your hands away from your eyes and never turn your backs to me when I am addressing you."

He waited as the guests kept their eyes on Todd.

Kenpachi said, "I shall now retire to my quarters to await the television cameras. One of you will be executed every hour until my *seppuku* is shown on Japanese and American television. I suggest you pray the storm does not delay the arrival of the press. As for any rescue, this castle is a fortress. It is impregnable. There is no way in or out except through the front gate, which is now locked. The drawbridge is up. You cannot escape and I strongly suggest you do not try."

He clapped his hands again. Several of his men stepped forward and pulled a handful of guests from the stunned group. One of those shoved toward Kenpachi was Nosaka.

Kenpachi looked them over. "You will be taken to my quarters where you will have the honor of witnessing my *seppuku* and the reading of my *zankanjo*. Everyone else will remain here under guard. My men have orders to kill anyone who resists or causes the slightest difficulty. I go now to join Japan's immortals, those whose blood has watered the tree of Nippon's greatness. In the future you will worship me as a god and you will be proud to tell others that you were present here in this castle on this most auspicious occasion. Long live the emperor!"

Outside in the hall he said to a terrified Jan, "Tonight, Saga, I shall kill you before you have the chance to betray me."

He led the way back down the vast corridor. Jan was roughly dragged behind him by an incredibly strong Todd.

34

Tokyo, Night

DiPALMA STOOD IN THE DARK, fetid-smelling shack and watched as two uniformed Japanese policemen tore at the floor with crowbars. He and Shuko trained flashlights on the planking. As chunks of it came loose, they were tossed outside where Shuko's men waited in the downpour. There was no room inside for a pile of wood or an extra man.

The shack was an abandoned caretaker's hut in a grove of trees on the edge of a Shinjuku park. It had neither electricity nor heat and anything valuable had long since been stolen or removed. A locked door had protected a bare room covered with dust, cobwebs and rat droppings.

After the break-in DiPalma had taken a crowbar, pried loose the window boards and stared out into the rainy darkness. Shuko stood beside him silently. At first the policeman saw nothing. Then lightning lit up the center of the city and he saw it clearly.

Ikuba Castle. Barely a quarter of a mile away.

As DiPalma continued to stare through the window, Shuko ordered his men to tear up the floorboards in search of the trapdoor to a secret tunnel, a tunnel that DiPalma said led to the castle.

Rain leaked through the roof and plastered DiPalma's gray hair to his skull. Wind whistled through cracks in the shack. Once or twice the men glanced at DiPalma, then dropped their eyes back to the ground. He knew what they were thinking. But no one would say it in front of Shuko.

They were digging because the *gaijin* wanted them to,

because he believed there was trouble in the castle. What kind of trouble? They were all fools and the biggest fool was Shuko, who was letting his friendship for the *gaijin* ruin his career. His career would be finished when it was learned that he had attempted to sneak into the home of a man as important as Kenpachi-san, a man with very important friends. The smartest man in the park tonight was the one Shuko had assigned to sit in a police car and monitor the radio. Poor Shuko. *Hai*, the life of a fool was worse than death.

They don't have to like me, thought DiPalma. All they have to do is keep digging.

When the trapdoor, moss covered and made of iron, was discovered under the floor, the atmosphere suddenly changed. As the men pulled at the door, the policeman assigned to the radio rushed into the shack and spoke excitedly to Shuko. When he had finished, the men in the hut looked at DiPalma, who said, "Kenpachi has made his move."

Shuko nodded. "As you said he would. Copies of his *zankanjo* have been delivered to the press, to the emperor. A police car drove up to the castle where someone threw a head down from the wall. It was the head of a man, a westerner. Shall we enter the tunnel now?"

DiPalma nodded. "Tell your people at headquarters we're going through. We can't take too many with us. Too noisy, might alert Kenpachi. You, me and four of your men. Leave two here to wait for reinforcement. Tell them to be on guard in case Kenpachi attacks us from this end. We're to have at least fifteen minutes before anyone follows us."

He spoke softly, in perfect Japanese, never raising his voice.

This time no one waited for Shuko's instructions.

DiPalma removed his jacket, tie, shirt, then his shoes and socks. He took coins and keys from his pants pocket and placed them in his jacket. As he looked down at the opening in the floor, Shuko and four policemen also stripped to the waist.

DiPalma, flashlight and cane in hand, was the first to descend the wooden ladder leading down into the pitch black tunnel.

* * *

KENPACHI STOOD at his bedroom window, peering into the darkness at the stone walls ringing Ikuba Castle, and cursed under his breath. *Hai*, the castle was impregnable, but he did not like the rain. Four hundred years ago the rain had helped to defeat Saburo. It had hid the *ninja* attack and enabled Hideyoshi's armies to steal in undetected. Damn the rain.

And damn the press, which had not contacted him. The telephones were working. Kenpachi had spoken to the police, who were now outside the walls in their little cars, and he had spoken to someone at army headquarters, telling him what he planned to do at Ikuba Castle. He had attempted to reach the emperor and failed. No matter. The emperor had a copy of Kenpachi's *zankanjo*. The emperor would understand and approve. Kenpachi had prepared himself. He was pure enough to be a worthy sacrifice to Nippon. And he had Benkai. He must calm himself, remain in control and act the *daimyo*. Then, when the television cameras arrived, he would show the world how a warrior died.

He turned from the window to see Todd walk away from the hostages in the bedroom and stand in front of the closet leading to the secret tunnel. Kenpachi had not mentioned the tunnel to the boy, but he had no doubt that the boy knew of its existence. Even most members of the Blood Oath League did not know of the tunnel.

Todd grunted. His voice was deep, a man's voice.

"What is it?" said Kenpachi. He felt an ominous forewarning.

"*Ninja*." Todd's eyes were glued to the door. "They are coming through the tunnel."

Kenpachi pressed his fists to his temples. It must not happen again. How did they find out about the tunnel? He looked pleadingly at Nosaka, whose face held a strange smile. Kenpachi had to forcibly restrain himself from asking the industrialist what to do next.

But was not Kenpachi *daimyo* of Ikuba Castle?

He pointed to the closet. "Kill them, Benkai! Do not let them capture me alive!"

* * *

IN THE TUNNEL DiPalma led the way through ankle-deep water. The beam of his flashlight sent rats scurrying. The air was sickening and for the first time in weeks his stomach began to trouble him. He was weak from lack of food. His feet, cut by rocks hidden by the water, were in agony but he dared not stop.

He had slipped once and fallen, tasting rancid water and mud and he had almost vomited. He had willed himself not to throw up, to keep running. Concentrate. *Hai.* Concentrate on Katharine, on Tendrai's forge. He thought of all his years of kendo practice, remembering how he had wielded the sword until his arms ached, until he could not lift them, but somehow had continued to fight.

The darkness threatened him, brought him close to panic. Where was the darkness leading him? Was he leading five men to their death because of a dream?

The tunnel seemed to grow longer, to go deeper into the earth. His mind played tricks. He was lost inside a dragon and would never see the sun again. The tunnel was a fake, designed to lure the castle enemies to their deaths by leading them in circles. DiPalma would starve to death under the earth. *There is nothing around you but dirt, foul water and rats. The rats will feed on you after you die.*

He ran, breathing through burning lungs, and heard only the splashing water. He ran because if he stopped, he would lie down in the water and warm darkness and never rise again.

He thought of Hong Kong, of the day in the Kowloon hospital when Katharine had forced him to walk. Crawl, she had said. Limp. But don't lie where you have fallen.

DiPalma ran. *Splash-splash-splash.* He led and the others followed, taking their strength from him; they too were tired. They were ordinary men, not *ninja.* But with the right leader, they could equal the *ninja* in spirit.

When DiPalma thought his heart would shatter, when it seemed all the breath had left his body and his legs could no longer function, he felt the cool air.

In the beam of his flashlight he saw the small red brick room at the end of the tunnel. Drawing the cool air into his burning lungs, he staggered forward and out of the water, up an incline, then stumbled into the room and collapsed. Seconds

later a mud splattered Shuko and his men followed. The
sweating, dirty men looked half-dead.

Shuko, too tired to speak, touched DiPalma. The gesture
said, You have led us well.

DiPalma turned away, listening. His hand went up, commanding silence. All the flashlights were turned off. A second
command and the men dragged themselves to the wooden
ladder leading upstairs, flattening themselves against the wall,
waiting.

In the darkness DiPalma leaned against the ladder and felt
the vibrations as someone stepped on it and began to climb
down. When the man touched bottom, DiPalma reached out,
grabbed his shirt and yanked him close. He covered the man's
mouth with one hand and kneed him twice in the groin. Then
he smashed him in the head with the knob of his cane.

A scuffle told DiPalma that a second man was being dealt
with by Shuko's men. There was a clang as a sword fell to the
floor.

Then there was a scream, an animallike screech, and in the
darkness DiPalma heard someone leap from the ladder and
land near the tunnel. Quickly DiPalma yanked his flashlight
from his belt and switched it on.

Todd.

Standing at the mouth of the tunnel, teeth bared, the
Murasama held overhead.

A wolf at bay, exuding more evil than any man in the small
room had ever seen.

More flashlights were switched on and DiPalma heard the
click of a safety catch. He shouted, "He's my son! Don't
fire!"

He ran his flashlight over the floor and found a dropped
sword. With the sword in his right hand, the cane in his left, he
inched forward. "Keep your lights on him! On him, not me!
Try to blind him if you can! And don't go near him. He's
dangerous. He doesn't know what's he's doing!"

Two of Shuko's men climbed the ladder to get out of the
way. The others, pistols and rifles aimed at Todd, edged along
the walls, keeping far away from the boy and his sword.

With a ratlike quickness, the boy scurried to his left, out of
the light and into a patch of darkness. Before the flashlights

could find him again, Todd leaped out of the darkness and at his father.

The boy attacked, slashing at his father's left knee. *Clang.* Their blades clashed as DiPalma blocked the swing and felt the vibrations from Todd's powerful stroke race up his arm. Todd faked a stomach thrust, then slashed at DiPalma, who sidestepped, but was still cut on the wrist. A second's delay and he would have lost a hand.

He had no choice but to accept a frightening truth. Todd was now the more skilled fencer. And he almost matched Di-Palma in physical strength.

More terrifying, Todd was no longer his son or Katharine's. He was now a deadly swordsman, a merciless fighter, a cold-blooded warrior committed to serving his *daimyo*, Kenpachi, to the death.

Dai-sho. Two swords.

Karma. Fate.

Father and son inched toward each other, each holding three feet of curved, razor-sharp steel.

Because Todd was concentrating on the kill, Shuko's men could do as DiPalma ordered. Quickly running behind Di-Palma all aimed their flashlights at Todd's face.

The boy turned white in the garish light. He cursed, his face tight with hatred. An arm came up to shield his eyes. For that one instant he was helpless.

DiPalma switched weapons from one hand to the other. The cane in his right hand, the sword in his left. He charged, pushed aside Todd's sword with his own; then, with a mighty shout, he brought the cane down on the Muramasa, breaking it in half.

As though pierced by a blade, Todd screamed in pain. He staggered back toward the tunnel, followed by the light. DiPalma smacked his wrist. Todd dropped the broken sword, then DiPalma dropped his cane and sword and rushed him. He wrapped his arms around the boy's shoulders and lifted him off his feet. Todd kicked, twisted and fought with such unexpected strength that both father and son crashed into a wall, then fell to the cement floor with Todd on top. Cursing, the boy jerked an arm free, punched his father in the temple and almost knocked him unconscious. Before DiPalma could move, Todd punched him again, breaking his nose. The boy's strength was astonishing. Todd could beat him to death with his fists and DiPalma knew it.

With blood streaming from his nose DiPalma shouted, "Shuko! Shuko!"

The police captain, followed by his men, rushed forward and pulled at Todd.

Maddened, the boy fought back. He shoved one man back into the tunnel, dropped another to the cement floor with a kick to the groin and smashed his elbow into the face of a third. DiPalma pushed himself to his knees. Unbelievable. Todd was holding his own against six grown men.

Sucking air in through his mouth, DiPalma hesitated a second, then leaped on Todd, tackling him from the rear. As the boy went down, Shuko grabbed an arm and hung on. Three men fell on Todd's legs, pinning him down. DiPalma grabbed the other arm. Todd continued to fight. Face down, he thrashed as a policeman cuffed his hands behind him.

A jerk of Todd's wrists and the cuffs were broken.

"Cuff him again!" DiPalma shouted, then told them to put on a third pair.

DiPalma turned the writhing boy over on his back and tied his ankles with his sash. A strip of cloth was torn from Todd's kimono and shoved into his mouth.

DiPalma looked down at his wild-eyed son, who flung himself about on the damp concrete, rolling left, then right to escape his bonds. There was something bestial about the boy which made DiPalma shudder. His face was hideous, almost unrecognizable.

"He is Benkai," whispered Shuko. "And he has been strengthened by the *Iki-ryō*, by thoughts of evil and darkness."

"Kenpachi."

"And Nosaka, who gave Kenpachi the Muramasa."

DiPalma picked up a flashlight and flashed it around the brick room until he found what was left of the Muramasa. Then, as the policemen watched, he took the sword and smashed it against the wall until the blade was broken from the hilt.

Todd had grown calmer, but he followed every move made by his father.

DiPalma stepped in front of the tunnel and, after once more

looking at Todd, hurled the jeweled hilt far back into the darkness. When he heard it splash in the flooded passage, DiPalma turned and picked up his cane.

Without a word he began to climb the ladder.

* * *

IN KENPACHI'S BEDROOM the only light came from the four large white candles near the white screen and rug on which the film director was to die. Nosaka concentrated on a single candle and prepared himself for the warrior's task. Gone was the fear of twenty-four hours ago when he had jumped at the sound of thunder, when he had been terrified by the sight of the Muramasa blade. Gone was his sense of shame at having fled the *dojo*.

During the purification in the dojo, *I came to know the boy as Benkai. Thus he and I were enemies for he served the lord of Ikuba Castle as my ancestors had served Hideyoshi. I fled Benkai, the swordsman whom none could face. I beg your forgiveness.*

Muramasa's words. Spoken by Nosaka and accepted by Kenpachi. Admitting that the boy was Benkai had flattered Kenpachi; it was an admission that Kenpachi's power had brought Benkai to life.

And so Nosaka was a hostage, an observer at Kenpachi's planned *seppuku*. In truth, Nosaka was here to carry out Muramasa's commands. He was here because the hour of the death fury had come, a time calling for courage and greatness. Nosaka, descendant of samurai, of feudal warriors, of Nippon's first spies, was ready. Muramasa had commanded him.

Muramasa had also told him that Kenpachi was not samurai and unfit for a warrior's death.

And Muramasa had revealed to him the glory of the evil deed he was about to commit, evil bred of all the evil Nosaka had ever done. Urged on by his karma, he could only obey. His karma, born of the sinister and demonic, had been nurtured by the Muramasa weapons he had collected. Muramasa had said that Nosaka's karma now called for him to dye his hands in blood. Now.

In the bedroom Nosaka stepped up to a guard and pried a sword from his fingers. The guard nodded respectfully, assuming that the charade of Nosaka as hostage was over.

The gray-haired man held the sword up to his catlike face. As rain continued to pound the castle, he stared at the candlelit blade. *To know was to act.* He smiled at the hostages and guards, then began killing them.

He plunged the sword into the stomach of a shocked politician, withdrew it and slashed a guard across his right side, sending him bleeding and spinning toward the door. As screaming hostages scattered throughout the bedroom, another guard charged Nosaka. He sidestepped his rush and cut off the guard's sword hand.

A Japanese reporter tried to run but tripped over a teakwood chest. As he frantically tried to crawl away he knocked over a tall white candle, extinguishing its flame. Nosaka raced to him, lifted the sword high and brought it down, splitting the reporter's skull. Nosaka then chased an American actress, who fled toward the door. Two steps and he was on her. He hacked her across the back of the neck, dropping her to her knees.

Muramasa was pleased, but demanded more victims.

"*Nosaka-san!*" Kenpachi's voice broke as he cried out. Too stunned to move, he stood near the screen and the candles, his eyes shimmering behind his tears. Why had this man whom he revered, to whom he owed everything, suddenly turned insane. It was beyond understanding. It was a mystery so impenetrable that it left a shocked Kenpachi on the verge of a breakdown.

Nosaka had brought the boy to him. Nosaka had given him the bone from Benkai's throat. And Nosaka had given him the Muramasa blade. Kenpachi must reason with him before it was too late. Nosaka would not harm him. The old man loved him; it was time to show that love, to cease this slaughter which had already defiled the room and made it unfit for an honorable death. Those killed by Nosaka had not died in battle. They had died at the hands of one who was crazed and therefore impure. No one should have to die in such a manner.

Such a swordsman was the instrument of gods who wanted to punish.

Kenpachi held out his hand. "*Sensei*, I ask that you give me the sword. You have my respect, my love, and so I beg you not to defile this room any further. Please hand me the sword."

Nosaka let his sword hand drop. Only two people in the room were still alive. Kenpachi and Golden's daughter, who cringed near the tunnel entrance. Those who had not fallen victim to Nosaka's sword had fled the room.

Kenpachi, the pretender who would be a samurai. And his whore, who had betrayed the castle. Muramasa wanted them dead. Nosaka walked slowly toward Kenpachi.

Kenpachi ignored a growing fear and took one step toward Nosaka. Only one step. Smiling, Nosaka stopped and stared into the film director's eyes. Returning the smile, Kenpachi bowed. There was nothing to fear from his protector, from his mentor, who had been his whole world. He tried not to think about the horrible karma of one killed by the man Nosaka had now become. Such a death meant thousands of years of torment to come.

Nosaka's sword arm came up slowly. Then, as Kenpachi reached for the weapon, Nosaka speeded up his motion. The old man's face was a mask of revulsion. He could no longer stomach the unworthy Kenpachi. He struck. His sword stroke was strong and aimed at Kenpachi's neck.

The razor-sharp blade, a prize from Nosaka's collection, bit into Kenpachi's flesh and sliced his head from his neck. Blood spurted high into the air, then fell to the floor. The head flew into the screen, knocking it back into a candle. The candle fell to the mat, where its flame was doused by Kenpachi's blood.

In the dark room Kenpachi's headless corpse stood erect, blood spewing from the neck. Then it fell forward. The legs twitched and a straw sandal fell from one foot. In the light of one of the two candles still erect, the eyes in Kenpachi's severed head shone with an unnatural brightness. There was disbelief on his handsome face and his lips continued to move, as though still pleading with Nosaka.

Jan screamed, drawing Nosaka's attention. Smiling and happier than he had ever been, he shuffled toward her, the sword held high over his right shoulder. She backed away from the tunnel entrance and edged toward the window overlooking the courtyard. Nosaka slowly stalked her.

Jan knocked down a bamboo screen, then looked back at Nosaka. She wept and shook her head, but Nosaka kept coming. He stopped directly in front of her, alert, ready to move left or right. The window, the rain, the thunder and lightning were at her back. *To know was to act.* Nosaka lifted the sword high.

The closet door leading to the tunnel shattered, then gave way as DiPalma pushed his way through and into the bedroom.

"Frank! Oh, God, Frank!"

Nosaka's eyes narrowed and he turned to look at his new enemy. *Kill him, said Muramasa. You are my beast of prey. You are my wolf who slinks from shadow to shadow in search of a quarry. You are my sword arm.*

DiPalma gripped his cane and stepped toward the old man. He thought of Katharine and Todd, of what Nosaka had done to Shuko and Tendrai. And to others.

A life for a life. A wound for a wound. It was time for judgment, for punishment.

Nosaka's confidence grew. The stick could not stand against the sword. He sneered, aimed the point of his sword at DiPalma's throat and inched forward.

DiPalma, barely able to breathe through his broken nose, stepped forward slowly. Judgment and punishment.

Suddenly DiPalma lashed out with his cane. Not at the old man, but at the two remaining candles, and knocked them to the floor. One flame went out immediately. DiPalma stepped on the other with his bare foot. Now the bedroom was totally black.

Nosaka froze, confused. Then he began to swing the sword wildly in all directions, calling out Muramasa's name, hearing the voice of the great swordsmith. Lightning flashed and in the brilliant light Nosaka, who was facing the window, never saw DiPalma behind him. DiPalma lifted his cane. Thunder crashed as he brought the cane down and in that instant the room became dark again.

Nosaka grunted. The sword slipped from his fingers and fell to the floor.

In the darkness the cane was raised twice more and brought down in powerful strokes. Each time it found its target.

Shuko and his men entered the bedroom from the tunnel and in the beam of their flashlights found DiPalma near the window, his arms around a weeping Jan. A few quick commands from Shuko, and his men, guns drawn, fanned out across the room. From here they moved into the hall, where they encountered guards with swords who had come to deal with Nosaka. Shots were fired. A guard fell, then the swords were dropped to the floor in surrender.

In Kenpachi's bedroom Shuko shone his flashlight beam from corpse to corpse, from the dead to the dying. He lingered briefly on Kenpachi's severed head, then moved on. He was looking for Nosaka. The American, pressing Jan tightly against him, jerked his head toward the window.

Shuko looked out into the rainy night. He heard the sounds of his men taking control of the castle and moving out into the courtyard. There were more shots. A guard on the wall screamed that he had been wounded. In the darkness flashlights were trained on two of Shuko's men as they struggled to lift the huge crossbar which locked the iron gates.

Then, in the courtyard below the window, a flashlight found Nosaka's rain-soaked body. Something dark and wet seeped from beneath the old man's skull, then was washed away by the rain.

As Shuko stared down at the dead industrialist, DiPalma held Jan and stroked her hair.

"It's over," he said. "It's all over, Jan."

And immediately sensed that it wasn't.

EPILOGUE

December

IN MANHATTAN'S METROPOLITAN MUSEUM OF ART, DiPalma held Jan's hand as they and Todd followed a small group of formally dressed men and women through a gallery lined with ancient Greek gravestones. The museum was officially closed. But tonight it was the scene of a private champagne supper following the world premiere of *Ukiyo*. As with most premieres, things had gone wrong.

Some people had attempted to get in by using counterfeit tickets. A mounted policeman's horse had accidentally stepped on a photographer, and the film had been delayed because a studio VIP had been delayed. The elaborate supper would also be late. With little else to do DiPalma and the other guests wandered through the galleries.

DiPalma had shocked Jan by his agreeing to wear a tuxedo, to join the rest of the penguins, as he put it. Jan looked beautiful in a black dress which left her shoulders bare. Her only jewelry was a string of pale blue pearls and her wedding ring. DiPalma had thought they needed the rest a honeymoon would give them, but he wasn't pushing it. The film was important to Jan and she had to go on tour with it. After the first of the year, they planned a vacation in Aruba, if she could get away.

DiPalma had worried about her sitting through the film too many times. It could trigger bad memories. Tonight she had remained silent through the two-hour showing, but she had never let go of his hand.

Marriage had calmed her down. She didn't like parties any more and had lost all interest in Japan. She had sold her father's homes and was resisting pressure to move to Los Angeles. She clung to DiPalma, whether out of love or need he did not know, nor did it matter.

In the museum she looked at a collection of Greek coins. "I may not go on the tour," she said. She was upset at the thought of being apart from him.

"Your decision," he said. "I'll go along with whatever you want."

She touched the glass case covering the coins. "Was Nosaka insane?"

"Yes. He killed Kenpachi's wife and children before coming to the castle. Shuko said it was part of a samurai ritual. Said Kenpachi had an impure death. No sense going over all that. He killed six people, all told. What made you think of him?"

"I was thinking of my father. I wanted him here tonight. And I thought of what you did for him."

"All I really wanted from the files was enough to make a case against Nosaka and his spying. Nothing more. Shuko said the files were mine. Nosaka sure wouldn't be using them. No sense hurting anybody."

He grinned. "Besides, I think Shuko wanted to increase Nosaka's bad karma. But don't quote me."

Jan looked around. "Where's Todd?"

DiPalma looked left, then right. "Around somewhere. Hasn't smiled since we got back from Japan." He stopped a white-jacketed waiter, took a glass of champagne from a tray and handed it to Jan. "Good at his school work, though. Put him in private school. Thought it might be less of a culture shock. He's still strong on kendo. Does his homework. Good kid. Except he just won't smile. Doesn't make friends either. I don't push it. Wouldn't help him if I did."

Jan took his arm. "Don't worry. He'll smile. He's going to be gorgeous, I'll tell you that. A regular little heartbreaker. Let's find him."

They found him in the next gallery. He was staring at a wall hung with medieval Japanese weapons. DiPalma felt Jan's fingers dig into his arm, but she said nothing.

Jan began to shiver, then rub her bare shoulders. DiPalma

felt cold, too. It was freezing in here. Near the entrance a frowning guard squinted at a thermostat. "Jesus, that's weird."

DiPalma was afraid. "What's weird?"

Jan huddled near him.

The guard shivered and continued to look at the thermostat. "Impossible. One minute it's warm, the next minute the goddamn thing goes crazy. How can it be forty in here—"

He looked at DiPalma. "Sorry. What did you say?"

DiPalma stared at Todd, who now stood in front of a glass case that contained an ornate, Japanese feudal saddle.

"That saddle," said DiPalma. "The one the boy's looking at."

"What about it?"

"Tell me about it."

"Everybody's fascinated by that thing. Just got it in this week from Japan with a lot of other stuff. It's on loan from a museum over there. Some guy died and left a bunch of things to the government. Happens all the time."

DiPalma knew.

From across the room Todd smiled at him and Jan. The room grew colder.

The guard hugged himself and hopped from foot to foot. "One of the rarest saddles in Japan, that thing. Done by a real expert. Man called Muramasa."

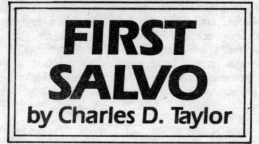